To Jol

All the best chum

Love Joy

Greg Carter grew up in Kent and Hampshire. Having been in the antiques trade since the seventies, he is also a respected cabinet maker and restorer. His interests include real ale, wine, cooking, flying, vintage aircraft and cars. Not to mention, real ale, wine and real ale.

In memory of Mum and Dad

To Bernice

Many thanks to the following for the information passed on to me:

Squadron Leader R. Brister
Flying Officer Kenneth Marsland (Malta 1942/43)
Sergeant Pilot Stan Bell (Chittagong 1943)
Kapitän Wolfgang Hessler – Kriegsmarine

Many thanks for their encouragement and support to:

Simone
Annie Clarke
Justin and Penny
Peter Farrow
Spud and Dawn
Bill Brindley
Mark Withrington
David Henshaw

Greg Carter

A GOOD IDEA AT THE TIME

AUSTIN MACAULEY
PUBLISHERS LTD.

A CIP catalogue record for this title is available from the British Library.

ISBN 9781785547270 (Paperback)
ISBN 9781785547287 (Hardback)
ISBN 9781785547294 (E-Book)

www.austinmacauley.com

First Published (2016)
Austin Macauley Publishers Ltd.
25 Canada Square
Canary Wharf
London
E14 5LQ

Acknowledgments

"Cockpit" - by Donald Nijboer

"Wings of the Pheonix" - by His Majesty's Stationery Office

"Aeroplane Magazine"

"Leader calling. Turning port, go!"

All six Hurricanes obediently followed the turn, straightened out when their leader did and trailed behind in a very loose line-astern formation.

All the pilots had their cockpit hoods slid back and locked open. The tropical heat they had left on the ground had been stifling. At three thousand feet it was still bloody hot. But with a comforting breeze coming into the cockpit, mixed with the smell of a Merlin engine throbbing with power up front, it was a fighter pilot's heaven.

Nevertheless, the day was not going very well. Nine Hurricanes had originally taken off, but within twenty minutes one of them, Sergeant Pilot 'Pip' Popham, had developed an oil pressure drop and had very wisely turned back to the airfield. In matter of fact, the engine seized up while he was taxiing to the dispersal area.

The second, however, was less fortunate. Flight Lieutenant 'Bobby' Graham was leading the formation and at the same time studying a map. He was well off course and had flown much further south than he'd intended. Having now turned his flight back in the direction he had just come, he realised he had overshot his turning point by a considerable distance. He looked down at his map again and then out the cockpit to the jungle below. He could vaguely make out three distinct hills to his right, which were prominent on his map.

'Pure genius old chap...' he said to himself, adding, 'though a little overdue.' He relaxed a little. He was just in the middle of briefing the flight on their position when his engine misfired once and then stopped dead!

At that particular moment in time the Hurricanes were in quite a tight line-astern formation. Flying Officer Hacker, who was flying behind Graham, found himself having to abruptly pull up as his leader lost flying speed and then watch him begin to fall away.

Graham reacted very quickly. He shoved the stick forward and the nose dropped, thus maintaining some flying speed. He looked around in vain, desperately looking for somewhere to land. There was nothing but dense jungle! He released his harness, unplugged his radio lead and bailed out. His parachute opened a thousand feet above the trees with a crisp bang.

As the treetops came up to meet him, Graham looked up to see the formation circle high above. Then he looked left and down just in time to witness his Hurricane completely disappear into the trees. This was followed by a much larger bang and a pall of smoke, marking his Hurricane's demise. Graham looked up once more to see the formation resume its course and then down again to see the branches coming up to batter him.

"Oh fuck!" he said resignedly. Then he was amongst them.

That's how Flying Officer Hacker came to find himself leading a flight of Hurricanes over the jungle, looking for a landing strip, which to all intents and purposes was the size of a playing card, or smaller.

"Oh well!" he said to himself. "It could be worse." And sure enough, it *was* going to get worse.

***

It was one of those things that had seemed like a good idea at the time.

A ferry pilot had fallen ill and the commanding officer needed a pilot. Having been stuck in the same transit camp for nearly a week waiting for orders, Flying Officer Hacker would have been mad to pass up an opportunity to fly.

15

Hacker was used to taking risks, he was a fighter pilot. Nevertheless, he would calculate the odds. Was the risk worth the prize? It would be remarkably stupid to take an unnecessary gamble which could cost you your life. On the other hand, one more fucking day in that lousy transit camp, with every conceivable bug and reptile known to man trying to sleep with you. Plus the mosquitoes making regular night and day attacks on him (which Hacker knew to be a personal insult as they had wings and they knew damn well that his were temporarily clipped) anything would be an improvement!

All things considered, the past few weeks had gone quite well, although his posting to India had come as quite a serious shock.

***

The Battle of Britain had been won, if by that you meant Jerry wasn't still trying to bomb the living shit out of you. The squadron he'd been with was having a well-earned rest. They had been at the forefront all through the fall of France and had seen a large majority of the squadron get killed. Then, having had their arses kicked out of France by Adolf, the squadron returned to England.

After a short period, they were re-equipped with Spitfires. New pilots were brought in to replace those lost. A lot of these pilots went through their training very quickly indeed. There was a serious shortage of fighter pilots and, rightly or wrongly, a lot of corners were being cut in their training to get them flying as quickly as possible. During the height of the air battle going on above England's beautiful countryside, nearly half the squadron went west again.

Later, the squadron went over to the offensive, doing sweeps over occupied France. These sorties took their toll as well. Though it was a good feeling to be on the offensive, rather than the defensive, at last.

The squadron also did its fair share of convoy escort duties, and bloody boring that could be.

Reconnaissance sorties were also required. In fact, there wasn't very much the squadron didn't do! More to the point, it would probably have continued that way had not a pen-pushing administration officer noticed that they were well overdue for a rest.

This came as a welcome relief to most of the pilots, especially those who had served in France who, by all accounts, felt they were living on borrowed time.

They quickly settled into a pleasant frame of mind. Sleeping better, going down to the local pub in the evening, knowing that they didn't have to be up at the crack of sparrows the next morning. Overdue leave was most welcomed. Some pilots went into London for the theatre or a drinking spree. Others took the opportunity to visit relatives or friends for a few days. The mess became a very relaxed environment; those pilots who were required to do any flying knew it would be just an engine check, or maybe instruments.

The only person not content with the situation was Flying Officer Keith Hacker.

**

Keith Hacker had been born into a reasonably happy family. By the time he had reached the age of three his father, a man with a huge chip on his shoulder and an intensely jealous nature, walked out on his mother, sister and brother. He was never seen or heard from again. This turned out to be something of a blessing. The family became much closer without his disruptive manner and sometimes aggressive mood swings.

They lived in Cornwall just outside Lostwithiel. As Keith grew up he slowly became the rock of the family. His elder brother, Malcolm, who was six years his senior, was a hard worker, both for his family and his boss, a blacksmith near the village of Lerryn. However, it was Keith who had the knack for scrounging things that made life that little bit more comfortable. Bacon, eggs, milk, the odd beef or pork joint. Petrol was the big profit. The family did not have a car or a motorcycle, but if he could lay his hands on some, it was always easy to sell or perhaps barter for something else. He became known as 'the fix-it man'. He was well liked and frequently made a point of checking on the older people in the village. Nobody knew where or how he obtained half the things he did, but then again, no thefts or illegal activities were reported so no one cared.

In early 1936, at the age of eighteen, his mother Irene was taken ill and was nursed almost full-time by his sister Claire. Irene had her good days and her bad days. But she was a strong-willed, resilient woman and tried hard not to give in to her illness. His brother Malcolm now had three jobs: working for the blacksmith, barman at the local pub and gardening for the local vicar. Keith did not wish to appear selfish, but now was the ideal time to pursue a proper career. He approached his brother and sister to discuss his moving out before talking to his mother. Both Claire and Malcolm said they would feel lost without him, but nevertheless they gave their blessing. His mother was obviously upset, but she had always known, deep down, that Keith was not the village type. He needed more in his life.

At school Keith was lazy but intelligent. He was also chief conspirator in nearly everything that went awry in the time that he was there. Sometimes the master or some of the teachers could prove his guilt. More often than not, he got away with whatever crime had been committed. But with all his faults and his carefree attitude, both the staff and fellow students liked him.

When he eventually left school, he had passed all his exams except for biology (the only part of the biology lessons he had paid any attention to was the reproductive system. This being something he wanted to experience as soon as possible).

Hacker had originally intended to apply for an apprenticeship in engineering or the like. What changed his mind was a casual conversation outside the local pub with the vicar's brother.

He was about thirty-five years old and an assistant designer for Rolls-Royce in the aero engine department.

"Well, it was great fun to begin with," he said to Hacker and at the same time reaching for his pint. "But now, quite honestly, I'm bored. I want to fly an aeroplane, rather than put engines in them. Alas, my company has informed me that I am indispensable due to some new engine designs coming up and I've been chosen to lead the team." He looked at his pint. "Quite flattering really, I suppose." He looked Hacker in the eye. "And apart from that, the RAF would class me as a fossil anyway. Seriously though, if there is one nerve in your body that has an inkling it wants to fly, give it the chance!"

Hacker gave the idea a lot of thought. A few weeks later, his decision made, he applied to the RAF. He was accepted and worked hard to achieve both his wings and his commission.

In October 1938 he was flying Gloster Gauntlets and Gloster Gladiators with the rank of pilot officer. At about the same time he received news from his sister that his mother had had a relapse concerning her illness. The local GP had suggested that a change of scenery and perhaps a different environment would help her recover. On his suggestion, his sister and mother moved to stay with his aunt in Jersey, leaving Malcolm to hold the fort as it were. That was a little under four years ago.

***

So, here he was, several weeks' leave available to him but bugger all to do with it. His mother and sister were in Jersey, which of course was currently occupied by the German army (who were not that keen on British fighter pilots popping round on flying visits to see their relations anyway). There was his brother of course, but Malcolm could be so incredibly dull. Moreover, the conversation he would offer would probably drive Hacker to drink, or worse. But what was much more to the point was the fact that his feet were on the ground and they were itching to be airborne. Hacker became more and more restless as time went on.

His CO noticed this when it was brought to his attention that Flying Officer Hacker had organised a game for his fellow pilots. The game entailed the use of two tractors, currently being used by the training squadron sharing the same airfield and normally used to tow bomb trolleys. On this occasion however, they had been appropriated by Hacker for a much more important mission. Sport!

Each tractor had a crew of six pilots on board, one was driving, one had his hands over the driver's eyes and all the others were shouting directions while desperately trying to maintain a firm grip on the tractor. The object of this particular game was to burst balloons, which were partially filled with water, which kept them reasonably secure to the ground. And burst more than the rival tractor, of course!

"Left... left!" shouted Hacker. "Come on Harry, stop driving how you fly, put some bloody effort in man!" Hacker had his hands firmly cupped over Harry's eyes.

"My dear chap, at no time did I say I was remotely capable of driving a tractor," Harry replied as he accidentally drove over three balloons in quick succession.

"There you go Harry! You're not completely bloody useless after all... turn right, you idiot!"

The opposing tractor had just made a near perfect beam attack on Harry's and missing by three feet, its crew shouting obscenities at the driver. At this moment both tractors had gone in opposite directions and then turned, as one. Both tractors came to a halt. They were poised, waiting to attack the remaining defenceless balloons. This was going to be the biggest massacre in balloon history. Harry revved the engine, the opposing tractor's engine took up the challenge and roared back, all the pilots were shouting at their respective drivers to attack, they were just about to move in for the kill when a car pulled up on the grass nearby. The duty officer stepped out of the car and eyed the situation with a look of disdain.

He stared at each tractor for a short moment and then purposefully walked towards Harry's. The engines were no longer roaring, just a gentle chug. A few feet short of Harry's tractor the duty officer stopped and stared straight at Hacker.

"The CO requests the pleasure of Flying Officer Hacker's presence in his office," he announced.

Hacker opened his mouth to make a flippant comment.

"Immediately!" added the duty officer without humour.

Hacker dismounted from his tractor and gave it a pat, as if it were a favourite pet, and then walked towards the car. As he did so, he looked over his shoulder and addressed the on-looking pilots:

"I expect he's just annoyed because we didn't invite him to join in!"

A cold silence came over all the pilots.

"Just a minute," said Harry, who was now standing on the metal seat of his tractor with his hands on his hips. "I thought you said the CO was at wing for a meeting?"

"He was," interrupted the duty officer, "but that was at 0630 this morning."

Harry looked flabbergasted. The other pilots looked at Harry, then the balloons and then the tractors. The car containing the duty officer and Hacker pulled away.

"Oh shit!" said one of the pilots.

***

"Now look Tony," said the CO of the training squadron on the other end of the phone. "I know this is a dull time for one and all, and there's just about bugger all to do around here. But my ground crew spent three and a half hours trying to locate those bloody tractors. My chief armourer wants your pilots for target practice. And I don't bloody well blame him!"

"If it was in my power Jim," replied Tony Miller, Hacker's CO, "I'd happily let him have them. As it is, I need them alive. However, the ringleader is on his way over here right now."

"Well be kind enough to kick the bastard up the arse as hard as you can. *If* you wouldn't mind."

"Consider it done, Jim. And I'll send a crate of beer to your 'Chiefy' with my compliments."

"Don't I get anything?" asked Jim Carver with feigned indignation.

"All right," replied Miller, "I'll send you a decent bottle of malt whisky."

"In that case I'll consider the matter closed."

Squadron Leader Miller placed the phone in its cradle. The door to his office was slightly ajar and his orderly gently knocked and looked around it.

"Flying Officer Hacker is here, sir," he announced quietly.

Miller, sitting at his desk, waved Hacker in. Hacker stood smartly to attention and, even more smartly, saluted.

Miller looked at him for a short moment with his elbows on the desk and his hands interlocked, supporting his chin. He then leaned back in his chair, stretched his legs, crossed them and folded his arms. He sat silently for a few seconds as if considering something. He looked up at Hacker.

"Bored are you?" Miller asked Hacker casually.

Silence seemed the best answer. Miller stared for but a moment and then said, "I'm having you transferred to RAF Seighford. It's near Stafford in case you didn't know. A training squadron. The CO there is not as tolerant as me. Dismiss!"

Hacker smartly saluted again and left the office. He walked down the hall in no great hurry.

"A training squadron!" he said to himself. "Bloody hell." He walked outside and stood staring at the control tower in the distance.

"A bloody training squadron!" he said out loud. He stood at the top of the steps for a few moments thinking. He'd go mad at a training squadron. He didn't want to sit with spotty little gits who were trying to kill him with their inept flying skills. The back of his mouth went dry with the thought. He methodically walked down the five steps, counting them as if they were distancing him from the inevitable.

As he reached the last step, his thoughts were shattered by the roar of a motorcycle. He looked up to see Harry White skid to a halt. Harry was an accident waiting to happen when he was on his motorbike. Nobody ever sat on the back.

"How did it go?" Harry asked. He was wearing his flying helmet with his goggles pushed up on his forehead.

"I've been bloody posted," replied Hacker.

Harry looked at him for a moment.

"Could've been worse, I suppose," Harry replied.

"It's a fucking training squadron!" Hacker exclaimed.

"Ah," said Harry thoughtfully. "So it can't get any worse."

Hacker's shoulders slumped. He looked at Harry.

"Where are you going in such a hurry anyway?"

"I thought it might be a good idea to get down to the pub before the CO sends for me. If a chap's going to be in the shit he might as well have a few beers first. Care to join

23

me?" he asked with a Devil-may-care glint in his eyes. Hacker smiled and got on the back. Harry was a little surprised.

"Just don't kill me!" Hacker shouted over the engine.

"If we go, we go together!" Harry shouted in reply, he revved the engine more than was necessary and let out the clutch.

Hacker just got his arms around Harry's waist in time as the bike lurched forward.

"I bloody mean it!" shouted Hacker.

Harry laughed aloud and changed gear.

When Hacker woke up the following morning, he found he had sustained a large bump to his head, a heavily scratched cheek and bruises to his left arm and leg. Not forgetting the obligatory hangover.

He and Harry shared a room. There was no sign of Harry. After a few minutes he sat up, then there was a knock on the door.

"Come in."

It was their batman with a mug of tea.

"Morning sir," he said, offering Hacker the mug. Hacker swung round and sat on the edge of the bed

"Thanks Morley." He took the mug in both hands and held it.

"Where's Harry?" Hacker asked.

"Having his leg plastered, sir."

"Why?" Hacker asked, not quite firing on all four cylinders.

"Same reasons he had his arm plastered, sir."

Hacker raised his eyebrows in surprise. He looked at Morley quizzically.

"You drove through the perimeter hedge last night, sir," Morley enlightened him. "And a small wall," he added. "Most spectacular according to the sentry. Mr White was airborne for some considerable distance."

Hacker's imagination took him to the hospital, he could see Harry in a hospital bed: one arm in plaster, his leg up and various sweet messages written by pretty nurses on his plastered leg. In fact, knowing Harry, the girls would be queuing up to offer their affections.

"Serves him bloody right," Hacker said softly.

"Beg your pardon, sir?"

"Serves him bloody right!" Hacker said a little louder. Morley raised his eyebrows.

"Well…" said Hacker, "he's a bloody awful driver isn't he? Bound to happen one day, wasn't it?"

"Oh dear," Morley said, gently shaking his head.

"What?" asked Hacker.

Morley had the beginnings of a grin.

"Mr White wasn't driving sir… you were."

Hacker looked at the floor and quietly groaned, "Oh bugger…"

Morley quietly left the room and closed the door gently behind him.

"Bad as each other," he muttered, "fucking idiots!"

Hacker slowly got himself together. He had a shower, shaved and got dressed. He then went straight to the MO's office.

"Oh he'll be fine, God's way of saying 'slow down'."

"Is it OK if I see him, sir?"

"Too late old boy. I've sent him off to Marlborough."

"Marlborough?"

"That's where his family live, he is on leave after all."

"Damn! I really did want to see him."

"Not to worry, as I say, he'll be fine. It's Hacker isn't it?"

"Yes, sir."

"He left you a note, I've got it here somewhere." The medical officer was patting all his pockets. There was a corner of an envelope showing from his top pocket.

"Er…" Hacker mumbled pointing.

"Ah yes, well done, here we go." He handed Hacker the envelope.

"Thank you, sir."

"When he gets back I'll be sure to give him your regards." He opened the door.

"Thanks very much, sir." Hacker left.

He walked towards the crew room, as he turned the corner Squadron Leader Miller was approaching. Hacker saluted. To Hacker's surprise and trepidation he stopped to talk briefly.

"No bones broken?"

"Er, no sir."

"Your luck must be changing. Still, what possessed you to get near Harry and his motorbike is beyond me. He's a bloody awful driver. Cheerio!"

"Sir," replied Hacker, confused.

He got to the crew room, sat down and opened the envelope and read:

And you call me an awful driver, I'll have to drink with the other hand now. The CO took it for granted that I was driving, you've got enough on your plate. He was quite good humoured about it. Said it should have happened years ago. You owe me a pint, take care, Keith, all the best.

Harry.

Hacker smiled. What a damned good chap, he thought to himself. He also felt very guilty. Harry was right though, if the CO had found out, he'd probably be making tea in a weather station in Scotland. He'd see Harry again he knew he would. Then they'd have a monumental party.

He sat pondering for quite a while, one or two pilots wandered through and said good morning or some such, but Hacker was miles away, his future looked a bit bleak. Out the corner of his eye he saw a pilot looking at a notice on the crew room board.

26

"No thanks," the pilot said humorously to himself. "I'm having a couple of weeks off!" He turned to leave and saw Hacker.

"How's Harry?" he asked.

"He's OK. The MO sent him home to his family."

"Good show. See you later." He left.

Hacker got up and walked over to the noticeboard. There was a memo in bold writing. It was asking for "interested parties" (nothing so crass as volunteers!) who would like a challenge with plenty of flying involved. Hacker immediately sought out the adjutant and requested an interview with the CO. To his surprise, the CO agreed to his request for permission to apply.

"If you're accepted," the CO said, "I'll cancel your transfer, if not, you'll be in the Midlands by next week. Good luck!" Interview over.

Hacker wrote and forwarded his application within an hour.

The interviewing officer was a squadron leader called Padshaw.

Padshaw had the look of a hard-working schoolteacher who took respect in his stride; almost an aloof arrogance surrounded him. He had in fact been a language master before joining the RAF.

He had a well-lined face from stress and hard work, dark hair, which was cut short and making its way slowly back over the dome of his head; it then made a flanking movement towards his ears.

But looks could be deceiving. He talked to Hacker with a mutual respect brought about by his own experiences fighting the foe.

Minus two fingers on his left hand and burns to his wrist, which then disappeared up his sleeve and reappeared just short of his left ear (Hacker was glad that he could not see the rest), plus a DFC and bar, Padshaw had certainly convinced Hacker that he was not being interviewed by a tired old pen-pusher with a bit of rank.

"Well Flying Officer Hacker," Padshaw said a little too brightly. "I must say you do seem to like to be in the thick of it, don't you, mmm?"

Hacker's file was sitting open on the desk in front of Padshaw. It was littered by asterisks on nearly every page, in fact it looked like an invasion of money spiders who had all stopped for breath at the same time.

Padshaw continued, "You have a very active flying record," he glanced at a page. "Four confirmed kills, two probables... and no doubt you've accounted for more than your fair share of enemy transport and the like." This, followed by another, "Mmmm."

"I've had some results," replied Hacker with unusual modesty.

"Modesty does not become you!" Padshaw stated with a hard, unexpectedly rough inflection to his voice. Hacker sat surprised and silent. A few seconds passed.

"I've read *all* of your file by the way," Padshaw added as though an afterthought, but in a softer voice (though emphasising the ALL).

Hacker frowned and squinted at the same time, giving him the look of a man who had just been caught for a crime committed in the distant past.

"Don't look like that, you've nothing to worry about. In fact, and I mean this quite sincerely, you are just what I'm looking for."

Padshaw picked up various pages from Hacker's file and very slowly began leafing through them. Hacker could see this was for effect, but was unsure why. On the other hand, the squadron leader did have his undivided attention.

"Squadron Leader Makepiece,' Padshaw opened. "Your CO when you were based in France."

Hacker nodded his confirmation of the fact.

"Well, that is to say, your first CO in France... copped it over Maastricht, didn't he?"

28

"Yes sir," answered Hacker.

"I never met him so I can't comment on him, but from the grave he has certainly made a comment or two about you, or should I say 'observations'."

"To quote: 'Full of self-confidence in the attack' –" Padshaw's eyes darted around the top page he was holding " – 'Flying Officer Hacker has always demonstrated natural skills in the air and, moreover, given the new boys and less experienced pilots a feeling of security when they fly with him. However, his disregard of various standing orders, unnecessary low flying, breaking formation without orders, etc. etc., does not help discipline. It is for these reasons I cannot approve a promotion.' Unquote."

Hacker just sat emotionless and listened. He'd heard it all before, he wasn't even bothered really. He gazed over the squadron leader's shoulder, out of the window. He was looking at an armourer getting what could only be described as seriously pissed off with a belt of ammunition, which he was trying to make adjustments to.

Squadron Leader Padshaw turned a page.

"Squadron Leader Banner!" he said in jovial fashion. "Now I know him. His comments on you are directed more towards your ground 'activities'."

Hacker remained silent; he was pretty sure what was going to come next.

"You seem to have a reputation for various unusual ways of passing the time when you're not flying." Padshaw paused for a moment. "Driving nurses from Abbeville around the perimeter track in an ambulance at breakneck speed, for instance."

"I was trying to break the squadron record, sir," Hacker said, attempting to bring some humour into the proceedings.

"Yes, so I see. In fact," Padshaw made the beginnings of a faint smile, "you said something similar to Squadron Leader Banner I understand. In point of fact, according to this, you set the record three weeks before."

A grin was beginning to appear on Padshaw's face as he perused another part of the page.

"You also make a habit of instigating your fellow officers and pilots into what I can only describe as 'pastimes detrimental to keeping their rank'."

He stared at Hacker with wide eyes and a broad smile, revealing a remarkably bright set of teeth.

This confused Hacker all the more as to what the bloody hell was going on.

"I see confusion in your eyes," Padshaw said as if on cue. "It's simple really, I've been given the task of forming a special squadron to operate in a different theatre of the War. The living conditions may not be as comfortable as you are used to here, but I can promise you bags of flying, a good tan and an easy-going atmosphere."

"North Africa?" Hacker offered.

"I'm not at liberty to say at this time," replied Padshaw. "But I will say this: you're an excellent pilot, it says so here, you have flown various types and adapt to these aircraft with great ability. Your other activities may well be a great asset for where you're going. Your application is approved." He added abruptly, "You'll find your instructions with the clerk, his office is down the hall. You may want to do some shopping. Shorts perhaps, or a sun lotion." The broad smile was still on Padshaw's face. Hacker felt tricked and bewildered at the same time. Bewildered being out in front.

"For the warm climate," Padshaw added. The squadron leader then stood up, his right arm outstretched.

"Good luck Flying Officer, you'll be leaving within the next three days."

Hacker was on his feet, his right hand being pumped rather than shaken.

"Thank you, sir," said Hacker and made his way to the door. As he opened it, he turned to the now sitting squadron leader who was now studying various files, Hacker opened his mouth to speak but nothing came out. He quickly saluted, walked out and quietly closed the door behind him.

Walking down the corridor, his brain came to life and caught up with current events.

The clerk would already have his movement orders. Padshaw had said so. That being the case, his application had obviously been approved prior to the interview. Not only that, but his catalogue of escapades did not seem to be deemed that important. Squadron Leader Padshaw, Hacker realised, had only touched the surface of his many, though be they minor, reprimands. Hacker was also fairly sure that Padshaw's comments on his flying abilities were sincere. For himself, Hacker had no ego in relation to his capabilities as a pilot. But he was good, he knew he was good and so did his peers and fellow pilots.

What bothered Hacker the most was that he had just had an interview with a senior officer he did not know until today. Who told him, basically, nothing! Padshaw knew, Hacker felt, more than he was prepared to admit, then approved his application in advance, did not tell him where he was going, but that he would be leaving in the next seventy-two hours.

No going back now. Bollocks!

"Well what the bloody hell is wrong with it, eh? Smallpox? Malaria? Amnesia? Overtired?"

"Not sure sir," replied one of the two men working on the engine.

"Could be dirty fuel," suggested the second man.

"Well the bloody thing has certainly forgotten how to fucking fly hasn't it?" The contained anger in Squadron Leader Marsland's voice was slowly coming out.

"We're doing our best, sir," came a calm voice from behind him, that of his chief engineer Pat 'Punchy' Jennings. He approached the CO with a casual indifference to the situation. He knew full well that Squadron Leader Marsland was not in any way upset with the ground crew or

31

himself. In fact, the CO was always full of praise for what they managed to achieve with their limited spares and facilities.

"All right 'Punchy'. Do what you can as soon as pos. But it's a bloody awful show when the Squadron takes off and the CO's plane won't even start!"

"God's way of giving you some time off to enjoy the scenery?" suggested Jennings, tongue in cheek. Marsland looked at Jennings briefly and then slowly did a full 360-degree turn and viewed the surroundings. A flat strip just big enough to land and take off (with the cannibalised wrecks of aircraft at each end – evidence of not such good landings and take-offs). Various tall trees created a wall of greenery on four sides, various tents and equipment were scattered about. Of the four bamboo huts one was the mess, one belonged to the CO, the second largest belonged to the medical officer and the last was occupied by Flight Lieutenant Hollingsworth, the squadron adjutant. Lastly, of course, was the ammunition dump on one side and the fuel dump on the other.

"You're right 'Punchy', such beauty should not be ignored. Adj?" he said to Hollingsworth, who was walking away from Marsland's office.

"Yes sir?" replied Hollingsworth politely.

"Have 'Punchy' court-martialled for bad humour while on active service immediately."

"At once sir," the adjutant replied. "May I be so bold as to recommend the firing squad as well, sir?"

"You may," Marsland said, adding: "I'll be in my office with my masseuse if you need me. And let me know as soon as that bloody aeroplane's remembered how to fly."

Marsland walked to his office, flying helmet and gloves in one hand and the other scratching his armpit. He opened the door, such that is was being constructed from bamboo and twine, to be met with a stack of paperwork and forms which were not there when he had left earlier.

He turned from the half-opened door to face the adjutant who was standing near the reluctant Kittyhawk, a look of total innocence on his face.

"What the bloody hell is all this, Holly?" he shouted, using the adjutant's nickname.

"Well sir," replied Hollingsworth, "what with the current situation with your Kitty. I thought it a prime opportunity to let you catch up with some of the paperwork."

"Holly?" said the CO.

"Yes sir?" replied the adjutant with the same innocent smile on his face.

"As soon as you've shot Punchy, please be so kind as to shoot yourself immediately afterwards."

"Yes sir," replied the adjutant as the CO slammed the door shut.

Punchy looked at the adjutant with a wry smile and said with some sarcasm, "He won't be inviting you to his birthday party, then?"

"That reminds me," replied the adjutant, "have we located any booze yet?"

"No," answered 'Punchy'. "But things are afoot."

Marsland sat in his office staring with little or no interest whatsoever at the piles of what he regarded as toilet paper in front of him.

The adjutant knew he hated paperwork and often covered most of it for him. Then it would simply require the CO's signature. Unfortunately there were always certain aspects only the CO could deal with.

"I could handle this a lot better with some decent gin inside me," he muttered to himself, and then started reading.

***

There was a knock on Group Captain Beecham's door.

"Come in," was his curt response.

"Squadron Leader Padshaw has just arrived, sir," the corporal announced.

"Thank you, Morris," replied Beecham. "Send him in will you. Oh, and rustle up a spot of tea would while you're at it."

"Yes sir," said Morris.

Three hours earlier, Padshaw had been in the middle of an important meeting discussing the logistics of transporting all the paraphernalia associated with forming his specialist squadron. Spares, tools, clothing, food, medical supplies, belly dancers and God knew what else. Plus he had to find a good IO (intelligence officer), a doctor, an orderly for the doctor, ground crew who were qualified on various types of aircraft and to top it all, he had to complete all this in a relatively short period of time. He also had to achieve all this without upsetting too many squadron commanders, whose staff he was, basically, going to poach.

He was just getting into the swing of things when he was interrupted with a message from an orderly.

Padshaw knew the orderly, whose name was Palmer. Palmer had knocked loudly on the door and entered without invitation. Padshaw knew Palmer to be courteous to a fault and always showed maximum respect to rank (even if the officer was an idiot).

For Palmer to enter the room in such a fashion was, to Padshaw at least, a message in itself that something was seriously wrong.

"Very sorry to interrupt sir, urgent message from group."

"Thank you," replied Padshaw, taking the sealed envelope offered to him by Palmer who now stood silent and alert waiting for instructions.

Padshaw slit the envelope with a paperknife and read the information it contained. That exercise took all of ten seconds.

"Bloody hell. It never rains but it pours," he said with frustration in his voice. "Have my car brought round immediately, Palmer." Palmer was already making his way to the door.

"It will be outside in ten minutes, sir." Palmer was well ahead of the situation.

"My apologies gentlemen," announced Padshaw to the assembled group. "Something has come up which may alter things somewhat. Please carry on without me. But do not put anything into motion without liaising with myself, first." With that Padshaw left the room and made off to his waiting car.

***

Group Captain Beecham was the officer who had given Padshaw the task of forming the special squadron.

Up until now Padshaw had done an exemplary job. Beecham had given instructions to specifically recruit pilots who either adapted quickly to different types of aircraft, or who were experienced on several types of fighter already in service. One of the reasons for this was having to take into account which aircraft were already available, plus whatever might be shipped out. It really was something of a mixed bag. Kittyhawks, Hurricanes, Brewsters, Bald Eagles, whatever was up for grabs.

Of course some aircraft would have to be adapted in various ways for the missions they would have to undertake, hence also the requirement for experienced ground crew.

The reason for forming this particular squadron was twofold. Firstly was the real need for more air power in the skies above and around India and northern Burma. It was a well-known fact, among the top brass at least, that a plan had been put together to advance south into Burma in the very near future. Air support would be vital. The second reason was very "hush hush". Beecham would inform Padshaw of this task when the time was right.

But right now, a quite ghastly scenario had come about.

The first thing Padshaw had completed in his list of tasks to form the squadron was to get his pilots. He had achieved this with great speed and already had them on a troopship bound for the East.

Group Captain Beecham was not looking forward to the next ten minutes.

Padshaw entered the group captain's office; the orderly quietly closed the door behind him.

"Have a chair, Terry," said Beecham, using Padshaw's first name with some familiarity.

"Thank you sir," Padshaw sat down.

Padshaw looked at the group captain with a little impatience and then said, "What's the panic?"

Beecham had his hands palms down on his desk and was looking at them. He clasped his hands together and drew himself closer to his desk and looked straight into Padshaw's eyes.

"Well Terry," he said, "to put it in a nutshell: you don't have any pilots and you've lost all your Hurricanes, to boot."

Padshaw's mouth opened in dismay, his eyes were wide open and his hands had a firm grip on the arms of the chair.

"Why?" Padshaw asked indignantly. "Who's snaffled my pilots?" There was a pause.

"The German navy," replied Beecham quietly. "I really am very sorry."

It took Padshaw a few seconds to digest this information. He was mortified. He had met every single man personally. He'd got to know two or three of them quite well. Losses happened every day but, to Padshaw, this was quite appalling.

At that moment the tea arrived.

"Thank you Morris," said Beecham.

Morris would normally have poured the tea, but with the sombre look on Padshaw's face and the attentive look on Beecham's directed at the squadron leader, Morris knew when to bugger off.

Morris closed the door and Beecham poured the tea. He then passed it to Padshaw, who remained silent. Holding his cup of tea in one hand and the saucer in the other, Padshaw looked blankly at the group captain.

"Are we sure, sir?" he asked. "I mean, are we absolutely certain?"

"I'm afraid so," replied Beecham, who was trying to keep his voice softer than normal.

"We had one troopship and two cargo ships," he explained. "The cargo ship containing your precious Hurricanes was torpedoed before the escort could do anything. They then managed to scare off two of the buggers but a third snuck in behind and bye-bye troopship. I have yet to receive any reports on survivors, but even if there were any, I doubt they'll be fit for any kind of duties for some time."

Padshaw was silent for a few moments. Then he piped up, "My sources tell me there are nine good Hurricanes sitting idle in a holding area quite close to where we wish to operate from. Why can't I have those, sir?"

"You don't have any pilots, Terry," Beecham replied calmly. "And those Hurricanes are allocated."

"I've got one pilot," stated Padshaw. "He's been sitting on his arse for a week waiting for orders." But even as he said it he knew his cause was lost.

There were a few moments' silence. It was Beecham who broke it.

"Look Terry," said Beecham, "nobody is happy about what's happened here. The thing is, and what you don't know, is that the brass upstairs had a particular task set out in conjunction with this new squadron, on top of teaching Johnny Jap not to trespass."

Padshaw placed his cup and saucer on the corner of Beecham's desk. He rested his elbows on his knees and clasped his hands together. He looked as if he'd aged two years in five minutes. He opened his mouth to ask the question.

Beecham raised a hand and waved Padshaw back to silence.

"The point I'm making Terry," Beecham continued, "is that despite this unpleasant setback, I cannot see the brass wanting to alter their plans. When they get a bee in their bonnet about something they can be a right pain. Anyway, I have to be in London for 1800 hours to meet with some chaps from the War Office. We've got several things to discuss including today's events. It might be to your advantage to join me. Perhaps you could say a few words yourself, give them your point of view, as it were? You never know, they might ask you to devise something else." Beecham paused for a moment, his face beamed with encouragement, then he added, "Well, do you fancy a beer in London?"

Padshaw had the look of a man who had just been given a sports car for a birthday present.

"Absolutely, sir," Padshaw replied.

"Excellent! You had better pack a bag. I'll meet you in the bar in three hours, we'll drive up together."

"Right sir, I'd better get a move on." Padshaw left the office. Beecham started putting files in a briefcase.

Squadron Leader Marsland was just coming to the end of his briefing. He had his pilots assembled in the shade of some trees beside the mess. They were sitting on ramshackle chairs, empty ammunition boxes or simply lying on the ground leaning on their elbows facing their CO. Marsland was standing next to an improvised tripod constructed of various branches lashed together with Jubilee clips and supporting a rather tattered blackboard.

"Right chaps, to reiterate: our main target are the sampans moored on this larger of the three waterways located at Akyab." Marsland indicated the area with his stick on the blackboard. "As you know, up to now Johnny Jap is unaware that we have a landing ground so close to areas he occupies... or likes to think he occupies." Some of the pilots smiled. "Let's keep it that way." Marsland continued, "On your return, Red section, led by myself, will fly in a westerly direction and then turn north for home. Yellow and Blue section, led by Miller and Harris respectively, will fly east and then for home. As you are all aware, we've had little or no opposition to date from the imperial Japanese air force. This does not mean they're having a holiday or that you can be complacent. Once the objective has been destroyed, providing we find the bloody things, do not waste ammunition. You might find a target on the way home, or more to the point, you might need what you've got left to get yourself out of trouble. Should we fail to find our initial target, you have a maximum of ten minutes to find another. All three sections are to split up and go hunting. *If* you do not find any suitable targets, come home. Ten minutes is the maximum!"

Marsland had raised his voice for effect. "Our fuel reserves are low. Don't forget, you have been fuelled up for about 600 miles each. We're expecting our fuel stocks to be replenished in the next few days. It's a round trip of 400 miles or so to and from the target. You're going to spend time over the target plus a detour on your return, so watch your fuel gauges. Lastly intelligence, if that's the right word for them –" there were smirks and chuckles from the assembled pilots "– intelligence," Marsland repeated gently, "have informed us that these sampans, if they are where they're supposed to be, are quite possibly protected by four or more other sampans equipped with heavy machine guns. Now I know we've heard this before and nothing came of it, but let's not take any chances. We've recently had great results in damaging the Jap supply routes on various rivers and trails. If I was them I'd be getting pretty well pissed off by now. So, on the first attack, Red section will go in first with Blue section at one thousand feet above, looking out for the defensive sampans. Yellow section will provide top cover. Red section will then take over from Blue and vice versa. Yellow section to mop up if we miss anything. Any Questions?"

There were none.

"One more thing: *if* anything happens to me, Flight Lieutenant Valentine takes over the squadron. Take off in twenty minutes, good luck!"

The pilots got themselves up, gathered their helmets and maps and walked towards their aircraft. Most of them were talking happily amongst themselves, on reaching their respective aircraft they were either waggling the rudder, kicking the wheels or generally looking their steeds over. One of the pilots, Colin 'Chancer' Harris (so called because of his fanatical love for gambling) climbed onto the wing as his rigger was just finishing polishing the inside of the windscreen.

"Morning Clarke," said Harris.

"Morning sir," Clarke replied cheerfully.

"Any idea what I've got on board today?" Harris asked.

"Well sir, 'Punchy' instructed all the armourers to load every third round tracer, sir, so I reckon that's what you've got."

"Jolly good!" replied Harris jovially. "I do love a good fireworks display."

Flight Lieutenant Charles 'Snobby' Valentine had left the briefing and gone straight to the latrines (his philosophy being *There's enough shit flying around doing this job so why take more with you?*). As he came out he saw the CO walking towards his Kittyhawk and intercepted him just before he got to it.

"I say old chap," he said with his usual total indifference to rank (whether it was a private or an air marshal, 'Snobby' didn't care), "I do wish you'd stop telling everybody I'm in charge if you get a problem. Firstly you're tempting fate and secondly you don't even have the manners or courtesy to ask me if I want the job or not! Bloody rude, if you ask me."

Marsland smiled. Valentine was renowned for his unusual humour and eccentric behaviour. On the ground he kept the Squadron amused and relaxed. In the air, however, Marsland was glad he was on their side.

"Awfully sorry 'Snobby'," Marsland replied. "I was under the misguided impression that, being the CO, everybody does as I tell them."

"Yes, well," said Valentine, "we'll forget about it this time, but don't let it happen again." With that he turned on his heel and walked towards his Kitty.

"Snobby!" Marsland called.

Valentine looked over his shoulder, "Yes old chap?"

"Don't let the boys fly too close together, if the Japs do have heavy machine guns on those sampans they won't be able to miss. OK?"

"Leave it to me Skipper, I'll keep an eye on them." 'Snobby' walked to his aircraft.

Marsland climbed up onto the wing of his P40, his rigger held his harness straps back as Marsland made sure his parachute was secure. He then clambered in and sat down.

In the cockpit of a Kittyhawk, when you sat down you were more or less sitting on the floor and you could stretch your legs right out in front of you. This made long flights quite comfortable for the pilots. There were even areas on the left and right in the cockpit where you could rest your arms (should people stop shooting at you long enough).

The other important thing to note about the Curtiss P40 was that everything, from the flaps and landing gear right down to the constant speed propeller and a majority of the other instruments, was controlled electronically.

An hour earlier, 'Punchy' Jennings had had his ground crew run up the engines on all the Kittyhawks. Some aircraft would still have enough charge in their batteries to turn the engine over. More often than not, the poor bloody ground crew would have to coax the engines into life by hand cranking them one by one, and in this sweltering environment, that was no mean feat. Marsland looked down from the cockpit at the NCO who had just come into view on his port wing. As he finished fastening his traps, his rigger nodded at him.

"Good luck, sir."

Marsland smiled at him. As the man clambered off the wing, Marsland checked all his gauges and set all the switches. He checked to his left and right, his rigger appeared at the end of his starboard wing.

"All clear?" Marsland shouted.

"Sir," the rigger replied giving him the thumbs up.

"Contact!"

Marsland pressed the start button. The Allison V12 engine roared into life. One thousand one hundred and fifty horsepower shook the airframe and yearned to get airborne. He looked to his left to see an 'erk' dragging a rather ramshackle fire extinguisher trolley to a safe distance. Marsland than looked at his instrument panel and began checking everything off. Landing gear warning light, fuel signal warning light, fuel tank gauges, oil pressure. The engine stopped! He abruptly looked up from the instrument panel and watched the propeller come to a stop. Marsland reset all the relevant switches and double checked everything as his rigger looked on.

"Contact!" he shouted again and pressed the start button. The engine popped and banged but refused to start again.

"Buggeration," he said to no one in particular. He looked at the rest of his squadron who were ready to take off. He couldn't delay them any longer; their engine temperatures would be slowly climbing up.

"Sorry chaps," Marsland announced, "my engine's packed up. Flight Lieutenant Valentine?"

"Yes old chap?" replied Valentine.

"You lead this one, I'll catch up if I can, over."

"OK, Skipper. See you for afternoon tea."

'Snobby' called to the rest of the Squadron, "Red section with me leading will take off first, followed by Blue, then Yellow. We will make one circuit of the airfield and then head towards the target, is that understood Blue leader?"

"Understood," replied Harris.

"Yellow leader?" 'Snobby' asked.

"Wilco," Miller confirmed.

"Right, let's go, Red section form up on me." Valentine swung his aircraft onto the airstrip, the propeller wash kicking up dust and dead foliage. The other three aircraft making up Red section followed him. Valentine opened the throttle and within a few yards his tail was flying, next minute he was airborne and climbing to port; he glanced over his left shoulder to see the last of Red section get airborne.

Blue section were lined up ready and Yellow were waiting their turn. Blue section was also made up of four aircraft. Yellow section three, Blue section started to build up speed as they ate up the airstrip. By this time Marsland had got out of his Kitty and was walking away from it in disgust. He stopped twenty yards away and took some pleasure in watching his squadron take off. Blue section were just clearing the trees at the other end of the strip as Yellow section just got to flying speed, a few seconds and they too cleared the trees and joined Red and Blue sections and then proceeded to do one circuit of the airfield. That completed, the squadron headed due south.

Marsland turned, and on seeing two men working on his aircraft, he walked back towards it.

After just over twenty-five minutes' flying time, Valentine was making good progress. He constantly kept

43

his eyes open for landmarks and was frequently checking his map. He looked ahead and saw three distinctively shaped hills. Up until now he had maintained radio silence, now he spoke to the squadron.

"Target in sight chaps, keep your eyes open."

All the pilots were turning their heads and twisting to get a good all round view of the surrounding sky.

"Yellow section, this is Red leader. Make angels and hold at three thousand. Over."

"Wilco Red leader. Yellow section climb, go!"

Valentine watched Yellow section climb away. Valentine was at two thousand feet.

"Right. Blue section. I can see the larger estuary up ahead. Follow Red section down to one thousand feet and hold at that height."

"Roger that, Red leader."

"Red section. We're going hunting. Get down to 300 feet and keep your eyes peeled. Their camouflage is bound to be good. Red and Blue sections… going down… now!"

The eight Kittyhawks made their descent, at one thousand feet Blue section levelled out, Red section kept falling. Valentine glanced up at Blue section for a brief moment.

"Spread yourselves out more Blue section. Don't bunch up!"

"Roger leader."

Blue section spread themselves right out. At 300 feet and 150 miles an hour, Valentine led Red section down the length of the waterway. Any faster, Valentine decided, and they'd miss a double-decker bus. He led Red section in from the mouth of the waterway, studying the banks and dense treeline, looking for any clue as to their target's position. On Valentine's left was Sergeant Pilot Don Spencer, a Canadian, flying as Red two. To his right was Pilot Officer 'Jiff' Verster, a stocky South African, flying as Red three, and just behind him was Sergeant Pilot Paul Cracken, an Englishman flying at Red four. They completed their pass of the suspected area and pulled up and to the left.

"Anybody see anything at all?" Valentine asked his pilots.

"Didn't see anything unusual," replied Cracken.

"Jiff?" Valentine asked.

"The only spot I saw that might be our target is the area off that bank where it seems to stretch further into the water," Jiff replied.

Sure enough, the banks were quite evenly matched on both sides. But there was an area in good shade stretching about 250 yards, which worked its way gently further into the water and back again.

Valentine studied the area for a few seconds.

"What do you think Spence?" Valentine asked his wingman.

"Well, there's one way to find out isn't there?"

Valentine made his decision. "Right Red section," he announced. "Spence with me, 'Jiff' and Paul 300 yards behind. We'll come in again from the mouth of the waterway. Spence, I want you slightly behind and above so as we can open fire at the same time, got that?"

"Roger."

"Same goes for you and Paul 'Jiff', keep it staggered, OK?"

"Roger that," replied 'Jiff'.

"Keep a slight bank on so as to make sure we can hit the target area below the treeline. Give the area three one-second bursts, no point wasting ammo if we've got the wrong spot. After you've made your attack, climb to port. All clear?"

"Clear," said 'Jiff'.

"Wilco," replied Cracken.

Spence, flying alongside of Valentine, waggled his wings and gave a thumbs up with a broad smile.

"Right," said Valentine. "Take position Spence. Let's see what we can find." Valentine dropped a wing and swooped down towards the shaded area under the overhanging trees. Spence faithfully followed every move. Valentine checked to make sure his guns were armed.

"Check your safety is off Spence."

"All set," replied Spencer.

"We'll close to 300 yards. When I say fire, start shooting!" Valentine ordered.

"Understood, leader."

The four Kitties ate up the gap between the mouth of the estuary and their supposed target in a few seconds. At 500 yards Valentine said, "Open fire!"

By the time he'd got the words out it was 300 yards and Spence was firing.

Small fountains of water splashed up as point five-oh ammunition sprayed about, clods of dirt and branches flew about in no particular direction. A small tree, its roots shot out, slowly fell onto the area they'd been aiming at. Tracer wove its way towards the target and was enveloped in the mud and water.

"Break left," ordered Valentine.

"Right behind you, leader," confirmed Spence.

Of the next pair 'Jiff' was leading. He and Cracken followed the same line and tactics as their leader. Verster turned in, sighted his target and moved his thumb to the gun button.

"Open…" That was as far as Verster got. His aircraft took twenty hits in less than a second. The noise of heavy machine gun bullets chewing up his Kittyhawk was frightening. Part of his engine cowling flew past his head, just missing the tail, his windscreen and gunsight disappeared. One bullet smashed through his canopy handle and ricocheted into the instrument panel; another re-arranged his headrest and the last damaged a control cable.

"Jesus Christ!" he shouted. What was intact were 'Jiff's' reflexes. He opened the throttle and pulled up hard to port, his Kittyhawk was sluggish in the turn. Damaged rudder most likely, he thought to himself. The rush of air through the front of his smashed cockpit was making his eyes run. He pulled his goggles down. "At least I can see where I'm going," he said to himself.

Cracken was following 'Jiff' as arranged. He was fortunate that their staggered formation protected him from the onslaught being thrown up at them. In fact, the two machine guns that opened fire let loose over 200 rounds, but fortunately the Japs firing them didn't allow for the Kittyhawk's speed and all the other rounds went wide. Cracken found himself flying alongside 'Jiff', whose aircraft was constantly sidling.

"Fucking rudder!" Verster shouted loudly.

"Jiff, this is Valentine. You OK?"

"Oh yeah! I'm bloody marvellous. I've got a howling gale in the cockpit, no instruments and I need a pee," he replied with indignation.

"Don't bugger about. Are you hurt?" shouted Valentine.

Jiff calmed down and said, "Sorry leader, no extra holes, but my rudder's spongy and my oil temperature is starting to rise."

"Understood," replied Valentine.

"Red four, escort Red three home, take the most direct route, any problems let me know. Over."

"Wilco leader, formatting on Red three now."

Valentine watched Verster and Cracken slowly fly away for a moment. Then he looked down at the target, Spence at Red two was flying alongside him. Neither Valentine nor Spencer could be expected to pinpoint the machine guns as they were flying away when Verster was hit. At that moment 'Chancer' Harris's voice came over the RT.

"Red leader, this is Blue leader. I've got the bastards! Over."

"Well done Blue leader. Lose height and make your attack. Myself and Red two will come in at a right angle to

47

the bank and make them keep their heads down as you turn away, understood?"

"Understood Red leader, going in... now!"

"Yellow section, this is Red leader, anything I should know about?"

"All clear Red leader."

"Blue leader, it's your show."

"Roger. Blue leader to Blue section. Line astern formation. I want 100 yards between aircraft, everybody weave on the approach. Give them a three-second burst then climb like blazes to port and re-form. Look out for Red section on your port side covering us on the way out. Clear?"

"Blue two, wilco leader."

"Blue three, roger leader."

"Blue four, roger leader."

Harris got his airspeed up to 200 miles an hour. He didn't want to fly any slower in case more heavy machine guns made an appearance, any faster and an accurate strafe was more difficult. Harris led Blue flight up the waterway; they were at 500 feet.

"Right Blue flight. Everybody get down to 100 feet and start weaving."

Harris dropped his nose; the rest of Blue section followed his lead. Harris kept his eyes fixed on the area around where the machine guns had opened fire on Verster. The Jap camouflage was very good indeed, nothing looked out of place. At 800 yards from the target one of the machine guns opened up, giving away their exact position. That was a mistake!

"OK Blue flight, now we can see the bastards!"

At that moment Harris thumbed the gun trigger and pedalled the rudder bar left and right, a swathe of bullets saturated the area of one of the machine guns. Just as Harris began to pull up, he saw a flicker of yellow and red flame lick from one of the camouflaged sampans.

Blue two was Sergeant Pilot Terry Cavendish. As soon as his leader broke away he began firing. He saw his tracer prance and duck and dive and then bury itself into the licks of flame. As he pulled away he saw out of the corner of his right eye an orange fireball rising.

Flying at Blue three was Phil Banner; at Blue four was 'Stubby' Hillman. Banner could see the flames rising. Banking slightly, he opened fire; one of the sampans erupted! Both Banner and 'Stubby' felt the air shove them over from the blast. They both opened their throttles and clawed for height. Stubby hadn't fired a shot!

Valentine and 'Spence', in what was left of Red section, were already approaching the bank head on, supposedly providing cover. Valentine could see men on fire diving into the water. All the camouflage netting was ablaze. There was no ground fire either. There was bugger all left.

"Red two. Break and climb port. Go!" Valentine pulled up and 'Spence followed.

"Well done chaps. Blue section formate on me, over."

"On our way, leader."

Valentine looked down at the carnage below. It seemed as if the whole riverbank was on fire. Ammunition was exploding everywhere.

"That'll teach the buggers," announced 'Spence'. Valentine smiled to himself.

"This is Red leader, we will all return to base flying north and then west. I want a loose formation. Yellow leader?"

"Receiving you, Red leader."

"Keep Yellow section 300 feet above and behind, over."

"Got that, Red leader. Yellow section loose height. Go!" Yellow section took up position behind Red and Blue sections.

Miller, as did the other pilots, felt marvellous. A successful mission and, providing Verster got back OK, no losses and home for tea. Even though Miller and his section had taken no part in the actual attack, the Squadron was a closely-knit team and everybody felt good about a job well done. Miller's earphones crackled into life.

"This is Red leader, everyone keep their eyes open. And keep a lookout for anything suitable to hit on the way home. Leader out."

Everybody continued to search the sky. It was easy to relax a bit after a successful action. It was also the worst thing to do. In the past few months the Squadron had seen very little of the Japanese air force in their area of operations, but that did not mean a couple of Jap fighters couldn't appear from nowhere.

A few minutes passed before something on the ground caught 'Stubby' Hillman's eye.

"Blue four to Red leader. I can see some movement on the ground at one o'clock." (There were six trucks)

Valentine stared for a few moments, then he too saw them. Unusual, he thought to himself. There weren't that many areas suitable for wheeled transport in this area.

"I see them, Blue four, but they might possibly be ours."

The whole Squadron was now looking at the same spot on the ground, looking for something that might identify them as friendly or Japs. Again it was 'Stubby' Hillman who saw something that might give the game away.

"Red leader, Blue four. There are men on bicycles." Japanese use of bicycles was commonplace and had played a decisive role in their invasion of Burma.

"I can see a nip tank as well," said Valentine. "That cuts it for me. Yellow leader, your turn. I suggest you fly downwind and come up from behind. They won't hear your engines until it's too late. Blue and Red sections will provide cover. Over."

"Wilco Red leader. Yellow section, turning starboard. Go!"

Yellow section peeled off. Miller led the flight quite a long way down wind.

"OK Yellow section," he said. "Let's get ourselves lined up. Yellow two stay close to me."

"Roger that, Yellow leader."

"Yellow three, I want you to stay 500 yards behind. As we fly over the troops on bicycles they will be looking at us and not you. They are your targets, got that?"

Dick Chalmers, flying at Yellow three, found this part of warfare distasteful. But he kept to a philosophy that every soldier he killed would have killed an Allied soldier, given the chance.

"Understood Yellow leader."

Chalmers throttled back to let the distance between himself and the rest of Yellow section grow to about 500 yards. He then opened the throttle to maintain the same distance.

"Yellow leader. Yellow three. In position."

"Right Yellow section, let's not push our luck, one pass only so make it count. Tallyho!"

Miller pushed the nose down and led Yellow section down to 250 feet. Trees were at various heights, some of them whipping past the wingtips. Lady Luck was surely with them. The Japanese column had reached an open clearing, allowing the pilots a clear view of their target and the opportunity to get lower.

There were six trucks in all and about forty men on bicycles lagging behind. The trucks had separated themselves into two columns of three next to each other, led by a light tank in the middle. They couldn't have made life easier.

"Yellow two, come up on my starboard side, we'll attack at the same time. You take the trucks on the right, I'll take left."

"Wilco leader." The trucks were trundling along on the uneven ground at about fifteen miles an hour. The route they had taken was that of an old trail long disused but sparse in vegetation. The clearing had offered the drivers an unexpected chance to put some speed on and make up some time.

In the back of the third truck in the right-hand column, two Japanese soldiers were sharing a cigarette and listening to the driver's mate shouting a joke through the open hatch in the back of the cab. The punchline had one of them in hysterics and laughing, he fell off the bench seat. He grabbed the top of the tailgate and pulled himself up. Still laughing, he looked up at the sunshine, the clouds, the birds. He nudged his friend and pointed to the sky. His friend leant out of the back of the tailgate and looked up.

The first Jap was still pointing when his mate's head exploded, throwing bits of brain and bone all over the inside of the truck, the same burst took off his own, still pointing arm and cut him in half right across the chest. The point five-oh calibre bullets carried on and chopped the driver and his mate into unrecognisable lumps of meat.

"Steady, Yellow two, steady... open fire... now!"

Streams of tracer leapt from the Kittyhawks' wings, both trucks at the back of each column were hit simultaneously; in the left-hand column the tail-end truck exploded as the petrol tank was hit by tracer. The second vehicle turned out to be a radio truck with aerials and communication equipment strapped all over it. The whole vehicle was ripped to pieces, the occupants suffering the same fate. The lead vehicle was carrying fuel and went up like a bomb.

Jimmy Parish, the only American in the Squadron, was Yellow two. He watched in exultation as his opening burst shredded the first vehicle. Before he could blink the second vehicle was twisted and burning. The last truck in the line just seemed to stop dead with no obvious damage.

Parish climbed and turned to starboard to get a view of the destruction behind him. The cab of the lead vehicle, which he thought he'd missed, looked like metal spaghetti.

The driver, if he could have seen him, made an excellent impression of a bolognaise sauce.

Chalmers in Yellow three couldn't miss. Miller had been right, all the troops were looking in awe and surprise at the mayhem before them.

He thumbed the gun button and pedalled the rudder at the same time. An invisible scythe slashed through bone and flesh. Bodies cartwheeled, mangled bicycles and butchered flesh were scattered across the ground and thrown into the air. As Yellow three pulled up he saw his last rounds cut down men who had escaped the first attack, he closed his eyes, pulled the stick back and opened the throttle. His Kittyhawk was followed by machine-gun fire coming from the light tank, but it was well off the mark.

"Yellow leader to Yellow section, regroup, regroup!"

After the attack, Miller had broken left, Parish and Chalmers to the right. It took a minute to spot their leader and get into position behind him. Yellow leader called them, "Well done chaps, bloody good show."

"This is Red leader, time for home, well done Yellow section."

Yellow section climbed and resumed position behind and above the rest of the Squadron.

Valentine couldn't believe it, two targets destroyed and no losses. He slapped his own face.

"We're not home yet chaps, stay awake," he said. With his own words he became more alert. War doesn't stop for anybody. They were getting close to home when Red two saw something very unusual. In fact he had to look twice.

"Red leader, this is Red two. Bogeys at twelve o'clock!"

Valentine laughed to himself. Bugger all happens for weeks and in one sortie the whole world wants to come out and play. He checked his fuel gauge. Enough for home and a gnat's bollock more to spare. The rest of the Squadron would be about the same.

"I read you, Red two. We'll go straight at them, throw what we can at them and then make straight for home. All sections spread out. After we've hit them regroup on me."

"Yellow leader, this is Blue two, they could be ours, couldn't they?"

Valentine hesitated for a moment. He stared as the distance between his squadron and the other aircraft diminished, he could clearly see seven aircraft. What he couldn't distinguish was the type.

***

Group Captain Beecham was already waiting in the bar. "Ah! There you are Terry. Fancy a Scotch before we get on the road?"

"Thanks very much sir, a malt if they've got it," replied Padshaw.

"My driver's waiting outside, but there's no hurry," said Beecham. He raised a hand to get the barman's attention.

"Two large Glenmorangies, old chap."

"Yes sir," replied the barman.

Another officer with the rank of squadron leader approached Beecham and Padshaw.

"Barman," said Beecham politely, "make that three if you would."

"Of course sir," he said reaching for the bottle again.

"Terry, this is Graham Hawkins, Graham, Squadron Leader Padshaw."

"Ah," said Hawkins, "a pleasure to meet you at last, Group Captain Beecham's told me a lot about you."

Padshaw was pleased and a little wary at the same time. "I'm sure he left out my bad side," replied Padshaw politely. They shook hands.

Beecham was immediately aware that Padshaw's defences were up. The last thing he needed now was an unnecessary confrontation due to lack of information.

"Squadron Leader Hawkins," Beecham said, addressing Padshaw quickly, "thinks he can help us with our current situation, in fact all three of us are going up together." Beecham gave Padshaw a humorous nudge with his elbow. "He's on our side, Terry," Beecham said with a smile.

Padshaw visibly relaxed, Squadron Leader Hawkins insisted on buying the round.

"The meeting starts at six o'clock," Beecham informed them, "so we'll tuck these away and talk in the car." He briefly looked at his glass and then glanced at Padshaw's and Hawkin's glasses and then said, "Down the hatch, chaps!" Beecham swallowed just once.

Both Hawkins and Padshaw stared for a moment. Both thinking *What a waste of malt whisky!* looked at each other, nodded and knocked them back.

"Onward," said Beecham, who then smiled to himself as he made for the door. Hawkins and Padshaw followed him out.

On the drive up Beecham invited Padshaw to explain from start to finish all the aspects of his operation to Hawkins.

"Well, I'm certainly not going to give you the long version," Padshaw opened.

"Just the rudimentaries will do just fine," replied Hawkins. "I simply need a bit of background information before we enter this meeting later."

Padshaw thought for a few moments and then began, "Right, well, in short: a few months ago Group Captain Beecham approached me and asked if I would be prepared to be temporarily attached to his staff for the sole reason of undertaking the forming of a new squadron. For a time I commanded my own squadron in France and during the Battle of Britain," Padshaw informed him. "Unfortunately I received a few injuries and was taken off flying duties."

"Squadron Leader Padshaw is being modest," Beecham said addressing Hawkins. "He's credited with two confirmed kills in France and three probables. During the summer of 1940 he shot down three aircraft, all confirmed."

Squadron Leader Hawkins looked impressed.

"And as for his injuries," Beecham continued, "they were sustained when he ran out of ammunition and rammed the tail section of a Dornier 17 which had just started its bomb run."

"Bloody hell!" Hawkins said before he could stop himself.

"Pray continue," Beecham said to Padshaw.

"Thank you sir," Padshaw replied, wishing Beecham had kept his mouth shut. "Anyway, the first hurdle was getting my hands on pilots with combat and 'type' experience. I managed to wangle and beg a dozen pilots; mind you, I upset a few people at the same time. As you can imagine, squadron commanders don't like letting go of their experienced pilots."

"No, I'm sure," said Hawkins with a grin and a raised eyebrow.

"I arranged to have them shipped off to India," Padshaw continued. "Next was the aircraft, as it turned out Group Captain Beecham –" Padshaw gave the group captain a respectful nod "– pulled a few strings and obtained a dozen Hurricanes. As for ground crew, supplies, etc., up until a few hours ago I was making some progress. That's it really. Oh... except the whole bloody lot's in Davy Jones's locker!" As he said it he felt guilty. 'On the other hand,' Padshaw thought to himself, it wasn't his fault. Chalk one up to the bloody Kriegsmarine.'

Hawkins looked thoughtful. Beecham leaned forward and, looking at Hawkins, said, "Why don't you tell the squadron leader what you have in mind?"

Padshaw looked interested.

Hawkins gave a small, indifferent shrug and said, "There were two squadrons based in Burma and then southern India. Both took a bit of a mauling a few months ago. So basically, they amalgamated into one. Pilots, aircraft, surviving ground crews, spares, you name it. One of the COs, a chap called Marsland, remained as CO of the whole lot. The other CO was flown home. Unfortunately he died in hospital from his injuries. The remaining pilots, however, make up Marsland's squadron. By all accounts he's turned them into a very efficient team. As far as I know, thinking about it, they don't even have an official squadron name.

"I'm hoping we may be able to convince the brass to let us continue to reach our objectives by using Squadron Leader Marsland and his squadron."

Padshaw looked Hawkins straight in the eye. "*Our* objectives?" he enquired.

Hawkins looked a little uncomfortable. He was saved from replying by Group Captain Beecham's timely intervention.

"If you recall our earlier conversation, Terry," Beecham said, "there was a particular task for your squadron which I have not yet discussed with you. *If* tonight's meeting goes in our favour, I will explain all to you then. To do so before would be superfluous."

"As you wish sir," Padshaw replied. Though it was obvious Padshaw wasn't entirely happy. For the rest of the journey, Beecham kept the conversation revolving around the latest shows in London, some minor scandals involving ranking officers and his family's recent hotel purchase in Scotland.

"We'll be there in five minutes, sir," Beecham's driver announced.

"Jolly good," replied Beecham.

Just under five minutes later, the car pulled up outside some heavy marble pillars, the door opened as soon as the car stopped. An imposing MP was holding the door open. "This way please, gentlemen." It was more of an order than an invitation.

The three of them left the car, Beecham first. The MP who opened the door faced them and held his left arm horizontal, indicating the direction they should walk in. Beecham complied without comment. Padshaw and Hawkins took their cue from the group captain and followed him, with the MP bringing up the rear.

They walked down the cobbled passageway, which eventually turned ninety degrees to the right. In front of them stood two large oak doors flanked by two more MPs.

"Your identification cards please, gentlemen," said the MP on the right. As they reached for their ID the mirror image on the left stepped forward, his left hand open, ready to examine their paperwork. The MP examining their ID took but a few moments. "Thank you gentlemen," he said and opened the right-hand door.

"Please follow the hall to the end, turn right and you will be met at reception," he added. Beecham nodded purposefully, all three MPs snapped to attention. Padshaw and Hawkins nodded more casually and followed Beecham.

A very attractive and efficient secretary was standing in front of her desk, holding three identically bound folders.

"Good evening, gentlemen," she said. Before Beecham could reply she was handing him and the others a folder each and talking ten to the dozen. "Unfortunately the meeting started early so you have some catching up to do. Please read all the contents underlined in red, your seats are allocated." A corporal appeared and saluted. "This way please, gentlemen."

They were led into a conference room. Officers of various ranks were talking amongst themselves, a few raised voices could be heard but no one was being unpleasant.

There were three empty chairs. Beecham took the centre chair flanked by Hawkins and Padshaw. Another group captain sat opposite Wing Commander Peters (who Beecham knew from before the War) to his right. The room very quickly went quiet. The group captain stood up and addressed Beecham:

"I do hope you won't think me rude, but it was I who moved the meeting to five thirty. I have to be at an emergency meeting with the air vice marshal in an hour. I believe you know Wing Commander Peters?"

Beecham gave an affirmative nod.

"Good, he'll fill you in. Which one of you gentlemen is Squadron Leader Padshaw?"

"Sir," Said Padshaw.

"I just wanted to wish you all the best with your ventures and every success. My apologies again, but my car's waiting." With that he left the room. Padshaw looked a little bewildered. Beecham gestured to Peters.

"Right, sir. Having had the loss of our pilots and Hurricanes confirmed, it was decided that we carry on with the initial plan. We would like to thank Squadron Leader Hawkins for bringing us up to date on a Squadron Leader Marsland, whose squadron is based in southern India. A priority message has been sent to him with instructions to expect more aircraft and await briefing and further orders. We are at this moment ferrying him nine Hurricanes. I'm afraid these particular pilots won't be very happy when they find out they're staying with the squadron. They are under the impression they'll be flying the old aircraft out." A few grins broke out around the table.

Padshaw gently nudged Beecham and started to speak, "Nine Hurricanes? Sir…"

Beecham gave him a sly look and smiled. Padshaw shut up.

The wing commander continued, "Informing them of course is Squadron Leader Padshaw's happy duty, as it is *his* operation."

Padshaw's eyes were wide and his jaw had dropped a little. He quickly regained his composure.

"I take it you are prepared to remain in command of this operation," he said smiling at Padshaw, already knowing the answer.

"Delighted, sir!" Padshaw replied.

"Good," said Peters. "But you do have some problems," he started. Padshaw started taking notes.

"First problem is the size of the airstrip. Marsland already operates ten or more Kittyhawks, he's going to have problems dispersing nine more aircraft. Secondly, these Hurricanes are MKIICs, armed with 20mm cannon. They're going to need spares. As you are aware, Marsland's Kittyhawks use .50 calibre, so you'll need ammunition for the Hurris too. Thirdly..." the wing commander looked at Beecham for a brief moment, Beecham gave a nod of approval, "we would like to move Marsland's squadron as far forward, or further south east as is possible, without the Japs knowing. This will give him a larger area of targets. To the best of our knowledge, Marsland's current position isn't known to them at this moment, so it may prove wiser for him to remain where he is. We leave that decision to you..."

Padshaw was listening intently.

"... this relocation of his squadron may prove totally impossible, but we request you look into it."

Padshaw was about to ask the reasoning behind such a difficult proposal, but Peters cut him off:

"We are hoping to receive confirmation that our forces are going to move south towards the Japanese positions in a few weeks or so. If this proves to be the case, they'll need as much air support as we can give them! You, Squadron Leader, will brief him yourself."

"Yes sir," Padshaw said at once. Just for a split second Padshaw imagined Squadron Leader Marsland being flown back to Blighty to be briefed. This idea quickly faded. It also struck him a little odd that he was personally required to brief this Squadron Leader Marsland. They could easily do that themselves. Oh, well.

"Squadron Leader Hawkins will be your liaison officer over here." He then addressed Hawkins, "Anything Squadron Leader Padshaw requires is to be provided as quickly as humanly possible."

"Yes sir," replied Hawkins.

"Excellent. Well, as far as you two officers are concerned, this meeting has ended. Anything of relevance you may have missed is contained in the folders you were given on your arrival. You've both been booked into the same hotel, which, by all accounts, is very comfortable. A car is waiting outside to take you there. I suggest you use the opportunity to put your heads together."

Both Padshaw and Hawkins stood and saluted.

"I'll speak with you both tomorrow," said Beecham.

"Yes sir," said Hawkins. Padshaw nodded politely.

They left the room and were led down the hall by the same corporal. They walked past the MPs and the marble pillars to where a car was waiting, the engine was running, and the driver was holding the door open.

"Efficient, aren't they?" said Hawkins.

"Quite so," replied Padshaw.

They got into the car and the driver closed the door. He then got behind the wheel and drove off. Padshaw and Hawkins settled back to enjoy the drive.

After a few minutes Padshaw asked the driver, "Where exactly are we staying?"

"I've been instructed to take you to the Grosvenor House Hotel, sir."

"I think he may possibly mean the Grosvenor Hotel by Victoria Station," Hawkins suggested politely.

"No sir," the driver said, "the Grosvenor House Hotel, Park Lane."

"Bloody hell!" exclaimed Hawkins. "That must cost twenty-five bob a night."

"We didn't book it," said Padshaw calmly, "so we're not paying!" So much had happened in the last twenty-four hours, Padshaw had become immune to anything.

"I believe Group Captain Beecham arranged it personally, gentlemen," the driver informed them.

"I hope that includes the bar bill," Hawkins said under his breath. Padshaw smiled and said, "After all that's happened today, I should bloody well hope so." They finished the rest of their trip in silence.

Chapter 2

Sergeant Bell briskly trotted up to the side of Major Connors' jeep. His face looked pained, not from exhaustion but dismay.

"All right George," said Connors. "What's the delay this time?"

"Another bloody puncture, sir," replied his sergeant. "At this rate we'll need somebody to supply *us* with spares and supplies."

Connors was sitting half in his jeep and half out, casually tapping his left knee with a swagger stick. This was the third puncture in fifteen miles. On two occasions they'd had to dig a truck out of mud and on the second occasion one of his men had slipped and suffered a broken arm. Who, to make matters worse, was a damn good driver. For two days now, Connors had struggled to get his men and supplies to their various objectives. Having gone as far south as he dared, to supply small units of men harrying the Japanese advance, he was now making his way back north. And it seemed like it was taking forever.

"How much further do we have to go?" Connors asked, already aware of the answer.

"Including the last pick-up? About a day and a half, maybe two, depending on the weather, sir," the sergeant replied. Connors stared in the direction of their destination. He looked at his sergeant. "Get it fixed as quickly as pos, and be so kind as to tell Captain Blackman I wish to see him now."

"Sir!" Sergeant Bell trotted off.

Connors turned to his driver, Corporal Burns. "Time for a brew up I think, pass the word back, Burns."

"Very good sir, an excellent idea if I may say so, sir."

Connors smiled. Corporal Burns had been his driver for two months now, there was a mutual respect and friendship between them despite the difference in rank.

Connors walked around the jeep, stretching his legs. Captain Blackman approached him. Connors gave him a friendly nod and pulled out a pack of cigarettes. Blackman pulled out a lighter.

"This trip is turning into a right pain in the arse 'Blackie'," he said, passing a cigarette.

"Thanks," said Blackman, taking the cigarette. He lit his lighter and offered it to Connors first. Connors cupped his hands and puffed his cigarette into action. Blackman lit his own.

"Just a social call Don, or have you run out of matches?" asked Blackman.

Connors was studying the road (if you could call it a road) ahead. He looked at Blackman and said, "Take the other jeep, 'Blackie'. There's no way we're going to make the time up today. Find a suitable spot to bed down for the night, take someone with you."

"I'll find us a nice hotel," replied Blackie.

"Don't take too long," Connors added, "I want to move out in about half an hour, OK?"

Blackman gave him the thumbs up and at the same time called, "Private Naylor!"

"Sir?"

"Get your rifle and get in this jeep!"

"Yes sir."

Captain Blackman clambered in and sat behind the wheel, he fumbled with the ignition switch and pushed down on the starter button located on the floor. He was revving the engine as Naylor trotted up.

"Would you like me to drive, sir?" Naylor asked politely.

"Not at all, you just sit back and relax, take in the scenery."

Naylor clambered into the passenger seat and stared anxiously at the captain.

"I'm quite happy to drive, sir," Naylor added hopefully. Blackman smiled genially back at him and said:

"Wouldn't hear of it."

He then proceeded to over-rev the engine and at the same time push down on the clutch. Naylor winced as Blackman ground the gearbox into surrendering first gear, he then got as many revs as possible from the engine and dropped the clutch. The massive lurch forward ricked Private Naylor's neck. Blackman raced past Connors' jeep just as Corporal Burns passed the major a cup of tea.

"Sergeant Bell had already got the lads to brew up, sir."

Connors took his mug. Burns was looking at the jeep driving away.

"I thought Captain Blackman couldn't drive," he said.

"He can't," replied Connors nonchalantly.

"Oh dear," Burns commented with a touch of fatalism in his voice.

Blackman's jeep proceeded to fishtail its way into the shadows.

"Lieutenant Portman!" Connors called. Portman was talking to the driver of the truck directly behind Connors' jeep. Portman had only recently been promoted to lieutenant and this was his first active posting.

"Yes sir?"

"Lieutenant, pass the word we're going to bed down for the night, Captain Blackman is looking for a suitable spot. Also I want you to organise sentries. You never know, some cheeky Jap officer may decide to collect a prisoner or two or simply want to spoil our day."

"I'll get on to it right away, sir," the lieutenant replied.

Twenty minutes later Captain Blackman returned, in the passenger seat. He exited the jeep just before it stopped and addressed the major:

"Right sir," he said, the 'sir' was there out of respect of the fact that junior ranks were present. "We've found just the spot," he continued. "Good cover, reasonably flat and what looks to be a safe water supply close by."

"Well done," replied Connors.

"We also found something else, sir," Blackman said in a more serious voice.

"What was that?" Connors asked.

"An RAF Hurricane, sir, or what's left of it. More importantly, it's only recently come down."

"What makes you think that?" queried Connors.

"Some parts of the wreckage are still hot," Blackman explained, "and the surrounding undergrowth shows that the fire's only recently gone out."

"The pilot?" asked Connors.

"Not in it, thank God," Blackman said. "Which means he's not far away. Request permission to search for him, sir?"

"Definitely not!" Connors said firmly.

"But sir, he could be less than half a mile away."

"Yes he could," Connors said. "He could also be two miles away in any direction, maybe he broke his neck on landing, maybe his 'chute didn't open, you could search for a week and never find him."

Captain Blackman knew Connors was right, but the idea of doing nothing left a bad taste in his mouth. He had a brother who was a pilot in bomber command, so he felt a certain attachment to any pilot.

Connors could see his captain wasn't happy with his decision.

"I'd like to talk to Captain Blackman alone," Connors said politely.

Corporal Burns, Private Naylor and two drivers in earshot made themselves busy elsewhere.

"Look Blackie, I respect the fact you want to try and find that poor bastard, but you'd be wasting your time."

"You're probably right," Blackman said. "I just hate to not even have tried. That's all."

Connors thought for a few seconds. "Tell you what," he said, "we'll follow you to the bivouac site and then you can take four or five men and check around the area. It'll be dark in four or five hours; make sure you're back there in two, OK?"

"Thanks Don," Blackman said and made his way toward Sergeant Bell.

"Oh Blackie, how come Private Naylor drove back and not you?"

"Ah," Blackman said smiling. "Private Naylor made it clear to me that he would rather desert and happily face a firing squad than risk another five minutes more of my driving. I think he was serous! So I let him drive."

Connors smiled and lit another cigarette. "On your way 'Blackie'. Quicker you go, quicker you're back."

Blackman walked briskly away shouting orders.

Chapter 3

Padshaw and Hawkins checked into their hotel and went to the bar for a drink. "What's your poison, Terry?"

"I'll have that large malt we wasted earlier," Padshaw replied. Hawkins smiled and said to the barman, "Make that two."

"Yes sir," said the barman. "Please have a seat, gentlemen. I'll bring them over to you," he added.

Hawkins and Padshaw took a table in the corner away from the other guests. "Well," said Hawkins, "it looks like you've got your Hurricanes and pilots after all, plus a gaggle of Kittyhawks for good measure."

"It would appear so," replied Padshaw. "First things first," he continued, "how fast can we get spares out there?"

Hawkins smiled. "As luck would have it, there's a supply unit on its way to Marsland's squadron right now. However, we'd have to intercept it with all the required equipment, after which they could continue to Marsland's landing ground."

"What about a parachute drop?" suggested Padshaw. Both men leaned back in their chairs as the barman arrived with the malt whiskies.

"Thank you," Hawkins said. They clinked glasses and drank.

"I don't think a parachute drop is going to be possible, not with such short notice. But we are going to try. Meanwhile I've already sent instructions to transport all the equipment required as soon as possible to rendezvous with …" Hawkins took some handwritten notes out of a pocket

"… a Major Connors who is in charge of the supply column. He has a reputation for being very efficient when the chips are down. Hopefully he will have received instructions to that effect."

"I'll drink to that," said Padshaw and then added. "What about me?"

"Group Captain Beecham is arranging to fly you out in a few days, maybe even tomorrow if he can wangle it."

Padshaw wasn't the least surprised and sipped his whisky. Then he asked, "This Squadron Leader Marsland, I hope he won't feel that I'm interfering with the running of his squadron. Don't you think that perhaps he may feel that I'm undermining his authority?"

Hawkins was ready for this question. "The communiqué sent to Marsland explains in some detail that you are there to brief him on what we have in mind. We've emphasised, as must you, when you meet him, that you are there in an advisory capacity only. Of course, all operations in relation to our earlier meeting will be overseen by you. Also, you have authority to release all information you deem necessary to forward the smooth running of this operation." He paused. "One thing that might help you break the ice…" Hawkins grinned.

"What's that?" Padshaw asked.

"Squadron Leader Marsland is quite partial to gin," Hawkins said.

"I'll take a case with me," said Padshaw

Hawkins rolled his glass between the palms of his hands. He was still wearing a grin and thinking. Padshaw looked at him quizzically. Seeing this, Hawkins voiced his thoughts:

"I was just thinking. If I were Squadron Leader Marsland, I'd be quite pleased to see nine new Hurricanes. I'll bet you he'll be more than happy."

Padshaw looked at Hawkins and thought to himself, You've never had your own squadron, have you? But he didn't voice his thoughts and said, "I hope you're right."

"Red leader, this is Yellow leader. I can't identify them yet."

"Wilco, Yellow leader."

Bugger! thought Valentine. If they are Japs they might want a prolonged fight and we don't have the fuel. And if we have a scrap and just one of them tails us home, we've given our position away. The chances of them being allied aircraft weren't very good and Valentine was also losing the element of surprise. Much closer and they'd be spotted, if they hadn't already. In matter of fact, Hacker had seen them. He had tried calling them up several times on the frequency he'd been given before they'd taken off, but to no avail.

"This is Hacker. I reckon they're Kittyhawks judging by their noses, you can't mistake them!"

"Ferry three to leader: I think we should identify ourselves. Over."

"I agree," replied Hacker. "I'll do a slow roll and display my roundels... rolling now." Hacker opened his throttle to put a little distance between him and the rest of the flight and then started to do a slow roll.

Valentine wasn't going to take any chances. Moreover, he also reckoned that their current heading would take them too close to the squadron's landing ground (LGI). He was just about to give orders to intercept when...

"Red leader. This is Yellow three. The lead aircraft is doing a barrel roll!" All the pilots stared in surprise.

"They're Hurricanes, Red leader! They're Hurricanes!"

Valentine was surprised and pleased at the same time: "Blue leader. Take Blue and Yellow flights and head for home now. Red two stay with me and we'll try to make RT contact.

"Wilco Red leader. Blue and Yellow flights turn port. Go!"

70

Valentine and 'Spence' took up position to the left and slightly above Hacker.

Valentine, oddly, managed to get RT contact immediately.

"Hurricane flight, this is Kittyhawk leader, Hurricane flight, Kittyhawk leader."

"Receiving you, Kitty leader," answered Hacker.

"What is your destination, Hurricane leader?"

Hacker gave Valentine the map reference he'd been given. Valentine was silent for a moment. Surely the CO would have briefed him about this?

"Hurricane flight, follow me."

"Message received, Kitty leader."

Hacker felt relieved. At least now he didn't have to find the landing ground. Valentine called again, "Hurricane leader, for now you will identify yourselves as Green flight, and I am Red leader, over."

"Roger, Red leader."

"Green flight turn port. Go." Valentine turned for home.

Chapter 4

Squadron Leader Marsland was still sitting at his desk, heroically fighting against overwhelming odds. No sooner had he completed signing one set of forms than reinforcements were there to replace them. He was almost at the point of calling a truce when the adjutant came into his office without knocking.

"Sir, we've got problems," Hollingsworth announced.

Marsland saw that his adjutant was worried, he stood up and walked out the door gesturing Hollingsworth to go first and asked:

"What's up, Holly?"

"Sir, we've just had two radio communications. We're to expect nine Hurricanes to fly in today!"

"What!? Are you sure?"

"Yes sir," Hollingsworth said quickly, "and 'Jiff' Verster's been shot up. He's due back any minute. I've briefed all the ground crew to be ready for him."

Marsland could see ground crew running about grabbing fire extinguishers and hatchets.

"Oh bloody hell," he said, " where's the doc?"

"Getting himself organised, just in case," replied Hollingsworth.

"Just a minute, Holly," Marsland said. "Where the hell am I going to put nine Hurricanes?"

The adjutant looked at a loss. Then he said, "I recommend we deal with one problem at a time, sir."

The faint sound of an Allison engine misfiring could now be heard.

"Red four to Red three. Try your undercarriage 'Jiff'."

"Lowering undercarriage now." 'Jiff' was relieved to feel the drag of his wheels coming down slowing his Kittyhawk slightly. He stared at the remains of his instrument panel. "Bugger!" he said to himself, softly.

"I don't think the wheels have locked, Paul," he said dropping RT procedure.

"Keep her level Red three, I'll take a look."

Cracken deftly took position below 'Jiff's' battered Kittyhawk and scrutinised the landing gear. "Looks OK from here 'Jiff'," he said. Cracken then resumed station on 'Jiff's' port side.

"You're a bit slow 'Jiff', open her up a bit."

'Jiff' nudged the throttle. His ASI (Airspeed Indicator) was smashed, as was his altimeter.

"I'll come in with you," said Cracken, "as soon as you're on the ground I'll pull away. Just try to match my speed and descent."

"Roger that," replied Verster. Both Kittyhawks turned as one. Cracken was slightly ahead of his leader so that Verster could judge his speed and descent better.

"Flaps down," said Cracken.

Verster lowered his flaps. The rush of air through the front of his smashed cockpit was stinging his face. There was also the odd splash of hot oil getting thrown back, occasionally hitting his goggles. Cracken, meanwhile was so concerned with looking after his leader, he nearly brushed the treetops, missing by a couple of feet at most. "Jesus! That was close!" he said aloud, adrenalin surging through him.

Verster missed the trees by ten feet, but had witnessed Cracken's near miss. "Bloody awful nursemaid you are," Verster joked.

"Start rounding out, Jiff," Cracken instructed.

Verster started to round out.

"You're drifting left, Jiff. Give it a bit of right stick and rudder."

Verster tried to depress the right rudder pedal. It wouldn't move! "Oh for Christ's sake!" he said in despair. He looked down. There were various parts of his instrument panel littering his cockpit floor. Verster tried to correct with a little bit of right stick. The gods were not with him, the gentle crosswind increased a little. He was committed. Something was fouling his control cables, his right wing was low and his tailplane was getting pushed to port. This was going to hurt!

Marsland and Hollingsworth were watching.

"Get those vehicles moving!" Marsland shouted. Two very tired, open-top Austin trucks with various ground crews and the doctor manning them, pulled away and raced after the now crabbing Kittyhawk.

Verster throttled back and gently pulled the stick back in an attempt to slow the Kittyhawk so that it was almost stalling. He was still fifteen feet up and was running out of airstrip, when his engine died. He fell out of the sky like a shot pheasant.

"Oh fucking hell!" said Marsland emptily.

The Kittyhawk landed right wing down, its wingtip and starboard wheel brushing the ground at the same time. As it shed half the wing, the whole machine started to pirouette. The tail came up and the propeller buried itself for a short moment before momentum threw the Kittyhawk into a cartwheel. The tailplane was ripped away, the port wing crumpled, various pieces of aeroplane were discarded in every direction. The Kittyhawk came to a rest over a hundred yards from where it first hit the ground.

The two trucks were moments away. Verster sat in the remains of his cockpit. He hurt everywhere. He reached, in what seemed like slow motion, for the canopy release. It was smashed and jammed. The cockpit stank of fuel. In fact his feet were swimming in it. Electrical leads were severed and dangling all around him. All of a sudden Verster was terrified!

"Oh God no!" he shouted. "Not like this! Please God! Not like this!"

Yellow flame licked out of the remains of the engine cowling in front of him. Verster pulled out his revolver. There was no way he was going to burn to death. He was just cocking it when a hatchet came flying through the side of his canopy.

"Smash it open, quick!" someone shouted. Another hatchet flew in from the other side. Verster could see two men close to the engine using fire extinguishers. Another was throwing buckets of wet earth onto the roaring flames. A man appeared with a crowbar and forced the canopy off its runners.

"Get him out!" Verster heard. Hands flew into the cockpit. Somebody punched and pulled at his harness release so hard it hurt. He felt himself being roughly manhandled out of the cockpit. There was a small bang.

"Run you daft bastards, run!" came another shout, this time in earnest. Verster felt himself being dragged away by one arm and a leg. Everybody stopped and threw themselves to the ground. What seemed like a few seconds passed and then the Kittyhawk blew up with a dull thud, spewing flames everywhere.

The next thing Verster knew the medical officer, Doc Holden, was leaning over him.

"You're not a pretty sight, are you!?" he said, loading a syringe.

"Jesus it hurts!" Verster moaned.

"Oh, don't be so childish," the doctor said nonchalantly. "I've been doing this for fifteen years, it never hurt me once!" Holden emptied the syringe into Verster's arm and the lights went out.

Verster was placed on a stretcher mounted on the back of one of the trucks and taken straight to the MO's hut. As the MO's truck drove past Marsland and Hollingsworth, Marsland shouted, "Will he be all right, Doc?"

"Ask me in an hour," Holden replied without smiling.

"Nothing we can do," said Hollingsworth, seeing the concern on Marsland's face. He quickly changed the subject. "But we'd better make some space and damned quick!"

Marsland turned and was about to shout out orders when he saw 'Punchy' Jennings backing up a truck to some of the remains of Verster's Kittyhawk. Various ground crew were throwing bits of debris into the back of it. Other men were using shovels to dig jagged bits of aeroplane out of the ground. Another truck pulled up and the driver and his mate started dragging a chain to the still-smoking remains of the engine. Jennings seemed to be shouting orders to everyone at the same time.

"Get that chain around the engine and drag it over to those trees." He was pointing to a deserted spot in the corner of the LG. "Jones, Carver, Massey: get the roller over here as quick as you can!" All three men moved quickly without answering. "Morrell, Jarvis, give those men a hand with that wing."

Marsland turned to face his adjutant, "I'm glad you didn't shoot him, Holly," he said. Hollingsworth smiled.

"Right adj, get whoever you can and strike all the tents. Collect everybody's personal belongings. They can sort it out amongst themselves later. With the tents down we should be able to squeeze a few in, we can hack out fresh areas for the tents later.

Cracken flew overhead and then completed a low circuit of the airstrip. He then brought his aircraft in for a smooth landing to the right-hand side of the carnage.

"As soon as Paul's parked up tell him he's in charge of dispersing the aircraft as best he can."

"Right you are sir," the adjutant replied.

"And find out what those Hurricanes are doing here," Marsland added.

Hollingsworth pulled a piece of folded paper out of his pocket and offered it to his CO.

Marsland sighed, "Do I really want to read that?" he asked. Hollingsworth screwed up his face and frowned.

"In that case give it to me later," Marsland said. He then walked towards the radio tent. He pulled open the tent flap and walked in. "Get me Flight Lieutenant Valentine," he ordered.

"Do my best, sir," replied the radio operator "but as usual the signal's a bit hit and miss."

"Just try," Marsland said curtly.

"Sir," replied the radio operator.

Marsland lit a cigarette and stepped outside the tent. Things were happening quickly. Most of the wreckage had been, or was being, removed. The tents were being struck, NCOs were shouting instructions and men were competently carrying them out. He looked around at his squadron, something not short of a fierce pride suddenly came to him, he took a deep breath.

"Sir? Flight Lieutenant Valentine," the radio operator interrupted. Marsland grabbed the mike with one hand and held one of the earphones to his ear. "Snobby, this is Marsland. Get back as soon as you can. You're not going to believe this, but nine Hurricanes are due here today!"

"I hate to sound cocky old boy, but its seven Hurricanes and they're right behind me," Valentine replied.

Marsland was lost for a second or two. Valentine interrupted his thoughts, "I've sent Blue and Yellow sections on ahead, they should be with you about now, we're about five minutes behind. Over."

"How's your fuel?" Marsland asked.

"How's your gin supply?" asked Valentine.

"Understood," replied Marsland. "Just take as long as you can getting here, right?"

"Wilco. Out!"

Marsland passed the headset back to the radio operator and said, "Contact Blue and Yellow sections, tell them to land as quickly as possible. They are then to taxi to the right of the field. Inform them that Sergeant Pilot Cracken is in charge of dispersal, got that?"

"Yes sir," he replied.

Marsland left the tent, he could see Yellow and Blue sections coming into circuit. The adjutant walked over to him.

"We've got the field cleared sir, Well, most of it."

"Well done. As soon as this mayhem is over, I want to speak to the men responsible for getting 'Jiff' out of his kitty."

"I'll get the details, sir."

"I'd like to see 'Punchy' as well," Marsland continued. "And as soon as the officer in charge of the Hurricane flight has landed, send him straight to my office."

"I'll see to it sir. Might I recommend you read this first though, sir?" The adjutant was holding the same piece of folded paper. Marsland stared at it but didn't take it from the adjutant's hand. "What does it say Holly?" he asked.

"I really think you should read it, sir."

"Holly!" the CO raised his voice.

"Basically," Hollingsworth began, "we're to expect nine new Hurricanes being flown in today." The CO's face twisted into a picture of impatience. Hollingsworth hurried on, "And we're to keep the pilots!"

A puzzled look came over Marsland's face. The adjutant said, "They think they're ferrying aircraft out, sir. But we've received orders to put them on the squadron strength."

Marsland was getting a little confused.

"Plus they're sending an officer from Blighty who's coming to brief you personally on specific targets on top of our current orders!"

"I'm not sure I like all this," Marsland said.

"I must say it is a little unusual," agreed the adjutant. "Still," he added, "it'll be good to have nine Hurricanes on the squadron."

"Seven," said Marsland.

The adjutant looked at his piece of paper, "Definitely nine sir," he said.

"Definitely seven," Marsland replied emphatically. "Flight Lieutenant Valentine is leading them in now."

"Valentine?" the adjutant said in surprise. He gave his CO a quizzical look.

"Buggered if I know!" said Marsland. "I'm just the squadron CO, so it's got sod all to do with me."

The adjutant looked at a loss and concerned at the same time. Marsland, seeing this in his face, said, "Oh, never mind Holly, don't worry about it. I'm sure everything will fall into place after we've debriefed everybody."

Yellow section drifted over the trees.

Marsland made his way to his office. As he did so he looked over his shoulder and said to the adjutant, "I'll meet all the new pilots one at a time. After I've spoken to the Hurricane leader. I'd like you present, Holly."

"Of course sir, I'll get my paperwork."

Marsland entered his office and sat down. He was thinking hard. Whatever was going on, it was happening very quickly. Which meant the top brass were either in a panic, or someone had ticked the wrong box in the 'How to run the Royal Air Force' questionnaire. Either way, the buck would stop with him. But then again, it always did.

Andrew Marsland had been in the RAF for seven years. Before that, he'd had a good education ending at Oxford. His family had moved to Ascot during his education, having previously lived in Stratford upon Avon. His father had made a handsome income from buying property requiring renovation. Some he had sold and some he rented out. After investing wisely on the stock market, he had gone into semi-retirement. He was just getting bored when one of his old school chums had offered him the job as the managing director for a company importing and distributing timber, hence the move to Ascot.

On arriving at his family's new house, having finished his final term, he and his father had been sitting in the garden enjoying a sherry when a biplane flew, slowly overhead.

"I say," he said to his father, "that looks like fun, where did he come from?"

"There's a private flying club about two miles away," his father replied. "In fact I recently met the chief flying instructor at a town meeting. I'll introduce you if you'd like."

Two months later Andrew Marsland went solo. He continued flying at the same club for some months and soon decided his career would be more fun in the air than on the ground. With this in mind he joined the Royal Air Force. His supervisor realised quite quickly that he had a natural talent for flying and dealt with situations on the ground and in the air with a calm efficiently. He was popular and everybody thought highly of him. Promotion came quickly.

By 1938 he was a flight lieutenant. During 1940 he was attached to eleven group, where he finally attained the rank of squadron leader. His next posting was North Africa, where he remained until he moved yet again to Burma in February, 1942.

Due to some foul-up with paperwork and the usual red tape, he was left kicking his heels for a few weeks before eventually being sent to take over a squadron whose CO had been killed. He arrived to take over the squadron just in time to see it lose five pilots and six aircraft and then witnessed two raids, which accounted for the deaths of a large number of ground crew and the loss of most of their equipment. He found himself left with a few tatty Mohawks and a couple of over-tired Curtis Tomahawks. At the same time a neighbouring squadron had also suffered similar casualties, including their CO.

On hearing this he pulled what was left of the remaining pilots' aircraft and ground crew together and had them operate from one landing ground. No sooner had he done this than they had to pull out before the Japanese overran them. Apart from relocating, the situation hadn't changed much. This forced retreat turned out to be a dark cloud with a silver lining. A wounded officer who had been in charge of the equipment and stores had told 'Jiff' Verster of some heavily camouflaged Kittyhawks that had been earmarked for Burma's defence, but had never reached their destination. Now down to five aircraft and pitifully few spares, Marsland simply took them.

The more Marsland thought about recent events the less it bothered him. His biggest problem, which was more or less insurmountable, was the position of his landing ground. To reach any worthwhile targets in southern Burma meant flying over dense jungle and mountains. Get an engine failure there and it's all over. On top of that, the hills, mountains and valleys played havoc with RT communications.

(During the Japanese invasion of Burma in May, many allied bases at Meho, Namsang and Toungoo were open to surprise air attacks by the Japanese partly because of the lack of efficient RDF (Radio Direction Finder) and other communications.

(Even the telephone could be unreliable)

To cap it all, Marsland also realised that without proper intelligence information he had a limited number of targets to hit. The bomber squadrons were getting good results with few if any losses, but of course they had significantly more range.

Maybe things are about to change, he thought to himself...

Chapter 5

The supply column had settled into the area located by Captain Blackman. Sergeant Bell walked up to Connor's jeep:

"Sir, we've just received this on the radio," he passed on the message. Connors read it and frowned, "I'll be holding a briefing as soon as Captain Blackman returns," he said. "I want you and Lieutenant Portman present as well."

"Yes sir," replied Bell and then added, "Grub's up sir, if you're hungry."

"Famished Sergeant, lead on. What is it tonight? Flambéed duck? Steak rossini? Or are we lowering our standards to steak and chips?"

Sergeant Bell smiled and replied, "It's some sort of curried animal with biscuit and some unusual vegetables which look worse than they taste, sir."

"Variety is the spice of life I say," Connors said. "More importantly, Captain Blackman has found us this excellent spot, where there are various places where I can puke up unobserved so as not to upset the cooks!"

Captain Blackman had volunteered Private Naylor, a Corporal Pitt and three other men to 'secure' the area surrounding the bivouac position. Each man had a rifle and a machete.

"Right chaps, all aboard," Blackman said politely, gesturing at the jeep. Private Naylor stared suspiciously at his officer.

"Private Naylor," he said, "you drive."

"Yes sir," replied Naylor. "Thank God for small mercies," he said to himself. Blackman got into the passenger seat as Naylor started the engine, the other four men made themselves as comfortable as possible in the limited space behind them.

"Drive as far as the stream we found Naylor, we'll have to go on foot from there."

"Right you are, sir." Naylor pulled away and drove along the path leading into the undergrowth. Ten minutes later Naylor pulled up by the stream.

"Everybody out," Blackman ordered. He got out and walked around the front of the jeep. "Right gentlemen, we'll split into pairs. Now, about one hundred yards over there, amongst those trees, is the remains of a Hurricane." He gestured vaguely to his left. "The pilot, thankfully, is not in it. I want you to slowly fan out and walk for ten minutes. Keep looking up, he could be floating above your head. Naylor and I will walk in a straight line as best as we can, from the front of the jeep. The rest of you keep to my left and right. As soon as ten minutes is up, you come straight back to the jeep and wait. If by some miracle you find the pilot, get back to the jeep and sound the horn three times. Should you run into any serious difficulty, fire off one round and everybody else will converge on your position. Any questions?" There were none. "Right, let's move out!"

***

As 'Bobby' Graham drifted down towards the trees he instinctively raised his feet. The top branches of the trees were thin and the foliage they produced was soft but dense. This helped to break the speed of his fall. He pulled his arms up to shield his face. The sound of fifty or sixty small branches breaking his fall reached his ears, shattering the silence of his descent.

His left leg, just below the knee, hit something that was not thin, but it was hard. In fact it was rock hard! The pain was excruciating. He involuntarily let out a sharp, agonised howl. He continued to fall, bouncing off various branches which were getting bigger as he fell, the parachute snared something above and he stopped, his feet only six feet off the ground.

"God's teeth!" he shouted at the surrounding trees. The pain in his leg was intense, his arms were badly bruised and two fingers on his left hand looked to be broken, or at least dislocated. Blood was running into his right eye, he wiped it away with his right arm. His head ached and he had trouble focusing on his surroundings. One moment he could see straight, the next he had double vision. He sagged in his harness and looked at the ground. Now what? he thought to himself.

The pain in his leg slowly subsided to a bearable ache. Sharp, shooting pains were coming from his left hand, but soon they too became more intermittent so long as he didn't move it. Graham raised his head and looked about him, as was to be expected he couldn't see much, except for trees and undergrowth. Four of five minutes passed before his brain fully engaged and took in his situation.

He couldn't stay here, that was obvious. He had to release his parachute and drop the last few feet. Under normal circumstances he would have already done this, but his left leg was now sending him throbs of pain to remind him of what was to come when he hit the ground. He couldn't reach any of the branches, which would help break his fall and the ground below him did not look terribly inviting. On top of that, only his right hand was fully functional, if he could fall right side first, he could give himself some support when he hit the ground, maybe protect his leg and arm a bit. He hung there for another fifteen minutes.

The more he thought, the less he cared. It was getting hotter, he was sweating now and beginning to itch in places he couldn't reach. Mosquitoes or some other anti-social insects were starting to eat him. Without consciously making the decision to do so he released his parachute and dropped the last few feet. At this point sod's law took over. He landed on his left leg! Agony took control as his left hand reached to the ground for support, his two damaged fingers clicked. Lightning bolts of pain shot up his entire arm. What was left of pure instinct in him pulled his hand away from the ground that had caused such pain. With no support at all, the left side of his body twisted as he fell, his head hit something solid and all the daylight disappeared, the pain with it.

When he awoke it was dusk, or maybe morning. He had ended up, more or less, face down, in mud and leaves. He tried to move but his body wasn't taking any instructions from his brain that might cause more suffering. Just when he needed an ally, treachery reared its head. Graham made a momentous effort to roll to one side. His leg screamed pain at him. He pulled his left arm from under his stomach and supported the left side of his body. A small corner of his brain forwarded a message saying his hand no longer hurt. An improvement he thought. With this encouraging development he slowly and gently rolled himself onto his back. The pain in his leg had reached a point where it couldn't get any worse. He dragged his elbows back and supported himself in a semi-upright position. Looking around him, he was shocked at how helpless he felt. He could hardly move, the blood from his injured head had dried around his eye and he could hardly see out of it. There was no way he could walk and he doubted he could crawl very far. The sounds of various birds and animals around him making their various calls was both soothing and worrying at the same time.

Could be worse I suppose, he thought to himself. Birds suddenly took flight from the trees and a deep growl silenced the animals.

"Fuck me God!" Graham said in a whisper "Anything else?"

There was a rustling in the undergrowth and it was coming nearer. Graham fumbled for his service revolver.

***

Padshaw and Hawkins met for breakfast at eight a.m. Padshaw was already seated and drinking tea when Hawkins approached their table.

"Any more in the pot, Terry?" he asked.

Padshaw looked up from his paper. "Morning Graham, yes of course!" He put his paper down and poured Graham a cup.

"Thanks," Graham said as he accepted the cup. "I've just been to reception to see if we have any messages," he continued, "apparently there's a car coming for us at nine thirty sharp."

"That's a shame," replied Padshaw. "I was just getting used to the good life, what would you like for breakfast? I haven't ordered yet."

"Well, taking into consideration we've got at least an hour and it's unlikely we'll eat this well again for a long time..." Hawkins deliberately paused and let a grin spread across his face. "I think we should try everything, don't you?"

Padshaw leaned back in his chair and opened the breakfast menu. His eyes quickly scanned what was on offer. He looked at Hawkins with a feigned look of surrender. "Oh if you insist, but I do it under duress you understand."

Hawkins got a waiter's attention and began ordering. An hour later they were both drinking coffee and eating toast with a rich creamy butter and Cooper's marmalade, when Padshaw saw a corporal approach the head waiter. There was a brief conversation and the corporal was gestured in their direction. He walked quickly towards them. Padshaw noticed a large parcel in the corporal's left hand. Padshaw got in first, "Good morning corporal," he said.

"Morning sir."

"You're early," it was ten minutes after nine. Hawkins casually glanced at his watch.

"Yes sir, sorry sir. I was instructed to arrive a little earlier and to give you this package, sir." The corporal politely handed the parcel to Padshaw. "Compliments of Group Captain Beecham, sir," the corporal added.

Padshaw looked at the brown paper package and the string holding it loosely together with suspicion.

"Is it your birthday, Terry?" Hawkins asked satirically.

"And this is for you, sir," the corporal said, producing a brown envelope and handing it to Hawkins. "Again with Group Captain Beecham's compliments, sir. I'll be waiting outside with the car for you." He respectfully saluted both officers and left the restaurant.

Padshaw began to pick at the string. At the same time Hawkins slit the envelope. Hawkins began reading the first of several pages. After a short moment his eyebrows raised and before he could tell his mouth to shut up, he blurted: "Bloody hell! That was quick!"

"You're not bloody joking either," said Padshaw.

Hawkins didn't look up from his papers. Quietly he said, "According to this, we are arranging a parachute drop with Connors' supply train, plus I'm to drop you off at some naval base as soon as we leave here. How odd!"

"I don't suppose your naval base has Sunderland flying boats based there, does it?" asked Padshaw.

"It doesn't say. Why?" he asked looking up. "Oh lord!

Padshaw was holding up a brand new RAF-issue tropical uniform.

"Doesn't waste any time, does he?"

"No," replied Padshaw, "he doesn't!"

Half an hour later both officers were being driven south, out of London. Hawkins was reading intently and occasionally stopping to brief Padshaw when, and where, it concerned him.

"We're to meet Group Captain Beecham in Thorney Island," Hawkins said. "Remind me…"

"Next to Hayling Island," Padshaw interrupted. "I believe the navy get up to all sorts of skulduggery there."

"Mmmm…" Hawkins pondered the thought, then continued, "… makes one wonder how much of this was all in place before last night's meeting, doesn't it?"

Padshaw looked up.

"Well, I mean, what with parachute drops, your Hurricanes and your pilots, getting YOU moving lickety split. It does make you think, eh?"

"It makes me think that I'm not simply going out there just to brief Marsland and oversee anything he couldn't do himself. From what I gather, Squadron Leader Marsland is more capable than a lot of squadron commanders I've met. Which draws me to conclude that there's a sight more going on here than meets the eye and I'm in the dark. Moreover, and I was thinking about this last night: MIIc Hurricanes are ground-attack aircraft, come to that, Kittyhawks are bloody good at it too. Those P40s are versatile aircraft." Padshaw fell silent and started thinking to himself, 'Where the bloody hell did he fit into all this?'.

A few seconds passed and Hawkins felt a little uncomfortable. He said, "You might well be right that there's something afoot Terry, but there's damn all you can do about it right now, so just relax till we get to where we're going. Besides, I need you to help me drink this!" He reached into his briefcase and pulled out a full bottle of Glenmorangie. Padshaw smiled.

"I took the opportunity of putting this on my room bill." He passed the bottle to Padshaw and pulled out two small glass tumblers. Padshaw stared and started to speak but Hawkins stopped him. "And I found these on the bar, I never could stand drinking out of the bottle."

Padshaw pulled the cork and poured the whisky.

"Cheers," he said.

"Cheers," replied Hawkins.

Padshaw put the cork in the bottle and sat back, looking into his glass. What will be will be, he thought.

Just over two hours later their car pulled up at a pole barrier. Armed guards were scattered about and looked to be very alert. Padshaw lowered his window as the duty sergeant walked up to the car. He then politely asked for their identification cards, taking a few moments scrutinising these before handing them back. The sergeant gestured to a corporal who was standing by a motorcycle. The corporal quickly put on his helmet, mounted the bike and kick started the engine into life. The sergeant then said, "If you would be kind enough to follow the corporal, gentlemen, he knows where you have to be."

"Thank you," replied Padshaw.

The sergeant took two steps back and saluted. A sentry then raised the pole barrier and the car slowly pulled away.

Five minutes later, after driving past several ugly office buildings and various workshops, the corporal pulled up by a smart building with two armed guards flanking the large, opened door.

As they stopped, Padshaw saw a very smartly dressed naval lieutenant come out of the door, followed closely by an orderly, and make a beeline straight to their car. The lieutenant opened the door and stood to rigid attention. "Good morning, gentlemen. If you would like to follow me please, I will escort you to Group Captain Beecham. My orderly will take care of your bags."

Padshaw looked at Hawkins and said, "He gets around doesn't he?" Hawkins replied, grinning, "He probably found out about the Glenmorangie!"

They got out of the car and followed the naval officer into the building. Two minutes later they got to an office door, painted bright red. The lieutenant knocked gently and entered.

"Squadron Leaders Padshaw and Hawkins, sir," he announced.

Padshaw and Hawkins walked in, the lieutenant saluted and left, closing the door behind him. Two MPs appeared and took station outside the office. Beecham was sitting behind a large, heavily carved oak desk.

"Good morning, gentlemen. I hope your hotel was to your liking?"

"Yes sir," replied Hawkins quickly.

"Very generous of you sir," said Padshaw. "Most relaxing."

"I'm glad you enjoyed your evening. You're looking quite refreshed Terry. Good to see. Please, both of you sit down." Hawkins and Padshaw sat.

"I'll cut to the chase," Beecham continued. "Firstly, Terry: your orders in reference to the possible relocation of Marsland's squadron still stand. However, more importantly, the powers that be are already looking at going back into Burma and kicking the Japs out. Now I know that's no secret but we've put together a list of targets, which will need to be hit as soon as possible. All the details are in there." Beecham passed Padshaw a leather case. Padshaw immediately went to open it.

"Read it later," said Beecham.

Padshaw placed the bag on the floor.

"In short," Beecham continued, "a large majority of these targets are obviously going to be heavily defended. At the moment Marsland's squadron is carrying out successful, but occasional raids on Akyab, that's on the west coast. We need more intense attacks on this area."

"Why that particular area, sir?" asked Hawkins.

"Simple really, Akyab is a very important rice export centre. Bugger that up and Johnny Jap fights on an empty stomach. Not literally, but it makes his life bloody uncomfortable. Moreover, there are other prime targets. Airfields, rice mills, docks. We can seriously damage their supplies and just as important, their morale."

"With all due respect sir," said Hawkins, "from what I understand, our Blenheims and Wellington bombers are already doing that quite successfully."

"Yes they are. In fact, bloody well, with almost no losses. But if we can repeatedly hit these targets with low-level bombing and persistent strafing of their supply trains, it might make them bring in more troops and defensive fighters into that area. Thus taking pressure off other units. You must understand that communications for both sides are limited, we should be able to knock out their aircraft on the ground before they know we're there if we use fighters. The more we take out, the less they have for air defence."

"Sir?" Padshaw queried.

Beecham looked at him attentively.

"I quite understand the necessity for these types of operations, but surely Squadron Leader Marsland is more than competent to carry out these missions without my interference, don't you think?"

"You're quite right. He is more than competent. But he's got more than enough on his plate getting his new pilots up to scratch and organising them as a team." Beecham seemed to look for a better answer for a few seconds. He then piped up, "Besides, you're his new intelligence officer."

Padshaw stared, his mouth slightly open.

"In point of fact," continued Beecham, "you're his only intelligence officer... he's never had one!"

"I see sir," said Padshaw, not overly impressed.

"You are also charged with the job of emphasising the importance of these targets and making damn sure they're hit. Regularly!" Beecham's voice had changed from his normal, soft, even friendly tone, to one of intense concern.

"There are also other targets we want hit. They're all listed for you to read in your own time. Some may be out of range of Marsland's aircraft, but we're making arrangements to supply him with extra drop tanks, both for the Kittyhawks and the Hurricanes." Beecham sat back in his chair.

Padshaw took the opportunity:

"It would appear I have a lot of reading to do, sir," he said.

Beecham's face changed to a bold smile. "Oh, I think you'll find you have plenty of time to read all that. I've managed to snaffle a Sunderland flying boat from Lough Erne in Northern Ireland."

Padshaw looked at Hawkins and gave him an *I told you so* look. Hawkins frowned.

"Much to the annoyance of their CO I'm sure. It landed twenty minutes ago. As soon as they've refuelled and stocked up you'll be on your way."

Padshaw looked impassive.

"They'll be making various stops on the way, fuel, other passengers etc. But they will get you as close as they can to your destination, after that it's cross country. Right! Let's get some lunch. I'll brief you later Hawkins, let's go!"

Two hours later Padshaw was standing on a narrow jetty about to board the short Sunderland flying boat. Beecham had already bade him farewell and was in yet another meeting. Hawkins was there to see him off.

"Well Terry, I hope you have an uneventful flight and all goes well."

"Thanks, I dare say we'll be hearing from each other soon."

"We're ready to leave as soon as you're aboard, sir," said the air gunner leaning out of the doorway.

"I'll be right with you," replied Padshaw. Then, looking at Hawkins, he said, "I'd rather be drinking scotch back in the hotel."

"That reminds me: there's six bottles of Tanqueray gin in the box marked 'life vest' with your personal kit. Something to help you pave the way, you might say."

"Thanks Graham, I'd completely forgotten."

"Well, I am here to supply you with whatever you need." Graham handed Padshaw a small briefcase. "There are various items I've organised on your behalf, anything else I can help you with, let me know."

"Thanks very much, I'd better push off, they've probably got the meter running. All the best."

They shook hands.

"All the best to you too, and make sure you get a good tan... cheerio!"

Padshaw entered the Sunderland and was seated by a sergeant air gunner. A few minutes later he was flying south.

***

"Green leader, this is Red leader."

"Receiving you, Red leader."

"Green leader, myself and Red two will land first as we are short on fuel. It looks to me that our dispersal arrangements have been changed. When you've landed, follow whatever directions you're given. I look forward to meeting you old chap. Red leader out. Red two, you're first."

"Wilco leader."

'Spence' turned onto his final approach; he lowered his undercarriage and checked it was locked. He gave himself plenty of height and trimmed out. As he drifted over the trees he realised just how crowded the landing ground was getting.

Paul Cracken was doing an admirable job in dispersing the aircraft of Yellow, Red and Blue sections, which had all landed in quick succession. He was doing his best, but there was only so much space to play with. There were various ground crews milling about, and 'Spence' could see the other Kittyhawks being manhandled into the tightest corners of the airstrip. He immediately took in the situation and gave his Kittyhawk left rudder, right stick and a little throttle. His aeroplane deftly fell into a controlled sideslip. Just at the last moment 'Spence' opened the throttle, corrected the stick and rudder and flared out to perfection. The wheels ran and he saw ground crew to his right gesticulating which direction he should go in. He called up Valentine:

"Red leader, Red two. It's getting quite busy down here, over."

"Roger that, Red two. Green leader, we're getting rather cramped down there old boy, think you can manage? Over."

"We'll manage Red leader. Green section, land at three-minute intervals. Take your time on the approach and give yourselves bags of height. Don't rush it and don't rely on your brakes. I will follow Red leader. Green leader out."

Spencer had no sooner stopped his engine than the ground crew started pushing his machine backwards. He slid back the hood to hear Cracken's voice, "Come on Spence, I need all the hands I can get."

"On my way," he replied. As 'Spence' clambered out of the cockpit, he glanced at Valentine touching down. A perfect three-point landing.

"Cocky git," he said approvingly.

Directly behind him was Hacker, he lowered his undercarriage and flaps, judged the trees to perfection, gave his Hurricane just the slightest of sideslip, straightened out to a nicety, gave the Merlin just a hint of gun on the throttle and performed a second perfect three-point landing.

'Spence' witnessed that landing as well, somewhat impressed. 'That's all we need,' he said to himself, 'two cocky gits on the squadron!'

Hacker taxied off to one side to where he had been directed. The next pilot to come in was Sergeant Pilot Dick Vine, an Englishman who made a safe, though bumpy landing, following him was Sergeant Pilot Brian Brandon from Canada. He very nearly undershot completely and did well to rescue a good landing out of a sticky situation. Next was Sergeant Pilot George Tillman, again a Canadian, he overshot and had to go round again. Second time lucky. Following him was Sergeant Pilot 'Clem' Decker, an Australian; he, basically, threw his aircraft at the ground. 'Punchy' Jennings, who was watching the new pilots land, screwed his face up. 'Bloody vandal,' he said to himself.

After Decker was Pilot Officer Gerald Hayward, an Englishman, he made a near perfect landing spoilt only by a rogue crosswind as he flared out. Last to land was Pilot Officer Michael 'Midge' Midgeham. Both he and Hayward had the dubious honour of 'pranging' one aircraft each, while training on the same squadron on the same day, within ten minutes of each other. Midgeham's landing was textbook.

Squadron Leader Marsland was in his office talking to the adjutant:

"Well, I must say, I'm bloody impressed!" He was sitting on a chair with his feet on the desk. "Cracken and 'Punchy' have worked a small miracle. Trouble is, how the bloody hell are we going to be able to operate efficiently? No spare clothing for the new boys, and unless you know something I don't, damn all ammunition or spares for the Hurricanes. Come to that, what are our food stocks like? If it's anything like my gin supply we're buggered, aren't we?"

Hollingsworth answered with a calm confidence, "Our food stocks are actually quite good, and I'm sure if we've been given these Hurricanes then the necessary spares shouldn't be too far behind."

"And my gin?" Marsland asked with little humour. Before Hollingsworth could answer, the MO stuck his head round the door. Marsland's face went to one of concern.

"Jiff?" he said, with some apprehension.

"Well, he's pretty knocked about," the MO replied as he stood in the doorway. "A fractured leg, a fractured left arm, four or five cracked ribs. Plus a badly bruised collar bone, a dislocated right arm, which I've put back, a few stitches in his head and some loose teeth. Not forgetting a foul temper."

Marsland gave him a blank look.

The MO shook his head and sighed. "He seems to think that I should be able to fix him just as quickly as he broke himself. Anyway, I just thought I'd pop over and fill you in. I'd better go back and top up his morphine before he finds out he's in agony."

"Thanks Doc, let me know if there's any change."

"Will do. Oh, by the way, there's a Flying Officer Hacker waiting outside to see you. Shall I send him in?"

Marsland glanced from the MO to the adjutant.

"The officer leading the Hurricane flight, I believe," Hollingsworth advised.

"Ah yes. Thanks, send him in if you would."

"This way old chap," the MO said, glancing outside. He then gave Marsland a courteous nod and left. Hacker walked in carrying his flying helmet and gloves in his left hand and a large leather satchel over his left shoulder. He stood to attention and saluted.

Marsland casually returned the salute and said, "We're not on a parade ground here, Flying Officer. Relax, it's too hot for ceremony. So long as everybody understands that I'm the CO I'm happy."

Hacker dropped his salute courteously and stood in a more relaxed stance. Marsland looked at the adjutant.

"I am still the CO, aren't I, Holly?"

"Yes sir," Hollingsworth replied with encouragement and wide eyes.

"Have a pew," said Marsland.

"Thank you, sir." Hacker sat down.

"So... Mr?"

"Hacker, sir."

"Sorry, yes. So, what brings you to our tropical paradise?"

"Er, well..." Hacker was surprised by the question. "We're delivering your new Hurricanes, aren't we, sir?"

"No other orders or instructions as to what you do next?"

"I was told we'd be ferrying your Kittyhawks out, sir."

Marsland glanced at the adjutant. The adjutant stared back at Marsland with a look that said *Oh dear, I suppose you'd better tell him* etched all over his face.

"Unfortunately it's not that simple I'm afraid." He paused as he thought of the best way of how to break the good news.

Hacker politely asked, "Are some of the Kittyhawks u/s, sir?" glancing first at Marsland and then at the adjutant.

"No, nothing like that," replied Marsland.

Hacker had a polite, but quizzical look on his face.

Marsland continued, "To be brief: firstly we only recently received information that we would be getting these Hurricanes, otherwise we would have made better arrangements for your arrival." Marsland then looked Hacker straight in the eyes and said, "We also received orders that you and all your fellow pilots are to be put on my squadron's strength with effect from now!"

To Marsland's surprise, Hacker's face lit up. "That's great sir!" Hacker said with feeling. Marsland sat back and looked at his adjutant, Hollingsworth's eyebrows were raised; he turned to meet Marsland's gaze with a face suggesting Hacker needed medical help. Marsland looked at Hacker and said, "Well I hope your associates feel as pleased about it as you do, mm?"

"If they've spent any time at all in the same transit camp as me, I would think they'd be quite relieved not to go back... sir."

"Well," said Marsland with sarcasm creeping into his voice, "you're their senior officer, eh? You know them better than I do. You can give them the good news, yes?"

Hollingsworth was staring over Hacker's head; his hand was covering his mouth, which was grinning like a Cheshire cat. Hacker's face was no longer lit up.

"As a matter of fact, sir, I didn't know any of them until today. In fact, I wasn't even supposed to be leading!"

"Pray tell," Marsland quipped.

"Well sir, originally there were nine of us. One of the chaps developed an oil pressure drop and turned for home shortly after taking off, so he either 'pranged' or coaxed his Hurricane home. Then our leader, Flight Lieutenant Graham, had an engine failure and had to bail out over the jungle."

"Not a good day then?" Marsland said.

"We're pretty sure he's OK sir, we circled him once as he went down. His parachute opened OK but we lost him in the trees."

"Well don't bloody well do that again and that's an order!" Marsland said harshly.

Hacker was perplexed.

"Sir?"

Marsland drew his feet off the desk, clasped his hands and in a genuinely soft voice said, "Think about it: if some poor bastard is unlucky enough to be left with no option but to bale out, taking into account the Japs are everywhere, the last thing he wants is his 'chums' marking his position for them, mmm?"

Hacker wasn't smiling at the thought. "Oh Christ! I didn't think of that!"

"Well bloody well start thinking, as of now you're an acting flight commander."

"Sir?" Hacker was nothing short of dismayed.

"Listen carefully…" Marsland continued, "I've got a mixed bag of ranks and pilots on this squadron. Who, between them, have an even more mixed bag of flying experience. I've got sergeant pilots, pilot officers, flying officers, fairies, pixies, leprechauns and even a goblin with three kills. Now, in just a couple of hours, I've got seven new Hurricanes, with seven new pilots to boot. I've got no extra tents for them, no clothes and no ammunition for their aircraft except for what they carry. On top of all that, I've now got to inform them of all this, AND tell them they're going to be stuck here for the foreseeable future. In view of all this, you can help me share the good news!"

Marsland's face said, *If I'm going over the top, so are you!*

"Thank you, sir. I'm very grateful sir," Hacker replied in a deadpan voice, heavily drenched in undisguised sarcasm.

Marsland grinned. "Nice to see you have a sense of humour Hacker, you'll need it!" Yet at that moment he seemed to be tired, his shoulders slumped, his hands dropped loosely by his sides, he sighed gently and with no real interest whatsoever he flippantly came out with, "I don't suppose you brought any gin with you?"

Hacker flashed a wicked smile, which got both Marsland's and the adjutant's attention. He casually removed the satchel from his arm and methodically placed it on his lap. Marsland had leant forward and raised his head to get a better view over his desk, his eyes were wide with anticipation and interest, Hollingsworth was one step up from curious. Hacker slowly undid the straps and sat the satchel upright, he pulled back the flap and, on putting his right hand in, said:

"I tried to get Tanqueray sir, but they'd sold out unfortunately, so I had to make do with Gordon's." He pulled out the bottle and casually handed it to Marsland. Marsland's eyes were ready to pop out.

"Jesus bloody Christ! I don't believe it! Where the bloody hell did you get that? And how did you know I like gin?" Marsland was half-heartedly trying to be indignant but the broad smile wasn't helping. Hacker's hand was again coming out of the satchel as he answered his CO:

"Well, I got your gin from the same place as I got the adjutant's Irish whiskey, sir" He pulled out and handed Hollingsworth a bottle of Bushmills.

"I say!" said Hollingsworth with sincere gratitude.

"And the answer to your second question, sir…" Hacker continued "… the officer in charge of flying at the transit camp warned me, over a drink of course, not to get too close to you if you have a hangover brought on by gin. Apparently you throw things, sir."

Marsland knew whom Hacker was talking about; they'd been on several serious drinking sessions together.

"Whoever he is, he's a lying scoundrel, dismiss anything he said and any other rumours you may have heard. Immediately. And that's an order!"

"Yes sir," said Hacker. He could see Marsland was delighted. Hollingsworth was staring at his Bushmills as if it were a newborn baby. Marsland opened one of the drawers of a solitary filing cabinet and pulled out one glass and two chipped mugs. He blew into them and put them on the table. Hacker was a little surprised to be included and slightly flattered.

"I'm not in the habit of drinking with subordinate ranks Flying Officer Hacker," Marsland said in a semi-serious voice. "So, by the powers not invested to me, and witnessed by the adjutant –" he was pouring gin into the mugs "– I promote you to the rank of acting squadron leader for the next ten minutes."

"Duly witnessed," commented Hollingsworth smiling.

Marsland finished pouring and passed them both a mug. He raised his glass, looked briefly first at his adjutant and then at Hacker.

"Cheers," he said.

"Cheers," they replied simultaneously.

Marsland took a mouthful of gin and washed it around his mouth, he then pouted his lips slightly and repeatedly moved his tongue side to side letting the gin leap over his taste buds again and again. He closed his eyes and swallowed as slowly as he could, then gave out a contented sigh and smiled. He held his glass with both hands and leaned back into his chair, looking very relaxed. Hollingsworth was looking at him with a smile; he liked to see his CO happy. Marsland's eyes were closed for a moment; he opened them, looked at Hacker and politely said:

"Well, I suppose you had better tell me something about yourself, hadn't you?"

"I'm not sure where to start, sir," Hacker replied.

"Well we don't need a life history," the adjutant said. "Just some information on your flying experience. What 'types' you've flown for instance, that sort of thing." Hollingsworth put his mug down and took out a pen and writing pad and looked enquiringly at Hacker. Hacker thought for a few moments and then started:

"Well I joined the air force in the late thirties, I've flown Gladiators, Gauntlets, Spitfires, Hurricanes. I've also got a small number of hours on Bristol Blenheims, Fairey Battles and Ansons. Plus various private aircraft." He glanced at the adjutant busily writing.

"What about combat experience?" asked Marsland.

"Well I served with the squadron in France right through to the retreat to Dunkirk–"

"Any kills?" Marsland interrupted.

"One Stuka confirmed and a possible Dornier."

"Well done. What then?"

"Once we were back home we re-equipped with Spitfires. Then of course there was the Battle of Britain–"

"Any luck there?" this from Hollingsworth.

"One Messerschmitt 109 confirmed and a possible Heinkel."

"Bully for you!" Hollingsworth said encouragingly.

"Then we went on to do convoy duties and fighter sweeps over France," Hacker continued. Both the CO and the adjutant looked at him expectantly.

"Two confirmed kills, a Junkers 88 and a Messerschmitt 110."

"I say, you have been busy," Hollingsworth said, still writing.

"And then you ended up here." Marsland said, sipping his gin.

"Yes sir."

"What the bloody hell did you do wrong?" Marsland asked.

Hacker immediately felt and looked guilty. "I volunteered," he said hesitantly. Hollingsworth nearly choked on his gin, at the same time Marsland blurted, "Bugger me! What DID you do wrong?"

Hacker looked at his CO and said as casually as he could, "Nothing really."

Marsland sat up. "'Nothing really' in the Royal Air Force dictionary means 'got caught buggering about'. Am I correct?"

"Yes sir," replied Hacker.

"Right, well, don't get economical with the facts with me again. Got that?"

Hacker nodded, looking uncomfortable. Marsland watched him squirm for a few seconds and then added, "And besides, I don't bloody care. Anybody that brings me gin can't be all bad."

"Hear, hear," said Hollingsworth.

At that moment 'Snobby' Valentine walked in. "I say. Gin! Where's mine?" Hacker stood up. Marsland introduced them as he produced another mug from the drawer.

"Flying Officer Hacker, Flight Lieutenant Valentine."

"Pleased to meet you old chap," Valentine said as he thrust a hand forward. They shook hands.

"How do you do, sir."

"I do very well. Ah, thanks awfully," Valentine said as he accepted his mug of gin. "Down the hatch!" He took a large swig and then looked at Hacker. "Do sit down old chap, you're making the place look untidy."

Hacker sat back down. In the few seconds of Valentine entering Marsland's office, Hacker felt relaxed and at ease, he also knew that Valentine was a man you could trust with your life.

"He's awfully polite isn't he?" said Valentine.

"Yes he is," Marsland replied. "So don't go teaching him your wicked ways."

"As if," Valentine said, with a roguish look in his eyes. Marsland smiled at him and said, "Sit down 'Snobby', we've got a few things to sort out." 'Snobby' pulled up the last chair and sat down, leant back and crossed his legs.

"Firstly," Marsland continued, "I've made Hacker up to acting flight commander."

"Well done chum!" Valentine glanced at Hacker. "Twenty minutes on the squadron and promotion already, you'll be an air vice marshal by next week."

Hacker's eyebrows went up.

"Not now 'Snobby'," Marsland said. "Leave it for later."

"Can't help it skipper. Carry on."

"Apart from Mr Hacker's unexpected arrival, we also received information that all the pilots who have ferried in these Hurricanes are going on the squadron strength."

Valentine said, "We don't have much space left to operate with so many aircraft." It was a statement.

"I realise that. We'll just have to do our best. The other point to make is that none of the pilots, except Hacker, know they're staying. They think they're flying the Kittyhawks out!"

Valentine laughed evilly.

"I thought that might appeal to your sense of humour … the other information we received was that an officer is being shipped out from Blighty to brief us on specific targets on top of what we're hitting."

That got Valentine's attention. "I presume his arrival has something to do with our shiny new Hurricanes then, don't you?"

"Possibly… Hacker?" Marsland looked at him expectantly.

"Sir?" Hacker was looking a little lost.

"Didn't you pick up any rumours at all?"

"No sir. I wasn't even supposed to fly today. One of the ferry pilots was ill so the CO needed a pilot. I haven't flown for weeks so I took his place."

Hollingsworth asked, "How come you've not flown recently?"

"Well the troopship had some engine problems, so that journey took a few days longer..."

"How long have you been in India?" Marsland interrupted.

"Just the week, sir."

"I see. So, what exactly was your posting here supposed to entail? You must have been given some idea of your duties, surely?"

"I'm not sure what I can tell you, sir."

"Try."

Hacker thought for a moment. One thing he was sure of, he wasn't going back to the transit camp without a fight.

"Basically sir, I volunteered for..."

"Volunteered!" Valentine exclaimed sarcastically.

"'Snobby'," said Marsland with a *belt up* look on his face. "Go on, I'm listening."

Hacker decided to be honest, "I got caught 'buggering about' as you put it sir –" Valentine nodded to himself, contentedly, and smiled at Hacker in understanding "– and I had a sort of choice, a training squadron or here."

"Right, now we're getting somewhere," said Marsland. "So what were the details of this posting? I mean, where were, or are you, supposed to be?"

"I've been waiting for orders for a week. I kept asking the CO if he had received any instructions for me, but all he said was that there had been a delay in getting the other pilots to India, and that he'd let me know if there was any change."

Hollingsworth, as were the others, was intrigued. "What other pilots?" he asked.

"For the…" Hacker stopped himself.

"For the what?" Marsland asked brusquely.

"I'm not at all sure I'm supposed to discuss it sir, I mean, I'm sure…"

"Hacker! What was your briefing?" Marsland asked impatiently.

"All I know is, sir, that there are supposed to be several pilots, including myself, who are part of a special squadron that has been formed for particular operations in India. That's all I can tell you, sir."

Marsland thought for a moment. He hadn't quite put two and two together yet, but he was as near as damn it. He looked at Valentine. "'Snobby'. Are you thinking what I'm thinking?"

"I'm thinking there's been a great big colossal cock-up and we're on the receiving end of it," 'Snobby' replied.

"Holly?"

"Looks like it, doesn't it?" Hollingsworth said.

"Have we been given any indication as to when we can expect this officer's arrival?"

"Not really," replied Hollingsworth. "But we only received notice of Mr Hacker's arrival today, so your guess is as good as mine."

"Bloody hell!" Marsland said defeated. "See what you can find out, Holly?" he added: "Possible arrival time, when can we expect spares for the Hurricanes, anything at all, OK?

"Right sir. Now?"

"No, let's get this day's shenanigans finished with first." He took another mouthful of gin and savoured it for a moment. The others took the opportunity to do the same. Marsland was firing on all cylinders again, he looked at Valentine. "How did you get on today, 'Snobby'?" he asked.

"Bloody good show actually. Completely destroyed the target, which was exactly where intelligence said it would be, I'm still suffering from shock. And then we shot up a small Jap convoy on the way back! I reckon we accounted for about seventy percent of them. Then we bumped into these chaps. How's 'Jiff' by the way?"

"Not so good," replied Marsland. "The Doc's working on him now. He's going to be OK, but I don't see him flying in a hurry."

"Well, that's better than I expected, looking at the remains of his Kitty." There was a short silence.

"Right, to business," Marsland said. "Let's get on with meeting and briefing the newcomers. 'Snobby', Hacker, sit this side with 'Holly' and me, we'll see them together."

'Snobby' and Hacker dragged their chairs around.

"Just before we continue," Hollingsworth said, "I really do think we should …" He was opening the Bushmills.

"Of course! How rude of me." said Marsland. He finished his gin and the others did the same. Hollingsworth poured.

Hacker raised his mug. "Cheers," he said.

"Cheers," Marsland replied. "Welcome to the squadron."

They drank.

***

The rustling in the undergrowth was getting nearer; Graham levelled his service revolver in the general direction of where the sound was coming from. Just holding the weapon was something of a feat. He really did hurt everywhere. It was like holding a ten-pound weight, his hand started to shake a little.

Corporal Pitt turned to Private Joyce, who was just off to his right, and said, "This is a waste of bloody time this is."

"Couldn't agree more, Corp," Joyce replied.

Pitt stopped suddenly. "What the bloody hell was that?"

"Sounded like a tiger," Joyce replied anxiously.

"Shit!" Pitt took the 'safety' off his rifle.

Joyce immediately did the same.

"Keep it quiet!" Pitt snapped at Joyce in a hoarse whisper.

"You don't have to tell me!" Joyce said under his breath.

Pitt pointed in the direction of where the sound had come from and directed Joyce far to the right, motioning with his rifle. Joyce stealthily made his way through the light foliage; Pitt was just to his left. Joyce was none too happy and was muttering to himself:

"Fine fucking idea this is! Can't see where we're going, don't know what we're gonna find, stink like pigs, what a way to fight a w... Jesus Christ!" he exclaimed before he remembered to shut up. With the snapping of small branches and twigs, Joyce fell into a large ditch. He fumbled for his rifle. "Bollocks!" he said quietly. He found his rifle and slowly stood up. Pitt glared at him from the edge of the ditch.

"Sorry Corp," Joyce said in a whisper, "I didn't see it."

"Well keep your bloody eyes open you idiot," Pitt said as he offered Joyce a hand out.

"Who's there?" came a voice from the undergrowth in front of them.

Pitt and Joyce stared at each other in surprise. Pitt leaned over, offered Joyce his hand and heaved him out of the ditch. They slowly walked forward. Pitt cautiously pushed some branches to one side with his rifle. He was confronted with the sight of 'Bobby' Graham, lying on his back pointing his revolver straight at him.

Pitt was wide eyed. "It's all right now sir," Pitt said, as he lowered his rifle. "We're on your side," he assured him.

Joyce came up to Pitt's side and said, "I'll be damned."

Graham lowered his revolver; a broad smile came over his face. For a moment, he had no idea what to say. Then he said:

"Hello chaps. You wouldn't happen to have a stretcher would you? The leg's a bit buggered, you see."

Corporal Pitt quickly sized up the situation.

"Joyce? Get back to the jeep and sound the horn three times as ordered. Explain to Captain Blackman that we've found the pilot but that he's got some injuries and we'll need a stretcher. Get back here as soon as possible. Off you go!"

"Right Corp," Joyce disappeared back into the jungle.

Captain Blackman turned to private Naylor and asked, "Did that sound like a tiger to you?"

"Yes sir."

"Mmm. Well I think we've made the effort, but we'll just move off to the right a little and then–"

The jeep's horn sounded. Blackman glanced at Naylor and then bolted back in the direction of the jeep.

"Come on Naylor, put your skates on!"

Naylor ran after him. As Blackman came out of the shadows, Joyce and the other two men were waiting with their rifles in hand, trained in his direction. On recognising their officer they lowered them.

"Sorry about that sir," said Joyce. "But you never know."

Blackman smiled. "You've found him?"

"Yes sir. Corporal Pitt's with him now, just up there to the right." Joyce was pointing in the direction from which he had just come.

"Bloody marvellous! Well done. Drinks are on me!"

Joyce had never seen Blackman so happy.

"He's a bit broken I'm afraid, sir."

"How bad?"

"Difficult to tell sir, certainly a broken leg. He's also got a head wound, but it's probably worse than it looks. Corporal Pitt told me to get a stretcher."

"Right. You two: take the jeep back to the bivouac area and get the MO. Make sure he brings a stretcher. Got it?"

"Yes sir."

"Naylor."

"Sir."

"You go too."

"Right sir."

They got into the jeep and drove off.

"Right Joyce. Lead on."

"This way sir." The sound of the jeep's engine faded behind them.

Major Connors was sitting on the ground with his back against the side of his jeep. He was re-reading the message that Sergeant Bell had passed him. Lieutenant Portman wandered over to him, he was holding his mess tin in one hand and a fork in the other.

"Cook wants to know if you'd like anything more to eat, sir?"

"No, thank you. My guts are already trying to defend themselves against the first attack!"

Portman turned and looked over to the cook and shook his head.

"Come into my office," Connors said. Portman sat down beside him.

"Anything of interest, sir?" Portman asked gesturing with his fork at the slip of paper.

"Well, I'll brief everybody later, but it appears we are to divert to this map reference." Connors was pointing at reference numbers. "Once there we're to expect some other supplies to be dropped by parachute."

"I see, sir."

"Well I'm glad you do, because I don't!"

"Am I missing something, sir?"

"According to this, we're also to meet up with another supply train, and then all of us are to make our way to the RAF landing ground at this map reference." Portman looked at the numbers.

"I'll get some maps," Portman said. As he stood up, the other jeep's engine could be heard approaching quite quickly. Portman looked at the area where the engine's sound was coming from. It appeared out of the trees at quite a brisk pace and then slowed to a halt. Portman observed immediately that there were only three occupants.

"Something must have happened sir, there's only three of them."

Connors drew himself up and stared but for a moment.

"Sergeant Bell!" Connors shouted. Bell looked up from checking the damaged tyre of the disabled truck.

"Sir?"

Connors pointed at the jeep and started walking to meet it. Sergeant Bell immediately started handing out orders:

"Bowyer! Clemence!"

"Sarge?"

"Get your rifles and follow me!" Both men quickly grabbed their weapons and followed Bell.

"Jenner!"

"Yes Sarge?"

"Get the MO. Just in case."

"Right Sarge." Jenner ran towards the MO's truck.

"You men! With me!" Bell ordered, and ran towards the stationary jeep. By the time he reached it, Connors was there too.

"Where's Captain Blackman?" Connors asked the driver.

"He's back there sir." The soldier turned and pointed uselessly at trees behind him. Naylor shook his head and said:

"We found the pilot, sir."

"Good lord!" said Connors, genuinely surprised.

"Captain Blackman's with him now, sir," he continued. "He ordered us to get the MO and a stretcher, sir."

"Sergeant Bell…" Connors began.

"Lieutenant Mercer's on his way now sir," Bell said and looked over his shoulder as Mercer trotted up.

"Got a message I might be needed, sir," he said.

"Captain Blackman's found the pilot," Connors explained.

"That's good news, sir," Mercer stated.

"You'll need a stretcher, apparently."

"That's not such good news."

"Either way Doc," Connors said, "get your show on the road, tout de suite!"

"Yes sir."

Sergeant Bell looked at Bowyer and Clemence. "All right lads, false alarm. Dismiss."

"Sarge," Clemence said, saluting. He and Bowyer went back to their duties.

"Naylor..." Connors started.

"Sir."

"... you can find your way back to their position?"

"Yes sir."

"Right, you take this jeep... Burns?"

"Sir."

"...you follow with the Doc."

"Right sir."

Mercer put his bag in Burns' jeep as another man strapped a stretcher to the back. "On your way," Connors said, giving Naylor a pleasant nod.

"Sir." Naylor turned and headed back towards the trees. As Mercer sat back, Burns dropped the clutch and followed. Connors and Bell watched for a moment.

"Right then... let's have another brew up," Connors said, smiling contentedly.

"On its way sir," Bell replied and then walked back to the vehicles.

***

After just one hour in the air, Padshaw had almost got used to the throb of the four Bristol Pegasus engines reverberating right through the Sunderland's huge interior. He had also resigned himself to the fact that he was going to get little or no sleep.

No sooner had the sergeant air gunner seated him, and he'd strapped himself in, than the Sunderland was moving.

"Make yourself comfortable sir, I'll pop back when I've finished my chores."

"Thank you, Sergeant."

That was an hour ago. Padshaw decided to kill some time reading the contents of the briefcase Hawkins had given him; he'd already decided to read Beecham's instructions when he got closer to his destination. He opened the bag and put his hand in, glass chinked. He pulled out the bottle of Glenmorangie.

"Hah! Graham, you deserve a medal!" he said to himself. He held the bottle in his left hand and put his right hand back in the bag. There was another chink. This time he pulled out a full bottle of Glenlivet.

"Forget the medal! You deserve a bloody knighthood!" he said aloud.

"Beg your pardon, sir?" said the approaching sergeant. Padshaw thrust the bottles back into the briefcase.

"Sorry Sergeant, just talking out loud."

The sergeant stared at him for a couple of seconds, slightly amused, and then said, "I'm just putting out some soup, sir, and there's a stew on the stove which should be ready in about ten minutes. If you'd like to come through next door to the galley..?"

"Lead on," replied Padshaw as he got up and followed the gunner. Padshaw had never been in a Sunderland before and it was far bigger than he had imagined.

"Don't you ever get lost in here?" he asked the gunner. The gunner smiled and said, "You get used to it sir. Mind you, it does tend to get quite busy if we spot a U-boat or something."

"Have you seen much action lately?"

"We helped sink a U-boat about a month ago, but the navy laid claim to actually sinking it. We found the bugger, but they said that they were already tracking it and that our help was appreciated but not required,"

"Ungrateful lot," Padshaw replied.

"That's what our skipper said sir, although he put it in a far more colourful way."

Padshaw raised his eyebrows and said, "I don't blame him."

"He also told them," the gunner continued, "that if we see another U-boat, we'll let them deal with it on their own. He also explained that we can only pick up so many survivors at a time, and would they be kind enough to supply us with the complement of their ship in order for us to get enough help to pick them out of the water?"

"A little strong. What did they say to that?"

"Some naval officer tried to pull rank, but the skipper soon stopped that."

"Really? How?"

The gunner opened his mouth to reply, but was interrupted by a stocky sergeant pilot had just walked into the galley.

"I told the pommie bastard to fuck off!"

"Sir, this is the skipper." The gunner left.

Padshaw knew what Australians could be like and immediately decided to forget any respect for rank. Besides, looking at the man before him, he wasn't likely to get a 'sir' out of him anyway.

Surprisingly, the big Australian stood up, offered his hand and introduced himself:

"Jack Stone. The boys call me Jacko."

Padshaw took the offered hand and shook it. The Australian's grip was firm but friendly. Padshaw too had a strong grip, but there was no competition between them.

"Terry Padshaw," he said, and just caught a glimpse of surprise in the Australian's face, brought on by not introducing himself by his rank.

"Fuck me!" Stone said, "a pom officer who hasn't got a stick of ginger stuffed up his arse! Have a seat. Would you like some rum?"

Padshaw was surprised, not by the language, but the offer of rum. He sat down. "That's damned civilised. Thanks very much." Padshaw hated rum. "What are we drinking to?" he asked as Stone poured rum into two heavily scratched glasses.

"You!" replied Stone.

"Me? Why?"

"If it wasn't for you, we'd still be in Northern Ireland. Have you been there?"

"Not since I was eight."

"Well you're not missing much!"

"I remember it being quite picturesque."

"Don't get me wrong Terry. The people are the nicest in the world. The countryside is breathtaking. The weather is shit! The quarters are shit! The lack of action is shit! The lack of women is shit! And on top of that, everything we get from ops is–"

"Shit?" offered Padshaw.

"You got it. When we were told we had to pick up some pom officer and take him to a meeting, we just thought 'more bullshit'. Wasn't till we got to Thorney that we found out where we were actually going. Me and the boys think you're a real bonzer bloke." He held up his rum.

"Up your chuff Terry."

"Cheers," Padshaw put on his best false smile and drank. Red-hot barbed wire went down his throat. "Jesus!" remarked Padshaw, almost in a whisper. "That's got a serious kick!"

"Sure has. One of the boys does something to spice it up."

Stone knocked his back, poured himself a small measure and topped up Padshaw's glass. He saw an inquisitive look in Padshaw's face.

"The rum?"

Padshaw nodded.

"Well, this is a boat as much as an aeroplane, so we have slightly different regulations. Not that we take too much notice of regulations anyway..." Stone gave a crooked smile and let the silence speak. Padshaw replied with an understanding nod.

"Here, try the stew. Lenny the rear gunner made it. He's a marvel. Used to cook for some fancy restaurant, he's no chef, but he's better than the rest of us."

Stone ladled some stew onto a plate and passed it to Padshaw with a spoon and fork.

"Thanks. Am I to assume the rear turret isn't manned?" Padshaw queried.

"No worries. We take turns to eat, so we get another member of the crew to man the turret while Lenny's cooking. When Lenny's eaten, he goes back to his turret and so on for the other gunners and crew."

"Ah," said Padshaw satisfied. "How many men do you have in the crew?"

"Ten in all."

"Ten? Where do you hide them all?"

Stone grinned. "Well, you've met Lenny. There's Josh Pelt; Josh is the flight engineer. Colin Rustin's my co-pilot. Then there's Don Lipman, he's our 'sparks'; Chris James is the navigator and bomb aimer. Jimmy Creed and Dean Parlow are the waist gunners. 'Vinny' Hardcastle, he's the mid-upper gunner which leaves Mike Illman in the nose turret. You won't meet a better group of misfits anywhere!"

"I didn't realise Sunderlands had so many gunners!" Padshaw confessed.

"We've got ten guns in total. Not including a couple that Mike 'acquired' for emergencies."

"Emergencies?"

"Mike's philosophy is, 'You can't have too much fire power!' Apparently Jerry calls these boats 'Flying Porcupines'. Whether that's true or not I don't know."

"I'm not surprised." Padshaw spooned some stew into his mouth as Stone helped himself to a plateful. He gestured with a fork at Padshaw's plate, "What do you think?"

Padshaw swallowed. "Excellent!" In fact Padshaw *was* impressed. It even reminded him a little of how his mother used to make it. "Compliments to the chef," he added. Padshaw hadn't long eaten, but saying he wasn't hungry might be taken the wrong way.

"What are your orders?" he asked Stone.

Stone's mouth was half full. "We've got a few refuelling stops to make on the way," he replied. "And originally we were supposed to pick up some passengers on the way and drop them somewhere else, but we've been told that might have changed. What we're really looking forward to is playing with some nice, shiny new depth charges they've put on board!"

Padshaw's face assumed a concerned look.

Stone caught this and said, "Don't worry. We've been told you're a priority, so we won't misbehave until we're on our way back."

"Well, I certainly don't want to spoil your fun, but I do have some serious business to attend to, otherwise I'd quite like a bit of action myself. I've been stuck behind a desk for some time."

"But not always?" Stone said, pointing at Padshaw's missing fingers and his burns.

"I flew into a Dornier," Padshaw replied, shrugging his shoulders indifferently. He really didn't want to go through it, now.

Stone looked into Padshaw's eyes. He knew there was more to it, but even he knew when not to ask. There was a gruff respect in his voice when he spoke.

"Should have looked where you were going then Cobber. More rum?"

"No… thanks." Padshaw appreciated the reply and the change of subject. "So, what's new about these depth charges?" he asked politely.

"Well, up until now, a lot of the boys have had some problems with the bloody bombs bouncing off the water and hitting the bloody plane after they've bloody dropped them!"

Padshaw's eyes widened.

"I'm serious!" Stone said with feeling. "The best place to bloody well be when we attack is in the bloody sub!"

"I take it these new charges are an improvement?" Padshaw replied, concerned.

"I bloody hope so. According to the boffins, once you've dropped them, they go down to whatever depth you set them at, and *then* they explode."

"I hope they're right."

"So do I. We had several boxes of them delivered to our base two days ago. The boffins wanted the squadron to test them. The CO gave us the job… which means he either thinks they're going to work, or we're expendable. Probably the latter."

Padshaw smiled and said, "I'm pretty sure your CO knew what he was doing when he gave the job to you."

The big Australian gave the beginnings of a smile.

"How many Australians are in your crew?" Padshaw asked.

"Apart from Lenny, we're all Australian," he replied.

At that moment Lenny walked back into the galley area.

"Stew all right, sir?" he asked Padshaw.

"Very good, thank you."

"I'm going back to my turret, Skipper. I'll send Jimmy back to eat and then he'll relieve Terry in the nose gun."

"Righto Lenny. Soon as I've finished I'll get back up front and spell Colin."

"Righto Skip... sir!" Lenny addressed Padshaw as he excused himself. Padshaw gave him a courteous nod.

Stone smiled and said in an almost fatherly voice, "We're working on him. One day we hope he'll grow up to be as loud and as disrespectful as the rest of us."

Padshaw grinned. He liked this Australian. They had just finished their stew when Jimmy and another crewman arrived to eat.

"Come on Skip, we're starving! Shift your..."

Padshaw turned to face them with a friendly smile.

"This is Squadron Leader Padshaw," Stone interrupted. "Our guest on this trip."

"Pleased to meet you cobber," Jimmy said loudly. "Would you like some rum?"

"I've had some, thank you," replied Padshaw.

"Well if there's anything you need, just holler and we'll do our best."

"That's very kind..."

"No worries!" Jimmy interrupted, "We reckon you've changed our luck."

"I hope that proves to be the case," Padshaw replied frowning at Stone. Stone picked up on the frown and said, "What the boys mean is, we haven't seen any real action in five sorties! And four of those were at night. Just to be flying in daylight is an improvement, plus there's a good chance of getting a tan!"

Padshaw raised his eyebrows in humour.

"Seriously. We've been bored rigid mate!" Stone stood up and slapped Padshaw on the back.

"You and us cobber, we're gonna get on fine!"

At that moment, for some odd reason, Padshaw felt he was giving them something that wasn't his to give and taking the credit for it. He moved the conversation on. "Which route are we taking?" he asked Stone.

"You'd better come and meet our navigator. He'll show you. I just point the boat where he tells me!"

118

Stone made his way out of the galley and gestured to Padshaw to follow him. As he stood up, Padshaw said to the other crewmembers:

"No doubt I'll see you gentlemen later."

"You can count on it cobber!" said Jimmy.

Padshaw followed Stone as he made his way up towards the cockpit.

"I'll get Chris to brief you on our route and then see you in the cockpit, OK?" said Stone.

"Fine," replied Padshaw.

"Oh, I nearly forgot..." Stone continued, "I borrowed this for you, you may need it for the first leg of our trip." Stone picked up an Irvin flying jacket and passed it to him.

"Thanks," Padshaw said and put it on.

"Chris!" Stone called loudly. Chris James turned from his navigation table. "This is Chris James. Chris, this is Squadron Leader Padshaw."

"Just call me Terry," Padshaw said.

"Nice to meet ya, Terry."

Stone smiled and said, "Brief Terry on our route and stops and then give me our position before you eat, OK?"

"Right Skipper."

"See you in a minute." Stone said and climbed into the cockpit. Padshaw nodded and stood over the navigator, one hand on the edge of the navigator's table. "What flight plan have we got?" asked Padshaw.

"Right, well... firstly we're taking the quickest route possible, but at the same time trying to avoid any trouble."

"Glad to hear it," Padshaw said pleasantly.

"You won't be when you hear the route!" James replied sardonically. Padshaw looked at him, the words *bloody Australian humour* going through his head.

"I take it we're not flying over Occupied France!" Padshaw said facetiously. James grinned:

"No, not quite that bad. First stop is Gibraltar. We'll be keeping a fair distance from the coastline on the way down,

Jerry's got regular patrols over the Bay of Biscay and we don't want to attract their attention if we can help it."

"How long do you think that will take?" asked Padshaw.

"I reckon it's about fifteen hundred miles give or take, and we'll be flying at around a hundred and fifty, so, ten hours all but I reckon."

"How long will we be in Gibraltar?"

"Long enough to refuel and get some sleep. Next stop is Alexandria, stopping at Malta on the way."

"Malta!" Padshaw interrupted.

"Yeah. The skipper's got orders to pick up some dispatches in 'Gib' and drop them off with some staff wallahs on Malta. Besides, it's well over two thousand miles to 'Alex', and the skipper doesn't like swimming."

"Out of interest," Padshaw asked, "what is our maximum range?"

"Around two and a half thousand fully loaded. But we very rarely clock up more than two thousand on a sortie. It's always a good idea to have a margin in case we have to divert for bad weather, or suffer a duff engine."

"Sensible," replied Padshaw. "Where to after 'Alex'?"

"Aden. The skipper intends to fly the length of the Red Sea all the way down to Aden…" James was indicating the route to Padshaw on his map with a well-chewed pencil. "Stay over for a night, refuel, and then Karachi."

"I take it I'm on my own from there?" Padshaw said.

"No idea cobber," James replied with a sly smirk. "But I think you'll find the skipper's always wanted to see Calcutta." James laughed out loud and added: "Relax chum, we're taking you as far as we can. And further if no one finds out!"

"Believe it or not," Padshaw said sincerely, "I'm very glad to hear that."

"We're glad to have you. We reckon you've changed our luck."

"So people keep telling me," Padshaw said with an uncertain smile.

"Either way," James said, "as far as the last couple of hops of our trip are concerned, very much depends on any additional orders, and the weather of course. It's a bit wet over there this time of year, but the monsoon should be coming to an end soon."

"Well, I appreciate you taking the time to brief me. I think I'll go and admire the view from the cockpit."

"No problem. Anything you want, just ask." James was writing on a piece of paper. "I'll follow you, I've got to give the skipper our position."

Padshaw stood to make room for James. James stood and then slid past Padshaw, adding a respectful nod.

On a Sunderland, the navigator, engineer and wireless position were all behind the pilot. They all had their own stations, but sat on the same level apart from a slightly raised level for the pilots.

"Skipper!" James shouted and passed Stone a piece of paper with their position. "Brest is well off to our port side."

Stone looked at his heading, glanced at the figures on the piece of paper and turned back to face James. "Thanks Chris. Go and get some tucker." Stone tapped his co-pilot on the shoulder, "you go too, Colin."

"Righto 'Jacko'." Rustin got up, squeezed between the seats and followed James. As he passed Padshaw, he beamed at him and said:

"All right chum?"

There wasn't much Padshaw could say in reply, but he was saved of trying by Stone:

"C'mon Terry, d'ya wanna fly her or not?"

Padshaw looked at the empty seat for a split second, smiled generously at Stone and clambered into the co-pilot's position. He gently placed his hands on the control wheel.

"All yours cobber!" Stone said, and let go.

Padshaw hadn't felt so content for God knows how long. He gently pushed the wheel forward. For such a large aeroplane, the Sunderland reacted very quickly. Padshaw then, just as gently, pulled the wheel back.

"She's very responsive," commented Padshaw.

"Crank her up to two hundred miles an hour and she's quite a handful," Stone replied. Padshaw was back where he belonged, he suddenly realised just how much he missed flying. Stone glanced at him, smiled to himself and remained silent for a few minutes. Then he said:

"I'll sit here and get some paperwork done. You fly her for an hour or so."

"Thanks Jacko," Padshaw replied.

Nearly half an hour had passed and, although Padshaw was enjoying himself, he had come to realise just how much concentration was required to fly the Sunderland. His own sorties in fighters had been short, sharp engagements, preceded by an anxious wait, then a sprint to the aircraft, a mad dash to intercept the enemy and then straight home to do it all again. If you relaxed for just a moment it could easily be enough time for a Messerschmitt to sneak up and put holes in you and save you the trip home.

Flying a Sunderland required a different sort of pilot. Sure, it had an automatic pilot, nevertheless you had to keep up a high level of concentration all the time. The job could be monotonous; you would fly for hours looking at an empty sky and a deserted sea in the hunt for the enemy. You had to remember that you weren't on your own. You were responsible for your crew and they were responsible for you.

Padshaw's thoughts were broken by Chris James:

"Coffee!" Chris shouted. Stone turned in his seat and took both mugs. He passed one to Padshaw saying:

"There you go Terry, something to warm you up."

"Cheers, just what I needed." Padshaw took a mouthful and swallowed. It was laced with rum; quite a lot of rum. Oh well, he thought to himself, when in Rome... He knocked the rest back in four large gulps and passed the mug back to James.

"Would ya like some more?" James asked, taking the mug.

"No thanks, that just hit the spot nicely."

"Skipper?"

Stone was about to reply when–

"Rear gunner here. I've got three bogeys at five o'clock high!" Every crew member dropped what he was eating and drinking and scrambled to his position.

"What course?" Stone asked as he gave the dregs of his coffee to James.

"They seem to be shadowing us, Skipper. They've got twin engines. Could be 88s."

"Keep an eye on them Lenny, Let me know–"

"Skipper, there's six of them! Three more just came out of cloud!"

"Mid upper here. Definitely Junkers 88s Skip!"

Stone took in the situation and started handing out orders.

"Don! Get a message off, tell Thorney what's happening."

"Roger Skip!"

"Josh, keep an eye on the engines cos I'm going to need every rev you can give me."

"They're waiting for you Skipper."

"Colin, get back up here now! Sorry Terry, you're–" But Padshaw was already getting out of the co-pilot's seat as Rustin came into the cockpit.

"All yours," Padshaw said to Rustin. Rustin didn't respond, he got into his seat and fastened his harness.

"Gunners! Report in!" Stone ordered. Gone was the laid back, indifferent and undisciplined Australian.

"Rear gunner ready!"

"Mid upper ready!"

"Port waist gun ready."

"Starboard waist gun ready."

"Nose gun ready!"

Padshaw, now sitting beside the navigator, was impressed by how professional the crew were. They all knew what to do and how to do it, and they certainly didn't need to be told.

Stone opened the throttles to maximum power, the Pegasus engines roared and the airframe came alive.

"Rear gunner here. Bandits coming down, now!"

"Roger. Keep me posted on distance and position."

"Wilco Skipper."

James nudged Padshaw and, with a huge smile, said:

"I told you you'd change our luck!"

Padshaw just stared wide eyed.

Stone was flying at six thousand feet. He wanted to keep some height to give himself more room to manoeuvre. He could go down to sea level, thereby forcing the 88s to make diving attacks, but if that failed they'd be swimming.

At seven thousand feet, four of the 88s levelled out. The other two broke away in different directions. Lenny continually kept updating Stone.

"Two of them have broken formation Skipper. Four in orbit; looks as if one of them's going to try a beam attack while the other comes in astern."

"Roger that."

The first 88 had flown off to the Sunderland's starboard side, it had gone about a mile before it turned back to intercept. The pilot had positioned himself so as the Sunderland would fly from his left to right as he made his attack, he also gave himself a couple of hundred feet above the Sunderland which would present him with a larger target area. The second 88 had broken left and let the Sunderland pull away from him; now, as he saw his leader turn into attack he opened his throttles wide. The maximum speed of the Sunderland was just over two hundred miles an hour. The Junkers 88 could top 280. The distance between them began to close up.

Hardcastle in the mid upper turret was all eyes:

"Eighty-eight coming in at two o'clock, slightly high."

"Roger that," replied Stone calmly.

"That second 88's coming up astern Skipper, about a thousand yards!"

"Wilco. Mike! Vinny! I'm gonna turn hard starboard and dive slightly, that should give you both a field of fire. Let him get as close as you can and then let him have it!"

"Ok Skipper."

"The other one's all yours, Lenny!"

"Roger, Skipper."

"Jimmy!"

"Yes, Skip?"

"Look out for Lenny's 88 breaking above and to our left, he'll have nowhere else to go."

"Roger."

"Turning now!"

The big flying boat began its turn. The 88 making the beam attack suddenly found himself losing the angle for his attack. He pushed the stick forward and opened fire. His opening rounds peppered the top of the Sunderland's fuselage.

Hardcastle saw tracer dance towards him. The next thing he knew, the top of the fuselage between him and the cockpit was full of holes. The sound of his own guns rattled in his ears. He gave himself plenty of lead ahead and slightly high of the 88 and watched his own tracer rip into the cockpit. He was casually aware of Mike Illman's tracer making a mess of the 88's starboard engine. Hardcastle's opening burst had taken half of the 88's pilot's head off and killed the dorsal gunner. With its starboard engine on fire, the 88 started to yaw to the right, presenting its belly to Illman's guns. Illman fired a prolonged burst and was rewarded by pieces of wing flying away from the 88 as his bullets struck. More by luck than by judgement, Illman corrected slightly and one of its elevators fell away. The 88 began to spin.

As Stone began the turn, Lenny concentrated on allowing for it. He would be leaning slightly to his left and tail high. If the 88 still wanted to get in a good burst, he too would have to turn to the right and dive so as the Sunderland would fly into his bullet stream. Lenny readied himself for this.

The second 88 was holding its fire till the last moment. At eight hundred yards the 88's pilot saw the Sunderland start dropping to the right, he started to turn too late and saw his target slipping away, he decided to give the Sunderland a couple of quick bursts, leapfrog it and make a second attack on the turn. He thumbed the gun button twice and saw his tracer just miss the Sunderland's port engines. Before he could correct, four streams of tracer began washing over his head and then began chewing into his port wing.

Just as Lenny was about to open fire, he saw the 88's right wing drop in an attempt to hold his target in its sights. He saw that the 88's aim was off and judged the deflection to a nicety. A few rounds flew wide of the bulbous glass cockpit, but he quickly corrected and saw his bullet's slamming into the 88's port wing and engine. Smoke began pouring from it as the pilot pulled up and started to turn to the left.

At that moment the flying boat was coming hard over to the right.

Lenny shouted, "He's coming your way Jimmy!"

Jimmy had but a split second to prepare as the 88 came over him. Stone now had the Sunderland standing on its right wing tip and the 88 displayed its underside to Jimmy's gun; it was so close, Jimmy couldn't miss. He saw his tracer disappear into the smoking engine and wash over its belly, part of the engine cowling flicked past the 88's tail. The 88's pilot turned away from the Sunderland and began to lose height. Stone held the flying boats turn so as to come back into his original course.

He was just coming out of it when Lenny's voice came over the intercom, "Bandits overhauling us, Skipper. Starboard side, three o'clock high."

Stone looked up to his right, "I've got them! Vinny, Mike, don't take your eyes off them!"

"I'm watching the bastards!" replied Hardcastle.

"I reckon they're going to try their luck from head on, Skipper!" Illman shouted.

"Could be…" replied Stone. He and Rustin pulled hard back on the control wheel. He'd lost a few hundred feet in his turn and he needed all the height he could get. He shouted to Rustin, "If they do come head on, I'm going to try diving below them, that'll give 'Vinny' a better field of fire from the top turret."

"Right Skipper."

"Mike here, they're splitting into pairs!"

Padshaw got up from where he'd been crouching and, standing behind Stone's seat, looked up and saw two of the 88s break away to the right. For the first time in his life he felt useless. There was nothing for him to do but keep out of the way. Of the two 88s that broke formation, the lead aircraft flew downwind of the Sunderland, while the second continued to fly away.

"They're not going to take any chances this time," Stone said. "They'll try to split our fire."

The 88 pilots had been shocked by the loss of their flight leader. All that remained of his aircraft was the tail section, which was slowly sinking in the sea below.

The second 88's pilot was last seen trying to nurse his aircraft back to France, but from the amount of smoke coming from it, that looked unlikely.

Stone's voice came over the intercom, "All gunners! If these first two 88s make a head-on attack I will dive in front of them. Short, sharp, accurate bursts; don't waste ammo. Look out for the other two making attacks off our beam or stern!"

Stone heard his gunners come back to him, but at the same time he was working out in his head all the variables. Unlikely all four will attack at the same time, certainly not from astern and head on, just as much chance of hitting each other – a beam attack yes, but not astern.

"Lenny! Keep a close eye on that 88 down wind. I want to know if he lights a cigarette!"

"Wilco, Skipper."

The 88 pilots had decided on their tactics. Two of them would attack head on, side by side and slightly staggered, while the third would make another beam attack on the Sunderland's starboard side but coming in from a higher angle. He would then break left and high. Of the two attacking head on, one would break left and climb and the other would break right and dive. The fourth 88 would come in from astern and below the Sunderland, attacking on the climb, as the others broke away.

Stone and his crew watched and waited. They didn't have to wait long: "Lenny here, Skipper. That Jerry's turning to come up astern, he's quite a way off and low."

"Righto Lenny."

Vinny had tried to keep the third 88 in his sights but had lost it for a few moments, now he found it again.

"Bandit! Two o'clock high!"

Illman in the nose came on the intercom straight after Hardcastle: "Those two Jerries up ahead are turning back on us now, Skipper!"

Stone watched them turn in the distance up ahead. With a closing speed of over four hundred miles per hour, they'd be on each other in seconds. Mike in the nose braced himself. The two 88s positioned themselves into their arranged staggered formation. At a thousand yards the one on Illman's left opened fire; much too early at that distance. A new boy, Illman thought to himself, and decided to concentrate on the one on the right first.

Vinny Hardcastle had his eyes firmly fixed on the 88 coming down on them. In an instant he was working out distance and deflection. He was also taking into account that Stone would dive. With any luck he could swing round and help Illman in the nose after this 88 had made its attack.

Hardcastle, watching the 88 come down on him, was briefly aware of tracer flying past him from left to right. At that moment Stone dived. Hardcastle opened up on the 88. His opening burst missed, just falling short of the cockpit and port engine, but it was enough to throw the 88's pilot off his aim. A few rounds again hit the Sunderland's fuselage and then carried on, holing the port wing, but the rest were well off. Hardcastle traversed his guns to the left.

Illman had just opened up on the 88 to his right. Both the 88s were firing at the same time. The flying boat's nose dropped and Illman corrected his fire. The 88 on his left was firing ineffectually and Illman concentrated on the other; he and the 88 traded fire. Illman's turret took a couple of hits and he flinched as the rounds missed him by inches. He saw bits flying away from the 88 as he saw his own fire strike home, at the same time he could hear pops and bangs as the Sunderland was hit again and again. Smoke and flame flowered from the 88's port engine as Illman's Vickers made their mark, the 88's pilot abruptly pulled up to Illman's right straight into Hardcastle's Brownings. Hardcastle's marksmanship was extraordinary. From the first opening rounds of a two-second burst, round after round pumped into the 88's starboard wing and engine. The 88 started to roll. Just as it became inverted, the starboard wing came away, taking the engine with it and then began to spin. There were no parachutes.

Stone knew he and his crew were up against it and continually shouted encouragement; part of the cockpit to his right took several hits and some of the instruments shattered in front of him.

"Good shooting gunners! Don't let up!" Plexiglass from the windshield flew around the cockpit.

"Jesus Christ that was close!" shouted Rustin.

Lenny in the tail let the 88 astern have everything he'd got, but this pilot skilfully jinked left and right and Lenny's bursts missed. As the nose went down, tracer whizzed past to his left, some rounds striking the tailplane and the rest disappeared into the distance. He lost the 88 for a couple of seconds. That was long enough. Stone's dive played right into the pilot's hands, who now found himself with the exposed hull of the Sunderland filling his gunsight, a blind man couldn't miss! He fired a two-second burst into the flying boat's hull.

Jimmy Creed briefly glimpsed the 88 dive away from the Sunderland's port side but couldn't bring his gun to bear. He swung his Vickers to the left, hoping a target would present itself. The first few rounds from the 88 took Jimmy's left foot clean off and then entered the top of his right leg, smashing bone and an artery before lodging themselves in the aircraft's skin. The rest took out his ribcage, lungs and heart in less than a second. Jimmy's carcase fell amongst the shell casings on the floor.

Parlow shouted frantically over the intercom:

"Jimmy's hit! Jimmy's hit!"

Stone turned and shouted at Padshaw, "Terry…!?"

Padshaw raised his hand at Stone and made his way to Jimmy's position. Having made his attack, the 88 dived away and then turned to the left before climbing again. The other 88s were regrouping and he went up to join them. Out of the corner of his eye he could see one of his fellow pilot's 88 on fire, spinning to oblivion.

Stone pulled hard back on the control wheel. It was a fight, the elevators were working but something was fouling the control cables and it was taking all of Stone's strength to pull the control wheel back.

"Pull back harder, Colin! Harder!" Stone shouted, looking across at Rustin. He saw Rustin's face was a grimace of pain. For the first time Stone saw blood all over Rustin's right hand.

"You're hit!" Stone shouted.

"Just a nick!" Rustin shouted back.

The flying boat graciously pulled out of its dive. All of a sudden the controls worked freely, the nose came up and Stone levelled out.

"Josh!" said Stone, "Come up and check on Colin."

Pelt grabbed a medical kit and went forward. He got behind Rustin and leaned precariously over the back of his seat, "Where'd ya get it?"

"Right arm!" Rustin replied in some pain.

Pelt could see the right sleeve of Rustin's flying Jacket ripped open and saturated in blood.

"I can't patch him up here Skipper!"

"Get him out of that seat!" Stone ordered.

Rustin was now feeling faint, otherwise he would have argued. Pelt helped him to his feet. Padshaw had just reached Jimmy's position behind the galley and was met with the sight of Jimmy's body, covered in blood and bright white bits of bone, lying amongst used shell cases. Dean Parlow was leaning over him. Padshaw dropped onto his knees beside them. It was now that Padshaw could see there was nothing anybody could do. Jimmy's eyes were still open, Parlow was staring into them, but Jimmy saw nothing.

"Get back to your gun!" Padshaw ordered with more force than he wanted to. Parlow looked at him. "They haven't finished with us yet!" Padshaw shouted.

Parlow looked at Jimmy's face once more. He then looked Padshaw in the eyes, nodded and got up. Padshaw took Jimmy's helmet and intercom and put it on.

"Stone. It's Padshaw. Jimmy's bought it."

Whatever Stone felt personally, it didn't show.

"Colin's copped one as well…" Stone replied "… get back up here!" Padshaw unplugged the intercom and then looked at Parlow.

"I'm all right sir!" Parlow shouted.

Padshaw nodded and made for the cockpit. The three remaining 88s had now regrouped and were in orbit high on the Sunderland's port side. Stone was watching them intently as Padshaw climbed between the seats and sat down.

"What about Colin?" Padshaw asked loudly.

"Copped one in the arm! He'll be OK, get strapped in."

Padshaw pulled the shoulder straps over himself. The right one was slippery with blood.

"When we get to Gib," Padshaw said, "I'm going to stand you lot a blowout!"

"I admire your confidence, Terry," Stone replied not taking his eyes of the 88s. "Right now I'd just settle for a decent drink."

Padshaw smiled to himself and then said, "I'll see what I can do."

The three 88s peeled off one by one and took up a line astern formation, diving towards the Sunderland's port side. Stone was about to shout into the intercom but was beaten by Hardcastle:

"Bandits! Coming down, now! Ten o'clock high."

Illman was watching the 88's descent. Hardcastle's blood was up, his head was throbbing, adrenalin pumped through him. It didn't matter what happened now. Jimmy was dead, Colin had copped one too, he'd had enough. Who's fucking sky was it, anyway?

"This is Stone. I'm going to climb up to meet them and shall then turn to starboard. That should give Mike and Vinny a chance to harry them a little. Open fire on my order, I'm then going flat out for the deck and draw them in. Turning now!"

Stone and Padshaw both heaved on their respective control wheels and pulled up and left. Whatever tactics the 88s had in mind, the sight of the Sunderland coming up to meet them was not expected. There was no way the Sunderland could hope to match the angle in which the 88s were coming down at, the flying boat's climb was too flat. What it did do was to force the 88s to change their angle of descent.

"Open fire!" Stone ordered.

Both Illman and Hardcastle realised they were well out of range to have any effect, but they both opened fire when Stone ordered. Tracer wove and whiplashed its way up to the 88s and fell short. The 88s wobbled a little, yet at that moment Stone, not quite, but almost, pulled off a near perfect stall turn to starboard. The great flying boat dropped out of the sky.

"I'll get it right next time!" he shouted at Padshaw.

"You do that!" Padshaw replied smiling.

The 88s now found their target falling away from them at an attitude they could not match for a good interception. The leading 88 tried to dive and turn to get in a shot, but his wings lost their bite and he started to skid. Dean Parlow, at Jimmy's gun, gave the 88 a long burst which cut in front of the cockpit and tickled the port wing. The pilot instinctively tried to turn to his right, but the airflow over the flying surfaces gave little response. Lenny, in the tail, was presented with a gift from God. Hardcastle also saw his opportunity. The 88 drifted into their gun sights.

Hardcastle fired five short, accurate bursts. He could see small bits of the 88's port wing fall away, then the port undercarriage unceremoniously dropped and caused the 88 to yaw wildly. Before the pilot could correct, Lenny opened up. His four Brownings ripped through the port engine and the cockpit. The 88 was so close that Lenny could actually see his rounds turning the cockpit into a slaughterhouse. As the 88 passed him he continued to stitch the fuselage, but the 88 was now just a piece of falling scrap.

Before Dean Parlow could get a bead on the last two 88s, they had managed to get slightly astern and below the Sunderland, as the flying boat passed over them the 88's rear gunners were firing continuously.

There was an enormous bang, and Padshaw instinctively raised his right arm. The starboard inner engine was smoking and throwing sparks out of the exhaust. A second bang and the propeller stopped dead! Flame began to creep out of the engine cowling. Padshaw opened his mouth to speak. Stone shouted:

"I'm on it!" and hit the extinguisher.

Padshaw stared at the engine looking for signs of fire. "Looks to be OK," he said.

"Keep an eye on it!" Stone replied and continued to take the Sunderland down to 300 feet.

"Anybody see 'em?" Stone asked.

"Off to our port, Skipper. Nine o'clock," Hardcastle replied.

"What are they up to?"

"They're just sitting there, Skipper."

The last two 88s followed at a safe distance for the next minute or so, then as one, they turned for the coast.

"They're flying away, Skipper!" Lenny announced.

"Stay on them!" Stone ordered.

"Wilco."

"What do you think?" Stone asked Padshaw.

"Probably low on fuel," Padshaw replied, then added, "and I think they've had enough!"

"How's that engine?"

"Looks to be all right at the moment. I'll keep an eye on it, though."

"You take her Terry, I'm going back to check on Colin."

"I've got her."

Stone unstrapped his harness and made his way back. Rustin looked up as Stone approached.

"How's the invalid?" Stone asked. Rustin gave a twisted smile and replied, "Not bad Jacko. Worse than it looks."

Stone looked at Josh Pelt.

"He's going to need some stitches Skipper, and he's lost a fair amount of blood, but I've patched him up as best I can."

"Well done Josh… I'm just going back to see Jimmy."

"Righto Skipper," Josh said quietly.

Stone made his way to the galley.

Chapter 6

Hollingsworth's orderly, Corporal Monk, had assembled all the new pilots outside Marsland's office. He popped his head round the door and said:

"They're all here, sir."

"Thank you Corporal," replied Marsland.

"Sir!" Monk disappeared.

Marsland looked at Hollingsworth, "Might be better if you and I address them as a whole, to the situation, before we meet them individually."

"Right you are sir." Marsland and Hollingsworth drew themselves up.

"Far be it for me to make a practical suggestion, but I do think we should hide the medicine from the peasants," Valentine said, gesturing at the whiskey and gin.

Marsland sniffed and said, "Top drawer. And I know how much is left!"

Valentine gave Marsland an indignant stare, his mouth slightly agape for effect.

"I haven't forgiven you for finishing the last bottle yet," Marsland added. He and Hollingsworth walked out and closed the door. Valentine asked Hacker:

"Do you prefer whiskey or gin?"

"I'm quite partial to both actually."

"Good!" Valentine said and took a large swig from the gin bottle. He passed the whiskey to Hacker. Hacker hesitated and then took a large swig himself. Valentine took the bottle from him and placed both bottles in the top drawer.

"Evaporation! It's such a curse," Valentine said.

"It's the heat," replied Hacker.

"I didn't realise you were an educated man."

"Oh yes. I used to get top marks in hairdressing!"

"Really! Tell me more …"

Marsland and Hollingsworth stood on the makeshift veranda outside the door to the office. The six pilots had saluted when Marsland appeared and were now standing at ease, looking up at him.

"First things first, gentlemen…" Marsland started, "… Welcome to our tropical paradise!"

Some of the pilots gave wry grins or frowned. Marsland gave his best smile. "Secondly! I have to inform you that you are now all on this squadron's strength and will be for the foreseeable future."

"You are joking sir!" said one of the pilots.

"No, I'm not. We received orders earlier today to that effect."

"Bloody hell!" said another pilot.

"I'll meet you all individually, now! Holly?"

"Right, sir."

Marsland walked back into his office and closed the door.

"Names and ranks please, gentlemen?" Hollingsworth asked.

Three quarters of an hour later, Sergeant Pilot George Tillman was the last pilot to leave the office. Hollingsworth followed him outside to the other waiting pilots.

"Right gentlemen. As you can see, we are having to make some adjustments to fit you all in."

Various ground crew and some officers were hacking at the foliage to make more space near the aircraft.

"We're all one happy family here which means everybody pulls their weight. We'll try to get you some personal kit, but for the moment you'll have to make do. We hope to get some more tents, camp beds etc., in the next few days, but in the meantime it's going to be a bit cramped."

Pilot Officer Colin 'Chancer' Harris approached the adjutant holding a machete.

"Ah, Colin!"

"Adj?"

"Perhaps you could help these chaps settle in?"

Harris nodded. "Be a pleasure Adj. Follow me chaps, I'll get you all a machete." Harris walked away smiling, the pilots shambled after him looking none too happy. Hollingsworth turned and went back into the CO's office.

"Well," Marsland said, "what do you make of them, Snobby?"

"I think they'll be OK. After all, some of them were expecting to get back to the UK on various other postings. Must be a bit of a blow."

"True," said Marsland.

"Can't say I take to that Australian chap much," Hollingsworth said. "Bit of a line shooter, if you ask me."

"Time will tell," replied Marsland and turned to Hacker. "Hacker?"

Hacker looked slightly unsure of what to say.

"We simply want your opinion, old boy," Hollingsworth said pleasantly.

"Well, Hayward and Midgeham strike me as being efficient and capable pilots. They've both seen action with eleven group during the Battle of Britain and have some kills under their belts, so that speaks for itself. Vine's a new boy. Bit nervous maybe, mind you it's his first operational posting. He needs to get some hours in, give himself a bit more confidence. Then there's Brandon and Tillman, the Canadians. They appear to have seen a fair amount of action but none of it seems to include any aerial combat."

"Those two were due leave weren't they?" Marsland interrupted, aiming his question at Hollingsworth.

"Yes sir. Two months overdue."

"Too bad. They can join the club. Carry on!" Marsland added, looking at Hacker.

"Then there's the adjutant's Australian chum."

Hollingsworth was wide eyed.

"He's either all he says he is or he's full of bullshit!"

"Snobby?" Marsland prompted.

"No real way of telling until we see him in action. He reckons he's something of a marksman though, doesn't he, and how many types did he say he's flown?"

Hollingsworth looked at his notes, "Twelve"

"Mmmm. Keep an eye on him," said Marsland. "I don't want him cocking up at somebody else's expense!"

There was a silent pause for a moment, then Hollingsworth asked:

"How do you want to allocate the aircraft?"

"I'll get round to that," Marsland replied. "For the time being we'll carry on as we are. Let's see how things pan out, so to speak."

"Fair enough," said Valentine, "but what about sections? We've got ten operational Kitties and the seven Hurricanes."

"Four sections of four aircraft I suppose," said Hollingsworth. "With one in reserve."

"I'm a little uncomfortable with flying the Hurricanes with no spares at all," replied Marsland. "The other point of course is the Hurricanes are all fitted with long-range tanks, as are ours of course. But we've no spare tanks for them, so if they do have to drop them their range is going to be somewhat limited."

"On the other hand..." Valentine began, "we've been damn lucky with the weather. If the rains hadn't eased some, we wouldn't have managed today's little shindig. Personally I don't think we'll get much done till the weather buggers off."

"In point of fact, sir," Hacker interrupted, "we only received orders to fly this morning."

"Holly?"

"Personally sir, I think we've got an ideal opportunity to get ourselves organised on the ground prior to this other officer's arrival. If we get some reasonable days that allow us to poke Johnny Jap in the eye then we can continue with the P40s until the Hurri spares arrive."

"Right," Marsland said, "Well, we'll leave it at that for the moment. Maybe we'll receive some more information tomorrow." At that moment Corporal Monk looked around the door again.

"Begging your pardon, sir?"

"What is it Monk?" asked Hollingsworth.

"Sir. You asked to see the gentlemen responsible for getting Mr Verster out of his aircraft, sir."

"I did indeed!" replied Marsland with feeling. "Show them in."

"This way, lads," said Monk.

The four ground crew trooped in and stood to attention. Hollingsworth politely reminded Marsland of their names:

"Clarke, Jones, Carver and Massey, sir."

"Relax gentlemen." All four stood at ease. "You are all a credit to me and this squadron, gentlemen. Without your unselfish actions today, Mr Verster would with no doubt at all have been fried to a crisp. Your quick response to the fact he was trapped and to the danger he was in, was an exemplary display of bravery and teamwork. I'm sure when Mr Verster has recovered he will wish to thank you himself. Until that time, I'm doing it for him. Thank you gentlemen." Marsland had never been so sincere.

"Rest assured that your actions today have been noted and I will do my best to ensure that they be recognised." The four ground crew were either looking at their feet or smiling uncertainly.

"Thank you again, gentlemen, no doubt I'll see you at supper."

They mumbled their 'Sirs' and made their way out. Monk held the door open and then followed them.

"Good lads they are, sir," said Hollingsworth.

"Yes they are… if and when we manage to snaffle any booze, make sure they get a good ration, Holly."

"As good as done sir."

"I hope they're around if I have a similar problem," said Hacker quietly. Valentine and Marsland glanced at each other and smiled briefly. Then Valentine said:

"I do believe you're going to fit in nicely, old boy." Hacker opened his mouth to ask what he meant when 'Punchy' Jennings walked in unannounced.

"You wanted to see me, sir?" he asked, wiping his hands on an oily rag.

"Yes 'Punchy'," Marsland replied, "I just wanted to say you did a brilliant job clearing the field so quickly. Could have been a bit sticky that, otherwise…"

Jennings saw the three mugs and the glass on Marsland's makeshift desk. "You've got booze!" he interrupted.

Marsland sighed and stared at Jennings with feigned disdain.

"Does my sincere thanks and gratitude for a job well done mean nothing to you?"

"Not when you've got booze, sir," Jennings said very courteously.

Marsland nodded at Valentine who was leaning against the filing cabinet and then looked at Jennings again.

"Mercenary bugger!"

"Thank you, sir."

Valentine pulled out a very tired willowware teacup with no handle.

"Whiskey or gin?" asked Valentine.

"Whiskey. Thanks very much!"

"Blast," said Hollingsworth irritably.

"Who do we have to thank for such fayre?" Jennings asked, taking his cup of whisky from Valentine.

"Mr Hacker," Marsland replied, pointing at Hacker. He introduced them.

"Hacker, 'Punchy' Jennings, our resident engineering genius."

"Flattery and whiskey! Must be my lucky day. A pleasure," Jennings replied nodding deeply at Hacker. Hacker nodded back in the same manner. Jennings took a mouthful, swallowed and then drank the rest in one go. Hollingsworth looked as if he'd been robbed.

Jennings passed his cup back to Valentine and, looking at Marsland, said, "Cracken's Kitty's got a few extra holes in it, so that's off line at the moment. Dick's Kitty's got a cracked fuel line, we're working on it now and yours is now fully serviceable, sir... Dirty fuel," he added apologetically.

"Thanks 'Punchy'. See you in the mess."

"Right you are sir." Jennings left.

"I don't see that there's much more we can do today," said Marsland. "I recommend we introduce Mr Hacker and his associates to the rest of the Squadron later and then start a new day tomorrow, mmm?"

"Suits me sir," said Hacker, adding, "Any idea where I can find a bunk for the night, sir?"

"I believe Flight Lieutenant Valentine is your host this evening," Marsland answered, mimicking a well-educated butler. Before Hacker could make a comment, Valentine asked, "You don't snore, do you old chap?"

"Not while I'm awake."

"Good! And please don't cut your toenails in my company. The parings end up everywhere."

"I'll do it outside," Hacker assured him. "But I did have a pedicure recently, so… "

"Enough!" Marsland said in a voice of despair.

"Bugger off, both of you!"

Hacker slung his satchel round his shoulder, picked up his gloves and flying helmet and stood up. He walked around the desk followed by Valentine. "See you in the mess, sir," Hacker said politely.

Marsland nodded. Valentine asked Marsland:

"Would you like me to look after your gin?"

Marsland didn't even bother to reply, he looked at Valentine, his face saying *fuck off and take your humour with you.* Valentine smiled and, holding the door open as Hacker left, said:

"I'll be on my way then… but if you should need any company later, you know, someone to discuss the War with?"

"Snobby!" Marsland shouted. Valentine left.

"Bloody hell," Marsland said to Hollingsworth. "It was bad enough with just 'Snobby'! Now we've got two of the buggers!"

"Fancy a whiskey?" the adjutant asked. Marsland slumped back into his chair. He looked at his adjutant and, with his fingertips, nudged his glass towards him. "Gin!"

Valentine led Hacker towards his tent. Valentine was fortunate that his billet did not interfere with the day's events and so was still intact.

"How long have you been out here 'Snobby'?" Hacker asked.

"Too bloody long old boy. I've forgotten what England looks like!"

"The grass is still green and it still rains after you've washed the car." At that moment a few spots of rain fell.

"Now you've done it! Never mention rain! This way!" Valentine started trotting to his tent, which was about eighty feet away.

"Come on," he egged Hacker on. The skies opened. A wall of water began to fall from the heavens. Valentine was half soaked as he pulled back the flap to his tent and scrambled in. Hacker was right behind him.

"Bloody hell," said Hacker. "I thought the monsoon was over!" Valentine sat on his camp bed.

"Obviously not," he replied. Valentine rolled up his single blanket and pulled the edge off the bed in an invitation for Hacker to sit.

"Thanks," said Hacker. "I promise not to use the word 'rain' again!"

"Good. You do that." Valentine wiped his face with a well-used towel. He passed it to Hacker.

"Thanks awfully." Hacker mopped his neck and face and passed it back. "I reckon we'll be swimming by morning," Hacker added.

"In case you didn't notice old chap, I've placed my tent on the highest area on the landing ground. The rest of the chaps think I just like to be eccentric by being up here on my own. Well, I was born eccentric; I can't help that! But one thing I can't stand is waking up wet in the morning."

"I'm with you!" replied Hacker.

There was a few moments' silence. Hacker tied his flying helmet and gloves to the tent pole. Valentine took off his boots and put them on top of a door-less cupboard.

"I must say, that was damned decent of you to bring some decent booze," Valentine said.

"You're welcome. Shame I wasn't flying in a Dakota. That would have been a real party!"

Valentine smiled and looked at Hacker mischievously:

"Can you keep a secret?"

"Yes, of course."

Valentine pulled out a bottle of Plymouth gin from under his pillow, there was about an inch left.

"Enough for a mouthful each," Valentine said.

Hacker laughed gently and said, "Is that the bottle the CO thought you'd finished?"

"Yes, actually, it is. Still, not likely to be charged with the same crime twice, am I?" Valentine passed Hacker the bottle.

"Cheers!" Hacker drank about half and passed the bottle back. Valentine raised the bottle to Hacker and said, "Up yours!"

Hacker bowed his head graciously as Valentine finished the gin.

"All good things come to an end," Valentine stated and tucked the empty bottle under his bed. In the same movement he pulled out a spare blanket and passed it to Hacker, saying:

"Keep an eye out for snakes and other various unpleasant bugs, they can be very anti-social!"

"Thanks for the warning, but to be honest, I've been lodging with them for a week."

Valentine grunted. The tent flap moved and Monk came in with a camp bed.

"Here you are, sir," he said to Hacker.

"Thanks very much," Hacker replied sincerely.

"It's on loan sir!" Monk said and disappeared into the rain.

Hacker looked quizzically at Valentine.

"It belongs to 'Jiff' Verster."

"Ah!" Hacker recalled the earlier conversation in Marsland's office. "He's going to recover OK?"

"'Jiff'? Oh, yes! He'll be back on his feet in no time. He's an arrogant bloody-minded South African git. He'll recover in record time, just so as he can piss us all off with his miraculous recovery stories."

Hacker gave a little grin and unfolded his bed. He rolled out his blanket and sat down. Leaning over, he picked up his satchel and put it on his lap. "Looks like we're going to be stuck in here for a while," Hacker said.

"Supper's in four hours," Valentine replied. "Plenty of time for me to recite my life story."

"Can you keep a secret?" Hacker asked.

"Yes, of course."

Hacker pulled out another bottle of Bushmills. Valentine's face lit up. "Just stick to the interesting bits," said Hacker.

"I'll abbreviate. Where's those tin mugs...?"

Chapter 7

Connors, Portman and Sergeant Bell were all looking at a map, spread out over two crates of bully beef. They were under a large tarpaulin strung between two trucks. The rain was coming down so hard that after twenty yards everything you looked at was blurred.

"Right sir," Lieutenant Portman began. "The map reference puts them right here." Portman made an 'X' on the map with his pencil. "Just south east of Chittagong."

"And where are we due to meet the other supply train?"

"East of Chittagong. Just here." Portman put another 'X' on the map.

"Any more information on that parachute drop, George?"

"Yes sir. Someone's been using their head for a change. Same map reference as the supply train but later in the day. Mind you, it was sheer luck we got the last message, sir, you know what communications are like!"

Connors frowned, "Mmm."

Captain Blackman walked up and joined them.

"I knew it was too good to last. This monsoon's going on forever."

"How's your pilot, Blackie?" Connors asked.

"Pretty good actually. Seems he came down today or yesterday..." Connors's eyebrows went up. "He's not sure, bit of a bump on the head, I think."

"Ah."

"He'd like to see you when you have a moment."

"Later. Have a look at this."

Blackman leant over Portman's shoulder. "Blimey Don! They couldn't get much closer to the Japs' lines could they?"

"You're not kidding. Anyway, here's how I see it: we've got one more pick-up from some of the locals tomorrow; we'll try and be there for about midday. Then with any luck, we can be in position for the parachute drop between three and four. The drop's not due till five."

"And the other supply train?"

"Ah! That's where they've made life easy. Same map reference, just earlier in the day. I can only presume we're all to move out together."

"Well it seems straightforward enough. Apart from the rain, the Japs and the mosquitoes."

"We're going to have problems with the vehicles tomorrow, sir," Sergeant Bell warned. "I mean, it's going to be mud on mud after a night of this."

"Well, we'll just have to do our best. If we look like losing too much time, Lieutenant Portman can go on ahead with the mules and make the rendezvous. We can meet up again later."

"What about the pilot, sir?" asked Sergeant Bell. Connors looked at Blackman.

"Maybe we could drop him at Chittagong?" Blackman suggested.

"We'll see. That's a hell of a detour in this terrain," replied Connors thoughtfully. "We'll play that by ear," he added.

The last thing Connors wanted was detours. He could vividly remember an occasion when a small footbridge had come down in a storm and he and his column had to divert. It was only a mile upriver to a crossing and then back down again, but it had taken ten hours and he lost two mules and the supplies they carried. He had been doing this job for over a year. It was only recently that he'd been equipped with vehicles. Generally speaking they were more trouble than they were worth on some routes. The word 'road' was

147

flattering, nothing more than a wide track. The going could be soul destroying. Some days he could cover several miles, others just yards. Men died from malaria, accidents, some of them simply weren't looking what they were doing and got lost...

The surroundings could be incredibly inhospitable and at the same time, quite beautiful.

"Well I'm going to try to get some shut-eye," Connors said. "We'll convene at 0800."

"Sir." Sergeant Bell went off to check his NCOs and the sentries.

Portman collected his maps and said, "See you in the morning, sir."

"Goodnight Lieutenant."

Portman trotted away and disappeared into the rain.

"Cigarette, Blackie?"

"Thanks Don."

Blackman got his lighter out and added, "I'm definitely going to buy you a lighter for Christmas."

Connors smiled and passed Blackman a cigarette.

"Don't forget the pilot." Blackman reminded him.

"Bugger, completely forgot! We'll smoke these and then go and see him. What's his name?"

"Flight Lieutenant Graham."

Chapter 8

As Valentine walked out into the rain he said, "I'll see you in the mess old chap. I'm going for a pee first."

"I'll be right there 'Snobby'." Hacker was very thoughtful. In the last few hours of conversation with Valentine, Hacker had come to realise just how strong willed you had to be to survive in this particular theatre of the War. Valentine himself had achieved something of a reputation as being a little eccentric, on occasion. Having listened to some of the things that he'd been through, Hacker wasn't surprised.

Valentine had told him about his time in Calcutta, before moving across the bay to Chittagong, and then to the Squadron. At one point he and his fellow pilots had received orders to use Calcutta's Red Road as a landing strip. The Red Road ran parallel to Calcutta's main street and wasn't even the width of a Hurricane's wingspan. During the same period, pilots would assemble in the Grand Hotel on the Red Road, waiting for the scramble order! Taking off and landing was not for the fainthearted. Several aircraft got tangled up in the front of a house or fence.

Even then, when the scramble did come on most occasions, the pilots had only been in the air for twenty minutes when it was found that all the plots they were intercepting were friendly. Another fruitless scramble, a quick descent, and a seriously difficult landing, with nothing to look forward to than repeat the entire farce again later that day or tomorrow. In fact, truth be known, it wasn't until all the fighters based in Calcutta for defence had been transferred elsewhere that the Japanese successfully bombed Calcutta and, of course, there were no fighters to defend it. Bad timing. Bad luck. Some of the pilots felt quite bitter. A lot of blood, sweat and tears and Johnny Jap still got one over on them.

Before that, Valentine had been heavily involved in shipping strikes in the English Channel and various occupied ports. On this subject however, Valentine had been reluctant to go into any detail and Hacker wasn't going to push the subject.

Hacker sat on his bunk for a few moments. Squadron Leader Padshaw drifted into his head, or at least, his words did. 'You are just what I'm looking for,' he remembered Padshaw saying; Hacker gave a gentle snort and grudgingly said under his breath: 'Smart Bastard!' He then tucked the bottle of whisky under his bedroll and left the tent. Hacker stood for a few seconds and got his bearings. He could see some of the other pilots walking into the hut that was designated as the mess. A few pilots stood outside, oblivious of the rain that was teeming down, and were casually eating and chatting as if it were a summer's day. He made his way over to them.

"Well, from what I hear," Cavendish was saying, "our chaps are going to push south soon and give the Japs a good kick up the arse!"

"News to me!" replied Parish. "And even if it's true, there's not a lot of progress to be made in this weather!"

"Besides," said Hillman, "I haven't seen any indication at all that we've got the equipment or supplies to mount an offensive."

"Bet you a quid we have ago at the buggers before Christmas," Cavendish said to Hillman.

"All right, you're on," Hillman replied.

"What's going on here?" Harris asked as he came round the corner of the mess hut.

"It's against King's Regulations to have a wager without consulting with me first. Come on, what's the bet?"

"Terry reckons our chaps will have a go at the Japs before Christmas," Parish answered.

"Aha! Well, I'm with Terry. But I reckon we'll have a go before the end of the month. A fiver! Any takers?" Parish looked at the rain coming down in buckets. They were already well into October and the monsoon hadn't buggered off, yet. Why not?

"A fiver it is," he said.

"Me too," said Hillman.

"I look forward to taking your money off you chaps," Harris said as he walked into the mess, adding, "And I don't want to see you spending my money before the end of the month!"

Cavendish looked at Parish and Hillman and said, "You silly buggers! What possessed you to take a bet from Harris?"

"He's lost before," Hillman said defensively.

"Yes he has. Twice to my knowledge," Parish said, backing Hillman up.

"And both pilots snuffed it before Harris could pay," Cavendish informed them.

"That's just bad luck!" said Hillman.

"So's gambling with 'Chancer' Harris!" Cavendish said, grinning like a cat.

"Good evening," Hacker said as he approached.

"Can't say it's good, but good evening to you too," replied Cavendish. Jimmy Parish put his fork in his mess tin and offered his hand to Hacker. "Hi. Jimmy Parish."

"Keith Hacker." They shook hands.

"This is 'Stubby' Hillman," Parish continued.

"Hello chum," Hillman put his hand out and shook Hacker's warmly.

"And this stuck-up Englishman is Terry Cavendish." Cavendish had his hand out. "Hello old boy." They shook hands.

Hacker asked, "What's the routine for grub around here?"

"No pecking order here," replied Cavendish, "except for the CO of course. Just help yourself."

"Fine, thanks, I will. What's on?"

"Bully beef and potatoes," Parish answered.

"No change there then," Hacker said as he walked into the mess.

"Seems like a reasonable chap," said Cavendish. "I wonder if he's any good?"

"From what I heard," Hillman said, "he's only been out here for a week."

"Doesn't mean a thing," Parish said. "For all we know he might be a flying genius."

Valentine had walked up beside them. "Well, whatever else he is," Valentine said, "he's got more kills than you lot put together."

"We were just curious 'Snobby'," Hillman said politely.

"Well bloody well ask him then!" Valentine walked into the mess.

"He hates the rain, doesn't he?" Hillman said.

"Hello Hacker," Hollingsworth said. "Have some grub." He passed Hacker a loaded mess tin with a fork sticking out of one of the potatoes.

"Thanks Adj."

"Don't lose that fork or you'll be eating with your fingers. Thieving buggers they are, around here."

"I'll try to remember that," Hacker filled his mouth.

"CO wants to see you and 'Snobby' at nine tomorrow morning, his office."

"I'll be there," Hacker said with a full mouth.

"Come and meet the rest of the chaps." Hollingsworth steered Hacker towards a group of pilots who were talking to Jennings and Valentine. Hollingsworth did the introductions.

152

"Right chaps! This is Flying Officer Keith Hacker, came out from Blighty a week or so ago. This is Phil Banner, our resident Australian."

"How are ya?"

"Good, thanks."

The adjutant pointed out each man as he introduced them.

"Dick Chalmers." Chalmers smiled and nodded politely.

"Dave Miller."

"How do you do," said Miller. Hacker shook his hand.

"'Chancer' Harris." Harris had his mouth full and casually touched his forelock with his fork.

"'Snobby' you know... Paul Cracken." Cracken shook hands and said, "A pleasure old chap."

"Don Spencer."

"Nice landing," said Spencer.

"Thanks, mind you, I find it helps if I keep my eyes shut."

Spencer smiled pleasantly.

"And of course our engineering genius 'Punchy' Jennings, who you met earlier."

Hacker and Jennings shook hands for the first time.

"And what an asset to the Squadron you are," Jennings said with a knowing smile and the taste of Bushmill's whiskey still in his mouth. Hacker gave a broad smile in reply. Some of the others had curious looks on their faces.

"You'll get to know the ground crew over time," Hollingsworth continued. "They're all good chaps... Ah, here's the CO." Marsland had walked in and was making a beeline for the adjutant, Valentine and Hacker and he didn't look too happy. Valentine had seen the same look far too often.

"Oh bloody hell," he said, under his breath.

"What's up?" asked Hacker.

"When the CO looks like that," Valentine replied, "it means we're flying in this shit again!" Before Hacker could comment, Marsland was standing in front of them.

"We're flying tomorrow," Marsland said brusquely. "Briefing my office. Thirty minutes. You too, 'Punchy'." Marsland turned and walked straight back out into the rain.

"Are we really going to fly in this?" Hacker asked.

"As a matter of fact," Spencer said, "we fly in this muck more often than not."

Hacker looked at Cracken, Cracken merely shrugged his shoulders. Hacker looked outside at the wall of water endlessly falling from the sky, he was about to say something like 'Don't the conditions play havoc with taking off and landing?' when he remembered the wrecks at each end of the landing strip and stopped himself.

"I think I'll write my will," he said flatly.

"Actually, taking off and landing is the easy bit," said Miller, reading Hacker's mind. "Flying in storms is when it gets dicey."

"You'll be fine," said Harris, "in fact, I bet you a tenner, you have no problems at all and land without a scratch."

"That's very encouraging of you," Hacker replied dryly.

"Not at all. Besides, if you prang you can't collect your winnings, can you?"

"You're all heart," said Valentine.

"You know me 'Snobby'. Charity's my middle name."

'Punchy' Jennings and the assembled pilots laughed. In all fact, and Hacker didn't know it yet, some of the flying conditions in which these pilots flew were nothing short of atrocious.

During the Allies' retreat from Burma, the Royal Air Force and the remnants of the AVG. (American Volunteer Group) were constantly on call to keep the Japanese at bay. Their aircraft were extremely limited in number and type. Spares were in such short supply that it was not uncommon for the ground crew to purchase nuts and bolts from local flea markets, just to keep aircraft flying. Oxygen bottles for the pilots were rarely half full which would often prevent them from being able to intercept the Japanese bombers. Conditions on the ground, already incredibly difficult, became a living hell as the monsoon settled in. Scores of airmen suffered from jaundice and dysentery.

Early 1942 was one of the hottest ever recorded in India, death was commonplace. Sunstroke and disease was everywhere but ground crews and pilots struggled on. With the monsoon now upon them, it was nothing short of a miserable existence. Everything from blankets to cigarettes were, more often than not, wet through. Marsland's squadron were luckier than most, in as much as the landing ground was on the site of an old deserted village. Bamboo huts were more or less still standing and took little time to rebuild. Even to have any kind of a building to hide from the rain was a luxury. Marsland's pilots and ground crew knew they were lucky in this respect, and were very grateful. In recent weeks a Dakota aircraft had started dropping supplies to allied units, but there were pitifully few of them to do the job and what aircraft there were flew around the clock. Mobile workshops had recently been delivered, which helped no end in the maintenance of the aircraft, but it was still not enough.

Every day, ground crews and pilots alike, were up against it.

Chapter 9

The remainder of the flight to Gibraltar proved to be more or less uneventful. Various aircraft were spotted and reported to Stone, but none showed any interest, or for that matter got close enough to be identified. Not much was said amongst the crew until the rock of Gibraltar came into view.

Stone had instructed Don Lipman to radio ahead, informing the powers that be that they were down to three engines and had sustained casualties. As he came onto his final approach, Stone was grateful that the sea was on his side for once and was reasonably calm with very little swell. As he touched down, the great Sunderland settled comfortably without so much as a tremor. If Padshaw hadn't known better, they could have been landing on a runway. Not that that would do a Sunderland any good, he thought to himself.

"Nicely done Jacko," Padshaw commented.

"Done it before," Stone replied without humour. Padshaw kept silent. He knew how Stone felt. He'd been there himself, more times than he cared to count. Nothing he said would help or make any difference. Padshaw had seen most of his friends die, when he'd got his own squadron he watched his pilots die. He remembered all the letters that he'd had to write to the parents and families of all the pilots and ground crew he'd lost. He even wondered if he himself had become removed from it all, and that maybe he was so hardened to men dying that now, perhaps, they were just pieces on a gaming table to be discarded.

He looked at Stone, who was staring emptily at the control wheel. Stone was hurting inside. Padshaw opened his mouth, but before he could speak Jimmy's words came back to him. 'We reckon you've changed our luck!' At that moment Padshaw felt some pangs of loss himself and was grateful.

"Come on Jacko. The boys deserve a drink, and so do you."

Stone's sombre face turned to look at Padshaw, looking briefly into Padshaw's eyes, Stone saw the reassuringly gritty resilience of the man. A crooked grin came over his face, and then he said:

"I reckon you're right, and as I recall, you said you were buying!"

Two hours later Padshaw and Stone were sitting on a low wall outside the hospital. Padshaw put his hand in his briefcase and pulled out the bottle of Glenmorangie. He offered it to Stone:

"Fancy that drink?"

"Bloody right I do, cobber." Stone took the bottle and pulled the cork. "Cheers!" he said flatly and took a large mouthful and swallowed. He sat holding the bottle and looked at the floor in silence for a minute or so. Padshaw said nothing. Stone took another large swig and passed the bottle back.

"Cheers," Padshaw said and drank a couple of mouthfuls. He offered Stone the bottle again.

"Maybe later," Stone said and gave Padshaw the cork. Padshaw whacked it home and put the bottle back in his case. A medical orderly came up behind them.

"Squadron Leader Padshaw?"

"Yes."

"He's going to be fine, sir. He's lost a fair amount of blood and he'll have a stiff arm for a month or so, but apart from that he'll be up and about in no time."

"Thanks very much for letting us know."

"You're welcome, sir." The orderly turned and walked back to the hospital.

"Looks like you might be my co-pilot for the rest of the trip!"

"I'd rather that than be a passenger, but I dare say there's probably an unemployed pilot around here somewhere."

"Well he'd better be bloody good or I'll toss the bastard overboard. C'mon Terry, I'm starving!"

"You and me both, let's see what we can poach." They both stood up, at the same time an Austin truck pulled up beside them. A voice called from the back:

"Skipper!" Lenny Sullivan's head appeared. "Vinny's found somewhere to eat!"

"Perfect timing," Stone said to Padshaw.

"Climb up!" Lenny said and offered Stone his hand. Josh Pelt appeared and offered his hand to Padshaw, saying:

"C'mon Terry. You can pull rank on the MPs when we get into trouble," Padshaw took Pelt's hand and heaved himself up into the truck.

"That's very encouraging. How can I refuse," Padshaw replied sarcastically and sat down.

"Where are we going?" Stone asked Lenny.

"Vinny didn't say. All he said was that he'd been told the food was good and they've got enough booze to float the *Queen Mary* on." Padshaw and Stone glanced at each other. Stone's face said, 'Suits me'. Padshaw brought his left hand up to his face and covered it, except for his right eye, which peered at Stone between his fingers.

"I do believe I may regret this," he said to Stone, who smiled.

"Apparently Vinny got the information from some chaps at the supply depot," Lenny continued, "It seems that quite a lot of crates get damaged and then get thrown out, and, unfortunately, on occasion of course, nobody has thought to check the contents. Very sloppy!"

"And no doubt the contents of some of these crates have found their way to the aforementioned eating house to which we are headed, mmm?" suggested Padshaw.

"Just a rumour," Josh Pelt said with all the innocence of a choirboy.

Stone could see that despite the slight grin appearing on Padshaw's face, that he was also a little concerned.

"Relax Terry. The boys won't misbehave tonight. Besides, if they get that engine fixed we'll be flying tomorrow. And on top of that, I'm tired!"

Padshaw resigned himself to the fact that he was going to be entertained 'Australian style' whether he liked it or not. "Who's driving?" he asked.

"Chris," Lenny replied.

"Lead on Macduff!" Padshaw shouted. Apart from Lenny, the others stared bemused.

"Never mind," Padshaw said.

James worked his way up the gears.

No sooner had they moored up and stepped onto the pontoon than several hospital staff with stretchers appeared and, nodding courteously, boarded the Sunderland. Facing Padshaw and Stone were two army cfficers and a well-dressed civilian.

"Squadron Leader Padshaw?" the civilian enquired. Padshaw quickly realised that his flying jacket concealed his rank. Stone opened his mouth to say something facetious, but Padshaw got in first:

"That's me," he took his jacket off.

"Boring sod!" Stone said.

"Welcome to Gibraltar."

"Thank you." They shook hands.

"This is Sergeant Pilot Stone," Padshaw said, introducing Stone.

"How do you do old chap." The civilian shook Stone's hand as well.

"I've had better days," Stone replied, looking at his battered Sunderland.

"Yes, so I see." The Civilian politely followed Stone's glance at the flying boat. "Still, we'll fix it up in no time," he said pleasantly.

"And my gunner?" Stone asked.

"Not my department I'm afraid, that comes under 'divine intervention'."

Stone stared at him wide-eyed, but the civilian simply smiled back at him understandingly, totally unperturbed by Stone's abrupt manner.

"Any chance of a cup of tea?" Padshaw asked quickly.

"Yes, of course. Please, come with us gentlemen, we'll organise a billet for your crew as well."

Padshaw and Stone spent the next hour or so being debriefed in separate offices. Stone was congratulated several times by various officers for his part in the engagement with the 88s, Stone then filled out and signed his report and was given a list of items to be dropped off in Malta en route. Rustin, he was assured, was being treated for his wounds at that very moment. There was the usual blurb of sympathy on losing a crew member, which, basically, went straight over Stone's head. What did they know about it? So long as they got a result they were happy. Fuck the lot of them...

To his credit Stone nodded, shook his head, and filled in the yesses and nos where required. As he left the office there were a few more 'well dones' and 'jolly good show's' thrown at him. He closed the door behind him and looked up and down the corridor, hoping to see Padshaw. A clerk was walking towards him.

"Have you seen a Squadron Leader Padshaw?" Stone asked.

"He's in the office at the end of the corridor. He shouldn't be long."

"Thanks." Stone walked casually to the end of the corridor where it then opened up into a waiting area. There were several wicker chairs and a couple of tables scattered about, on one of the tables was a recent copy of *The Times*. Stone sat down, put his feet up and went straight to the sports section.

Padshaw was on his second cup of tea and had just concluded his summing up of the day's events.

"All in all their professionalism against such odds was exemplary," Padshaw was saying, "I will of course be recommending them for decorations sir, which I'll get written up and then pass on to your office in the morning."

The Wing Commander gave a broad smile and replied, "As soon as I receive it, I shall forward it with my own commendation. We've had some pretty sticky times hereabouts recently, I can tell you, so it's a breath of fresh air when we hear that the Luftwaffe just received a good kick up the arse." The Wing Commander was still smiling but had seen a thoughtful look in Padshaw's eyes. "Something I can help you with?" he asked politely.

"I was just wondering, sir… who was the civilian that met us on our arrival? I mean… we didn't expect a welcoming committee or anything, but I was a little surprised to be met by a–"

"Well, let me stop you there old chap," the Wing Commander interrupted. "I can't tell you too much, but, basically, he works for various government types. You know what I mean. The 'old boy' fraternity, awfully hush hush. Anyway, he needs to get to Malta ASAP, and the aircraft that was to fly him out overshot the runway this morning and is currently doing permanent submersion trials!"

Padshaw raised his eyebrows.

"My little joke," said the Wing Commander, adding, "Either way, he likes to see things for himself which is why he wanted to see the damage to your aircraft and meet the crew. It was I who suggested he fly out with you once it has been repaired."

"I see sir. Thank you for explaining."

"He's quite a nice chap actually. Well-travelled, smart, and he's got a sense of humour. Thank God! Most of these cloak-and-dagger types take life much too seriously. Just don't ask him too many questions."

"I won't!" Padshaw answered emphatically.

"Good, good," the Wing Commander said jovially. "Well, I think that's everything. Perhaps you'd care to join me in the mess for dinner and a couple of drinks?"

"That's very kind of you sir, but I promised our colonial friends I'd stand them a few beers."

"Absolutely! Got to keep the chaps happy." The Wing Commander stood up and offered his hand. "Give them my best. Probably see you in the mess for breakfast."

Padshaw shook hands. "I look forward to it, sir." Padshaw left the office and turned to see Stone engrossed in his newspaper. He walked over. "Anything interesting?" he asked.

Stone looked up. "Not much. This bloody war's playing havoc with the horseracing. Have they finished with you?"

"For the moment? Yes. You?"

"Yeah. I'm a free man again. Any idea where Colin's being held?"

"Yes. Apparently he's about two hundred yards up the road. Shall we?" Stone put his paper down, got up and followed Padshaw out.

"You make it sound like he's under arrest," Padshaw said, humorously.

"Well he can't get a beer so he might as well be."

Padshaw grinned, he was secretly pleased to see the Australian's carefree manner and sense of humour slowly returning.

Two and a half hours later, however, Padshaw's humour was dissipating as quickly as his rump was, which was currently being bruised by the unpadded wooden bench seat in the Austin truck. It was dark now, and there was still no sign of the hostelry they were looking for.

"For crying out loud! Where the bloody hell is this dump?"

"I'm doing me best Skipper. It's not going to be advertised, is it?"

Padshaw, looking aimlessly out the back of the truck, caught a glimpse of the civilian they'd met earlier entering, to all appearances, a blacked-out house. As the door opened to let him in, a blaze of light leapt across the road and was quickly swallowed up as the door closed.

"Pull up!" Padshaw shouted.

James did just that, but rather more sharply than he intended. Hardcastle hit the back of the cab, Pelt hit Hardcastle and Padshaw was sprawled across Pelt. Lenny, sitting opposite Pelt, was half on and half off Don Lipman.

"Jesus Christ!" shouted Lipman.

"What's up Terry?" Stone asked, as he got off his hand and knees.

"Sorry about that chaps, but I think we just overshot our target."

"Where?" asked Stone.

Padshaw pointed at the blacked out building.

"You reckon?" Pelt asked sceptically.

"I do," replied Padshaw, giving Stone a knowing smile.

"Green light fellas," Stone said. "Bale out!"

There was no problem getting in and, on entering, they were welcomed by the proprietor who was smartly dressed in a white linen suit, white shoes and a black rollneck. He wore a very thin moustache and just the beginnings of a beard on his chin, yet what Padshaw noticed most was that he spoke with his hands as much as he did with his mouth, and that was a considerable feat taking into account he never stopped babbling. He hustled Padshaw's group to a large farmhouse table surrounded by an array of wooden chairs and stools and sat them down. As he turned away from their table, still talking ten to the dozen to no one in particular, two casually dressed waiters turned up, one holding two ceramic jugs overflowing with froth and the other with a clutch of wine bottles, both white and red. Immediately following them was a middle-aged woman carrying a tray of tankards and various glasses. Stone's crew got stuck in with relish and a lot of noise. Stone, sitting next to Padshaw at one end of the table, filled two large glasses with red wine and passed one to him.

"Cheers Terry. Well spotted!"

"My pleasure!" They toasted each other and knocked them straight back.

"Yeah, well done Terry!" shouted Hardcastle. They all banged the table a few times and then got on with the serious pastime of drinking.

Padshaw was just in the act of refilling their glasses when Stone nudged him and gestured towards the civilian sitting on his own in the far corner of the bar. Padshaw glanced over just as the civilian looked their way. Padshaw politely nodded in recognition and the man responded with a relaxed smile and then pointed at an empty chair at the very end of the bar. "Be our guest," Padshaw said loudly and beckoned him over.

"I hate civilians!" Stone said. The civilian walked towards them carrying his bottle and glass in one hand and dragging the chair with the other.

"Unless they're Sheilas of course," he added.

"I suggest you give him the benefit of the doubt," Padshaw said gently. Stone looked curious and replied:

"If you say so, Terry."

"Good evening Squadron Leader."

Padshaw and Stone half stood as he sat down. Some of the crew looked on but were more interested in drinking.

"Please, call me Terry... and this is Jacko."

"John Smith," said the civilian. Padshaw didn't blink, but Stone's face immediately took on a look of understanding. Smith caught the look and quickly said:

"Seriously! My name really is John Smith. Couldn't ask for a better name in my job when you think about it."

"Dare I ask you anything about your job?" asked Stone.

"No, not really... sorry and all that... besides, most of it's all bullshit and what isn't is incredibly boring."

"Somehow, I find that hard to believe," said Padshaw. Smith gave his pleasant smile.

"Any idea what's good to eat in here?" Stone asked.

"They'll bring whatever they've got in the kitchen," Smith replied.

"They don't keep a set menu as they never know what they're going to get in. Sometimes it's meat, sometimes fish, if you're lucky, both."

Padshaw looked a little uncomfortable, Smith leaned over and said quietly, "The Wing Commander eats here occasionally... as do some of the staff wallahs." Padshaw visibly relaxed. Smith looked at Stone:

"I'll tell you what you ought to try."

"Go on," replied Stone.

"They do a dish called 'Calentita'. I believe its origins are Italian."

"What's in it?"

"It's made up of chickpea flour, olive oil, water and various seasonings. There are various ways of cooking it but here they bake it, goes well with anything. In my opinion." Right on cue, the babbling man came to their table.

"All eat? All eat? Yes yes yes!?"

Everybody nodded or gave the thumbs up; babbling man counted heads and walked away. Smith shouted, "Calentita!" Babbling man repeated the word 'Calentita' all the way to the kitchen.

Twenty minutes later they were all eating a spicy meat stew (nobody knew what was in it and nobody wanted to ask). This was accompanied by a pan-fried fish, several flat breads of Calentita and various bottles of wine. Smith was more relaxed and talkative, he was aware of the fact that both Stone and Padshaw had a fairly good idea of what he got up to, but also that they knew better than to ask.

"I don't suppose you've had the chance to see any places of interest or sample any of the local haunts, have you?" he asked.

"Not really," replied Padshaw. "Too many other things to sort out."

"Shame. The architecture is so varied. Moorish, Georgian, Victorian, a spattering of Italian influence…"

"I'm surprised you get time to notice," Padshaw said

"Normally I don't, to be honest. But I've been sort of hanging around 'Gib' on and off for a few months now. Almost a holiday you might say… except for the odd bomb dropping from the sky now and then and spoiling it."

"The only thing I've noticed," said Stone, "is an awful lot of monkeys… and right thieving bastards they are!"

Smith surprised them both by bursting into laughter.

"Something we missed?" asked Padshaw.

Smith stopped laughing and looked down at the table. A cheeky grin came over his face and he slowly raised his head, leant back in his chair and said:

"Sorry about that. You may hold me partly responsible."

"I don't understand." said Stone.

Smith hesitated for a moment and then continued: "Well I don't suppose I can get shot for this…"

Padshaw and Stone were very attentive.

"It's quite simple really… a few months ago there were only two or three apes left on Gibraltar. All the rest had died off."

"Good job too!" said Stone.

"Quite. Well, I happen to agree with you. However, legend, or rumour, or whatever you want to call it, has it that when there are no more apes on the Rock of Gibraltar, the British people would lose the island to the enemy. Which enemy God knows, but people really believe it. So I was charged with the job of helping reintroduce them."

166

"You're kidding!" Stone's face was a picture of disbelief.

"No, I'm not. In fact it was a direct order from the Prime Minister himself – no joke!"

"I'll be damned." Padshaw said.

"The thing is…" Smith continued, "morale is paramount both military and civilian."

"I haven't seen any civilians," commented Stone.

"That's because they were all evacuated… well, nearly all," Smith looked over at 'babbling man' welcoming some new guests, "most of the civvies that are here are up to no good, or running bars."

"Thank God for some of them then," said Padshaw.

"Quite so… anyway, one more drink and then I'm having an early night."

"Busy day tomorrow?" asked Stone.

"I'm flying out to Malta in the morning."

"I hope you have a pleasant trip," Stone said, filling the glasses from a fresh bottle.

"I'm sure I will. I have total faith in your flying ability."

Stone was wide-eyed. "We're not flying tomorrow! The boat's crocked."

"I think you'll find they're working on it right now. In fact it'll be finished by three a.m., of that I can assure you." Smith's voice had taken on a cold matter-of-fact tone, "And we're leaving at 0600," he added.

"Bugger me!" said Stone.

"Not on a full stomach old chap," Smith quipped with humour.

Padshaw grinned and said, "One more bottle for the road, Jacko?"

"Make it two!" Stone replied gruffly.

Smith gave his smile.

At eight o'clock the following morning, Connors and Blackman were sitting on the bully beef boxes, having a cigarette. Though the rain had eased considerably, the tarpaulin was completely drenched and Blackman was continually getting up to displace the build-up of water in the centre.

"You're very restless this morning, Blackie."

"I'd just prefer to be on the move rather than sitting around here doing nothing."

"So would I. But until Lieutenant Portman's recce'd ahead we're stuck here. Not much point moving out with all the vehicles only to find we can't cover more than a few hundred yards."

Blackman grunted.

"And besides, if we're being delayed by this wonderful weather, so's everyone else."

"I guess so."

Connors smiled to himself. He knew only too well that Blackman had a very low threshold for boredom.

Half a minute later, Corporal Burns walked in out of the rain, carrying the lid off one of the wooden crates that he was using as a tray.

"Tea's up, sir!"

"Thanks," said Connors, taking a full mug off the tray.

"Don't mind if I do," Blackman said smiling. He held the mug to his mouth and looked at Burns.

"No bacon sandwiches?"

Burns raised his eyes to the sky thinking *Miserable sods, never happy!* and then replied in a deadpan voice: "Sorry about that, Captain, we've run out of bread."

Connors spat out a mouthful of tea, laughing. Blackman grinned and said:

"I suppose eggs benedict is out of the question, then?"

Burns simply ignored him and took a mouthful of tea instead. Looking at Connors, he asked:

"Any idea how long till we move out, sir?"

"Soon as I know what state the track ahead's like, then I'll make a decision... impatient buggers!"

Burns had a look of bemusement.

A few moments of silence passed and then Sergeant Bell walked in and saluted.

"Sir!"

Connors looked up.

"Yes George?"

"All vehicles serviceable sir, and all the men have been fed... and Lieutenant Portman's just got back, sir."

Connors could see Portman approaching over Sergeant Bell's shoulder.

"Thanks George, hang around for a moment... we'll see what the lieutenant's got to say."

Portman walked in.

"What do you think?" Connors asked straight away.

"It's not as bad as I thought it would be, sir. It'll be slow going in places but we should be OK."

"That's good enough for me."

Connors saw Portman frowning and biting his bottom lip.

"I think we've got time for another brew then."

Connors quickly finished his tea and passed his mug to Burns.

"Yes sir," Burns said, who then went off in search of more tea.

"You have something on your mind, Lieutenant?"

"Yes sir. The radio operator just informed me that he received a garbled message earlier this morning, concerning one of our supply trains. He's only just told me because he was expecting more information."

"Well there's only two I know about. And we're one of them! What did he get?"

"Not much I'm afraid. It was in code of course, but the interference was such that he only picked up snippets of it. It might not even have been meant solely for us."

"Well what 'snippets' did he make sense of?" Connors asked impatiently.

Portman quickly replied, "It appears that only one of the supply trains needs to be at the drop zone, but we don't know if it's us, or them or someone else."

"Excellent!" Connors said sarcastically. He let his shoulders slump.

"Doesn't make much difference really, Don," Blackman said. "I mean, it's almost on route to the LGI anyway, and we still have a local pickup on route."

Connors' head came up. Portman winced.

"The local pick-up's cancelled! That much we did get," Portman said.

Connors stared into nothing.

"Has the radio op had any luck in making contact again?" Blackman asked.

"No... he hasn't. The information came from an RAF Lysander. One of the men reported seeing one floating about earlier. I can only assume it was doing its best to contact other units as well as ours."

"I bloody well hope the Japs have as much trouble with communications as we do," Connors stated.

"I damn well hope so!" Blackman said, adding, "Otherwise it's not bloody fair!"

Sergeant Bell stared at his CO, an out and out soldier, he would fight anybody he was told to, but he could find no humour in war.

"What are your orders, sir?" asked Portman.

Connors thought for a moment and then looked at the lieutenant.

"Work out a route from here straight to the RAF landing ground. I'm not going to waste any more time on what might be a wild goose chase, as soon as you've done that we'll move out."

"Right sir, I'll be as quick as I can," Portman left.

"George?"

"Sir."

"Have the men ready to move out at a moment's notice."

"Yes sir." Bell saluted and walked away in the direction of the vehicles, barking orders.

"Blackie? You scout ahead of the column and keep your eyes peeled."

"Right Don, I'll take Naylor with me, I know how much he enjoys my company."

"Just let him drive!"

"Wouldn't have it any other way."

"Tea sir?" Burns walked up with two mugs.

"An ice-cold beer would go down well!" Blackman said.

Burns couldn't argue with that; like everyone else, he was sweating before he'd even woken up.

An hour after moving out Connors had managed to cover, at most, two miles. Considering the conditions, he'd done bloody well. There were very few areas of track that were in a straight line or even flat. Some parts were actually reasonable to drive on, others were nothing more than a quagmire of mud, some full of deep ruts, some not. Blackman, as ordered, had scouted ahead for a distance and then waited for the column to catch up before moving on again. The mules would quite often reach him before the vehicles. Twice one of the trucks had lost any kind of grip and had begun to slide, back end first, towards a shallow drop. Had it of gone any further they would never have got it out. Losing a truck would not be the end of the world, but unloading it and trying to disperse its contents amongst the other vehicles and mules in these conditions?! No bloody thank you!

Blackman had found several sections of track blocked by young trees whose roots had been washed clean of soil which had caused them to either collapse or slide onto the track. On the first occasion he'd driven back to the column for extra men to help, and then got down to the laborious job of cutting the trunk and branches into pieces small enough to move. From then on he kept two extra men in the jeep with him in case it happened again. It did. Four times. The going was arduous for everyone, but more so for 'Bobby' Graham. He'd been made as comfortable as possible, but even a slight jolt was agony, his leg was killing him and his ribs were aching like mad. Originally, he'd had a shot of morphine, which had made life quite bearable, but that had worn off and he didn't see much point in having any more until he was desperate; on top of that, it was in very short supply.

Lying beside him in the truck was a young private who'd been taken ill the previous night. It was obvious he was coming down with malaria, and, judging by the smell, that wasn't his only problem. Graham had tried a couple of times to hold a conversation with him, but all the man could do was mumble incoherently and occasionally moan.

"He can't hear you, sir," said Lieutenant Mercer's orderly, Lance Corporal Fenn.

"...How are you feeling, sir?"

"I bloody hurt... but I'll manage... any idea where we're headed?"

"A 'Raff' landing ground, so I'm told."

"Which one?"

"No idea I'm afraid, sir. I expect Mr Mercer knows. Would you like me to ask him?"

"It's not important... thanks anyway though."

The truck hit a deep rut that sent a wave of pain down Graham's leg

"Shit and bollocks!" Graham let out.

Fenn smiled sympathetically.

After another three hours the terrain had improved a little in some places, but it was taking its toll on the drivers and the vehicles. A buckled wheel had had to be changed and a radiator hose on Connors' jeep split and had to be replaced. Blackman was aware that they were making slightly better progress, but it wasn't by much. He was continually wiping sweat from his eyes and swatting at the endless supply of mosquitoes.

"Bugger!" Naylor remarked. Then, without warning, the engine stopped dead. The jeep came to a halt.

"Don't tell me..." said Blackman, "the engine fell out?"

Naylor glanced at his CO.

"I think it's the fuel line, sir."

The smell of petrol reached their nostrils.

"Well let's get it fixed," Blackman said, getting out.

Despite his sarcasm and occasionally arrogant comments, Blackman was an officer who would happily get his hands dirty and would always lead from the front, something that all the men respected him for, although sometimes grudgingly. Blackman raised the bonnet, Naylor stuck his nose in.

"Fuel hose has come off," he said, "this'll only take half a minute."

The others were about to get out of the jeep.

"Stay put," Blackman ordered. "Won't be long."

They sat back down. Naylor fiddled with the fuel line and secured it.

"All sorted sir."

Naylor stood up and Blackman dropped the bonnet. They both got back in and Naylor started the engine.

As it turned out, the minor problem with the jeep was something of a blessing. Naylor was just changing into second gear as they approached quite a sharp bend in the track.

As they started to round it, Blackman was surprised, and, momentarily pleased to see a stretch of track going on for quite a distance which was reasonably flat and almost straight. He also noticed that the trees died away dramatically on one side and left the area very exposed. Now he was not so pleased!

Before the jeep could break cover, Blackman shouted:

"Pull up Naylor!"

"Sir."

The jeep came to an abrupt halt. Blackman came close to hitting the windscreen. He looked at Naylor. "Well done." He smiled. He clambered out and then stood beside the jeep and stared ahead.

"Stretch your legs chaps," he said casually.

The men clambered out and stood by the jeep. Blackman took his binoculars out of their case, which was slung round his neck, and studied the track and surrounding area.

To the right of the track the bank was steep and thick with trees. To the left the ground fell gently away, but there was very little cover for 150 yards out, at which point the trees became very dense again. The lack of cover went on for about 600 yards in length.

"Can't say I'm that keen on this bit," he said to himself under his breath.

"Beg your pardon, sir?" said Naylor.

"What do you think?" Blackman asked Naylor gesturing ahead with his binoculars. Naylor walked up beside his CO.

"Nice to see... but not inviting."

"My sentiments exactly."

Blackman raised his binoculars again. After a few moments he said:

"You chaps stay put. If I'm not back in thirty minutes, get back to the column ASAP."

"Yes sir," replied Naylor.

With that, Blackman stooped and made his way forward, after a few yards he was crawling.

Connors, meanwhile, was having his share of problems too. The rain had, at last, stopped. Having encountered various delays with the vehicles, Connors had instructed Lieutenant Portman to go on ahead with the mules, meet up with Captain Blackman and they would catch up as soon as they could. Generally, the mules could make slow but steady progress, whereas the four trucks and the jeep would

174

make quick time for seven or eight hundred yards and then get bogged down, or start to overheat, or suffer a stroke.

On this occasion, however, both the trucks at the back of the column had become thoroughly bogged down and it was going to take some time to unstick them. To compound the problem, one of the trucks contained the malaria-stricken private and the injured Graham.

Connors had just made his way to the rear of the column even that was slow progress as his boots were caked in soft mud.

"How's it going, George?"

"We're just going to try and pull the first one out now sir."

Both the trucks that were free of the mud had been secured together by a chain, another chain attached them to the nearest bogged down vehicle.

Connors looked on and then nodded.

"All right lads," Bell said, "take up the slack slowly."

The engines revved. Both trucks started moving slowly forward. As the chain lifted out of the mud and took up the strain, so the driver in the first stuck vehicle gently let out the clutch. Slowly, painfully, it began to extricate itself out of the mud. Fifteen minutes later it was clear. Connors, with his hands on his hips, spoke encouragingly.

"Bloody good show George! Now for an encore!"

"You heard the Major, fingers out!"

Another thirty painstaking minutes later and they were moving again.

Lieutenant Portman on the other hand was making quite good time. He had the advantage of leading the mules around the more difficult areas. Once or twice one of the animals would get itself into difficulties and would sometimes have to be unloaded, before ropes would be lashed around it and then brute force would free it. This was by no means unusual and invariably could cause the animal some distress. On this occasion, two of the men had

175

tried to calm the animal while two more tried in vain to load it up again. Bucking and pulling, it eventually managed to break free, but not before kicking one of the men and cracking two of his ribs. It then plodded of a short distance and stood still, labouring for breath.

"All right! Leave it!" ordered Portman. "How bad are you hurt?" he asked.

"Not too bad sir. Hurts when I breathe deeply, that's all."

"As soon as the Major catches up I want you in one of the trucks, got that?"

"Yes, sir."

"Meanwhile we'll rest up here."

The men gratefully removed their packs and sat or lay down wherever they comfortably could.

"Shall I start a brew-up, sir?" Corporal Pitt asked.

Portman looked at the men.

"Yes, why not? I think we've got time."

Pitt looked up. The sound of aero engines could be faintly heard. Some of the men and Portman raised their heads, the noise of engines got louder. There were very few gaps in trees above to see much at all. For a split second, six aircraft could be seen... and then they were gone.

"P40s," said one man.

"Oh rubbish Sid, they were bloody Hurricanes."

"Bollocks! I know a P40 when I see one."

"You need glasses chum."

"I need glasses!"

Portman, smiling, looked on at the two men. So long as they were arguing about which type of *Allied* aircraft they were, he didn't the least bit care. Now, if they were Japs, he'd be worried.

Just under fifteen minutes later, Connors caught them up. Portman told Connors about the injured man and had him put in a truck. He then started to explain as to why he'd had delays, but Connors had been through it all a hundred times before himself and wasn't the least bit surprised.

"Well, we're going to press on," Connors told him.

"As soon as we've made contact with Captain Blackman we'll find a spot to rest up and wait for you."

"Right you are, sir. See you later then."

"George? We're moving on!"

"Sir."

"Captain Blackman must think we've got lost," commented Burns.

"He's probably fast asleep or got his feet up enjoying a bit of peace and quiet," Connors replied jovially.

At that moment Private Naylor was getting concerned. It was nearly forty minutes since Blackman had gone on alone. He knew he should really have headed back, as ordered, but he couldn't bring himself to leave without his Captain. As a precaution, he'd got the other two men to take cover either side of the track and keep their rifles at the ready. Naylor kept a steady vigil in the direction Blackman had gone.

A few more minutes passed and Blackman came into view, stooping. As he got closer to the jeep he stood and looked at Naylor.

"What the bloody hell are you still doing here?"

Naylor swallowed.

"My watch must have stopped, sir."

"Is that so?" Blackman replied sternly.

"The jeep broke down again?" Naylor offered lamely.

The other two men emerged from the undergrowth either side of Blackman.

"And I suppose these two were looking for rare butterflies?"

Naylor stood motionless.

"When I give an order, you obey it to the letter! Understood?"

"Yes sir," Naylor replied.

"Don't let it happen again!"

"I won't, sir."

"If you start going out on a limb to look after an officer in this manner, you could end up being promoted. And you don't want that, do you?"

Naylor's eyes widened and his eyebrows went up.

"As punishment you're my driver until I say otherwise... or some bastard promotes you and spoils the rest of your life!"

Naylor saw the makings of a smile.

"Make some tea," Blackman said in a relaxed voice. "I'm gasping."

"Yes sir," Naylor replied respectfully, grinning to himself as he turned away.

Naylor was just passing Blackman his second mug of tea when the distant hum of engines could be heard.

"Cheers," said Blackman, taking his tin mug and knocking it against Naylor's.

"Cheers sir," Naylor replied, a little surprised by the gesture. "Sounds like the Major's catching up, sir."

"About time too. I half expected him to have been here by now. No doubt he's had his fair share of setbacks as well."

Blackman walked to the back of the jeep and leant leisurely against the spare wheel attached to its rear. He sipped his tea while casually watching Connor's jeep and the trucks approach. As Connors pulled up, Blackman pulled out his lighter, held it between two fingers and swung it in a pendulum motion. Burns turned the engine off. Connors got out of the jeep and walked up to Blackman, at the same time taking a pack of cigarettes out of his top pocket.

"Want one Don?" Blackman asked, raising his tin mug.

"No thanks Blackie."

Blackman put his mug down on the jeep and indicated with his head and eyes towards the way ahead.

"You need to see this."

Blackman walked back the way he'd just come. Connors, following him, watched Blackman stoop down and did the same. Blackman then got on his belly and crawled, Connors crawled up beside him and stared at the terrain ahead.

"Not nice," Connors stated.

"That's how I feel. Have a gander." Blackman passed his binoculars.

Connors scanned the whole area meticulously.

"Can't see anything. But that means bugger all."

"Pretty quiet. No birds, nothing," commented Blackman.

"Have you been out and had a look?"

"Yeah. Just got back. Couldn't see any sign of Japs."

"But you're still not happy?"

"They've sent patrols further up than this before. And we were briefed that our chaps were possibly going to push south. Johnny Jap might well have got the buzz on that and moved some of his slant-eyed dwarfs north to have a look-see."

Connors was still holding the binoculars to his eyes and studying every leaf and tree.

"Point taken, Blackie. Either way, we can't stay here forever."

"What do you want to do?"

Connors thought for a moment.

"We'll have to take a chance and go for it Blackie. We can't go back, that's for sure. Plus... if we run into any trouble, Lieutenant Portman's got plenty of warning."

"OK Don. You're the boss."

"I'll lead in the first jeep, then the trucks and then you bring up the rear. Tell the drivers to keep a good distance between vehicles. Should we hit any trouble and one of the vehicles gets disabled, leave it."

"Drive like Billy-o for the far end. Got it?"

"Got it."

"As a precaution..." Connors paused for a second or two, "... have some men positioned on the left-hand side of the trucks with their rifles at the ready. Some defence is better than none, probably worrying about nothing, still... Right, let's get back and have that cigarette."

As they crawled away, both Connors and Blackman missed the reflection of sunlight from the trees.

Connors explained to Sergeant Bell the position and gave him his orders. Blackman, meanwhile, went to brief the drivers.

"Give the Major twenty-five yards' head start and then follow him. Second truck same distance and so on. *If* we run into any trouble, drive like hell! Got it?"

"Yes sir," the drivers replied as one.

"Right then, get in your cabs and wait for Sergeant Bell's order to start up."

They walked off to their respective vehicles.

Blackman approached Connors.

"All ready here, Don."

"Time to go then. See you shortly."

Blackman nodded and turned for his jeep. Burns started the engine as Connors got in.

"Once you're in second gear, stay there," Connors ordered. "We may need to move quickly."

"Right sir."

Sergeant Bell gave the signal for the drivers to start up and got into the second truck.

As Connors' jeep broke cover, Burns shifted up into second gear and rattled along at a bumpy but respectable twenty miles an hour. The first truck followed, bouncing and bucketing twenty yards behind, the second truck emerged twenty-five yards behind the first and Sergeant Bell was already doing what he did best. He was leaning out of the cab window shouting orders.

"Don't take your eyes off those trees. Look for trouble!"

As the third truck just came into the open, the bonnet on Connors' jeep seemed to twist and buckle at the same time.

"Jesus! What the...?"

"Bullet strike!" shouted Connors. "Get your foot down!"

Then all hell broke loose.

The officer in charge of the Japanese patrol had already made his decision to return to his own lines. He had been given orders to harass the enemy supply lines and if possible take prisoners. To his surprise he had advanced a lot further than he had thought possible without encountering his enemies. On the other hand, maybe he'd simply been unlucky.

He had ordered his men to stand down just short of the clearing. And get something to eat before heading back. Under his command he had thirty-five men and a type ninety-five light tank, the commander of which had wandered off for a pee. He was just doing up his fly when he thought he heard an engine. His immediate glance took him to his tank, but he wasn't thinking. He looked towards the furthest corner of the clearing. The engine stopped! He ran back to his tank and climbed onto the turret. He took of his glasses and held up his binoculars, for a minute or so he saw and heard nothing, then he spotted a small movement in the undergrowth. He raised his hand to get the attention of his officer. The officer looked at him. The tank commander pointed to the corner of the clearing to indicate in which direction the officer should look.

More movement. The officer smiled and, waving in acknowledgement to the tank commander, went back to quickly brief his men. Having briefed them, all he could do now was wait.

Nearly an hour later, the Japanese officer's patience was getting a little frayed. He very much wanted to engage his enemy, move in for the kill and then return to his own lines. Maybe they had turned back and he and his men hadn't heard the engine, perhaps they were planning to move on after nightfall. Even better! He had star shells and an open killing ground. He also had time.

Suddenly an engine started, then another, then maybe two more, he couldn't be sure. His men were all ready, most were armed with rifles, though a few had sub-machine guns.

The tank commander had been given instructions to let the first vehicle cover 200 yards before opening fire. He was then to pick off the lead vehicle before concentrating on the others. This was all very well but they had no idea how many vehicles there would be, or whether he could get a clear shot at them with so many trees clouding his lines of fire. He said as much to his officer, but to no avail.

"Break cover if you have to. Use your wits!"

If he was to use his wits, he wouldn't break cover, he thought to himself. A jeep came racing into view. Everyone held their fire. Then a truck, and another. A third appeared, the tank's turret traversed slowly from right to left, following a line of fire just forward of the lead vehicle. Allowing for speed and distance, the tank commander waited, as ordered, for the jeep to make up the required distance before opening fire. At 150 fifty yards the officer dropped his hand. Machine guns rattled, the crack of rifles filled the air. The tank's thirty-seven millimetre gun fired.

Squadron Leader Marsland was sitting at his desk when Hollingsworth, Valentine, Hacker and 'Punchy' Jennings walked in. Valentine immediately occupied a chair and put his feet up on Marsland's desk (to nobody's surprise). The others casually stood around attentively. Marsland finished reading and looked up.

"We've just received information that the Fourteenth Indian Division has been given orders to achieve a line between Buthidaung and Rathedaung. Exactly how old this information is I have no idea. They are currently advancing south towards those positions."

"Bloody slowly considering the terrain," Valentine commented.

"That's as maybe," Marsland continued. "Nevertheless, we've been given orders to supply air cover whenever and wherever it's required. The other airfields at Chittagong have received similar orders. We've also received orders to intercept and escort a transport aircraft directly to Chittagong. I'm assuming there's brass on board and the bigwigs upstairs are jittery."

"Probably contains their month's booze supply," Valentine said.

"Well, whatever it's carrying, it's our job to deliver it...'Punchy'?" Marsland looked at Jennings. "I've decided to make two of the Hurricanes operational for this sortie plus four Kittyhawks."

"Right you are, sir."

"Hacker?"

"Sir?"

"You're flying one and I leave you to decide which you take with you."

"Yes sir."

"I'll lead, but we'll operate as two sections. The Kittyhawks will be Red and you will be Green."

"Right sir."

"What about me?" Valentine asked indignantly.

Marsland smiled broadly.

"You, 'Snobby', are flying my desk!"

Valentine's mouth opened wide, as did his eyes.

Hollingsworth, Hacker and Jennings grinned at the surprise on Valentine's face. It didn't happen very often.

"Relax, 'Snobby'," Marsland said, having enjoyed the moment, "intelligence also came through with information that two, maybe three, Japanese patrols have been spotted further north than was originally reported –" Marsland picked up, and read, a typed memo "– and according to this report, Jap fighters have been making appearances and making something of a nuisance of themselves... so I doubt you'll have a quiet day."

"I'd better not!" Valentine replied, staring hard at the top drawer of the filing cabinet containing the booze.

"I've hidden it," Marsland said immediately.

"You cad!" Valentine said, as if he were a child who'd had his sweets taken away.

"What time are we off, sir?" Hacker asked.

"Good question. I expect to receive confirmation of our rendezvous time in the morning... talking of the morning...'Snobby'?"

Valentine grudgingly took his eyes away from the filing cabinet.

"Brief Hacker and his pilots on the wonders of the Jap fighters we're up against before we leave –" Marsland looked at Hacker "– they have certain attributes that Jerry fighters don't. They also have various failings."

Valentine nodded at Marsland and turned to face Hacker.

"First thing in the morning?"

"Sure thing. I'll make sure they're all there."

"Right then, " Marsland said, "let's get back to the mess."

As they left Marsland's office, they noticed that the rain was starting to ease.

"That would be nice," Hacker said, looking up.

"Just don't mention that word again," Valentine replied.

"I won't."

As they approached the mess, Hacker was trying to make up his mind who to take with him the following day. No doubt they'd all want to fly. They entered the mess hut and conversation took the thought from his mind.

Eight thirty the following morning, Hacker and his pilots had gathered in the mess hut. The rain had eased considerably and it was promising to bugger off altogether.

Hacker, standing in the doorway, was watching 'Punchy' Jennings and various ground crew checking the condition of the airstrip prior to them taking off. He could also see some of the ground crew manhandling sheets of Marston mat to create a path from where the Hurricanes were parked to the runway area. Marston mat was also known as PSP, or pierced steel planking. Each sheet could be interlocked to another to create a firm and stable surface on which vehicles could drive and aircraft could land and take off. (That was the principle, anyway)

Valentine came around the corner.

"All here?"

"All present and correct," Hacker replied.

"Decided on a pilot yet?" Valentine asked.

"Yes. I thought I'd take Dick Vine. He needs the experience, and, with a bit of luck, we should have an uneventful trip."

"There you go again! Putting the kiss of death on what was going to be a quiet day."

Valentine went inside, Hacker followed him, smiling.

As Valentine walked around the sitting pilots, some of them started to stand to attention. He lazily waved his hand for them to sit.

"Right, gentlemen. I'm going to make this as short and as painless as possible."

To Valentine's left was Marsland's tattered blackboard with various tired pictures of two Japanese fighters pinned on it. Using a stick, he indicated to two pictures of each aircraft at different angles.

"This aircraft, for those of you that don't know, is the imperial Japanese air force's Nakajima Ki43 fighter, which we lovingly call the 'Oscar'. The one below –" Valentine tapped the lower two of the pictures with his stick, "– is the Mitsubishi type 0 fighter, known by us as the 'Zero' or 'ZEKE'. Some of you, I know, already have air combat experience. I am not trying to teach you how to suck eggs, but, if you use the same tactics against these buggers as you may have used over France, the CO will be writing very short letters to your families back home!"

Hacker was paying attention to what Valentine was saying and at the same time looking at what were, now, his pilots, to see that they were doing the same.

'Clem' Decker, the Australian, Hacker noticed, was cleaning his nails and paying little or no attention whatsoever. Hacker was not impressed.

"Now, both the Oscar and the Zero are exceptionally manoeuvrable machines, far more so than us, especially in the turn. If you intend to try to out turn either of these aircraft, please write your will first. Rate of climb: both types can exceed three thousand feet per minute, so they've just got the edge on you.

"If you find yourself pursuing one on the climb in a Hurricane, fine, you've got cannon. If you're in a Kitty, make damn sure you're close enough to finish the bastard! If he's pursuing you, get the bloody hell out of his way."

"Sir?" Vine interrupted.

"Yes?"

"I've heard a lot of people back in England, and at various transit camps, saying that the Japanese aren't suited to flying and that, well... basically... they're not much good."

"Drivel!" Valentine said annoyed. "Anyone who believes that won't last a day! Whatever any of you has heard to that effect had better forget it."

Vine flinched. "Yes sir."

"Japanese pilots are bloody good, and they've got little or no consideration for themselves, and nothing but contempt for you. If you have to bail out, do it as low as you can, they will make every effort to kill you even when you're hanging under your 'brolly'."

Some of the pilots moved uncomfortably.

"Firepower," Valentine continued. "The Oscar is armed with two twelve point five millimetre machine guns. Whereas the Zero has two seven point seven millimetre machine guns and two twenty millimetre cannon. Do not get into a one-on-one dogfight with either, always fly in pairs... is that clear?"

The assembled pilots nodded with 'Sirs' or 'Yesses'. Except Decker, who seemed to be miles away. Valentine wasn't blind. He looked hard at the Australian and asked in his usual aloof manner:

"Am I boring you, old chap?" The hut went silent. The other pilots' attention switched to Decker.

Decker looked up and opened his mouth to reply but Valentine got in first.

"Am I keeping you from an important date... your manicurist, perhaps?"

"No sir," Decker replied.

Valentine stared at Decker threateningly:

"Listen to me very carefully –" Valentine had an unusually cold and ruthless manner in his voice "– if you, in any way, shape or form, endanger the lives of anyone on this squadron with your self-conceited, arrogant, egotistical, self-opinionated attitude, I, personally, will have your balls for a tennis court and use your lungs for the net. Is that understood?"

"Yes sir," Decker replied, his face going a little red.

Valentine continued to stare at Decker for a moment, Decker looked away. Valentine gave the others a broad smile.

"Now for the good news," he glanced at Decker. Decker now gave his best impression of someone who was listening. Valentine continued, "both the Oscar and the Zero have two major weak spots. Neither of them have any armour plate, nor do they have self-sealing tanks. I've seen Zeros fall out of the sky with hardly a scratch on them.

"It's not impossible to pop off a few accurate rounds and find your target suddenly blow up in your face. Be wary of that! You also have an advantage in the dive. They cannot outdive you. The Zero especially has been known to break up at over 400 miles per hour. However, I am not suggesting you make a competition out of it."

The pilots smiled.

"All that said and done, its normally the Oscar we've come up against and those occasions they have been few and far between... just the same, keep your eyes open and your wits about you. Right, you're all dismissed except Vine."

Vine looked up.

"You're flying today."

"Yes sir," Vine replied enthusiastically.

"No doubt your flight commander would like a word with you."

Hacker smiled at being addressed as flight commander.

"Just a little chat," he said to Vine and turned to leave.

"'Hack'!" Valentine called.

"'Snobby'."

"Squadron briefing in twenty minutes"

"Righto." Vine followed Hacker as the other pilots filed out. The rain had stopped. Vine looked up and then back at Hacker.

"I say, it's actually stopped..."

"Don't say that word," Hacker cut him short, "Squadron orders!"

Twenty minutes later Marsland was briefing all of his pilots on the current situation. He had a large map pinned against one wall of the hut.

"Right gentlemen. As of last night, we have been informed that our troops are making their way south to push the Japs back." Parish and Hillman glanced at each other and then raised their eyes to the ceiling. 'Chancer' Harris smiled to himself. "This squadron, and others, are under orders to assist in any way we can. This will probably mean a lot of ground strafing and, where possible, the bombing of enemy positions."

There were enthusiastic murmurings from the pilots.

188

"Also keep an eye out for the Jap fighters! It appears they've become more active recently, as have some bombing raids aimed against our supply lines, which, God knows, have a difficult enough job without their interference, so keep your eyes open."

"Now..." Marsland was indicating positions on the map, "our chaps are trying to achieve a line between here... and here, so we may have to cover quite a lot of ground. I have been led to believe that we are due to be supplied with bombs, new extra fuel tanks and ammunition, on top of our usual supplies. These are in fact overdue, nevertheless, we will be putting up as many sorties as our current supplies will allow. As of today, we will have four aircraft at readiness from dawn to dusk on top of any planned missions. I leave that to you, 'Snobby'".

"Such faith in my ability," Valentine said airily.

"Today's sortie will involve six aircraft. Four Kittys and two Hurricanes. Hacker and...?"

"Vine sir," Hacker said.

"Hacker and Vine in the Hurris, Hillman, Parish and Cracken with me. We are to rendezvous with, and escort, a reconnaissance aircraft to Chittagong. On the way there and back keep your eyes open. As I've already said, the Japs have been putting up more fighters, maybe they've got wind of what our ground forces are up to, maybe not, either way, if we run into any while we're on the way out, leave them alone unless they want a fight! Our priority is escort duty. Our interception point is here –" Marsland indicated a point on the map "– write the map reference down in case we get separated. Rendezvous time is approximately twelve thirty, we will take off at eleven thirty. Lastly, if anything happens to me, Flying Officer Hacker takes over."

"He never asks does he?" Valentine said loudly to Hacker, who grinned in reply.

"Any questions?"

The hut was silent.

"Right... let's get on."

As everybody made for the door, Marsland walked up beside Vine who was standing next to Hacker.

"Has Mr Hacker had a word with you?" he asked pleasantly.

"Yes sir," Vine replied.

Marsland raised his eyebrows.

"... He told me not to crash taking off, not to get shot down, and don't crash when I land... sir."

"Excellent!"

Marsland gave Hacker an approving nod and walked on.

Hacker, followed by Vine, casually walked towards the parked Hurricanes. 'Punchy' Jennings and various ground crew were clambering over them, polishing the canopies, checking the engines, topping up the fuel tanks. The men were all in shorts and soaked in sweat. Hacker's eyes were stinging and, as he wiped the sweat away from his brow, Padshaw's words came to him yet again: 'You are just what I'm looking for...'

"Clever bugger. I think I'll kill him," Hacker said out loud.

"What's that?" Vine asked.

"Oh... nothing, just thinking of someone I met in Blighty."

"Ladybird?" Vine enquired, meaning a WAAF, "Popsie?"

"No..." Hacker laughed a little, "no one as pleasant as that."

Vine let it go.

However, the more Hacker thought about what Padshaw had said, the more he realised that Padshaw had been right. He'd been in India less than two weeks and he was already adapting to the climate quite well. He'd made a reasonable impression on his new CO, and the rest of the Squadron already regarded him as a piece of the furniture. The fact that he had more or less immediately been made an acting flight commander had caused no waves amongst the other pilots, which was also encouraging.

He mulled over this recent turn of events for a few moments, then the only other alternative popped into his head...He'd have been posted to a training squadron in the Midlands! As he walked towards his waiting Hurricane the waft of engine oil and petrol drifted under his nostrils. He inhaled deeply. The smell was intoxicating. "The bloody Midlands!" he said to himself. "Not ruddy likely!"

"On second thoughts," he said happily, "I might buy him a pint."

Vine stared at him with a look of amusement on his face.

In mid October the Fourteenth India Division was, with great difficulty, making its way into the Arakan. They had indeed received orders on the seventeenth of the month to achieve a line between Buthidaung and Rathedaung, this objective was to be attained before the beginning of December. The hardships that confronted them could not be overemphasised. The terrain was quoted as being a "measure of hell". The heat, rain, illness and lack of supplies all contributed to a horrendous existence which had to be personally overcome by each individual and, at the same time, reach a military objective.

Supplies were being dropped as often as was possible, which, in most other theatres of the war, would have been classed as common practice. Yet even this proved difficult simply from the lack of aircraft and, moreover, parachutes, with which to drop supplies safely.

Various ways were improvised to 'free' drop various items. Some aircraft would approach at near stalling speed and as low as possible to reduce the chances of sacks splitting on impact, accurately dropping containers on dense foliage to break their fall, was also practiced.

Any and every way possible was used to help the ground forces. RAF fighters were regularly called upon to strafe and bomb areas of jungle at the army's request. On many occasions the pilots felt these sorties to be superfluous as they could not see their enemy or any kind of visual result for their efforts. Their attitude changed quite quickly, however, when information would filter back to them as to how grateful the army was for their help in knocking out formations of Japanese troops, and sometimes armour.

Once they realised how effective these strikes were, they carried them out with a new resolve. Life for the pilots was difficult enough, but for the men operating on the ground, it was nothing short of a living hell. Whatever they could do to make the footsloggers' life that little bit easier, was carried out with a new enthusiasm

At around the same time the war in the Mediterranean was turning more in the Allies' favour. During the month of August, various operations were successfully carried out against enemy shipping and some ports. 'Operation Pedestal', a convoy of over fifty Allied ships, fought their way through to Malta. Twelve ships were lost but vital supplies were delivered.

In the same month sixty-plus Spitfires managed to reach Malta to aid in her defence. During September, Rommel had been stopped by General Montgomery at Alam Halfa.

Nevertheless, in late September and during the most of October, the German and Italian forces threw everything they had at Malta to try and force her surrender.

Chapter 10

Unfortunately, there were no available gunners to replace Jimmy Creed, but a new co-pilot had been found to replace the injured Colin Rustin.

His name was Simon Pither. He was a sergeant pilot who'd originally been the pilot of a Bristol Beaufort. After making an attack on enemy shipping, his aircraft had been hit several times, knocking out one engine. Having nursed it back to Gibraltar he had ordered his crew to bale out. This done, his intention had been to point the aircraft towards the open sea and bale out himself.

It was at this time he realised that his parachute had been damaged by shell splinters, he had little choice but to attempt a landing.

All in all he did quite well to overcome the loss of one engine... and half an aileron... and half an undercarriage! The pillbox to the side of the runway however, proved to be insurmountable.

Once he'd left the hospital, he'd been given a desk job while he recuperated. He wasn't sorry to leave it.

Chapter 11

Padshaw and Smith were both seated in the galley. Padshaw was reading the instructions supplied to him by Hawkins, Smith was doing much the same thing with the contents of a folder which had been passed to him just prior to boarding the Sunderland.

Every few minutes Smith would let out a snort, or a short sarcastic comment. If he wasn't doing that, he was shaking his head in wonder.

After ten minutes, Padshaw had almost finished reading his orders, which was just as well as his concentration was slowly disappearing due to Smiths constant, meaningless, narrative.

"I take it you're not overly impressed by whatever it is you're reading?" he said politely.

"Hmm...? Oh, sorry. I'm afraid I have an inane habit of making disconcerting noises when I have to read total drivel that's supposed to be my instructions from above."

"I can only assume you've been given a difficult task."

"Difficult..?" Smith replied with his smile. "No, difficult is standard procedure. If I can achieve even half of this tosh, it'll be nothing short of Homeric."

"Given you something of a tall order, have they?"

"Understatement..." Smith said lethargically. "I just wish they'd all talk to each other first... before they send me on my way. Problem is, half of the brass don't confide in each other long enough to agree anything, so, as far as I can see, what they all do is write their requirements down on little bits of paper, shove them into a big box and then some bloke with a white stick has to pick a few out at random,"

"Just like playing tombola," Padshaw said sarcastically.

"I'm only half joking, Terry. Some poor bastard has to collate all the information required from numerous departments, some hush hush, some not. Some are simply looking for accurate figures on results from information they've previously acted on, various ranking officers want to know what Hitler had for breakfast, or does Mussolini really like Mae West!

"The thing is, and I'm not being big headed, there aren't enough of us to go round who have got the experience to succeed."

Smith paused for a moment, not for effect, more from frustration. Padshaw let him continue.

"Anyway, when the poor bastard, whoever he is, has sifted through all the bumf, he then has the job of allocating it as best he can." Smith casually glanced at his paperwork again and then looked directly at Padshaw, "I think this time I was at the back of the queue, so to speak."

There was no smile.

Padshaw put his paperwork away, picked up his briefcase and produced the remains of the Glenmorangie.

"Would this help the grey matter?"

Smith's smile returned.

"Can't hurt." He took the bottle. "Thanks very much." He held the bottle up, there was an inch or so left.

"Are you sure?" Smith asked.

Padshaw patted his case.

"I have reinforcements," he said.

Smith took the cork out.

"Cheers!"

Chapter 12

"Right chum, you take her," Stone said.

"I've got her," Pither confirmed.

"Good, cos I've got a hangover... I'm going back for coffee, want one?"

"Yes, thank you."

Pither was desperately trying to accept what a different environment flying a Sunderland was to anything else he had experienced, and even more so the casual attitude of the Captain and crew. He'd even heard Stone, who was the same rank as him, address a squadron leader as 'Terry'!

As Stone squeezed between the seats, he glanced at Pither and asked flippantly:

"I take it you like rum?"

"As a matter of fact I do. Why do you ask?"

But Stone had already gone.

"Coffee, Chris?"

Chris James looked up at his skipper. His face looked as if it had been sucked of all its blood, except for his eyes which were bloodshot and looked ready to fall out. With some effort, he opened his mouth to reply.

"I'll make it a large one," Stone said, saving him the trouble.

James nodded. Apart from the fact that they'd all had to get up for an 0600 departure, the morning had got off to a good start. Some of the crew had got appalling hangovers and were continually ribbed by those that didn't. As it turned out, those that didn't were still pissed and they would suffer later.

Pither was introduced to Stone and the rest of the crew half an hour before they took off from Gibraltar. He kept getting their names confused but half of them didn't even notice. Smith and Padshaw were waiting by the pier chatting when a bleary-eyed Stone appeared with his, mainly subdued, crew.

The Sunderland's engine had, as Smith had said, been repaired during the night. The damage to the holes in the top of the fuselage, wing and tail had been very professionally patched up, and had even had a lick of paint. Even the damage to the cockpit had been completed. Stone was impressed and said as much.

"They've done a pretty good job!"

"I told them I don't like draughty aeroplanes," Smith quipped.

Stone looked at him.

"It's a boat!" Stone stated, slightly louder than he meant to.

"I stand corrected," Smith replied courteously.

"All ready to go Terry?"

"I'm ready if you are."

"All I'm ready for is to drop dead."

"Try not to do that until we've reached Malta, old chap," Smith said.

"Well if I do, so will you, chum!"

"That's what I'm afraid of," Smith said quietly.

As Stone walked into the galley, Smith was just finishing the bottle. Stone winced a little.

"I'm pretty sure if I did that right now I'd save Jerry the trouble of shooting me."

"You did rather overdo it last night, Jacko," Padshaw said, reaching for some tin mugs.

"How many?"

"Three..."

Stone answered: "It was bloody well worth it. That was the best blow-out we've had in months... did we say thanks, Terry?"

"In a manner of speaking," Padshaw said, pouring coffee.

Stone's face looked puzzled.

"None of you puked in the restaurant," Smith added.

"Very witty," Stone said, reaching for the rum.

Mike Ilman came in.

Stone topped up the three mugs with rum and gave them to him.

"Take these to Chris and Simon, Mike."

"Cheers, Skip."

Padshaw took another mug from the metal cupboard and filled it with coffee. As Stone sat down he passed it to him.

"Thanks... God, my head's got a bell in it."

"Rum?" Padshaw suggested half jokingly.

"No!"

"Must be bad," Smith said.

"I've had worse... at least I think I have."

"How long till we reach Malta?" Padshaw enquired.

Stone confided in his watch. They were cruising at around 200mph. "About another three hours. Providing we don't run into any trouble."

"From what I've heard this morning." Smith said, "when you run into trouble, you deal with it rather well."

"Nice of you to say so, but I'm hoping for a quiet trip."

"My information is that Malta's still getting quite a pasting, so don't hold your breath," Smith said seriously.

"Oh well, the way I feel right now, if I get hit, I won't feel a thing!"

Smith smiled grimly.

Stone took a couple of mouthfuls of coffee and grimaced slightly as he swallowed.

"Anything interesting?" he asked Padshaw, pointing at the sheaf of papers in front of him.

"A lot of contradictory waffle which I, more or less already knew, before we left. Not that I've finished reading it."

"Nothing new there then."

Stone turned his attention to Smith, his eyes asking the same question.

"Don't ask," Smith said politely, sounding exasperated.

"I'm glad I'm just a common pilot," Stone stated.

"So was I... once," Padshaw said ruefully.

There was a short silence.

"One thing I can tell you..." Smith said, looking at Stone.

"Yes?"

"I'm not getting off in Malta anymore."

Padshaw's head came up attentively.

"Really?" Padshaw said. "When did that change of mind come about?"

Smith picked up his bundle of papers and waved them for effect.

"About page bloody six," he replied, none too happy.

"So, where am I dropping you now?" asked Stone with a disgruntled voice.

"Alex, and by this evening if you'd be so kind." Smith gave a courteous bow of his head and motioned his right hand in a regal fashion.

Stone simply stared at him for a moment, finished his coffee and stood up.

Padshaw and Smith looked up at him.

"I'm a bus driver," Stone said, turning and then making his way out of the galley, "just a fucking bus driver!" He headed back to the cockpit, muttering to himself.

"I like him," Smith said comfortably.

"He does have a funny way of growing on you, doesn't he?"

Smith glanced at Padshaw and asked, "Any chance of another...?"

Padshaw pulled out the fresh bottle.

Kapitän Lieutenant Matthias Hoch's U-boat was one of the few, if not the only, U-boat in the Mediterranean theatre of the War to be equipped with the Fa 330.

The Fa 330 (Focke Achgelis) was basically a kite with rotor blades, which could be towed behind the U-boat and reach a height of about 400 feet. This gave him the advantage of sighting shipping up to twenty to twenty-five nautical miles away, whereas the captain of a U-boat would normally only have a line of sight of up to five or so nautical miles in calm conditions. The kite had been given the nickname *Bachstelze*, meaning 'Wagtail'.

He had never bothered to use it up until now, mainly because he realized when it had been delivered, that it would also be visible to the enemy and could easily give away his position, thereby endangering his boat. It was, in his opinion, a double-edged sword.

His decision to launch the Wagtail was born out of frustration. He had been very fortunate at the beginning of his patrol, when he happened upon three freighters with a light escort. He had made short work of two and made good his escape. Five days later, he and two other U-boats had tracked and intercepted a convoy of twelve ships. Hoch had expertly got into an excellent interception point and fired a spread of four torpedoes, three of which were direct hits on three different ships, two of which sank and one was crippled... later to be finished off by one of his colleagues. They shadowed the remainder of the convoy for a short time and later attacked again, but this time his torpedoes were wasted and he and the others had been lucky to escape unscathed. That was three days ago and he'd just received orders to return home. Time was short.

His fellow officers and crew had the highest respect for him. Hoch was known to be calculating and efficient by his superiors and had a high success rate. His crew knew him to be a hard but fair man. They knew he would always look after them to the best of his ability.

Hoch had been awarded the Iron Cross second class, the Iron Cross fist class and the Knight's Cross. He was proud of his boat and his crew. His awards, though good for moral, meant more to his family and friends than they did to him. He classed himself as an 'old school' naval officer and had very little time for political agendas. So long as he had his boat, his crew and some torpedoes, he was happy. Though a target would be nice!

Hoch had been at periscope depth for a minute or so before he made his decision. The sea had developed something of a swell, nothing too heavy, but enough to prevent him getting a good view of any possible targets.

"Spieler?"

"Kapitän?"

"We will surface and launch the *Bachstelze*!"

"*Jawohl, Herr Kapitän...* Surface!"

"Scholz?"

"Sir."

"Tell the *Bachstelze* pilot to get ready!"

"Sir."

"Hartmann?"

"Kapitän!"

"Detail the lookouts and alert the gun crews!"

"Yes Kapitän!"

As the U-boat broke the surface, the pilot was pulling on his gloves. He picked up his leather flying helmet and binoculars and made his way stoically forward. Some of the crew members patted his shoulder and wished him luck, most simply smiled grimly. It was a known fact that if the U-boat was spotted and had to dive, the kite would be cut loose and the pilot left to drown. It had happened before and it would happen again.

As the boat levelled out, the conning tower and aft hatch were thrown open. The lookouts immediately took up position and studied the surrounding horizon.

The crewmen climbing from the aft hatch stood just behind the conning tower, where the kite was stored in watertight compartments, waiting for orders to assemble it.

Kapitän Lieutenant Hoch looked up, drew his binoculars and scanned the horizon and the sky. Spieler looked at the apparently empty sky and horizon and then at his commanding officer.

Hoch lowered his glasses and rubbed his jaw firmly with his left hand, thoughtfully. The pilot stood behind him, patiently. Sea spray gently drifted passed them, occasionally hitting their faces.

Hoch stared at Spieler for a moment, he knew he was taking a risk in deciding to launch the *Bachstelze*, but he didn't like the idea of heading back to port with half his torpedoes left.

"As quickly as possible, Konrad!"

"Yes sir."

Spieler shouted at the men huddled behind the conning tower.

"As quick as you can, boys!"

They were well trained. The six of them had the kite assembled and ready to launch in just under fifteen minutes. One of the men checked that the telephone lead was properly attached at each end and nodded to the pilot who was walking towards them.

"All yours!" said a crewman.

The pilot nodded, got in and sat himself down. He quickly checked the controls and gave the thumbs up.

"Full ahead!" Hoch shouted.

His orders made their way through to the engine room and the clacking of the Man diesel engines resonated louder than ever.

Hoch was the commander of a formidable boat. Apart from the powerful Man engines, it was also fitted out with two supplementary six-cylinder diesel engines. His surface range was well over 23,000 nautical miles. He was armed with four bow tubes and two stern tubes with an arsenal of twenty-four torpedoes.

On top of that, his decks and conning tower boasted a four point one-inch cannon, accompanied by thirty-seven millimeter and twenty millimeter flak guns.

As the U-boat ploughed forward, one of the deck crew started the kite's rotor blades on their way with a swing of his arm. He immediately found himself ducking quickly as they caught in the rush of air.

The kite suddenly lifted off, the pilot was constantly correcting the pitch and yaw. At a hundred feet the pilot had it under control and the cable was let out.

"Fifty meters only!" Hoch ordered.

At just over 160 feet the *Bachstelze* stopped climbing and hung almost motionless in the sky. The pilot held the stick with one hand as he reached for his binoculars. He looked to his left and carefully scanned slowly to his right, being careful not to lose airflow to the rotor blades and keep a good flying attitude.

Hoch lit two cigarettes and passed one to Spieler. Spieler nodded and took along draw on it. Both he and Hoch were looking up at the unusual sight above.

As the pilot twisted round to his right he inadvertently let the kite turn with him, this turned out to be extremely fortunate. In the distance he could see a mass of ships. One of them, however, was only about four or so miles off and appeared to be heading straight for them. He shouted into the telephone.

"Destroyer astern! Five kilometers!"

Hoch dropped his cigarette and shouted orders.

"Get him down, Spieler. *Schnell!* And throw that bloody machine in the sea!"

"Yes sir."

The pilot saw the men below frantically winching him in. He was a little surprised, but nevertheless he would be eternally grateful. Had it been an air attack they would have definitely dumped him in the sea. Kapitän Lieutenant Hoch was still shouting orders.

"Clear the bridge! Prepare for silent running."

The *Bachstelze* hit the steel hull at a precarious angle and pieces of rotor blade flew harmlessly into the sea. The pilot was physically pulled from his machine and man handled down the aft hatch as the *Bachstelze* was being unceremoniously pushed over the side. One of the crewman produced a pair of bolt croppers.

"Get below Spieler!" Hoch ordered. He looked over the edge of the conning tower as Spieler went below. Hoch was looking at the crewman with the bolt croppers. He was now the only man on the deck. To anyone else it looked like the man was hesitating, but Hoch had realised why, he was waiting for the discarded *Bachstelze* to clear the propellers. As it drifted past the stern of the ship, sinking gently, he got to work. Hoch shouted down through the open conning tower hatch:

"Dive! Dive! Dive!"

He stood up and again looked at the man on the deck. He was fighting with the cable as the U-boat began to rapidly submerge.

"Come on man!" Hoch shouted earnestly.

There was a dull click as the cable snapped, the man didn't hesitate, he threw the bolt croppers to one side and threw himself headlong through the hatch. His legs hadn't quite finished going through when a pair of brawny hands came up and dragged him in. Another pair of hands slammed the hatch shut just as water started pouring in. Hoch did much the same. But feet first.

"Port ninety! Depth fifty! Silent running!" Spieler ordered as Hoch appeared.

"Get me the pilot, Spieler," Hoch said quickly.

"Sir."

Thirty seconds with the pilot was enough for Hoch to realise that he had a marvelous opportunity, so long as the destroyer didn't catch him! As the pilot was dismissed, he looked Hoch in the eyes with respect and said:

"*Dankeschön, mein Kapitän.*"

Hoch smiled and said, "Get yourself a coffee."

The pilot saluted and went to the galley.

Half an hour later, the destroyer had either given up or it hadn't actually seen them. Either way, Hoch wasn't going to do anything rash.

The pilot reckoned he'd seen at least twenty ships. Maybe he had, maybe he hadn't, but even if it were close to that number, Hoch knew he would need help to account for more than two or three of them. The destroyer had obviously been scouting and there was bound to be two or three more and probably a number of corvettes.

Hoch also knew that there were at least eight other U-boats operating in the area. He needed to confirm the number of enemy ships and then make contact with them, as quickly as possible. First, however, he had to make sure he'd lost the destroyer. He would give it another ten minutes and if all was clear, he'd surface.

Chapter 13

Two hours later, despite the constant rumble of the Sunderland's engines and the occasional rattle of tin mugs and plates as various crew members ate and drank, both Padshaw and Smith had managed to doze off. They had been offered the use of any of the available bunks but had declined. Their slumber was rudely interrupted by the shattering bangs of four successive explosions that seemed to come from inside the Sunderland itself.

Padshaw was momentarily shocked, he'd been dreaming about his favourite pub, the Cat and Custard Pot and a barmaid he'd had his eye on when he was a pilot officer.

The skin on Padshaw's face was taut, he was temporarily lost as to what was going on, then reality returned and was driven home by another shell burst. His head jerked in the direction of Smith.

"I'd say duck, if I thought it would do any good." Smith said phlegmatically.

Padshaw gathered his wits. "Not again!" he shouted, his ears recovering.

"Does this happen often?" Smith asked in the same matter-of-fact voice, though his posture was slightly curled in defense of what was happening outside the airplane.

"What's happening?" Padshaw asked in a composed voice to Dean Parlow, who was looking decidedly pissed off.

"The Royal Navy!" Parlow replied.

Parlow saw the confused look on Padshaw's face.

"Well..." Parlow continued, "either we've got the flare colours of the day wrong, or they're blind, or they just hate airplanes!"

"Just another cock-up!" Smith said resignedly.

Padshaw glanced out of one of the galley windows at the sea below. He could see nothing.

The Sunderland shook again. A black cloudburst erupted in front of Padshaw's eyes, then a bang that made his ears ring. He turned to face Parlow again. Parlow shouted.

"The skipper's dealing with it!"

As he spoke, the Sunderland's four Pegasus engines magnified in noise and Padshaw felt the nose lift as it clawed for height.

"Are they blind?" Stone shouted indignantly at Pither as they pulled back on their respective wheels, the engines roaring.

"I don't know Skipper! But they've definitely got the twitch!"

Stone glanced at Pither, he saw his new co-pilot in a different light. In but a few seconds, he recognised a pilot who wasn't flustered easily, and took what was thrown at him in his stride. For no particular reason, Stone had implicit faith in a man he'd known but for a few hours.

"We'll climb for 500 feet and fire the yellows again," Stone shouted at James.

"OK Skip."

"I bet you'd rather be back in 'Gib' right now, eh?" Stone asked, looking at his co-pilot with the smile of a Cheshire cat across his face.

Pither, pulling hard on his control wheel looked across at Stone and, staring hard at him, shouted:

"With all due respect, Skipper. Fuck off!"

Stone smiled broadly and shouted back:

"Just a joke you pommie bastard!"

"I know that you Australian git!"

Shells burst in front of the cockpit. Pither shouted:

207

"Let's drop some bombs on the buggers!"

Stone's face was smiling and relaxed and he replied loudly:

"Are you sure you're not Australian?"

"You don't have to be Australian to be pissed off!"

Suddenly the sky was clear again.

"They're signalling, Skipper!" Lipman shouted.

"Oh, yeah! Would they like us to fly in a straight line to make it easier for them?"

Lipman ignored the sarcasm and replied:

"Actually, they're apologising and asking if we're OK."

"That's nice," Stone said, "ask them if they'd like us to strafe them as a good will gesture!"

Padshaw leant forward between Stone and Pither, Stone looked at Padshaw. Padshaw said nothing. Stone took a deep breath and said:

"Tell 'em we're OK... and tell 'em their gunners need a good kick up the arse."

"My sentiments exactly," Padshaw said agreeably.

Stone levelled out. Padshaw looked out of the port side of the cockpit down at the convoy. There were an awful lot of ships, but he wasn't counting.

"They've got a bloody nerve!" Lipman shouted.

Stone looked over his shoulder as Lipman approached him.

"What's up, Don?" Stone asked.

"Well, first they try to shoot us down, and now they want our help to locate a possible u-boat...bloody nerve of the bastards!" Lipman's face broke into a mischievous grin.

Stone glanced at Padshaw.

"Can't pass this up, Terry."

"I would have been surprised if you did," Padshaw replied indifferently.

"Ask 'em if they've got a possible position for us to work from, Don."

"I'm on it, Skipper," Lipman replied and returned to his set.

Padshaw stared at the convoy for a few moments and then said:

"I'll go and tell Smith we're going to be a little... delayed." He turned and made his way back to the galley, knowing full well Smith would not be happy with a possible delay to his schedule.

"Looks like we might get a chance to try out our nice shiny new depth charges after all," Lipman said as he passed Stone a piece of paper. "This is the position passed to the convoy by a destroyer scouting ahead of the convoy, Skip. Looks like they're heading straight for it."

"Right," Stone said. "We'll get down to a thousand feet and see what we can find."

Stone pushed forward on the controls, Pither matched his movements like a shadow as the Sunderland made its descent. Stone glanced at him.

"I have flown one of these before you know," Stone said with gentle sarcasm.

"No offence," Pither replied, "but if you get hit... I'm ready!"

Stone grunted in reply.

At a thousand feet Stone levelled out and began his search. Fifteen minutes passed, although it felt longer and they saw nothing. Another five long minutes went by.

Don Lipman was engrossed in studying the ASV (Anti Surface Vessel) MKII Radar. He and Pelt were taking turns.

"Is that magic box working or what?" Stone asked impatiently.

"It can't see something that's not there, Skipper! And you know as well as I do it's temperamental at the best of times."

Much like you! Lipman thought to himself.

Another ten minutes passed and still they sighted nothing. Lipman was in regular contact with the convoy below, who, understandably, were getting more and more concerned as time dragged on.

Stone was a mile or so ahead of the convoy when he announced to Pither he was going to turn to cover a different area.

"I reckon we're in the right spot, Skipper," Pither said confidently.

"What gives you that idea?"

"Well... I reckon that if that destroyer did see a U-boat, the chances are that the U-boat saw him and, maybe the convoy, at the same time. So he dived damn quick. There's a lot of ships down there and I think he'll wait for them to come to him or, maybe, he'll surface and use his communications system to try and get some help!"

Stone thought for a moment. Josh Pelt came forward with two mugs of coffee.

"Thanks," Stone said.

"Cheers," Pither took a mug.

"How's Chris' hangover?" Stone asked.

"He's fine, Skipper. At least that's what he keeps telling me."

"Rear gunner here! Periscope breaking the surface astern."

Both Pither and Stone passed their mugs quickly back to Pelt.

"You were right!" Stone said excitedly to Pither.

"Bloody well done! Don? Contact the convoy...tell them we've found the bugger! Give them our position and tell them we're going to attack."

"Roger!"

"Josh?"

"Skipper?"

"Get dean to help you 'bomb up'!"

Pelt quickly made his way back to the galley. Sunderlands were unusual inasmuch as all mines, bombs and depth charges they carried were actually stored inside the fuselage. They were then winched up and attached to racks which would then themselves be winched, through doors in the fuselage, to the underside of the wings from where they could be dropped.

Pelt reached the galley.

"We heard," Parlow said putting his plate down.

Padshaw stood up.

"Can I help?" he asked.

"Thanks very much, sir," Pelt replied courteously.

"See you later," he said to Smith as he left.

Smith nodded. Despite his reservations in the delay, he found himself wanting to be more involved in what was going on.

Stone was making a gentle turn to the right and then flying some considerable distance away from the U-boat, giving Pelt time to 'bomb up', and hopefully bringing him into a position where he would have a full view of the port side of the U-boat as it surfaced... if it surfaced.

At the same time, he was being updated with the U-boat's position by Sullivan in the tail and Hardcastle in the top turret.

"Conning tower's visible, Skipper. She's coming right up by the look of it!" Hardcastle announced.

Stone shouted into the intercom, "You ready, Josh?"

"Almost there, Skipper!"

Sullivan was staring into the distance at the vague shapes of navy ships approaching.

"Looks like the navy wants some fun too, Skipper!" he shouted over the intercom.

"Not before we've had ours they're not!" Stone stated emphatically.

"Winching out now, Skipper," Parlow said enthusiastically, "and Josh is on his way back!"

"Roger that! What's the navy got to say, Don?"

"They want the bastard sunk before he tells his chums, and there's a destroyer and two corvettes coming to assist *us*!"

211

Pither stared at Stone wide eyed and said, "That's very civilized of them!"

Stone too was a little taken aback. All the navy types he'd met up until now were stuffed shirts. His reply expressed this.

"Tell them we'll keep them occupied as long as we can Don!"

Lipman raised his eyebrow a little and passed on the message.

"I'm here Skipper!" Pelt said as he took up his engineer's position.

"Roger." With that Stone opened up the Pegasus engines into the red. Pelt's shoulders slumped and he looked to the sky in disgust as Stone thrashed his engines.

Stone's approach was bringing him into position to make a perfect beam attack on the surfacing U-boat's port side.

Chapter 14

Kapitän Lieutenant Hoch gave the order.

"Spieler, periscope depth!"

"Kapitän."

Spieler repeated the order and the U-boat began to rise.

"Gun crews first, lookouts second," Hoch instructed.

"Gun crews to positions," Spieler ordered.

The gun crews assembled themselves on and around the ladder leading to the conning hatch and the aft and bow hatches.

Hoch was ready at the periscope. As his boat settled, he raised it and did a full 360 degrees. Nothing in sight. He nodded affirmatively at Spieler.

"Surface!" Spieler ordered.

The U-boat came up very quickly, even before it was on an even keel the gun crews were climbing out.

U-boat gun crews were very well trained, and Hoch's gunners were acknowledged as some of the best.

As the second man climbed out he was instinctively looking at the sky, in the distance he saw the Sunderland approaching.

"Alarm! Sunderland on the port side!"

Hoch knew, as did the gunners, that he did not have time to dive. They were already making the guns ready, before Hoch reached the conning tower. The guns swung round to engage the flying boat, which was closing fast. Hoch ordered his lookouts to concentrate on the surrounding sea, he then turned his attention to the approaching aircraft as Spieler came to his side.

"Bad luck!" Spieler said with undisguised frustration.

"Understatement!" Hoch replied. "Open fire!"

The gap between the Sunderland and the U-boat closed.

Stone had briefed his gunners to open fire as soon as the U-boat was in range and to continue shooting as they flew away. Stone held the U-boat in his sights. His approach was perfect; his speed was spot on. His concentration now was solely aimed at when to release the bombs. He was talking to himself just as much as he was to his co-pilot.

"Steady... steady... nearly there... bombs gone!"

A sky full of accurate flak poured from the U-boat, pieces of the fuselage behind Lipman's gun exploded into fragments hitting the cockpit. Stone instinctively pulled back on the control wheel just as the bombs were released.

"Fuck me!" Stone shouted. "Break right!"

Pither followed Stone's lead on the controls. The bombs straddled the U-boat but caused no damage.

As water cascaded down around them and the odd round of tracer bounced of the hull, Hoch and Spieler watched the Sunderland fly off to their left, hounded by flak.

As Hoch watched the Sunderland pull away, he assumed that it was going to attack again, but he reckoned he'd now got time to dive. Besides, the Sunderland would alert the convoy and its escort as to his position, he was no longer the hunter.

"Clear the deck, Spieler! We are going to crash dive."

"Yes, Kapitän."

Had Hoch known he had more time than he thought he had, would have made no difference to his decision.

Aboard the Sunderland however, Stone was frustrated by the short delay, seconds could be vital. Parlow, assisted by James and Padshaw, were only just winching out the experimental charges. The delay had been caused by the simple disappearance of a crowbar to open the crates.

"All ready, Skipper!" Parlow shouted into the intercom.

"About bloody time! Where's the bastard now, Mike?"

Conning tower dead ahead skipper! About one thousand yards... He's almost under!"

"Down one hundred!" Spieler reported. "Hard to starboard."

Hoch was the most composed man on the boat. He was handing out orders as if it were an exercise. He noticed Scholz looking a little unnerved.

"Scholz!"

"Kapitän?"

"Get me a coffee," Hoch said politely.

"Charges gone!"

Stone pulled up and to the right and started to circle so as to get a view. A few seconds passed and the four charges exploded almost simultaneously. Tall fountains of frothing water leapt out of the sea like erupting volcanoes.

"Bugger me Skipper!" Parlow said, "They work!"

Stone looked down at the still foaming sea.

"Message from the destroyer captain, Skipper," Lipman announced. "They'll be about five minutes."

"Wilco... tell 'em we'll circle until they get here." Stone, looking down at the now settling sea, saw a dark mass getting bigger and bigger on the surface... oil!

"And tell 'em I think we got the bugger!"

Pither looked down at the oil slick and smiled.

"Well done Skipper!"

Padshaw was also looking down at the ever increasing oil slick. He smiled back at the other crew members who were grinning happily, but made no comment. His cousin was a submarine captain, and Padshaw knew him to be a sneaky, devious, cunning bastard! Inwardly, he very much doubted whether they had even scratched the paint...

The U-boat shook violently as the first charge exploded, a split second later the other three exploded with such force that the U-boat was tossed side to side like a toy. The inside of the boat was thrown into darkness. Spieler could hear that the tone of the engines had changed.

"Emergency lights!" Hoch shouted. "Get me a damage report, Spieler!"

Spieler didn't even reply. He made his way towards the engine room asking after damage reports and injuries.

Scholz found himself standing in front of his commanding officer holding what was, now, half a mug of well-shaken frothy coffee. The rest was all over his arm and chest.

"Kapitän," he said nervously as his shaking hand passed Hoch the mug. Hoch looked at the bubbles subsiding in the mug and said:

"I wouldn't tell the crew you know how to make coffee Italian style. They'll all want some." Hoch smiled broadly and took the mug. Scholz visibly relaxed, a nervous smile came over his face.

A few minutes later Spieler returned.

"Kapitän? We've lost a lot of diesel oil but we still have enough to make port. And the chief engineer reports he can only give us four knots. He's working on the engines now."

"That's still good. Injuries?"

"One broken arm and two concussions, sir. Also sonar reports a ship quite close but moving away from us."

"Thank you Spieler. Maintain silent running."

"Sir."

Kapitän Lieutenant Hoch and his crew were going home.

Chapter 15

The four Kittyhawks were at two thousand feet, the Hurricanes were 500 feet above them and slightly behind. The rendezvous time had been and gone and Marsland was getting a little impatient. He was also uncomfortable with the thought of having to hang around waiting for the transport aircraft which may not even have taken off. On the other hand, he was even more concerned that the moment he decided to return to the landing ground, the bloody thing would appear, closely followed by a flock of Japanese fighters.

"Bollocks!" he said to himself. He checked his position for the third time... spot on. He would give it another five minutes.

Ten minutes later he really had had enough.

"Red and Green sections, time to go home. Turn port and regroup at fifteen hundred feet. Turning port... go!"

As Red section turned, Hacker and Vine flew on a little further and then followed in a wide curve. Dropping their port wings and letting their aircraft shed height, they slotted in neatly behind Red section.

'Waste of bloody time, that was,' Hacker thought to himself.

Five minutes had passed when Cracken, flying at Red two, glimpsed movement on the ground.

"Red leader! On the ground! Ten o'clock!"

Marsland stared down, he could see a small pall of smoke and men making their way across open ground from left to right. He couldn't be expected to identify them from this distance, but he'd been in similar situations before and he knew exactly what to do.

"Green section! You're top cover! Orbit at fifteen hundred!"

"Roger."

"Right, Red section! Stay 800 yards behind me. Give yourselves 200 yards between aircraft and wait for confirmation to fire. Line astern... going down now!"

Marsland put his nose down, opened the throttle and pulled away from Red section. Cracken waited a few moments and then followed his leader. Hillman at Red three and Parish at Red four left it a couple of seconds each before diving after them.

Marsland's plan was simple: with the distance between himself and Red section, he had time to identify the troops on the ground and then brief his pilots. They in turn had time to get in a good strafe or simply pull away.

Marsland was almost on them. He could see some men running from left to right, some of them were falling, others were crawling on their stomachs. A small burst of flame caught his eye on the right-hand side, a cloud of smoke followed. Then he saw the unmistakable shape of a Willis jeep disappearing into the smoke.

Marsland shouted into the RT:

"Jap troops attacking from the left! Look out for our chaps on the right!

"Roger that leader! Tally-ho Red section!"

Burns had his foot on the floor, he could hear the fizz of bullets and the sharp crack of rifle fire. Connors twisted round to see what was happening. The truck directly behind was bouncing violently; he could see the driver fighting with the steering wheel trying to keep it on the track. A machine gun opened up and Connors saw the truck's front left wheel shred itself: it careered of the track and came to a stop so suddenly that the driver's mate flew through the windscreen like a rag doll.

Connors could now see the second truck returning fire. As he turned to look forward again, the track ahead erupted in flame. Burns had no chance to avoid the crater left by the exploding shell, a truck might have weathered it, but the jeep's smaller wheels dropped into the crater and buckled in opposite directions. Burns was flung against the steering wheel, knocking the wind out of him and leaving him semi-conscious. Connors had realised what was going to happen and had launched himself from the jeep, landing upside down in the undergrowth lining the steep bank.

Blackman, meanwhile, hadn't broken cover when the Japanese opened fire and had ordered Naylor to pull up. He had ordered Naylor and the two men in the back to follow him.

"Get yourself into some good cover, only shoot if you have a clear target! Don't waste ammo!"

"Right sir!" Naylor replied.

"I'm going forward." There was a loud explosion above the sound of the gunfire.

Hearing it, Blackman ran like the wind. The last truck wasn't moving, but he could see the men in it sporadically returning fire. He had almost reached it when their fire intensified, he looked to his left; at least a dozen Japanese soldiers burst into the open. Several of them were armed with machine guns and were firing from the hip as they ran. Two of the men in the truck were cut down.

Blackman shouted at the others.

"Get behind the truck and return fire!"

As they jumped down, Blackman ran on. The third truck was also stationary. Bullets cracked as they hit the trees to Blackman's right. A couple of stray rounds whipped up the mud in front of his feet. He hurled himself to the ground beside the truck. 'Jesus Christ!' he said to himself aloud. "Why aren't we moving?" he shouted angrily at one of the men beside the truck who was reloading.

"Can't sir!" he pointed ahead.

Blackman looked down the trail. 'Buggeration!' He pushed himself up and bolted. As he came into the open, various Japanese tried in vain to pick him off. The second truck was tucked up close to the disabled leading truck as Blackman ran up to them. Sergeant Bell, efficient as ever, had all the men behind the trucks and was methodically giving out orders.

"Whealer! Murdoch! Lane! Concentrate your fire to the right of their formation! The rest of you aim for the middle of them!"

Blackman knelt beside him.

"Well done Sergeant," Blackman gasped as he got his breath back. Bell and Blackman jerked their heads as a bullet ricocheted off the chassis of the truck. "I've got Naylor and two men back there who will be firing on their left as they approach–"

"Was that a mortar I heard just now?" Blackman asked.

"I may be wrong, but I think it might be a tank, sir."

Blackman looked at the trees.

"I bloody hope not!"

"Sir?" Bell said, gently gesturing towards the back of Connors' jeep.

Blackman's heart was suddenly in his mouth. He could see Burns' motionless body but no sign of Connors.

"I can't see the Major!" Blackman said.

"He may have been thrown out," Bell replied. The distance between the first truck and the jeep was about twenty yards.

Blackman studied the area surrounding the jeep. He glanced at Sergeant Bell. Bell read his mind and, raising his rifle at the same time, he shouted:

"Covering fire!"

Blackman was up and running. Bell and the others each fired five rounds rapid. Blackman threw himself behind the right side of the jeep. Lying on his belly he tried to see where Connors had ended up. He couldn't see any sign of him.

"Buggeration!" he said to himself loudly.

"Idiot," Connors said gently.

Connors was still lying upside down on the bank where he had landed, entangled in small roots and greenery. His upturned head was only four feet from Blackman's.

"Jesus Don, you scared the shit out of me!"

Several rounds slammed into the side of the jeep.

"Are you hit?" Blackman asked.

"Just a busted arm. Give me a hand."

Connors stretched out his right arm and Blackman pulled him down beside him. Connors shifted himself around so as he could see Burns. He looked at Blackman.

"Burns?"

"Dunno."

"How many of them do you reckon?"

They were both now looking at the trees.

"A dozen, maybe more... and maybe a tank!"

"Shit!"

Connors thought for a moment. He could see that the oncoming Japanese had been whittled down to seven or eight men who were now lying flat and laying down accurate fire on the trucks.

"Right Blackie. Tell Sergeant Bell to–"

Connors was cut short. Twenty or more Japanese emerged from the treeline shouting and shooting at the same time. The officer leading them drew his sword, he was gesturing with his left arm to advance.

Blackman leaned into the jeep and grabbed Burns' rifle, Connors pulled out his Webley revolver.

"This is getting a bit sticky, Don!"

"You're telling me!"

Connors looked to his left. Sergeant Bell looked at him and then turned to face the oncoming troops. Connors then stood up so his men could see him, Blackman leant over the spare wheel on the back of the jeep and picked out a target.

"Sergeant Bell!" Connors shouted.

Bell looked across at his CO. Connors had a big smile on his face. Bell knew this wasn't going to go their way.

"Sir?"

"Rapid fire if you please!"

The roar of an Allison engine almost drowned him out.

Connors looked up to see the Kittyhawk flying away. Sergeant Bell and his men were blazing away but they were off the mark. The Japanese were only sixty or so yards away now. Blackman loosed of a couple of rounds and, glancing at the fading silhouette of the Kittyhawk, said:

"He'll never get back in time Don!"

Just as the words left Blackman's mouth, the ground in front of them seemed to erupt as furrowed lines appeared from left to right, churning up huge clods of mud. The bodies of Japanese troops could be seen jerking violently as limbs were torn away, their weapons still clutched by dismembered arms. More furrows, more slaughter.

Connors and Blackman were agape. Again the sound of heavy calibre machine guns filled their ears as a second Kittyhawk left its mark.

"Talk about the nick of time!" Blackman shouted.

Connors was about to reply when yet a third Kittyhawk swooped in, guns blazing. Blackman was grinning with an overwhelming feeling of relief. He and Connors watched as it pulled away. Several of the Japanese ran towards the far corner of the open plain, their officer included. Sergeant Bell raised his rifle, aimed and fired. One of them fell minus the top of his head. The remaining Japanese turned, knelt down and began to return fire. Their officer was shaking his fist and apparently shouting at the trees.

Unbeknown to *both* Connors and the Japanese officer the tank Commander had, as he had anticipated, been unable to get a line of fire which wasn't hindered by trees. On ordering his driver to advance, the engine had stalled, thus leaving the ground troops committed to their attack without armoured support. His commanding officer was hysterical with anger. He had lost face. The Mitsubishi diesel engine suddenly roared into life. The officer stopped shaking his fist and pointed towards the British column. The tank moved forward slowly, it slipped and slid on the sodden ground. As it came into the open, the thirty-seven millimeter fired again.

Hacker momentarily looked down at the carnage below. He then looked up and continued scanning the sky. Vine too glanced down. He had never seen a strafe before and part of him was horrified. Hacker had completed one circuit of the clearing, just as Red section were engaged in their strafe.

Red section were re-grouping just as Hacker was finishing his second circuit, looking down again just in time to see a shell burst. He stared at the open ground searching for the cause. He didn't have to wait long. The type 95 appeared as if from nowhere, a small group of Japanese troops following in its wake. Marsland opened his mouth to alert green section but Hacker was already on the ball:

"Green two! The Japs have got a tank! Keep 200 yards behind me, got that?"

"Roger leader."

Hacker shoved the stick forward and opened the throttle. As he followed his leader down, Vine was suddenly filled with a feeling of trepidation and excitement all at the same time.

As the Hurricanes closed up the gap to their target, Marsland was wheeling Red section around for another strafe. Marsland knew it was down to Green section, with their cannon, to take out the tank, but he was going to make damn sure he mopped up the remaining Japanese troops. Hacker could hear his CO as he manoeuvered himself and Vine onto a good angle for their attack.

"Red leader here. Line abreast Red section! Formate on my port side by number. Go!"

Hacker concentrated on his target, the type 95 tank was now head on to him. At 800 yards Hacker opened fire. His four twenty millimeter Hispano cannon thumped out their tune.

The ground to the side of the third truck in the column exploded with sudden ferocity, ripping away part of its side and sending a body spinning into the air. Connors shouted at Bell:

"Get the men to fall back into the trees!"

Bell turned, shouting out orders. One of his men was trying to help a badly wounded man stand, Bell grabbed his arm and pulled him away.

"Leave him! You men! Fall back to the far end. Naylor, covering fire!"

Naylor and his men started blasting away as the others crawled and ran towards their position. The seven point seven millimeter frontal machine gun from the type 95 opened up. It was short of its target... but not by much.

"We need a bloody miracle now, Don!" Blackman said.

Connors, watching Sergeant Bell directing the men back the way they had come, glimpsed the outline of the two Hurricanes. Connors pointed up, but couldn't get the words out before the fast repetitive whop of multiple cannon fire filled the air.

For Connors, the sight of the two Hurricanes coming in to attack was something he would never forget. One moment he was visualising the death of his men, then, from the sky... salvation!

Cannon shells ripped the earth apart and then hammered into the type 95's frontal armour. At only fourteen millimeters thick, the twenty-millimeter shells tore into it as if it were cardboard.

As Hacker pulled up, Vine began firing. Just as his first shells reached their target the tank erupted in a ball of flame, tossing the turret to one side. Then the auxiliary fuel tanks strapped to its side threw up a wall of flame which enveloped him. For a split second he was terrified, but he was out of it as quick as he was in.

"Green two. You all right?"

"OK leader." Vine was a little shaken but more composed than he had ever been. "Might need a bit of paint here and there, though."

Hacker smiled to himself.

As Red section swept in and wiped out the remaining Japanese; Blackman, watching them fly past, turned to Connors and said, almost seriously:

"I'm going to start going to church."

"I hope you're not Catholic."

"Why?" Blackman said, puzzled.

"Because you'd have to go to confession first... and that could take weeks! Sergeant Bell?"

Chapter 16

"What have you got?" Beecham asked, sitting at his desk. Hawkins, clutching various files, pulled out several pieces of paper. Beecham waved Hawkins to sit.

"Thank you, sir. Well sir, it would appear that the extra drop tanks for both types of aircraft are en route, as are bombs and ammunition. I believe that by the time Squadron Leader Padshaw arrives, everything should be in place."

"Mmm..."

"Is there a problem, sir?"

"Not so much a problem... more an unexpected turn of events."

Hawkins' face asked for more.

"I've just received information that the Fourteenth India Division is advancing south as we speak... or trying to."

"I thought—"

"So did I. Maybe they got fed up with waiting, either way, there's not much we can do about it now!"

"What about Squadron Leader Padshaw's briefing sir, and his list of targets?"

"The targets and... some of his briefing still stand."

"Do you still require him to fulfill his role as intelligence officer?"

"I have something far more important for the Squadron Leader's talents."

"I'll try to make contact with him as soon—"

"That won't be necessary," Beecham interrupted.

Hawkins was something at a loss. He opened his mouth to speak.

"The Squadron Leader's new orders will be waiting for him in India," Beecham stated, "in the meantime you are to continue updating this office with information on supplies and operational conditions."

Hawkins hesitated before replying:

"Right sir."

"That will be all for now."

"Yes sir."

Hawkins stood up and left the office. As he walked towards the exit at the end of the corridor, he was wondering just what did Beecham have in mind for Padshaw? And how long ago had it been planned?

Chapter 17

Back at the landing ground, the Squadron had been surprised by the arrival of several trucks with supplies.

"We weren't expecting you," Hollingsworth said politely, standing by the front of the first truck.

"Actually...we got lost sir," the lieutenant replied sheepishly.

Hollingsworth raised his eyebrows.

"Well... not so much lost as separated," he added.

Valentine appeared smiling and said in a jaunty manner:

"We call it 'temporarily unaware of one's position'."

"Yes sir," the lieutenant said quietly.

"Guess what, Adj?" Valentine asked still smiling.

"What?"

"They've got drop tanks, and ammunition, and lots of other presents."

The lieutenant stared at Valentine, he didn't know quite what to make of him.

"I'm supposed to deliver all the supplies to Chittagong, sir."

"Well you've overshot somewhat, haven't you?" Hollingsworth replied.

"Yes sir," the lieutenant looked to his left to see various ground crew unloading his trucks.

"Sir. I really don't think—"

"Don't worry about thinking," Valentine interrupted, "we'll do all that for you."

"But sir..."

'Punchy' Jennings appeared. He was quite excited.

"What have you found 'Punchy'?" the adjutant asked.

"Tool kits, sir... for the Hurricanes!"

"Excellent," said Valentine.

"And..." Jennings teased, "Fuel! Bucket loads!"

The lieutenant was getting agitated.

"This is terribly irregular..."

Valentine put his arm round the lieutenant and placed his hand firmly on his shoulder.

"Well irregular is something we're very good at, here." Valentine winked at Hollingsworth and started to steer the unfortunate man towards the mess hut. "In fact I was born irregular. I remember my father saying to me when I was six, "'You look irregular.' It was much the same at school..."

"Poor bastard," Jennings said as he watched them walk away.

"Right 'Punchy'," Hollingsworth said firmly, "'Snobby' will keep him occupied for hours." The Adjutant glanced at Valentine steering his victim away.

"Let's get on with it."

Apart from the four pilots at readiness and the required ground crew, all the others mucked in to unload the trucks. Just over an hour later, Hollingsworth and Jennings were totting up their ill gotten goods.

"Just like Christmas!" Jennings said cheerfully.

"No ammunition for the Kittyhawks though," Hollingsworth commented.

"Well, it wasn't meant for us in the first place, was it?"

"Mmm..." The Adjutant was thoughtful.

"Penny for your thoughts?"

"I was just thinking... somebody's got to sign for all this."

"Commanding officer's job in my opinion," 'Punchy' said flippantly.

"He's not going to be happy signing for this lot!"

"Well, to my way of thinking... at the moment, 'Snobby's' the commanding officer, isn't he?" Jennings' face was a picture of innocence.

Hollingsworth brightened up and stared at Jennings.

"Get over to the mess. I'll get this typed up and meet you there."

'Punchy' wandered off towards the mess, whistling.

Twenty minutes later, Hollingsworth walked into the mess. Valentine was still talking to the lieutenant, who looked as if he was contemplating suicide. Jennings had his arms folded on a makeshift table supporting his head.

"And then," Valentine was saying, "I was posted to India! Now that really was irregular–"

"Ahem!" Hollingsworth ventured.

"Yes, Adj?"

"We're all done. Just need to get this signed up and the lieutenant can be on his way."

"Jolly good," Valentine replied jovially.

Valentine signed several pieces of paper with a flourish. The lieutenant pulled out some forms as well and offered them to Valentine, at the same time he opened his mouth to speak – not a hope!

"No problem," Valentine signed them without even looking. "Got to keep everything in order, eh?"

"Yes sir," the lieutenant mumbled. Maybe his day would get better... maybe the Japs would kill him, he thought to himself.

Hollingsworth and Jennings glanced at each other. Valentine hated signing for anything, he was worse than the Co, and they knew it. The adjutant bent over and whispered in Jennings' ear.

"What's come over him?"

Jennings shrugged his shoulders. Valentine put all the paperwork together, folded it neatly and passed them to the mentally numbed lieutenant.

"Perhaps you'd like to stay on a bit longer?" Valentine suggested smiling. "I mean, you've had a long enough trip already."

"NO! No, sir. We really ought to try to get to Chittagong."

"Oh well, as you wish. Thanks for dropping in."

They all stood up and trooped out to the trucks, the lieutenant leading. As they watched him drive away the adjutant said:

"Well done 'Snobby'!"

"Here to help, old boy. Here to help." Valentine wandered off.

Both Jennings and Hollingsworth were frowning at each other. Maybe Valentine wasn't feeling very well, the heat maybe?

It wasn't until the lieutenant reached Chittagong that he found out that Valentine had signed his name *Benito Mussolini*.

The roar of aero engines filled the air. One by one Red section, followed by Green, hedged over the tree line and 'beat up' the airfield.

"Looks like the boys have had some fun!" Hollingsworth said.

Half an hour later the adjutant, sitting on a box, was taking each pilots' report on the afternoon events outside his office. With him sat Marsland and Valentine. All the others were sitting on the ground cross-legged or lying on their sides supported by one elbow, a couple of cigarettes were being passed around.

The pilots, Hollingsworth noticed, were quite reserved in detailing the day's action, they were quite 'matter of fact' in their manner. The adjutant could vividly recall the excitement of pilots returning from air combat sorties in England who would be falling all over one another to get their version out first. But then again, he knew full well that ground strafing did not hold the same professional status to a fighter pilot as air-to-air combat.

As Hollingsworth finished taking his notes he said:

"Well all I can say chaps, is: bloody good show!"

Some nodded, some half smiled.

"OK chaps." Marsland said, "see you in the mess later... well done!"

As the pilots got up and wandered off, Hacker lay fully on his back and then propped himself up on both elbows. Marsland looked at him full on.

"You did a damn good job on that tank, today."

"Thank you, sir."

Marsland gave Hacker a respectful nod.

"You seem to have had an unusual few hours yourself Adj," Marsland said, turning his attention to Hollingsworth.

"Supply train, sir. Fuel, spares, tools, drop tanks and some tinned grub. Most welcome... and overdue, as you are well aware sir."

"All signed for?"

"Flight Lieutenant Valentine jumped into the breach there, sir."

Marsland paused for a moment, turned to face Valentine and said, skeptically:

"You... signed... official... documents?"

"I was acting CO. You know me... mustn't shirk one's responsibilities!"

"I see..." Marsland said, not the least bit convinced, "so we have plenty of ammo for the Kittyhawks but not for the Hurricanes!"

"Actually we've–" The Adjutant was cut short as 'Punchy' Jennings came up to them.

"We've got more cannon shells than we can count." Jennings stopped short as he saw the 'have we really?' look on the CO's face.

"...Ah!" Jennings said sheepishly, realising the CO hadn't been fully informed. "My wife told me my timing was bad... the result is twins... I guess she was right."

232

"Were those cannon shells I signed for?" Valentine asked Jennings indignantly, with a broad bright grin on his face.

"You know damn well they were!" Jennings snapped, biting hard on Valentine's bait.

"All right," Marsland interrupted genially, "I think we all know what's going on. No doubt there'll be merry hell to pay with some store's wallah somewhere down the line. Meantime, we've got seven fully operational Hurricanes that we didn't have a few days ago, which is more important than some pissed off pen-pusher! How many kittys have I got, 'Punchy'?"

"Ten sir. Dick Chalmers' Kitty isn't repaired yet."

"Fair enough."

"Excuse me, sir?" Neane, the radio operator had just walked round the corner of the hut.

"Yes Neane?"

"I've just received confirmation that a Lysander is going to try and reach us in the next couple of days sir –" Marsland's face was blank "– to collect Mr Verster, sir!" Neane added. Marsland looked at Hollingsworth.

"There's nothing we can do for him here, sir. Not with his injuries," the adjutant said softly.

"No... I guess not." Marsland looked at Neane.

"Anything else?"

"Not at the moment, sir."

"All right. Carry on."

"Sir."

Valentine and Hollingsworth glanced at each other.

Marsland looked to be deep in thought. Verster was one of the few pilots left who had served with Marsland since his posting to the Far East.

"The Doc arranged to ship him back to the base hospital as soon as was possible," Valentine said.

"Absolutely... best place for him," Marsland agreed thoughtfully.

There was a short silence.

It was Jennings who brought the conversation back to business.

"If they're sending a Lysander to pick up Verster, perhaps they could bring in some extra kit for the new boys?"

"Holly!" Marsland said.

"Right you are sir." Hollingsworth immediately made off after Neane.

"There's quite a lot of space in those things, isn't there?" Valentine said suggestively. "Maybe they can bring in some booze?"

"Find out if the Doc wants anything," Marsland said to Jennings.

"Yes sir."

Valentine looked at Marsland in mock disgust.

"You really must get your priorities in order, you know."

Marsland looked at him in the same manner as a headmaster would to a petulant child.

Hacker, still lying on the ground, looked at Valentine and simply shook his head.

In all fact, the Westland Lysander was ideally suited to the collection and delivery of both individual personnel and small quantities of varying supplies. It could take off and land in relatively confined areas, and, with long range tanks, it could cover a considerable distance. Designed for liaison/reconnaissance duties, it had proved itself more than once to be very formidable in the dropping of allied spies in France and other occupied countries. Its main drawback was its vulnerability to interception by enemy aircraft, its top speed was only just over 200 miles per hour, but its stalling speed of only 65 miles per hour made it ideal for when short take-offs and landings were required. For those operating in jungle conditions, it proved to be something of a godsend.

A hundred miles out from Malta, Stone and his crew were in high spirits. The arrival of half a dozen Spitfires, scrambled to meet them, only added to their sense of achievement.

Padshaw and Smith were both lying on bunks reading their respective 'bumf'.

"Nice to see them all happy," Smith said quietly as he turned a page. Padshaw smiled to himself and said:

"Ah well... boys and their toys!"

"Not convinced they hit it though, are you?" It was a statement rather than a question.

"I very much doubt it!" Padshaw got back to reading.

Nearly half an hour had passed when Smith sighed loudly and said:

"Well I've read enough of this contradictory poppycock! I don't think they've got a clue what they want."

"I know how you feel," Padshaw replied, putting paperwork into his briefcase.

Dean Parlow called to them, "Skipper says we'll be on the water in five minutes!"

Padshaw raised his hand in acknowledgement.

The Sunderland began its descent.

A large majority of Malta's capital, Valletta, was little more than a bombsite. Situated on a promontory and flanked by two major harbours, Grand Harbour and Marsamxett, it had been indiscriminately hit by several thousand tons of high explosive for some considerable period of time. What were once imposing buildings, with some of the most beautiful architectural lines, were now just heaps of rubble.

Because of Malta's strategic position in the Mediterranean, and the fact that it had several airfields and of course its formidable harbours, it had been bombed mercilessly by both Italian and German aircraft. Axis forces realised early in the War what a great threat Malta was to their shipping and, therefore, their supply lines. More bombs were dropped on Malta in two years than were dropped on Coventry during the entire War. By the end of 1942 it had been hit by over three thousand raids.

Civilian casualties on Malta were very high. Even though a majority had been moved to the middle of the island for safety, nearly 1,500 people died and over three and a half thousand were wounded.

Death was not always delivered from the sky, however. Because of the intense bombings, people were forced to live in cellars, bomb shelters, caves – anywhere, in fact, that stopped them from being blown up, smashed up or cut to pieces by large pieces of hot shrapnel. This unpleasant way of life led to an outbreak of typhoid, which contributed greatly to the death toll, especially amongst the children.

Despite all this, Malta and its inhabitants, be they civilian or military, would prevail, come what may.

As Padshaw, Smith and the others climbed the stone steps to the top of the harbour wall, the scene surrounding them was a lot to take in.

Burnt-out and still burning vehicles littered the dock area. Wafts of black and grey smoke swirled in the breeze, the pungent smell of burning rubber intermingled with that of charred flesh found their nostrils, backed up by a strong, heavy odour of burnt cordite. A flight of Spitfires flew overhead, two of them billowing smoke from their exhaust stubs. Alongside the wall, a half-submerged merchant ship was alive with men desperately trying to retrieve what they could of its cargo. Makeshift hoists, manufactured from timbers and steel girders, were working to lift crates from its hold. Masts from sunken ships protruded from the water. Cables, wires, broken mooring lines, lay strewn across them.

Holes the size of cars could be seen in some of the ships moored on the far side of the harbour. Locals, risking their lives between raids, were out in their small boats, collecting fish killed by the concussion of exploding bombs; there were pitifully few to collect. The crunch of broken glass and the chink of spent cartridge cases came from underfoot. No sooner had the crates been lowered when men, using crowbars and hammers, rushed to open them before the bombs dropped again. The head and front legs of a dog lay to one side, surrounded by flies. A captain trotted up to them.

"This way! Quick as you can!"

He turned and ran towards what was once a civilian bus. All the windows were blown out and various jagged holes covered the bodywork. As they clambered aboard, Smith noticed the smears of dried blood on the dashboard and headlining, the remains of several unfortunate drivers. Nobody spoke. The bus pulled away, all around them was a picture of urgency.

"Busy day?" Stone asked. There was no humour in his voice. The desperation of the people surrounding them was not lost on him.

"Fourteen raids so far..."

They looked at each other wide-eyed.

"... it was forty yesterday, so God knows what today will bring..."

They were silenced.

As they drove past the bombed-out buildings, another flight of Spitfires flew over, heading out to sea.

"Good luck," the captain muttered.

"Where are we going?" Padshaw asked.

"The Ditch," the captain answered as if that explained everything.

Everybody wanted to ask, but no one did. It didn't matter much anyway. 'The Ditch' was, in fact, the name given to the underground operations room, which was situated amongst the many natural caves beneath Valletta itself.

After ten minutes of working their way through the shattered street, the bus pulled up by a side street.

"See those two sentries?"

237

Padshaw looked where the captain was pointing and nodded.

"Their expecting you... run!"

Padshaw didn't hesitate, he ran. The others followed as fast as they could. The sentries hustled them into an entrance which wasn't visible from the bus. The whistles of bombs falling made Hardcastle and Pither look up. There were at least forty Junkers 88s overhead.

Sticks of bombs rained down, the first of which was a direct hit on the bus they'd been travelling in. It simply disappeared in a ball of flame.

"Poor bastard!" Hardcastle said.

"Get inside you stupid drongoes!" Stone shouted.

They ducked inside and followed the others.

A few minutes later the Sunderland crew were eating one hard biscuit and a small slab of bully beef each, accompanied by not much more than a mouthful of water. Stone handed over some documents to a squadron leader who had simply introduced himself as George.

"Thanks very much old chap, I'll sort all this out..."

He wandered off. Stone watched him disappear into a group of officers.

"Skip!"

Stone turned. Pither gave him a mess tin.

"Thanks."

Stone looked around. Smith was talking to two naval officers, there was much head shaking and gesturing of hands, there was also a lot of 'buggered if I know' looks as well.

Padshaw meanwhile was sitting in a corner with a group captain and what looked to be a naval intelligence officer. The discussion contained the odd smile accompanied by vigorous nods. The group captain then produced some maps and charts and much pointing with pencils commenced.

Hardcastle ambled up to Stone.

"Any idea what's going on, Skip?"

"Haven't the faintest idea –" the irregular crump of bombs could be heard "– but we're better off in here."

Dean Parlow joined them.

"Got anything?" Stone asked him.

"Not much Skipper... but from what I gather, this is the quietest day they've had for weeks."

"Jesus!" blurted Hardcastle.

"Well he's not exactly helping much either, is he?" Stone said sarcastically.

Padshaw walked over.

"Anything we should know, Terry?" Stone asked politely.

"Lots you shouldn't..." Padshaw replied.

Stone sniffed.

"... but I'm going to tell you anyway!" Padshaw added mischievously.

"Come into my office," Stone said, gesturing towards his crew who then walked over and surrounded them.

"Firstly," Padshaw began, "we'll be leaving as soon as possible."

"Provided we've still got a Sunderland," Lenny said, cocking an ear towards the resounding detonations above ground.

"Yes... quite. Secondly, I have been informed that you are all to be decorated for your actions concerning your altercation with various Junkers 88s–" Cheers stopped Padshaw in mid-flow.

Apart from Stone, they all clinked mess tins and congratulated each other.

"Jimmy?" Stone asked

The good humour stopped.

"Posthumous..." Padshaw replied gently. "His family will receive his decoration and whatever details the War Office can release."

Stone nodded and grunted at the same time.

"And lastly, you now have direct orders to take me all the way to Calcutta."

Stone was just about to speak when Smith appeared.

"And me!" he said cheerfully.

"Really?" asked Padshaw, surprised.

"It would seem so. Change of orders. I told you they haven't got a clue what they want!"

Stone glanced at Smith and then back to Padshaw.

"I'm just a fucking taxi. aren't I?"

"Yes old chap," Smith said, "but what an excellent cabbie you are!"

Before Stone could say something colourful, a young lieutenant interrupted them.

"Squadron Leader Padshaw?"

"Yes."

"Jerry's buggered off, sir." The bombing had stopped. "This way sir."

The lieutenant turned and walked briskly down the same tunnel through which they'd entered. They all placed their mess tins on a table and followed him. Stone, Smith and Padshaw were the last out.

"After you," Smith said to Stone condescendingly.

Padshaw smiled and walked on.

"On the contrary," said Stone in the same voice, "after you!"

Smith bowed his head and followed Padshaw. Stone followed them out, his hands held up in front of him mimicking strangling Smith.

As they emerged into the daylight, all that had changed was the amount of rubble. Another bus awaited them. Looking at it, it could easily have been the same one. Only this one had no seats, except for the driver's. The lieutenant sat at the wheel.

Stone was the last to climb in, as soon as his feet were inside, it pulled away. The bus bumped and rattled its way back to the harbour. Padshaw was looking out of his side of the bus at the new devastation on top of the old. Looking out the other side, Stone saw a man and woman crying hysterically while being held back by several civilians.

Twenty feet away from them, two army medics were looking down at a small boy, one arm and both his legs had been blown off, and most of his guts were hanging out of his side.

Stone closed his eyes.

"By the way," Padshaw said still looking out his side of the bus. "I'm afraid you can't claim the U-boat. No confirmation, you see."

"Doesn't matter," Stone replied quietly, his eyes still closed.

Padshaw turned in surprise at the mild reply, he was expecting some Australian abuse. He saw that Stone was upset. He looked out of Stone's side of the bus for an answer, but the tragedy had passed.

On the short trip from the Ditch back to the harbour, there had been little conversation; by the time the bus had pulled up there was total silence. As they got off, the first thing they saw was the now totally submerged merchantman. The mainmast was still visible, as were the bodies of several men floating in the water around it. A small launch containing a sub lieutenant and a sailor pulled up at the bottom of the steps, the sailor threw a rope to a waiting squaddie.

The bus pulled away. Stone momentarily watched it drive off and then looked at his Sunderland, bobbing gently in the light swell. Amazingly it hadn't received a scratch, it was, to Stone at least, a very inviting picture.

"Come on you lot. Let's get out of here!"

They all climbed into the launch. As it made the short journey out to the flying boat, the naval officer addressed Stone.

"We've refuelled her, but we're short on ammo I'm afraid."

"Not to worry," Stone replied very courteously. "Thanks for the fuel... I guess you're short of everything?"

"We have been, desperately. But things have really improved in the last few weeks."

Stone looked at the wrecks of ships surrounding him, some still smouldering. The flotsam in the water, intermingled with oil; dead birds and fish, littered the surface. Here and there, floating aimlessly, was a sailor's hat, or a piece of clothing, caught up on a jagged timber once part of a fishing boat.

Stone looked straight at the sub lieutenant.

"You reckon things have improved, huh?" The naval officer did not reply.

Another flight of Spitfires flew overhead, again heading out to sea. As they pulled up beside the Sunderland four more Spitfires flew very low over them. The sub lieutenant addressed Padshaw.

"They're for you sir!" he said, watching the four Spitfires climb away.

"Really? Are you sure?" Padshaw replied in a surprised voice.

"Our own fighter escort?" Stone asked quizzically as he climbed in.

Smith, following behind Stone, said:

"It's probably a regular procedure–"

"Special orders, actually," interrupted the sub lieutenant, "they'll be escorting you part of the way..."

Smith turned and gave the naval officer a vicious look that said 'shut the hell up!'. If Smith had wanted all and sundry to know that he'd arranged a fighter escort, he'd have bloody told them.

The officer fell silent. Padshaw, being last out of the launch, caught the glare on Smith's face. For the first time he saw Smith in a different light. The big smile, the sarcastic humour, the pleasant manner, it was all there to hide the real man whose job was very serious, bloody dangerous and totally thankless. In fact, Smith would always be expendable, he knew it, and so did everyone else!

As Lieutenant Portman emerged from the shadows with the mules, Connors and his men were still taking stock of the situation. Portman had heard the gunfire and explosions but had been too far away to help. He had then heard the growl of aircraft engines intermixed with what he thought to be heavy machine gun fire. Fearing the worst, he had very cautiously made his way towards Connors' position. The silence surrounding him added to his apprehension, it had been a good fifteen minutes since the last sound of gunfire. To Portman's relief, Private Naylor trotted into sight; Blackman had ordered Naylor to backtrack and make contact with him.

An hour later Portman, walking out into the open, was met with the sight of bodies scattered all around him, most of them were twisted and shattered. In a hollow to his left lay the bodies of two men he knew. One was the man who'd been kicked by the mule, the other was the young private who'd been taken down with malaria. Two men with stretchers walked past him and placed it on the ground next to the dead. As they lifted another body off the stretcher, Blackman walked up to him.

"Any problems?"

Portman looked up from the corpses. "No, sir."

"Good... we've had enough for one day."

"What's the score?" Portman asked softly.

"Four dead, six wounded... not including the Major."

Connors walked up behind Blackman, his left arm in a sling.

"... He's only got a broken arm so that doesn't count!"

"Thanks very much!" Connors said indignantly.

"No one made you jump out of the jeep," Blackman said flippantly. Connors ignored him.

"Get your mules down to the far end of the clearing and secure them," Connors ordered Portman, "then detail some men to shift the remains of my jeep and fill in that shell hole so as we can cross it."

"Yes sir."

As Portman walked away, Connors turned to Blackman:

"That was a rum do, wasn't it? All things considered, we got off pretty lightly I'd say..."

"It had its moments." Blackman replied, gazing at the empty sky. "I reckon we owe the Raff a few beers, though!"

"Mmmm... how's Burns?"

"He's all right. A few cracked ribs and a bang to his head. Lucky bastard though, wasn't he? Sitting in the jeep in full sight of them. Christ knows how he didn't cop a bullet, someone was definitely looking after him! By the way, I'd like to make Naylor up to corporal."

"Fine by me! George should have some stripes lying around somewhere."

"Thanks. I'm going to enjoy this! He's going to hate me for the rest of his life."

Connors raised an eyebrow and said:

"I think he'll be chuffed to bits and you know it!"

"You think?"

"Blackie," Connors said emphatically, "it takes more than a lot to earn your respect. And if Naylor's done that, which he obviously has, you should make that fact known to him."

Blackman looked at Connors, "Yeah, I know. I just hate being sincere. It's not in my nature."

Connors gave him a hard stare.

"All right, all right! I'll be sincere." Blackman gave Connors a resigned look, sighed loudly and then wandered off to find his new corporal. "Bloody hell," he said to himself, "I don't even know what sincere means!"

Sergeant Bell had organised the unloading of the disabled truck. This should have been a relatively simple task, but due to the angle at which the truck had ended up, most of its load had shifted and it was proving to be something of a battle. Bell had had enough.

"All right lads, we'll have to empty the crates first and then re-pack them. We'll be here all day otherwise."

"Fucking things!" said one of the men.

Bell couldn't agree more. Connors came up behind him.

"How's it going, George?"

"We're getting there, sir."

"How bad's the damage to the other vehicles?"

"Well, sir, the other jeep's OK. This truck's had it, the one behind has got a holed petrol tank. One of the lads is working on it now. The third truck has lost one whole side, but mechanically it's all right. We'll just have to lash everything down so it doesn't fall out, and the last one's suffered a few holes but nothing serious."

"Do you reckon we can get it all in the remaining vehicles?" Connors was watching some of the men unloading crates.

"Where there's a will, sir."

"What would I do without you, George?"

Bell had no ready answer to that. Instead, he passed Connors a piece of paper.

"I've made up a list of the wounded men, sir. The most serious is a chest wound. Mr Mercer's working on him now."

"Where is he?"

"Just over there, sir." Bell pointed to the truck with the damaged side.

"Carry on, Sergeant."

"Sir."

Connors made off towards the truck. All around him, his men were picking up discarded weapons and ammunition, checking the dead Japanese for bandages, cigarettes, maps, whatever they could use. Water bottles were a priority. There was no disrespect involved, anything that was useful would be collected and put to good use. Japanese rations made a change to bully beef and biscuit.

Although rice, tinned fish and some very obscure tinned vegetables weren't to everyone's taste.

As he walked around the side of the vehicle, he found himself confronted by two men holding up a blanket which they were using as a screen, both men were looking away from what was happening behind it.

"All right, chaps?" Connors asked encouragingly.

"Yes, sir." One of them answered as the other nodded and moved to let Connors through. As Connors walked past, he looked down. His face grimaced and he had to swallow hard. It was not a pretty sight. Mercer was being assisted by Lance Corporal Fenn, they were both on their knees and stripped to the waist. They were up to their elbows in blood, their shoulders and faces were smeared with dirt and more blood. Scattered around were blooded bandages and empty water canteens. Fenn had one hand on the man's forehead and the other pulling on part of his ribcage. Mercer had one of his hands inside the man's chest. Sweat was pouring from him. Tears were in his eyes, whether from the sweat running into them or frustration, Connors couldn't tell. Mercer twisted his body a little to get a better angle, his hand went in deeper.

"Come on! Come on! Where the fucking hell is it?"

The man's breathing was erratic. Fenn looked at his face, the eyes seemed to be fixed on an invisible object.

"Jesus fucking Christ!" Mercer shouted, "I can't find the fucking thing!"

Fenn looked up at Connors, a look of helplessness lined his face. Mercer refused to give up and persisted in his search. Fenn, still looking at Connors, gently shook his head. The man began to convulse, his breathing started to come in short gasps.

"Don't you fucking dare!" Mercer shouted at him, he was almost crying with exasperation.

The man coughed violently once, and then lay motionless. Mercer started at the open eyes for a few moments; they were still looking at the invisible object. He slowly pulled out his hand and let his shoulders sag. He was totally drained, mentally and physically.

"Oh bugger!" he said, quietly.

Fenn wiped his hands on his shorts and then slowly stood up. Connors saw two men with an empty stretcher and, raising his good arm, beckoned them over. He then leant forward with his arm outstretched.

"Come on..."

Mercer glanced up, he looked exhausted.

"...time for a brew-up."

Mercer smiled grimly and took Connors' hand. As he stood up, the two men lay the stretcher down and reached for the dead man's arms and legs. Walking away from the scene, Connors put his good arm around Mercer's shoulder.

"How's the arm?" Mercer asked, without any real interest.

"You tell me, you're the quack," replied Connors. Mercer pulled out a dirty rag from one of his trouser pockets and began wiping the blood from his hands.

"I'd better get on," Mercer said and walked off towards three or four men who were being bandaged up.

Fenn, standing on his own, looked up at the sky. Black clouds were drifting towards them. He took a packet of cigarettes from his shorts; they were sodden with damp, sweat and blood.

"Bollocks!" he said to himself quietly.

Captain Blackman found Naylor sitting with a somewhat bruised and blackened Burns. One of Burns' eyes was so swollen that it had closed right up. He looked as if he'd gone two rounds with Tommy Farr. Lying prone beside them was Flight Lieutenant Graham.

"How are you feeling, Burns?" Blackman asked.

"Not too bad, thank you, sir."

Blackman smiled at him. "You're a lucky bugger!"

"Yes sir." Burns' chest was on fire; he didn't feel that lucky.

Blackman looked down at Graham. Dried blood covered his face and his left hand was heavily bandaged.

"How's our fly boy?" he asked Naylor.

"He'll be OK, sir. He's got a concussion and he busted a couple of fingers. Luckily he was on the right-hand side of the truck when it was hit."

Blackman let his gaze move from Graham to Naylor.

"Come with me," Blackman said politely, then turned and began to slowly walk away. Naylor frowned and looked to Burns as he got up. Burns shrugged his shoulders and said, "No idea."

A few feet away, Blackman stopped walking and pulled out his cigarettes. He lit two, and as Naylor came alongside him he passed one of them to him.

"Thank you, sir." Naylor said wide-eyed.

"I'm not going to beat around the bush. I'm going to make this short and sweet." Naylor looked a bit worried. "You did a bloody good job today, and you have impressed me and the Major. Not just by today's actions but your commitment to this troop as a whole. I'm making you up to corporal as of now."

"Bugger me!" Naylor blurted.

"That's exactly what I will do if you let me down."

Naylor saluted smartly. "Thank you, sir."

"Don't. You will now have men who will look to you for orders. Who will expect you to make decisions that keep them alive. They come first! Understood?"

"Yes, sir," Naylor replied seriously.

"And in return I promise not to drive the jeep again. Deal?" Blackman's smile had returned.

"It's a deal, sir," Naylor agreed in a relaxed voice.

"Sergeant Bell should have some stripes somewhere. Get them sewn on as soon as pos."

"I'll do it now, sir."

"Bugger off."

"Yes sir."

Naylor turned and made off in search of Sergeant Bell. There was a new stride in him, he suddenly felt a confidence in himself that hadn't been there before. Walking towards him was Major Connors. Naylor saluted.

"Corporal," Connors said, returning the salute.

"Sir!" Naylor felt marvelous. Spots of rain began to fall.

Chapter 18

Not an hour had passed since Marsland and his pilots had landed and been debriefed than the skies had opened yet again. The pilots at readiness were sitting with their ground crew under the cover of the newly delivered portable workshop that had been hastily erected as the rain began to fall. The conversation revolved around the unexpected arrival of the supply trucks. All of them had known each other for such a long time that new conversation was difficult to find. Nearly every subject under the sun had been talked to death a hundred times over; football, rugby, cricket, the local pubs or bars they missed. Nobody wanted to discuss wives or girlfriends back home, that subject was almost taboo. Someone might mention a little bit of trivia they picked up in a letter, which would then be examined from all angles by those present until a bored silence would come over everyone. Many of the pilots and ground crew had originally owned books of one nature or another, which would get passed around. But with the constant humidity and everything inside the tents covered in a permanent mildew, paper did not last long. Even writing home would often prove impossible because of the sodden condition of the writing paper.

"I reckon 'Punchy' and the adjutant deserve a round of applause for wangling all this," Banner said.

"'Snobby's the one who should get the thanks," Cavendish piped up, "he played up a bit of rank to get it all, I know, but if it wasn't for him we certainly wouldn't have this –" he gestured with both hands "– and he did sign for everything, didn't he?"

"If I know 'Snobby'," Miller commented through his pipe, "he'll have pulled the wool over somebody's eyes. He's bloody good at that."

Harris was about to add his two pennies worth when Hillman and Parish ran in out of the rain, holding ground sheets over their heads.

"You chaps owe me a fiver each!" Harris said in a cocky manner.

"Keep your bags on," Parish said, "you'll get it." and then purposely shook the ground sheet so as Harris received a small rain shower. Harris ignored it.

"Cigarette, anyone?" Hillman asked, producing a fresh pack.

"I say, dry cigarettes. Thanks awfully old chap!" Cavendish took one. One by one they all took a cigarette.

"Damned generous," Cavendish said, "I might start to forget that twenty bob you owe me."

"What twenty bob?" Hillman asked wide-eyed.

"You bet Terry a quid," Parish reminded him. Hillman's shoulders dropped.

"Bugger! God this war's expensive!"

"As a matter of fact," Parish added, "there were several boxes of cigarettes in one of those trucks today, the Adj is going to ration them after he's sorted through it all."

"Any booze?" Banner asked with little optimism.

"Not that I've heard," replied Hillman, "but –" he hesitated for effect, everyone looked at him "– I'm pretty sure I did see tinned meat, and it wasn't bully beef!"

"Anything would make a nice change!" Miller said cheerfully.

"Hear, hear!" Banner chanted. Cavendish produced a lighter and lit his cigarette. As the lighter circulated, thunder rumbled in the distance.

251

Marsland and Jennings were both in Hollingsworth's hut, sifting through various pieces of paper, on which the adjutant had drawn up various lists of what had been appropriated that day. Unfortunately, they were in no particular order as the adjutant hadn't had much time to play with during the unloading.

"What's 'DTH' times twenty-four, Holly?" Marsland asked, waving a slip of paper.

"Drop tanks for the Hurricanes, sir."

"Oh... excellent!" Hollingsworth smiled at his CO.

"And cannon shells... LOTS?"

"That's 'lots', sir. I didn't have time to count them all."

Hollingsworth wasn't sure if Marsland was taking a rise out of him. "Hmm... nothing about gin?"

"No, sir," the adjutant said a little irritably.

Jennings tried not to smile as he read his list.

"Ah, tents!" announced Jennings.

"The chaps will be pleased to hear that," Marsland said.

"You'll be even more pleased by this," Jennings said as he passed his list to the CO.

"Bombs! How many, Holly?"

"Just the four, I'm afraid, sir."

"Four? What bloody good are four fucking bombs?"

"Crates, sir, crates," Hollingsworth replied almost melodically. Marsland stared at his adjutant who was wearing his 'I'm innocent of all crimes' look and then went back to his paperwork.

"Touché," Marsland said grudgingly.

Jennings failed to stifle a chuckle. Both Marsland and Hollingsworth looked at their own lists. They both wore twisted grins. A minute or so of silence passed, broken occasionally by the odd, studious grunt.

"There's going to be hell to pay eventually," Jennings said, putting down his paperwork. Marsland bit his lip thoughtfully.

"Well, we need the bloody stuff as much as anyone else," Hollingsworth said emphatically.

"I agree with you, Holly..." Marsland remarked thoughtfully, "however, the Hurricane squadron based at Chittagong only recently arrived from the Calcutta zone. I doubt if they're going to be too happy when they find out we've snaffled their supplies. I know I wouldn't!"

Hollingsworth and Jennings exchanged looks at one another.

"Not much we can do about it now, sir," Jennings said, turning his attention back to his CO.

"Hmm," Marsland mumbled to himself. A thoughtful silence descended. The adjutant took it upon himself to change the atmosphere.

"Well... only one thing for it then," he said as he proceeded to open one of the boxes lying on the floor. He pulled out three tin mugs and passed one each to Marsland and Jennings, the third he placed on his ramshackle desk. He then opened his foot locker and produced his bottle of Bushmills.

"Mugs! Tin! For the use of!" The adjutant then presented the bottle in the same manner as a wine waiter would with a rare vintage. Marsland smiled at him and said in an aloof voice:

"It's not true what they say about you, Holly –" Hollingsworth raised his eyebrows "– you truly are a gentleman and a–"

"Thank you, sir," Hollingsworth interrupted quickly.

The adjutant poured the whiskey. Marsland raised his mug and looked at it. Jennings was right, he thought to himself. There wasn't a damn thing he could do about it now, might as well get on with the job.

"Oh, well," he said, still looking at his mug, "here's to 'Snobby'!"

"To 'Snobby'!" they replied, mugs clinked.

After the debriefing, Valentine had gone back to his tent to try and write a letter home. He was sitting on his bed, totally lost as to what to write. This was the same letter he'd been trying to write for some time. Apart from the fact that the paper was invariably damp, making it nigh on impossible, he hated writing letters. Moreover, he felt he was unsuited to the task of comforting his cousin whose husband had just had one of his arms ripped off by flying shrapnel. All very well they were shipping him home, but she was confined to a wheelchair and he'd been a horologist in civvy life, what were the poor buggers going to do now? And what could he say that would make them feel any better?

"I hope my end's quick," he said to himself gently.

"Thinking of leaving us?" Hacker said as he ducked into the tent.

"You any good at writing letters, old chap?" Valentine looked up at him.

"Not really... problem?"

Valentine ran through his predicament.

"Well, if it was me, I'd offer my sympathies for his injuries, ask how she's keeping and wish them all the best."

"That's it?!"

"Well... you could also add that there are several thousand dead people who would happily have given up one arm to still be here, if you think that that may be beneficial."

Valentine burst out laughing. "You have a very good point old chap!"

"Whisky?" Hacker offered, smiling.

"Writing or drinking... one is faced with such difficult decisions in these precarious times. What if one was to make the wrong decision? What would be the consequences of such–"

"Shut up Snobby! Bloody well drink!" Hacker thrust the bottle at him.

Valentine was his abnormal self again. He smiled broadly, discarded the paper and took the bottle.

"Don't get shirty old chap... chin chin!"

The afternoon drifted into dusk and the sun finally went down. Valentine got up out of his camp chair.

"See you in the mess old chap."

"Will do," Hacker replied as he stretched out on his bunk.

Valentine made his way over to the pilots he'd had standing at readiness and their ground crew. The rain coming down would have spurred new boys on their way, but to Valentine and the regulars, it was just another day.

Banner, sitting on an empty crate, watched Valentine walking casually towards them. Massey and some of the other ground crew were playing cards.

"May as well call it a day, chaps," he said as he joined them. Hillman offered him a cigarette.

"Thanks very much."

Cavendish lit his lighter. "Maybe tomorrow will be a bit more eventful," he said as he lit up.

"So long as it stops raining, 'Snobby', tomorrow can do what it likes," Banner replied.

"I doubt if it will, this particular monsoon seems to have it in for us. See you chaps in the mess. I've heard a rumour there's a change of menu this evening, so don't be late or you might miss out." Valentine turned and walked towards the CO's hut.

"Fillet steak perhaps?" Harris quipped.

"Actually, 'Punchy' told me they'd found a couple of crates of tinned minced beef and also some tinned tomatoes," Parish informed them. There were mutterings of approval.

"Bloody good show 'Snobby'!" Marsland said approvingly as Valentine walked in. Both Jennings and Hollingsworth had joined the CO in his hut, having had enough of sorting out the day's booty.

"Where's the gin?"

"Bloody hell! You're as bad as 'Punchy'!" Marsland replied as he reached for the bottle.

"I taught him everything he knows," Valentine stated.

"I've always looked upon myself as a model pupil," Jennings said loyally as he offered Valentine a tin mug with his right hand and pushed another towards Marsland.

"Bloody parasites," Marsland said, pouring.

"Ahem!" Hollingsworth cleared his throat while producing a tin mug from inside his tunic.

"It's a fucking conspiracy!"

"Thank you sir," Hollingsworth said graciously.

"I was going to save some of this for my birthday," Marsland said irritably.

Jennings smiled at the adjutant. "Something is bound to turn up, it always does."

"What do they mean?" Marsland asked Valentine suspiciously.

"I haven't a clue. Who knows what goes on in the minds of menials?"

"Hmmm..."

"What's on for tomorrow?" Valentine asked indifferently.

"Ground strafing for the pongoes. We're still waiting for map references." Marsland glanced at Jennings and Hollingsworth, still not altogether happy.

"Who's flying?" Valentine asked.

"Make it three sections of three aircraft. You lead Blue section, 'Chancer' can lead Yellow and Hacker Green. And make sure some of the new boys fly. In fact, stick 'em in the Kittyhawks. Why should they have all the fun?" Marsland was getting more and more irritable as he spoke. Hollingsworth had seen him like this before and knew it was probably a good time to bugger off. He looked at Jennings seriously, took some papers from his top pocket and knocked back his gin.

"We'd better make sure all this stuff has been stored away 'Punchy'." He made his way to the door. Jennings took the cue to leave and downed his.

"Good point. See you in the mess, sir," Jennings said politely as he followed the adjutant out. Marsland grunted.

"What got into him?" Punchy asked walking towards a stack of crates.

"Well it wasn't us, that I can tell you. Leave it to 'Snobby', he'll wheedle it out of him." Hollingsworth stopped short of the crates and stared at them.

"Bugger this! Let's go to the mess."

"You've got my vote."

"Are you going to tell me what's biting you, or do I have to beat it out of you with your empty bottle of gin?"

"It's not empty," Marsland replied defensively.

"It bloody well will be if you don't tell me what's got on your tit!"

Marsland put his left elbow on his desk and propped his head in his hand. "What do you reckon's going on with this officer they're sending out here?" he asked calmly.

"Ahh! So that's what it is. I wish I could tell you–"

"He'll just be in the way as far as I can see," Marsland interrupted.

"Well there's no point getting worked up over it. They certainly wouldn't send anyone out from Blighty to take over the Squadron. There's more than enough adequately qualified idiots sitting on their arses in Calcutta, if that's what's bothering you."

Marsland was nonplussed. "I just hope he's not going to bugger up my war. I've put a lot of effort into it so far and I haven't finished with it, yet."

"Personally I think somebody's ballsed it up as usual and it'll all end up being a gigantic cock-up. That's my learned opinion anyway."

"You're probably right, 'Snobby'," Marsland said more relaxed, staring at nothing in particular.

A few seconds passed, then Valentine said, "Come on... I'm hungry."

Marsland replied with a resigned smile and stood up.

Though dimly lit by old cans filled with oil, petrol and rag, the atmosphere in the mess was nothing short of convivial. Hacker was the first person they met as they walked in.

"Evening, sir... 'Snobby'."

"What's on?" Marsland asked.

"It's an eastern take on a cottage pie, I think."

"Here you are chaps." Hollingsworth passed over two full mess tins.

"Eating irons," said Jennings, producing two forks.

"Thanks awfully," replied Valentine.

"Gentlemen," Marsland said, politely nodding at each of them in turn. Jennings and Hollingsworth smiled at each other. Marsland pretended not to notice.

"That's not half bad," Snobby said surprised. Marsland took a mouthful off his fork. "Bloody hell," he said with his mouth full, "That's not bad at all!"

"Loads more if you want seconds," Hacker added. Standing right behind Hacker were Cavendish and Parish.

"Any idea what's on tomorrow?" Parish asked Cavendish.

"Haven't heard anything. Chancer?" Cavendish called, interrupting Harris's conversation.

"Don't look at me chum, I'm just another mushroom."

Vine looked puzzled.

"Kept in the dark," said Midgeham helpfully.

"Ah."

A little later Brandon, Tillman and Hayward were talking shop with Parish and Harris in a corner, while forking mouthfuls of food down.

"Do you really fly in this crap?" Brandon asked, gesturing at the rain coming down.

"We do," Harris replied flatly.

"Is there a knack to it?" asked Hayward.

"Don't crash," Parish replied as if that answered everything.

"It's not as bad as you think, actually," Cracken said as he came over to them.

"You reckon?" Tillman asked unconvinced.

"Wait till you get caught in a storm," Cracken started, "the squalls are so rough, aeroplanes totally fall apart. No joke."

"Bloody hell...!" Hayward remarked. "I think I'm going to get my mum to write me a sick note for the CO."

"That's the spirit," Harris said encouragingly, slapping him on the shoulder, "keep it up!"

Jones and Morris were chatting amongst themselves when they were joined by two armourers, Toms and Carnegie, who were trying to calm down a somewhat seriously annoyed Massey.

"Good grub," Toms stated.

"Makes a nice change, eh?" Jones agreed.

"You look pretty well pissed off, what's up?" Morris asked Massey.

"That Australian tosser who just arrived! He talks to me like that again and he'll get my size nine boot right in his sweetbreads. Fucking prick!!"

Morris opened his mouth to ask what had been said but Toms saved him from asking.

"Massey simply asked the chap what made him join the air force."

"What did he say?" Jones asked.

"To quote: 'None of your fucking business you second rate grease monkey!'."

"You're kidding!" Morris said wide eyed, "Sure he wasn't having some sort of a–"

"He's a fucking arsehole," Massey said with conviction.

Morris glanced over to where the Australian was standing, he was looking over at them with a look on his face that could only be described as disgust. Morris looked away.

"What the bloody hell's wrong with the man?" he asked the others.

"Buggered if I know," Toms replied, "but if he's not careful he'll get my ruddy boot, too."

"And mine," Carnegie said, "both of them in fact."

"Leave it for now, lads," Morris said, trying to calm them down. "I'll have a word with 'Punchy' later, OK?"

There was a short silence.

"Yeah... all right," Massey agreed grudgingly.

"Good, now enjoy your grub. Besides, with that attitude, he won't last long around here."

As the evening progressed Valentine made a point, as he always did, of circulating himself amongst all the Squadron personnel. He wandered up to Clarke who was talking to two other fitters, Lennox and Bamford.

"All right chaps?"

"Yes thanks sir. Good nosh innit?" Lennox replied.

"Make the most of it," said Valentine, "we're probably back on gruel tomorrow."

The men smiled. Valentine saw 'Punchy' Jennings talking to the MO and made a beeline for him.

"Evening Doc."

"'Snobby'."

"How's Jiff?"

"I was just telling 'Punchy' he's doing pretty well actually. A bit better than I would have expected, over all."

"That's good." Valentine then turned to Jennings, "Any news on getting Jiff out?"

"Neane tried to find out earlier, but all he got was lots of static and a fair amount of gobbledygook. He's going to try again in the morning."

"He'd be better of sending smoke signals," Valentine said sarcastically. There followed an occasionally bitter conversation about the farcical state of Allied communications. An hour or so later, Marsland sought out his adjutant who was in the process of praising the cooks.

"Bloody well done chaps, not a morsel left!"

"Thanks, Adj."

"Adj?"

"Yes sir." Hollingsworth turned, smiling broadly.

"Have all the new chaps meet for briefing at 0800 hours, got that?"

"Right you are, sir."

"Six Kittys for the new chaps and Hurricanes for the flight leaders."

"Roger that."

"Goodnight Adj." Marsland turned as he spoke.

"Night sir."

"He's still got the bit between his teeth then?!" 'Punchy' said as he ambled up.

"It would seem so," Hollingsworth replied thoughtfully as he watched Marsland walk away. "Fancy a small whisky?"

"Such generosity... after you."

Chapter 19

It was nearly midnight. The bar was mainly lit by an awful lot of candles which were giving off quite a pungent odour. Stone looked up from his beer.

"I get the feeling we're in the way," he said irritably.

"There's rather a lot going on at the moment," Padshaw replied. "And I fear we're at the back of the queue, so to speak.

"Couldn't you have pulled some rank?"

"If I thought for one moment it would have done any good, I would have. May we have another round of beers please?" Padshaw asked a passing waiter. The man nodded politely and made for the bar. "There is a war on after all."

"Really? I hadn't noticed!" Sarcasm drenching every word, Stone slouched in his chair and looked around the bar. There were various different uniforms and ranks eating in small groups or playing cards or simply standing at the bar drinking. A group of nurses were being well looked after by a large contingent of young officers, some of whom were obviously recovering from wounds of one sort or another. The one thing that was most noticeable was an expectant buzz that seemed to fill the room, an air of confidence he hadn't seen for a long time, which seemed to fill everyone.

"I take it they're all chuffed 'cause Monty gave the Afrika Corps a bloody nose last month?"

"He did do rather well, didn't he?"

"Jesus! You pommies really are the masters of understatement, aren't you?"

The beers arrived.

"Thank you," Padshaw said.

"Do you reckon we'll get our fuel and ammo tomorrow?" Stone asked despondently.

"We'll have to wait and see," Padshaw replied.

"Well I hope they at least sort us out with somewhere to kip tonight, otherwise the boys will start a war all of their own!"

The flight from Malta had been relatively uneventful. Fifty miles out from Malta a gaggle of enemy fighters had spotted the Sunderland, but the escorting Spitfires intercepted them. Smoke could be seen coming from two or three aircraft in the distance, but who was hit was anybody's guess. They reached Alexandria in the middle of the evening.

On arriving they were met by what appeared to be organised chaos. Nobody really wanted much to do with them. It seemed they were an unnecessary burden. Stone's initial request to be refuelled and re-armed was met by the somewhat nonchalant attitude of a stores officer.

"My dear chap, I've got everyone screaming at me for just about everything. In fact, technically speaking, the cupboard, as far as you're concerned, is bare."

"What am I supposed to bloody do? Flap me ruddy arms?"

"If you think that would help..."

Stone's blood was getting up. "What sort of bloody answer's that, you stupid drongo?"

"Leave it Skipper!" Pither said quickly, putting a gentle hand on his shoulder. Stone shrugged it off.

"Now you listen to me you pommie bastard–"

"Get out!" the officer shouted as he stood up from his desk. Pither got between them

"Come on Skip."

Stone's face was thunder.

"Come on!" Pither repeated and guided him out. The officer slammed the door behind them.

"Bloody colonials," he said aloud.

"Fucking pommie arsehole!" Stone shouted back as Pither escorted him down the corridor. Much the same happened when he enquired about a billet for him and his crew.

"Well I'll see what I can do, but I doubt it."

"Jesus Christ, it's a simple bloody request! What the bloody hell is wrong with–" Pither to the rescue again.

Another waiter came over to Padshaw, and in broken English said:

"You... have... tables two... there, sir." He pointed at two tables which had just been cleared.

"Jolly good." Padshaw stood up, "Get the boys in Jacko, at least we can eat."

Stone grunted, got up and went outside to where his crew were drinking.

"Grub's up cobbers!"

"About time!" Hardcastle said. They marched in and sat down. Ten minutes later various types of fish came out on large wooden plates accompanied by slices of hard bread. A large bowl with a ladle sticking out of it was placed in the centre of the table along with some shallow dishes, most of which were cracked. Stone started ladling the contents into one of the dishes.

"Smells pretty good," he said, surprised, and passed it to Padshaw. As he took the dish, Padshaw realised it was leaking.

"Better hurry up Terry!" Stone said smiling, the others started laughing. Padshaw grabbed his spoon and got stuck in. Twenty minutes later they'd more or less cleared the table.

"All sorted!" Smith said jovially, as he sat down unannounced.

"What d'you mean?" Stone asked.

"Billets, fuel, ammunition... all done." Smith was quite matter of fact about it.

"How the hell did you wangle that?"

"You know, right word in the right place. Your aero plane–"

"Boat!" Stone said indignantly.

"Sorry, boat." Padshaw smiled as Stone took the bait. "Your 'boat' has been refuelled and is being re-armed as I speak and they are also tidying up a few battle scars."

"Well done," Padshaw said. "Have a beer." Padshaw raised his hand to get the barman's attention.

"How come he could arrange all that?" Hardcastle asked quietly.

"Don't ask," Stone replied.

"Never mind getting the fuel and stuff, how on earth does he know where to eat all the time?" Parlow enquired.

Stone looked at Padshaw for help.

"He used to write travel guides before the War, for tourists and the like."

"Ah," Parlow seemed satisfied.

"What does he do now then?" Hardcastle asked.

"Ask him," Stone said as Smith came back with his beer.

"Bit of a cushy number actually," Smith said, sitting down, "I have to look after various officers who need a bit of guidance, sort of make sure they don't walk down the wrong alley, that sort of thing."

"Hmmph," Hardcastle retorted, unimpressed and turned to his beer.

"I hadn't thought of that one," Smith whispered to Padshaw. "Thanks, I'll use that in future."

"No charge," Padshaw said.

Truth to be known, Smith had had to pull a lot of very big strings to get things done so quickly. Stone's efforts had fallen on deaf ears, his brash, in-the-face attitude didn't help. Nevertheless, he was simply trying to follow his orders. As soon as Stone had explained his lack of progress, Padshaw himself made some enquiries but met with the same result. It wasn't a case of being unhelpful, it was simply that the demands being made from other quarters took priority. It was at this point that Smith took Padshaw to one side.

"Leave it to me Terry. I'll get all this sorted out."

Padshaw knew better than to ask questions. "What a helpful chap you are."

"Meanwhile," Smith took a well crumpled address card out of his pocket, "take yourself and the chaps to this address. Tell the owner Mr Smith will be joining you later."

"What is it?"

"A dingy little bar that does pretty good food."

"I'm not sure my pockets are that big."

"You won't need money."

Padshaw raised his eyebrows.

"The owner and I have been doing business for some time," Smith added with a crafty smile.

"I won't ask."

"Don't."

Smith's biggest headache had been trying to locate the right officer to speak to. Various high-ranking men knew him for different reasons, but only a handful knew he was up to his neck in the skullduggery business. After much searching and bullshitting various clerks and secretaries, he eventually found who he was looking for. The clerk passed him the telephone receiver.

"Mr Smith?"

He took the phone and sat on the corner of the clerk's desk, his right leg swinging like a metronome.

"George, how are you?"

"Harassed!" There was a long pause, Smith stayed silent. The clerk looked on, puzzled and said:

"Something wrong with the line–"

Smith politely raised a finger to his lips, the clerk fell silent.

"If you had to have a pet, what wouldn't it be?"

"An ape," Smith replied.

"Just checking."

Smith smiled.

"What do you need?

Smith explained.

"It's as good as done."

"I appreciate that, thanks George."

"Don't mention it, good luck on whatever it is."

"Cheers George, bye for now." Smith put the receiver down, nodded at the clerk and left the office.

Smith really was sincerely grateful, he was well aware that right at this very moment Monty was about to launch his counter attack at El Alemein and all allied resources revolved around that.

As Smith walked out of the building, he paused for a moment and looked up at the moon. He let out a contented sigh. "I deserve a beer," he said to himself generously, and then walked into the night.

The following morning, Stone and his crew were wakened at five a.m. Much to their disgust.

"What bloody time d'ya call this?!" Stone asked the orderly brusquely.

"Five o'clock," he replied, nonplussed, as he offered Stone a mug of tea.

"What's the rush for Christ's sake?" Stone sat up and rubbed his eyes.

"You have orders to be on a launch to take you out to your aeroplane in one hour, Sarge."

"BOAT! It's a fucking boat! How many times do I have to–" Stone suddenly stared hard at the orderly who was now a little bewildered by Stone's outburst.

"Smith!" he exclaimed. "This is his fucking doing isn't it? He's having a fucking laugh at my expense isn't he? I'm going to toss him over the side at five thousand feet! They'll never find the bastard –" the orderly left quite quickly "– yeah, that's what I'll do! The bloody sharks will finish him if the fall doesn't."

At some distance, the orderly could still hear Stone ranting, "depth charges! I could depth charge the bastard! Nothing but bits..."

Forty-five minutes later a truck pulled up and Stone and his crew climbed in. Padshaw was already sitting in the back. Stone, climbing in first, looked at Padshaw.

"C'mon Terry, spill the beans and it had better be good 'cause I'm bloody tired."

"Jacko, I haven't got a clue," he replied sincerely.

Stone could see straight away that Padshaw was at a loss as well. He calmed down a little and sat down opposite Padshaw as the rest of the crew scrambled in.

"Tell me this has got nothing to do with that sneaky bastard Smith," he said in a tired voice.

"I haven't got a clue, really. First thing I knew about it was a mug of tea and a sandwich."

They all looked at him.

"It wasn't a very good sandwich," he added quickly. They all sighed or mumbled something incomprehensible and resigned themselves to a short, bumpy ride.

Ten silent minutes later they arrived at the quayside. Smith was sitting on a crate holding a clipboard and ticking items off as various army and navy types were loading the launch from the edge of the harbour wall.

"That's all of it sir," one of the men said to Smith.

"Jolly good, well done! Morning," he said, somewhat more jovially than was necessary, as the Sunderland crew shambled towards him.

"Morning," Padshaw replied politely. As he opened his mouth to speak again, Stone was just ahead.

"How the hell are we supposed to get in as well?" Stone was staring at the over laden launch.

"They'll take it all out to your... boat, and then come back for us."

Sullivan looked down at the launch.

"Bloody hell Skipper, that's a hell of a lot of fuel!" They all studied the launch. Before Stone got the chance to use his colourful English, Padshaw asked:

"Why the early start?"

"Tell you later."

"You'll bloody well tell us now!" Stone said curtly. "Or we're not going anywhere."

Smith let out a sigh through one side of his mouth. Padshaw immediately said to Stone:

"It may be, Jacko, that he isn't in a position to tell us."

Smith raised a pair of upturned hands in agreement. Stone put his hands on his hips, stretched, and stared at his Sunderland bobbing gently in the water.

"God this war's full of bullshit," he said, as the launch pulled away.

The squeal of brakes turned their heads. Two men wearing aprons got out of the cab.

"Breakfast," Smith said cordially.

"Thank God for that!" Hardcastle said. To the onlookers' surprise, folding tables and chairs were set up and then trays of food followed. They all sat down enthusiastically and got down to eating, except Stone and Padshaw. Stone looked at his men for a moment and began to feel uncomfortable. He turned and walked up close to Smith.

"Just what the bloody hell is going on...?" Stone asked in a voice of genuine concern, "because that looks to me like the last fucking supper!"

Smith genuinely felt for Stone, he could see his concern for his men in his eyes. Trouble was, technically, his own hands were tied, he couldn't just tell all just because he wanted to, or that they deserved to know. On the other hand, he didn't want to find another crew either. Stone's crew would do whatever Stone said, they certainly wouldn't tolerate him. Bloody colonials.

"All right," Smith said quietly, "once we're on board I'll brief you. And only then."

"Fair enough," Stone replied and turned to his crew.

"And Jacko..." Smith added.

Stone looked back over his shoulder at Smith.

"...you have my word I wouldn't do anything to risk your crew's lives unnecessarily."

There was a sincerity in Smith's voice which had never been there before.

"And this?" Stone gestured to his ravenous crew.

"My way of apologising for getting them out of bed early."

Stone grunted and then joined his men.

"He's just concerned for his crew," Padshaw said to Smith encouragingly, as Stone sat down.

"I realise that, he's a damned good chap, pity he's not English."

Padshaw grinned and said, "Well all I can say is you did a good job placating the bugger."

"For now."

"What do you mean?"

"Wait till I tell him where he's going next."

"Aden's the next stop, isn't it?"

Smith twisted his face in reply. Padshaw raised his eyes to the sky.

"Oh dear."

Chapter 20

"Sir?" Marston repeated to get his attention.

"Mmm?" Hawkins looked up from his desk.

"Latest reports sir. You asked me to bring them as soon as they were in, sir."

"Yes..." Hawkins dragged his wandering mind back into his office, "thanks very much... miles away." Hawkins took the file from Marston's hand. Marston smiled to himself and left.

"Right," Hawkins said to himself, "What have we got?" and began reading. Thirty minutes later he closed the file and made off for Beecham's office.

"Come in."

"Good afternoon, sir."

Beecham nodded. "What news?"

"Well, sir, Squadron Leader Padshaw's making good time, and Sergeant Pilot Stone and his crew seem to be making something of a name of themselves." Hawkins replied lightly.

"Pray tell."

Hawkins told him what he knew.

"Bully for them," Beecham said smiling. "I must be honest, I have seen a brief report on their exploits with some Jerry fighters, but I didn't know they were trying to do the navy's job for them, as well."

Hawkins was smiling.

"What was the pilot's name again?"

"Sergeant Pilot Jack Stone, sir. An Australian."

Beecham wrote his name down.

"What else?"

"Not much sir. Last reports say Major Connors' supply train is still en route, but there's no telling quite how old this information is. Communications, as you know, are awful at best."

"Quite so, quite so." Beechams's mind was going somewhere else.

"Close the door and have a seat," Beecham added cordially.

Hawkins closed the door and walked back to Beecham's desk. As he drew the chair back, Beecham took a few leaves of paper from a drawer and passed them to him.

"Read these later."

"Sir." Hawkins sat down.

"Meanwhile, I've decided that you need a change of climate." Beecham was very matter of fact. Hawkins, however, was wide-eyed.

"Sir?"

"You've spent some time working with transport command, I believe?"

"Er, yes sir."

"In fact your record shows that you spent three months with them."

"That I did sir, but I was sort of shunted around a lot, if you know what I mean. I never seemed to have a particular role, so to speak."

"Quite... you could say 'Jack of all trades but master of none'!"

"I suppose you could say that, sir," he agreed, a little apprehensively.

"Perfect!"

With Beecham's reply, Hawkins knew that whatever his fate was, it was already sealed.

"I want you to follow in Squadron Leader Padshaw's footsteps, so to speak."

"In what way, sir?"

"I want you to put together a team of men. These men must be experienced in the organization of moving supplies on a large scale by air."

"I see, sir." Hawkins was still a little wary.

"I don't care where you have to steal them from, I'm not remotely interested. However, whoever you recruit will be training or overseeing men who have limited, if no experience in large scale operations, so choose them and their rank carefully. About thirty will do for now."

"Very well, sir."

"You start now."

"Yes, sir."

"By the way, Hawkins..."

Hawkins cocked his head.

"I don't suppose you speak Chinese, do you? Mandarin and the like?"

"I'm afraid not, sir." Hawkins was surprised by the question.

"Just thought I'd ask. One never knows. That will be all, thank you."

"Right sir." Hawkins stood up, clutching his paperwork. As he pushed the chair in between the pedestals of the desk, a past conversation with Padshaw flew into his head.

"Funny you should ask me if I speak Chinese, sir..."

Beecham gave him a politely attentive stare.

"... I believe Squadron Leader Padshaw is quite fluent in Chinese languages. Pity he's not–"

"Thank you, Hawkins," Beecham interrupted. "I'm well aware of the squadron leader's knowledge of the Chinese languages." Beecham had a wry look on his face.

"Sir." Hawkins made for the door. As he opened it, he turned.

"You mentioned a change of climate, sir?"

"You have seventy-two hours to recruit your men," Beecham said with the same look on his face.

"Yes sir." Hawkins left the office, none the wiser.

Chapter 21

By morning the rain had stopped coming down like a waterfall and was contenting itself with falling out of the sky in buckets. As usual, Sergeant Bell had risen early and was busying himself organising the troops' moving out. Naylor was sitting on a broken wheel, staring out across the open plain that had been the previous day's killing ground.

"Corporal!" Sergeant Bell called to him.

Naylor drew on his cigarette, still staring.

"Corporal!" Bell repeated loudly.

Naylor's brain suddenly engaged and he jumped to attention, discarding the cigarette.

"Sarge! Sir! Sorry, Sarge!" Naylor eventually saluted.

Bell stared at him stiff-faced.

"I take it I won't have to repeat myself again, Corporal?"

"No, Sarge."

"Good. Now get a brew on and start waking the men."

"Right away, Sarge."

Bell nodded and walked passed him. Naylor relaxed as he saw Bell smiling to himself.

Yet again Connors, Blackman and Lieutenant Portman found themselves studying a map.

"Can't be more than a day or so, sir, now that the local pickup's been cancelled. Weather permitting, of course."

"Trouble is, Lieutenant, the bloody weather isn't permitting, is it?" Connors replied, looking out at the rain.

"No sir."

"What d'you reckon, Don?" Blackman asked thoughtfully. "Should we split the mules from the vehicles or just plug on?"

"After yesterday's little set-to I think we're better off sticking together. I doubt if any more Japs will turn up, but if they do, and they catch us in small numbers, it'll be a very short fight..."

"What time do you want to move out?"

"0730 hours," Connors replied, consulting his watch. "That's just over an hour."

"Just enough time for a mug of tea then," Mercer said as he appeared, holding four tin mugs.

"Cheers Doc." Blackman took two mugs and passed one to Connors.

"Thanks," Portman said as Mercer passed him a mug.

"Anything I should know?" Connors asked.

"Nothing new. I think another two of the men are coming down with malaria. I've given them a shot each, just have to wait and see." He took a mouthful of tea.

"Righto... well, let's see if we can get through this day without any hassle, eh?"

They all looked at him.

"Mmm," he added.

By lunchtime Connors found himself pleasantly surprised by their progress. They'd had the usual bogged-down vehicles and the odd temperamental mule, but, all in all, things were going well. Even the rain was letting off. Mercer was cutting away the old dressing on Bobby Graham's leg, or at least he was trying to. The bumping and swaying of the truck wasn't helping, neither was the fact that he had little or no room to move, due to the extra crates that had come from the disabled vehicle. He should really have changed the dressing earlier but, by the time he'd finished patching up the more serious cases, he was so dog tired, he'd simply fallen asleep. Connors had noticed this and gave orders not to wake him.

"Bugger!" Graham said painfully.

"Sorry old boy," Mercer said, having just stabbed Graham with a pair of scissors.

"Sir?" Fenn said, leaning over a crate, passing him a fresh dressing.

"Thanks."

Graham was gritting his teeth as Mercer, as gently as possible, fed the dressing under his leg.

"Almost done old boy."

Graham nodded encouragingly.

"There we are... how does that feel?"

"Not too bad." He lay back and relaxed.

"Any idea how long before we get to the LGI?"

"Well, all things being equal, which of course they're not, Major Connors thinks we'll be there by midday tomorrow."

"What then?"

"I expect you'll be transferred to base hospital in Calcutta, all things being equal."

"Which they're not."

"Well we'll just have to wait and see, eh?"

Graham closed his eyes. Fenn stared out the back of the truck, the rain seemed to be easing.

Morning came and it was, of course, still raining. All the new boys were waiting in the mess for the CO. Valentine, Hacker and Harris were outside on the partly covered veranda having a smoke.

"Visibility's going to be shit in this!" Harris stated.

"Seems to be easing a little though–" Hacker began.

"Doesn't really matter, does it? Besides, we've flown in much worse than this," Valentine interrupted. "What concerns me is that some of these chaps haven't."

Hacker looked over at the others as Marsland came around the corner of the hut.

"Morning chaps."

"Morning, sir."

276

"Sir."

Marsland was carrying a single piece of paper.

"What have we got?" Valentine asked.

"What we've got is some of our forward units crying out for air support." Marsland walked into the mess, the assembled pilots stood to attention.

"Relax, gentlemen. Right, as some of you may be aware, our chaps are making their way south, and bloody hard work it is too. However, this message –" Marsland waved the paper "– has just come through. It would appear that our forward units have got themselves a bit too far forward and are now somewhat ahead of the main advance–"

"Some people are so impetuous," Valentine said airily. Marsland ignored him.

"Maybe this inclement weather has something to do with it," Marsland continued. "Whatever the reason, they are now in something of a pickle and we're going to get them out of it."

Hollingsworth walked in with a blackboard under one arm, a map in the other hand and a mouthful of paper.

"Morning, Adj," Valentine said, knowing full well he couldn't answer. Hollingsworth's reply came out as a snort. He hung the blackboard on the wall and took the paper out of his mouth. "You'd better read this, sir," he said, passing it to Marsland.

Hollingsworth then proceeded to open up the map on a table, the pilots gathered round. Various Xs were scattered about, some with question marks beside them.

"Snobby?" Marsland passed the paper, Valentine read the short message and then said:

"Let's hope they're having the morning off." He passed it to Hacker and Harris.

"Right chaps," Marsland started, "the Xs with question marks are the positions of the forward units, at the time of receiving this message. Chances are they are still there. At least I bloody hope so. They have been given orders to take and hold position here." Marsland pointed to an area south of Cox's Bazaar. "The bulk of our forces are not far behind them, but it would appear that the Japs have sent their own forward units north and, of course, it's all ended in tears. Our chaps, fortunately, have radios and flares to help in directing us onto our targets. Now listen carefully, because this is important!"

They all looked up at the CO.

"A red flare indicates a call for help, a yellow flare will be fired in the direction of the area they want bombed and strafed. A white flare means you stop bloody quick! Got that?" 'Sirs' followed.

"Hopefully we'll be able to do without the flares, provided their radios work. 'Snobby', your call sign is 'Guillotine'."

Valentine smiled.

"Their call sign will be 'Fighting Cocks', so at least we know they have a sense of humour."

There were a few smiles.

"For those of you who are most probably new to this, it's very unlikely that you will even see the Japs you're strafing. But believe me, you will be hitting them where it hurts and the brown jobs will be grateful! 'Snobby'?"

"This –" Valentine took back the piece of paper the adjutant had brought with him "– is a report of Japanese aircraft active, right now, over and around Cox's Bazaar. Keep your eyes open and look out for each other. Got that?"

They nodded or sirred.

"This looks like being a long day," Marsland said. "And this will be the first of several sorties. As you will have noticed, flying conditions are less than perfect."

A couple of them looked out at the rain.

"*If* you're going to prang taking off, be so kind as to do it in the trees. Same applies to landing. DO NOT BLOCK THE STRIP!"

278

They looked for some humour, but Marsland's face was deadly serious. 'Punchy' Jennings walked in, soaked through and wiping his greasy hands with a couple of large leaves. The rain hid the fact that he was sweating like a pig.

"Nearly done, sir. The lads are just finishing 'bombing up'."

"Thanks 'Punchy'."

"Sir." Jennings turned to leave.

"'Punchy'!"

"Yes, sir?"

"Refuel and re-arm the others. Just in case we need them."

"Right sir." Jennings shoulders slumped. He walked outside.

"Bugger and fuck!" he said to himself. The boys were going to love him!

"I'll leave the rest of the briefing to you, 'Snobby'."

"Your faith in me never ceases to–"

"Take off as soon as you're ready!" Marsland interrupted and then went off to round up the rest of his pilots and brief them on what was going on.

Valentine then proceeded to the finer points of the sortie and comments on distances between aircraft during strafing. He then continued with quite a detailed briefing reminding them of the vices and foibles of the P40. Having done that, he finished with:

"And I want a staggered formation, give each other plenty of room, above all stick with your leader, don't lose him!"

They were all attentive, even Decker looked like he was paying attention.

"Finally – sections! I'll lead Blue section with Brandon and Tillman, Hacker, your Green with Hayward and..." Valentine pointed at Midgeham

"Midgeham, sir," he said helpfully.

"Midgeham, Chancer, you've got Vine and Decker in Yellow."

"Right 'Snobby'."

Valentine looked at the six of them.

"Take off in thirty minutes. Get yourselves something to eat, quick."

As they left, Valentine turned to Hacker and Harris.

"Keep an eye on them. Don't let them wander about."

"Will do," Hacker said.

"And Chancer..." Valentine added.

" 'Yes Snobby'."

"Keep a close eye on Decker. If he puts a foot wrong, I want to know about it."

"Will do."

"Come on, let's eat."

Just under an hour later, all three sections were making a beeline south for Cox's Bazaar. Valentine, with Blue section, was leading, flanked by Green section on his left and Yellow on his right. Harris was continually chivvying Vine to close up.

"For Christ's sakes close up Yellow two!"

Vine was having trouble getting used to the Kittyhawk's layout. Every time he looked down to familiarise himself with the controls and instruments, he inadvertently began wandering away from the rest of the formation.

"Sorry, Yellow leader." Vine corrected and got himself back into position.

"A staggered formation does not mean you staggering about over the Bay of Bengal, Yellow two," Harris said gently.

"Roger, leader."

Vine concentrated on holding position. All in all, he was a fair pilot, it was just that half of the 'doings' in the cockpit took some getting used to and he'd only got a few hours on Kittyhawks, and the weight of his bomb load made everything seem a bit sluggish.

Decker on the other hand was having no difficulties at all. He'd flown Tomahawks and Kittyhawks before, mainly during training, and had clocked up a fair amount of hours. He kept position well, Harris noticed, and gave no cause for complaint. Perhaps 'Snobby' was worrying over nothing, he thought to himself.

A few minutes later, flying at three thousand feet, Cox's Bazaar was coming up. Valentines voice came over the RT.

"Right chaps. Yellow section will stay at three thousand, your top cover, over."

"Roger that, leader."

"Blue and Green sections will lose height and reform at two thousand... going down... now!"

Harris watched Blue and Green sections fall away, a few minutes later Cox's Bazaar was behind them.

"Keep your eyes peeled chaps," Valentine said in a calm voice.

Looking down, Hayward could see nothing but trees. There was little or nothing from which to take any kind of a bearing to make any sort of attack. A little crackle in Valentines headset made him jerk his eyes to the ground.

"Guillotine, this is 'Fighting Cocks'. 'Guillotine'. 'Fighting Cocks', over."

"Receiving you, 'Fighting Cocks'. Over."

"'Guillotine', look out for yellow marker smoke... firing now!"

All the pilots scanned the trees below. A moment later yellow smoke could be seen rising from the trees.

"We see it!"

More by luck than judgment, the smoke shell had landed right amongst a large contingent of advancing Japanese.

"'Guillotine', that is your target! Repeat, that is your target!"

"Roger. Green section, make your attack first, over."

"Wilco, tally ho Green section."

Hacker opened his throttle and pushed the stick forward. Valentine gave it a couple of seconds and followed.

"Line abreast and keep it tight, Green section."

Hayward and Midgeham obediently came up either side of their leader.

At 500 feet and coming up nicely on the target, Hacker shouted into the RT.

"Fire and bomb at will!"

Before he'd hit his own gun button, tracer was whipping from the flanking Kittyhawks into the smoke and trees. Hacker's cannon thumped, he pulled the bomb release. His Hurricane suddenly felt more responsive, at the same moment Hayward and Midgeham dropped their eggs.

"Green section, break left and climb. Go!"

As Green section's bombs exploded, Blue section were already firing.

"Blue section. Bomb, now!" Valentine ordered. Brandon and Tillman dropped their eggs. "Now break right and climb."

Valentine opened his throttle. But a few seconds passed and Valentine's headphones cracked again.

"Hit them again 'Guillotine'! They're almost on us!" The voice was in earnest. Valentine reacted very quickly.

"Green section strafe again! Yellow section make your attack. Buster, Buster! Blue section, make angels, we're top cover."

"Going down Yellow section, we'll attack on the dive, over."

"Roger, leader."

"Wilco"

Harris opened his throttle wide and made a beeline for the smoke. Hacker had pulled Green section round in a sweeping curve.

"Green section open–" before Hacker had finished, Midgeham and Hayward were already firing. Round after round pummeled the area around the smoke. Vine was now full of confidence. With his throttle opened wide and the airframe vibrating, he was a knight in armour descending from the heavens to vanquish the enemy. All his nervousness had gone; he was totally focused on the destruction he was about to wreak.

"Green section, break left and climb. Go!"

As Green section broke away, Yellow section opened up. Vine's Kittyhawk shook as his guns hammered the target. He felt bloody marvelous.

"Bombs away!" Harris shouted.

Decker and Vine released their bombs simultaneously. Blue section had just leveled out as yellow section finished their attack.

"Fighting cocks… this is Guillotine… over." Valentine got nothing but static. He tried again, "Fighting cocks this is Guillotine, over!" Everyone was silent, their eyes pointlessly searched the trees for the impossible sign of movement. Bugger this! Valentine thought to himself. "This is blue leader… Yellow and Green sections will orbit at two thousand feet… Blue section will remain as top cover. Stay off the RT!" Valentine's thoughts were mixed. Perhaps they were overrun? Radio packed up? Both? He left it for another thirty seconds or so. He was pushing his luck and he knew it. There was still a good chance Jap fighters could turn up and spoil his afternoon tea.

"Sod it," he grumbled.

Hacker was staring more at the sky than the ground. He had implicit faith in Valentine, but he did it naturally, out of habit. A few more seconds passed which seemed more like minutes. Then:

"More smoke!" Vine shouted excitedly.

Valentine winced. "Yellow?"

"It's red, leader."

"I see it," Hacker said.

The pilots stared briefly at the red smoke coming up out of the trees.

"Can't see a yellow marker yet," Vine stated.

Valentine was getting pissed off. He knew they needed help, hence the red smoke, but where? A few moments passed and then Valentine was rewarded with another yellow marker. At the same time his RT crackled. The voice was so faint he could hardly hear the man: "Guillotine, east of smoke, rep– Of... five m–" The message faded to nothing, but it was enough for Valentine.

"Yellow section will attack first, then Green. Strafe east of the yellow smoke... Yellow section go!"

Harris dropped a wing. Decker and Vine followed and took position on his port and starboard side. Diving at their invisible target east of the smoke marker, Harris gave the order to fire. As he did so, he gave the rudder a couple of bootfulls and sprayed cannon shells all over the blanket of trees. Vine and Decker followed suit. Vine watched his and Decker's tracer pummel the area.

"Yellow section, break left and climb," Harris ordered.

Green section, following, opened up as soon as yellow section were out of the way.

Valentine was just about to order Blue section to attack again when 'Fighting Cocks' came over the radio, "Well done Guillotine... we are moving forward. Repeat: we are moving forward... fighting cocks out."

Valentine was mildly surprised. Half the time they didn't know if they'd even hit the target! "All sections make for home," Valentine ordered. "Well done chaps!"

Green and Yellow sections formed up at about 2,000 feet and began to cruise home. Vine was elated. He wanted to go back and do it all again. Decker, looking over at him, smiled grimly to himself and began searching the sky. Above them, in Blue section, Valentine was doing the same, but his eyes were on the weather, which looked like it was about to get worse. "Looks bloody awful up ahead chaps. Yellow and Green section make angels. All aircraft spread out. I don't like writing letters."

Unfortunately, Valentine couldn't have been more right. No sooner had Yellow and Green sections reached Blue section's altitude of 4,000 feet, the squalls were on them.

"Jesus Christ!" Hayward shouted at no one. It seemed as if a giant hand had grabbed his Kittyhawk and shaken it like a rattle. He fought with the stick and rudder to correct his attitude. As soon as he thought he was on an even keel, the aircraft yawed and tossed itself the other way. Hayward could not believe the ferocity being thrown at him. Again and again he was violently tossed about the sky. His visibility was just about zero, and his instruments were a blur. He concentrated on his altimeter and compass as best as he could, the latter seemed to be going north-east and south all at the same time…

It was the same for everyone, yet Vine was absolutely terrified. Gone was his earlier confidence. This was a hell he'd never dreamed of. His port wing suddenly dropped and was thrown violently up again before he could correct it. His nose started to drop and then reared up with such force that it jarred his spine.

Another almighty force shoved his tail up. Vine had no idea what was happening to him. For a split second he could see ahead. Tailplane! "Fucking Christ!" His propeller just clipped it and then it was gone.

Over and above the atrocious weather conditions, Vine could sense the fine vibration coming from his prop. He was shaking like a leaf and it wasn't the storm. His knuckles were white and his teeth clenched. Blood was coming out the side of his mouth where he'd bitten himself. Guilt began to seep in. Who had he hit, what had happened to them? Another jolt and another.

'Chancer' Harris, however, had been through this shit before. His rule of thumb was twofold: one – don't fight the

285

squalls by constantly correcting the aeroplane, because it was bound to trick you the other way out of spite. And two – he'd already made out his will.

After seven or eight minutes the squalls dissipated. As all the pilots came into clear weather, Hacker found himself flying next to Midgeham. In fact, he was only ten feet off his port wing, he edged away. He then noticed they'd all lost quite a lot of height.

Valentine was surprised to find himself behind a very spread-out Yellow section, whereas Vine was simply surprised to find himself still alive.

"This is Blue leader. All sections regroup at 3,000."

One by one they re-grouped. The rain had eased to a sticky drizzle. Hacker looked to his right to see 'Chancer' Harris come alongside. He was wearing a huge grin. Lunatic, he thought.

To Harris's right was Vine, who seemed to be having a fight in the cockpit. In fact, he had got certain parts of his anatomy twisted while being thrown about by the squalls and he couldn't get them untwisted.

This, technically, was a salutary lesson in ensuring your straps are tight before you take off. To Vine's right and slightly below, was Decker. He was constantly correcting on the rudder and stick because his aeroplane seemed to want to dive down to the left. It was Decker who concerned Valentine most.

"Yellow three, this is Blue leader."

"Receiving you, Blue leader," Decker replied.

"Yellow three, your port undercarriage is down. Try and raise it."

Decker kicked himself. 'Idiot!' He should have worked that out himself. He attempted to retract the undercarriage but to no avail. "Won't budge, Blue leader."

"Try lowering the other side."

Decker lowered the other side. After a few seconds the undercarriage showed as locked down. "Undercarriage down and locked, Blue leader," Decker said, relieved.

"No, it's bloody not! It's stuck halfway. Try the hand pump." Valentine had a clear view of the underside of Decker's machine. Decker reached for the auxiliary hand pump and pumped away earnestly but nothing happened.

"Give her a good shake," Valentine said.

Decker pulled up a couple of hundred feet and gave the airframe something else to think about. Again, no luck.

'That's all we need,' Valentine thought.

Decker persevered. "Bugger!" he said to himself.

"Leave it, Yellow three," Valentine called. "Anybody else?"

"Green leader here. We're two short. Brandon and Hayward."

"Roger that, Green leader." Valentine replied. 'Sodding hell!' he said under his breath.

Valentine continued to search the sky above and the trees below but saw bugger all. "Keep your eyes open everyone," he said encouragingly.

Midgeham, at Green two, was gutted at hearing Hayward was missing. He couldn't breathe for a couple of seconds. The two of them had been through a lot together; they'd come through some pretty tight scrapes, both had been shot down once and bailed out. They'd had various landings with damaged aircraft and five kills between them. To cop it because of a lousy storm was something he couldn't digest.

Tillman was looking for his countryman. Unlike Midgeham and Hayward, he hadn't known Brandon that long, but both of them had cut their teeth flying in some pretty awful conditions in Canada. Though nothing like what he'd just flown through.

"Yellow two here... I've got a dodgy prop."

Not much Valentine could do about that. "Keep an eye on it, Yellow two. Anybody else?" His voice had a hint of childish resignation mixed with impatience.

"Green two here, my rudder's playing up and the elevators are sticky."

"Understood." Nothing Valentine could do about that either. "All sections, head for home. Green section will lead."

"Roger Blue leader." Hacker checked his compass.

***

The sea was creating nothing more than a gentle swell as the launch pulled up against the Sunderland's hull. Vinny Hardcastle was the first crew man to climb up the ladder and into the hatch on the Sunderland's side.

"Up you come, sir." He offered Padshaw his hand who was following him.

"Thanks."

One by one the crew, in good humour after being well fed, boarded the Sunderland. Stone was last and pulled in the ladder as he watched the launch depart. The crew made their way to their respective positions. Lenny, however, found his way partially blocked by all the extra supplies brought in from the launch and found himself squeezing past various items. "No booze, I see…" he said quietly. "Someone should get their priorities right." He made his way back to his turret.

Pither made his way up to the cockpit. Josh Pelt began reading off various dials to himself.

"Josh," Stone said.

"Yes, Skipper?"

"If we run into any trouble, you take over Jimmy's position, right?"

"Will do, skip."

Stone turned to Smith. "Come into my office." Stone was firm but not antagonistic. He walked towards the back

288

of the Sunderland, out of earshot of the others. Smith and Padshaw followed. Stopping by a small workbench, Stone turned and leant against it. "You have my undivided attention," Stone said, folding his arms.

"All right..." Smith started with a sigh. "Firstly, my orders come from the very top. Those orders state in no uncertain terms to be in Calcutta as soon as possible. I am to use any means at my disposal to do so." Smith's voice held a heavy air of authority that Stone hadn't heard before. "I am, if necessary, to take any action I deem fit to complete that task ... and, with all due respect, YOU are at my disposal."

Stone drew himself upright with his hands on his waist. "Is that fucking so?"

"Yes, Sergeant Stone. It is."

"Who the hell says I'm going all the way to Calcutta?"

"I do," Padshaw answered gently.

Stone looked at him. Padshaw's face was relaxed but serious.

"Come on old chap... you've got orders to take me there anyway," Padshaw said.

Stone glanced back at Smith and then faced Padshaw again. "I know that, Terry," he said louder than necessary. "But no bloody 'civilian' is going to order me to do it!" Stone knew he was losing; he also knew his blood was reaching boiling point. He very responsibly sidled past Smith to make his way to the cockpit.

"Jacko," Smith said politely. Padshaw thought, Here we go...!

Stone turned and stared.

"Qatar," Smith said.

"Qatar?" Stone almost spat the word out.

"Then Karachi."

Stone waved a threatening finger.

"Look, chum, I've got my flight plan worked out and–"

"And it's not fast enough." Smith was still firm of voice but polite. "Alex to Aden is around sixteen hundred miles, cruising, at, let's say, one fifty?"

Stone glared.

"That's over ten hours. Aden to Karachi. That's all of seventeen hundred miles, eleven hours at least. Karachi to Bombay? Call it 500 –" Stone was mildly impressed but didn't show it "– three to four hours, and then it's still over a thousand to Calcutta. That's well over thirty hours' flying time alone by my reckoning and doesn't include the time it takes to re-fuel." Smith cocked his head slightly.

Padshaw, though he didn't want to, was just about to pull rank, when he noticed Stone gently bite his lower lip, thoughtfully.

"I'm listening," Stone stated curtly.

"Thank you," Smith replied courteously. "Qatar is fourteen hundred miles, give or take, we should be able to top up the tanks there and then. It's a thousand miles to Karachi–"

"What if we can't top up the tanks in Qatar?" Stone interrupted.

Smith gestured to the recently stowed fuel cans. Stone shook his head with a bitter smile on his face. "It's not enough if we have a problem," he said confidently, "and do you have any idea how bloody difficult it is to refuel at sea?"

"I know that this aircraft has a fully laden range of over two and a half thousand miles –" Stone felt mentally disemboweled "– and a final 1,400 miles to Calcutta," Smith added, "give or take." He gave a gentle shrug with his shoulders.

"You'll have us swimming, chum," Stone said resignedly, he glanced at the cans and boxes strapped to the hull. "Thanks to you, we're probably over weight!"

Padshaw saw Stone's face turn from mildly sarcastic to one of resolute Australian arrogance. Stone turned once again to the cockpit, he called out loudly, "Chris!"

"Yes Skipper?"

"Forget Aden… we're going to Qatar, and then Karachi!"

James peered around the navigation table at his approaching pilot.

"Right Skipper," he replied a little surprised. "It'll take me a few minutes to work out a course.

"Well, don't hang around," Stone's voice was filled with childish sarcasm. "Mr Smith's in a hurry."

Smith's pissed him off again, James thought to himself. "Where are you looking at stopping for–"

"Straight there! No stops. We don't want to delay Mr Smith any more than we have to!" Stone shouted loud enough for Smith to hear.

"Oh great…" James said to himself. "We're gonna end up swimming."

Stone reached the cockpit and strapped himself in. Smith, looking at Padshaw, had a satisfied smile on his face. Padshaw clicked. "You cunning bugger!"

"Years of practice old chap," Smith replied.

"*If* Stone gets wind you played him, he'll…" Padshaw was grinning as he spoke.

"I won't tell if you won't tell."

Padshaw smiled and asked, "Fancy a Scotch?"

Ahh, Smith thought back, these must be the reinforcements you mentioned.

"Or do you prefer gin?"

Smith feigned a suspicious look. "It appears I'm not the only cunning bugger."

As Padshaw opened the bottle, the engines on the great flying boat started coughing into life.

After two hours into the flight, Stone, who by now had calmed down considerably, glanced at Pither.

"I'll take her for a bit chum. You go and read a nice book."

Pither realised Stone needed time on his own. "Righto skipper." Pither undid his harness.

"We'll alternate every couple of hours. OK?"

"I'll put my alarm on." Pither made his way back.

To some extent the crew could relax on this particular leg of the journey. The chances of coming into contact with an enemy aircraft were remote. Lenny, in the tail, was scanning the sky every few seconds and was at the same time writing a letter home. Jimmy Creed came into his head, "All the best, Jimmy," he said quietly. To Lenny's way of thinking, people only died when you forgot about them.

Both Smith and Padshaw were lying on the two rear bunks. Both had agreed to stay out of everyone's way, especially Stone's. Smith appeared to be asleep. Padshaw swung himself up and around and sat for a few moments. He'd done a fair amount of long flights himself, but being a passenger was so bloody boring. "Oh well," he said quietly, "may as well finish reading this lot." He opened his briefcase and pulled out the last of the sealed files. He was just about to break the seal when Smith, still lying with his eyes closed, said:

"I really wouldn't bother wasting your time on that, Terry."

Padshaw looked at him curiously. "Why do you say that?" he asked, puzzled.

Smith snorted gently and cleared his throat

"Because it's all academic," he answered with a flat sigh.

Padshaw looked at the file, then back at Smith. "Explain." There was a mild curtness in Padshaw's voice. Smith opened his eyes and looked over. "Everything you've read, or been led to believe, is nothing more than a smokescreen –" Padshaw was wide eyed and somewhat taken aback "– a fabrication, to put it another way."

"I think you had better explain," Padshaw stated with authority. "Now!"

Smith sat up, as he opened his mouth to reply.

"And no more games," Padshaw added, with a stony face.

"No more games, Terry… you have my word."

Padshaw relaxed a little. A few seconds passed.

"Well," Smith began, "where to start?!"

"I find the beginning always a good idea," said Padshaw.

"Quite so… but we haven't got that much time." Smith gave his best wry grin. It was difficult not to like Smith, but Padshaw wanted answers, and right now. "Perhaps it would help if you could explain, at least in part, what your involvement, or your mission, in all this is?" Padshaw queried.

"My mission, Terry, is easy. It's you."

"Me?"

"Yes, always has been."

"I don't know quite what to say. In what capacity am I your mission? I mean… I don't see the sense of it."

"You may recall a certain meeting with 'Batty' Beecham?"

Padshaw's eyebrows went up, he'd never heard Beecham referred to as 'Batty' before and how did Smith know him? "Yes of course, but –"

Smith raised his hand. "Best you regard that meeting as an interview."

"Interview?"

"Yes. You see, Beecham specifically wanted you for this assignment –" Padshaw nearly spoke but decided to let Smith continue. He nodded encouragingly "– but he had to convince the bigwigs that you were the right man for the job. Hawkins too, for that matter."

"But what about this special squadron I was ordered to form –" Padshaw swallowed hard "– what about all those poor bastards I put on a troopship?"

Smith came in quickly. "Not your fault–"

"That's easy for–"

Smith raised both his hands this time. "The forming of a new squadron for operations in India had already been decided. Even now they're trying to get more pilots out to the East."

"What's Hawkins play in all this?" Padshaw asked, at the same time thinking, Is there anything or anyone Smith doesn't know?

"None of my business. One doesn't ask too many questions in this job. Anyway, as you may have surmised, you came through with flying colours."

"Oh bloody good show." Padshaw's voice was deadpan. There was a short silence.

"I'm led to believe you're quite fluent in Chinese languages?" Smith asked softly.

"I used to be a language master, so what?" Padshaw couldn't see the relevance.

Smith drew himself upright. "My orders are to get you into China."

"China!"

"Where," Smith continued, "you will attempt to negotiate certain military contracts and long term arrangements with Chiang Kai-Shek."

Padshaw really was speechless. Smith waited for him to digest what he'd just said. Padshaw quickly pulled himself together. "I know nothing about such things… what on earth was Beecham thinking?"

"No idea, old boy. Perhaps that's why we call him 'Batty'."

"Christ Almighty!" Padshaw went into silent thought for a few moments. He hadn't pulled the short straw; some batty bastard had given it to him. He didn't want to go to bloody China. Just then, all his years of service asserted themselves. "What happens when we get to Calcutta?"

'Batty' really did make the right choice, Smith thought. "I have to arrange transport north. Where, hasn't been disclosed yet. No doubt there will be some ludicrously pompous, stiff upper-lipped, low-ranking officer with delusions of grandeur of course, waiting right now, to let us know."

Padshaw gave the hint of a smile. A thought occurred to him. "One thing seriously concerns me."

"Please," Smith replied helpfully.

"I find it difficult to see how Chiang Kai-Shek is going to be remotely impressed by a mere squadron leader, to handle such delicate negotiations."

Smith smiled. "Good point," he reached under his bunk and, still smiling, pulled out an RAF tropical-issue tunic, neatly folded. He offered it to Padshaw. "Courtesy of 'Batty' Beecham."

"He's already given me one."

"Not like this, he hasn't."

Padshaw took it by the collar and gave it a shake. His jaw dropped. "Bugger me!"

"Congratulations, Wing Commander."

"I don't believe it."

Smith handed him an envelope. "Corresponding bumf I believe."

Padshaw was thoughtful and then smiled. "What will Jacko have to say? He doesn't even like junior officers at the best of times."

"Well he's going to be upset for a long time, then."

"How so?"

"That envelope you're holding also contains his promotion to pilot officer." Smith was grinning from ear to ear. "I'm glad it's your job to tell him, he'd probably shoot me."

Padshaw laughed out loud. "Don't be so sure he won't."

For a short moment they sat silently, but still smiling. Both comfortable in the company of another professional.

"Oh well... I suppose I'd better go and give him the bad news."

"Good luck," Smith replied sarcastically.

"Thanks very much!" Padshaw stood up. "On second thought…" he sat down again, "I think I'll wait till we've put a few miles behind us. Don't want him turning back out of spite, do we?"

Smith laughed.

***

"Corporal Naylor?"

"Sir." Naylor was still getting used to his new rank, but both Connors and Blackman had already noticed a marked change in him. Naylor walked confidently up to the jeep. Connors lowered his field glasses and tucked them into his sling. Naylor saluted.

"Sir."

"Blackie?" Connors said.

"You and I are going for drive, Corporal."

"Right you are, sir."

"Get plenty of fuel and some rations."

"Yes sir."

"Be gone."

Naylor nodded and trotted off.

"Good choice, Blackie."

"He'll do… Quick brew-up?"

"Why not?" Connors fumbled for his cigarettes.

Connors' progress for the rest of the previous day had been much the same as it had been in the morning. Nevertheless, the mules were beginning to tire and the terrain wasn't getting any easier. Connors had decided to bed down for one more night and aim to be at the LGI the following evening.

By late morning the following day Connors had continued to make good progress. In hindsight, it may have been more practical to have split the mules and vehicles, but he'd stuck with his decision and had been rewarded with no setbacks and no injuries. The rain had never really stopped, but there had just been a torrential downpour which had brought them to a complete halt, and had bogged down one of the trucks. This took some time to dig out.

By three o'clock it had become apparent, that short of an act of God, he wouldn't make the LGI before nightfall, not with the mules. The chances of Japs turning up again was also highly unlikely. In fact, after their earlier run-in, both he and Blackman discussed the confrontation in some detail.

Their original route had taken them well east and slightly south of their destination. Pick-ups and drops with various locals were not that uncommon, however, some locals would volunteer as guides or translators. Some tagged on to help forage in return for minimal reward, it didn't hurt to keep them sweet. Nevertheless, the Japanese unit they engaged had been some way north of any others reported before.

"Maybe they got lost?" Blackman suggested half joking.

"I doubt that, Blackie… he was up to something."

"Not now he isn't."

"Mmm…" he offered Blackman a cigarette. "Got a light?"

Blackman sighed and pulled out his lighter.

Burns had been driving, albeit one-eyed. They'd stopped while Sergeant Bell had gone ahead with three men to check the terrain. They had come across two different tracks up ahead. A choice had to be made.

"They're probably as bad as each other," Blackman commented, gesturing ahead.

"We'll see," Connors replied. Bell had sent two men to the left while he and Jenner took the right.

"Let's see about that brew up, eh?" Connors said as he clambered out of the jeep. Burns and Blackman followed. "This is as good a place as any. Plenty of cover, anyway."

They walked back to the vehicles and mules.

Mercer was walking purposefully towards Connors.

"This isn't good news," Connors said to Blackman under his breath.

"Go on, tell me the worst."

"Private Hurns just died, sir."

For a moment, Connors had to think. Hurns, yes, bit of a poet... always taking bugs out of his tent... bit of a recluse. "What happened?" he asked gently.

"Shock, I think. Took one bullet in the leg and another grazed his skull. Not enough to kill him, though."

Connors was quiet, he glanced at Blackman.

"I'll get on it," Blackman said softly and walked on.

"Must be close," Mercer said, looking towards the two trails and wiping his forehead.

"Not far. We'll bed down here for now, I've given 'Blackie' orders to go on ahead to the LG, let them know we'll be there tomorrow."

Mercer nodded.

"Tea?"

"Why not."

Half an hour had passed when Sergeant Bell returned. "Sir?"

"What do you reckon, George?"

"The track to the right is the best option, sir. Pretty flat, and wide enough for the vehicles. Only just... but..."

"But good enough?"

"Yes, sir."

"Well done. There's a brew on... get yourselves something."

"Sir."

Blackman put a wooden box into the back of the remaining jeep. He looked around. "Corporal Naylor!" he shouted.

"Coming, sir."

Naylor appeared out of the undergrowth and trotted up.

"Time to go."

"Yes sir." Naylor got behind the wheel.

"I hope you washed your hands?"

Naylor stared wide-eyed.

Connors sauntered over. "See you tomorrow, Blackie… with any luck."

"Hope so. If you haven't appeared by tomorrow evening, I'll report you AWOL."

Connors smiled. "See you tomorrow," he said, gesturing with his bad arm.

Blackman nodded and then looked at Naylor. "Corporal, if you would be so kind?"

"Sir."

Naylor revved the engine and dropped the clutch. Blackman's head jerked slightly. "And we'll have less of that!"

"Sorry sir," Naylor replied innocently, but with something of a grin. Blackman frowned at him.

Bell had been right, the track made for good time. Blackman was holding a map and marking it in various places, endeavoring to choose the right moments to do so in between ruts and holes, which the jeep was constantly bouncing out of. "Bloody awful driving Naylor."

"Thank you, sir."

Blackman pulled out his cigarettes and lit two. "Where do you hail from, Naylor?" he asked loudly over the engine.

Naylor took the cigarette. "Cheers, sir… Aldershot."

"Army born and bred, eh?"

"You could say that, sir." Naylor took a long pull on his cigarette. "Truth be told, I was going to be a gardener. Till this little shindig kicked off."

Blackman looked at him thoughtfully. "Maybe you still will… when this –" Naylor bounced in and out of a large hole. Blackman came out of and back into his seat. Painfully "– little shindig is over!" his voice was pained.

"Sorry sir, missed that one."

"No Naylor, you didn't," he replied through gritted teeth.

Both of them grinned wryly.

***

Marsland had briefed his remaining pilots on the possible order of the day and glanced up as the last of the three sections flew off. No prangs.

"On with the day then." He turned and found himself facing Hollingsworth.

"Trouble in the ranks, sir," he said.

"Oh... what's the problem?"

"Our Australian friend."

Marsland's eyebrows went up. "Shall we?" Marsland pointed to his hut. They walked towards it. Once inside, Marsland sat down. Hollingsworth remained standing. "Go on," Marsland said encouragingly.

"Well, it appears our colonial friend has little or no respect for the erks... been quite unpleasant, apparently."

"Says who?"

"Massey."

"I see..." Marsland knew Massey wasn't the sort of chap to make such comments idly. He thought for a moment. "Any idea why?"

"Haven't a clue."

"Any of the chaps been baiting him?"

"Not to my knowledge... seems to get on with the other pilots OK. It's just the ground crew from what I can gather."

"Mmmm... have Mr Decker report to me as soon as he's landed."

"Right sir."

"I'm not having his attitude undermine morale on my squadron."

"Quite so, sir."

"Conditions are difficult enough here as it is." Marsland slouched back into his chair. "Did Massey come to you?"

"No, 'Punchy'."

"What does he think?"

"He doesn't know either, sir. But you know how defensive he is of his chaps. I mean, if one of them steps out of line, 'Punchy's on them like a ton of bricks. On the other hand…"

"Tell 'Punchy' I'll deal with it."

"Will do, sir." Hollingsworth had yet more bits of paper in his hand. He glanced at them. "Erm…"

Marsland sighed. "Just tell me."

"All just to be signed, sir." Hollingsworth smiled.

Marsland took them, his eyes darted around his excuse for a desk. "Got a pen, Holly?" He looked up, Hollingsworth was holding one for him. Marsland grunted. "Any news on that Lysander?" he asked, signing everything very quickly.

"Tomorrow I believe."

"Good show… anything on how the pongoes are doing?"

"Nothing solid I'm afraid, still plugging on south. But I don't see them making much progress in the current conditions. Bloody weather. Still, at least they're advancing, eh?" Hollingsworth had a confident tone to his voice. Marsland didn't want to dampen it.

"That is encouraging," Marsland replied, but inwardly he didn't give much for their chances. But still, why spoil the adjutant's day? He passed back the dreaded 'bumf'.

"Well done sir, I'll be off."

"And I think I'll have a quick word with 'Punchy'." Marsland stood up, Hollingsworth followed him out.

By half past ten everyone was expectant of Valentine's return. Marsland stood with the other pilots, chatting.

"Sir?" Cavendish interrupted Marsland and cocked his head towards the approaching adjutant. Just beyond him, Marsland could see Neane, the radio operator, leaning against the tent pole, head down, smoking. What now, dammit!? As Hollingsworth approached he shouted out "'Punchy'! Fire Bell!"

On hearing this, the pilots quickly disappeared. Some went for extinguishers, or buckets of sand. 'Punchy' was ringing the bell madly as ground crew and pilots alike got ready for a possible forced landing.

"Who is it?" Marsland asked before 'Holly' could speak.

"Decker, his undercarriage is jammed half down. They're about ten minutes away."

"Righto… hopefully–"

"And Midgeham's got rudder and elevator damage. Don't know how bad."

"If his elevators are shot…?" Marsland could see a look in Hollingsworth's eyes, he stopped in mid-flow. "What else, Holly?"

"Vine's got a damaged prop… and we're two down."

Marsland's mouth opened a little.

"Brandon and Hayward, sir."

"It never rains…"

"No sir."

Neane called out, "Sir!"

Marsland trotted over, with Hollingsworth on his heels. "Go ahead."

"'Snobby's bringing them in now, sir. He's ordered the three damaged aircraft to land last."

Aero engines filled their ears.

"Right you are… 'Holly', brief 'Punchy'."

"Sir."

Marsland looked up as the first aircraft came over the trees. A Hurricane... 'Chancer' Harris. He was on the ground very quickly. Before he'd reached the end of the strip Tillman's Kittyhawk was flaring out. Next was

Hacker. Valentine was close behind. Both turned left off the strip and taxied as close as they could to the tree-line. Valentine pulled his mike to his mouth. "Yellow two… you first."

"Roger."

Vine turned into wind, the vibration from his propeller was now so bad it shook the airframe. As he flared over the trees there was an almighty bang and the engine revs dropped. He pushed the stick hard forward and pulled back just at the last second, resulting in a near perfect three-point landing. He then got as many revs as the labouring engine would give him and taxied out of the other's way. God his balls hurt! Still, small price to pay.

"Yellow three… your turn."

"Roger that."

Decker had deliberately set himself up for a long approach. Right up to the last practical moment he kept trying to raise his undercarriage, over and over. He kept trying the hand pump. "Bloody thing… hopeless. Here we go then!" Decker turned into wind. Not too much flap, watch the airspeed, little more stick.

Marsland watched him clear the trees, Bit high, he thought. Valentine was now standing on the wing of his Hurricane. "Come on, sideslip. You're too high!"

As if he had heard him, Decker gave it some right rudder and left stick. The Kittyhawk lost fifty feet. "Nicely done," Valentine muttered, "come on. Throttle back."

Decker corrected and then cut back the throttle: nothing happened. The throttle was jammed. The trees were looming at the end of the strip, he cut the engine and held the stick back. At stalling speed, the port wheel touched the ground and started to fold up. As soon as the starboard wheel hit the ground it came out in sympathy and collapsed. The stationary propeller then dug into the ground and the whole aircraft went arse over tea kettle. The fuselage split just behind the cockpit. The engine was wheezing and ticking. Spots of rain sizzled as they landed on the underneath of the engine cowling. Decker was hanging in his straps; he was pushed up against the side of the canopy. He tried to move, but everything seemed to happen too slowly. He watched his hand as if it were not his own, reach lethargically for the harness release. "Come on! You can go quicker than that!" he shouted but even that sounded like a gramophone playing at the wrong speed.

'Punchy' Jennings was racing for the stricken Kittyhawk with five or six men following behind. Ahead of him was Massey, a hatchet in one hand and a knife in the other. There was nothing Valentine could do; he ran to the radio tent. As he went in, Neane got up. He passed Valentine the radio. "Green two, you will have to orbit, we're a bit busy down here. Over."

"Understood. Out."

Midgeham had had a grandstand view of Decker's arrival. He was pleased to see there was no fire. That really was a shitty way to go. He started his first circuit. Massey reached the upturned Kittyhawk. As he crawled under the wing he could see Decker was conscious.

"Move back!" he shouted. "I need to smash the runner!" Massey gestured with the hatchet to the edge of the cockpit hood.

Decker's traitorous hand suddenly moved quickly, he pulled the pin and more or less fell on his side. At that moment his sense of smell came back. The stench of fuel was everywhere. Massey gestured again with the hatchet. Decker moved as far as he could to the other side, half kneeling.

Massey swung the hatchet against the runner as hard as he could. Part of the runner tore away. Again and again Massey wielded the hatchet. It was difficult to get a good swing. Next moment 'Punchy' Jennings was beside him. "Here!" Jennings produced a three-foot crowbar. "Use this!"

Massey dropped the hatchet and, taking the crowbar, forced the flat end into the jagged hole he'd made. He half stood and the two of them began levering away the side of the hood. Jones and Carver crawled in from the other side of the wing with another crowbar. As Jennings and Massey prized the hood from its runner the others, using the hooked end, pulled it further out. Massey grabbed his hatchet and smashed the framework.

"Lever it open, lads!" 'Punchy' shouted.

"Come on!" Massey shouted and grabbed one of Decker's arms. With Massey pulling on him and shouting encouragement, Decker crawled through the gap. He was still dazed and couldn't find his feet. Massey took him under one shoulder and Jones took the other. Decker half walked and stumbled as he was helped away.

No fire.

Valentine was now standing next to Marsland. He looked up at Midgeham's Kitty. "Elevators you say?"

"Rudder not too hot either." Valentine's voice held some concern.

"He'd still be pushing his luck even without that!" Marsland looked over at Decker's Kitty.

Valentine was sucking on his lower lip. Marsland turned to Neane.

"Sir." Neane passed his headset.

"Midgeham, this is the CO. Over."

"Receiving you."

Marsland looked at Valentine.

"He'll come a cropper if he tries to put it down."

"Agreed," Valentine replied seriously.

Marsland put the mike to his mouth while holding one earpiece to his ear. "I'm ordering you to bail out! Make as many angels as you can and point the bus towards the bay, over."

Midgeham had bailed out once before, he didn't fancy doing it again. He looked down at the strip, with Decker's wreck where it was. A landing would be pretty hairy anyway. Worst of two evils? Bugger!

"Understood... making angels."

That was easier said than done. Whenever he pulled back on the stick there was little or no response at all. He opened the throttle and started some wide circuits of the airstrip. His climb was very shallow and he had very little response from the rudder. He'd never land this in one piece! Best of two evils, then.

Decker was delivered to the MOS hut. He was sitting on the end of a cot. As Massey and Jones left, the MO held his hand up in front of Decker's bruised face. "How many fingers?" he asked, loudly. He had a clenched fist.

"Two," groaned Decker.

"Well done old chap."

Outside the rest of the Squadron was looking up. Two thousand five hundred feet at least, that's what the altimeter said. Midgeham slid the hood back. He really didn't want to get out, he was comfortable here; nice solid aeroplane, the Kittyhawk. Rugged, dependable. It wasn't a Hurricane, but it was just as tough. Two thousand seven hundred. The rain had more or less stopped. Midgeham took that as the signal to get out. He made sure he was pointed towards the bay and then unclipped his harness. He methodically removed his radio lead. He double checked his parachute harness, pulled his feet up and patted the side of the aero plane. "Goodbye girl!" And jumped.

"He's out!" Cracken shouted. Everybody stared. Almost immediately a long plume of silk appeared above the falling pilot.

"It's not open!" someone shouted.

"OH CHRIST!" Valentine said.

Marsland stared helplessly with gritted teeth.

Midgeham desperately tried pulling at the shrouds. "C'mon damn you…" Some men turned away. "Open you fucking bastard!"

A little over one hundred feet above the ground at the edge of the strip, the parachute deployed with a loud whop! Midgeham hit the ground awkwardly and with some force. Later, people said he actually bounced…

"Not our most auspicious start to a day," Marsland said. They were in Marsland's hut. Valentine had just given Marsland a report on the morning's events. "Still… the brown jobs are very grateful. So grateful, in fact, they've asked us to do it again."

Valentine looked over at Decker's Kitty. It was going to take some time to clear the mess and fill in the ruts. More work for the roller.

Marsland raised his hand. "Holly's told them we're grounded till tomorrow."

"Good."

The MO walked in.

"God bless all here… where's the gin?"

"I'm out of gin!" Marsland replied indignantly and glanced at Valentine.

"Not guilty," Valentine said in all honesty.

"Mmmm… how's…?" Marsland looked at Valentine again.

"Midgeham?"

"Midgeham."

"Broken angles, one broken leg, broken collar bone and his back's suffered. Not broken, though. Lucky bugger at that!"

"Sit down Doc… 'Snobby'?"

Valentine raised his eyebrows attentively.

"…Bottom drawer."

Valentine pulled the drawer open.

"I thought you just said you were out."

"I've been taking lessons." Marsland leant behind him and produced three tin mugs.

"What about Decker?" Marsland asked, as Valentine poured.

"Badly bruised around the shoulders and ribs... and an almighty lump on the side of his head. Blurred vision. I've grounded him for now."

"Mmmm... I still want a chat with that young man."

"Yes, I heard... none of my business mind you, but I'd wait a bit."

"Really? Why?"

"Well... we just had a little chat. I think you may find that our Mr Decker has a new attitude."

"Divine intervention?" suggested Valentine.

"No," he was smiling, "nothing so dramatic."

"What then?" asked Marsland.

At that moment Hacker and Hollingsworth walked in.

"I'm out," Marsland said straight away. And he was. The bottle was empty.

They both stared.

"Bad time?" Hollingsworth asked.

"No... just listen," he nodded at the MO, "pray continue."

"It's all a bit sad really, but, in a nutshell... Decker had an elder brother who was also a pilot. His aircraft developed a problem and he had to pancake. Due to faulty maintenance his undercarriage collapsed on landing. It flipped over and he was trapped inside... he burnt to death."

"I see," Marsland said thoughtfully.

"The ground crew involved were found to be negligent and were either court marshaled or reprimanded." He finished by gently shrugging his shoulders.

"... All right, we'll give him some time to settle in. What have you got, Holly?"

"Vine's Kitty's had it I'm afraid. Needs a new prop amongst other things. He's a bit upset as well, actually."

"What's his problem?"

"He reckons he flew into the back of someone in that storm."

"Hardly his fault. Did damn well to get it down. 'Hack'?"

"I'll have a word with him, sir."

"You do that."

"Is that it?"

"Just the paperwork for today's losses," Hollingsworth said in a quiet whisper.

Valentine snorted. Marsland ignored both of them

"Good... so long as that's all," Marsland emphasized the 'all' and stared at Hollingsworth, who then bowed in the manner of a patient valet.

"Right... let's get on."

***

In fact, it only took Hawkins a couple of days to locate the men he was after. Like Padshaw before him, he'd left a few disgruntled officers in his wake, after having pinched some of their most skilled men. Beecham had asked for around thirty men. Hawkins had located twenty-eight and was leaving it at that. Hawkins' office door was slightly ajar; he could hear the steady chatter of typewriter keys. He called out to his orderly.

"Marston?"

The chatter stopped, Marston came in. "Yes sir?"

Hawkins handed him the list of men he was about to recruit.

"Make transport arrangements for these men..."

"Sir."

"Quick as you can." Hawkins gave him a polite stare.

"Right away sir."

Hawkins picked up the phone. "Group Captain Beecham, please."

An hour later, Hawkins walked into the officers' mess. Beecham was standing by the fireplace with two subordinate officers. He gestured at them with his tea cup, emphasizing his final point.

"Really sir? I had no idea."

"Hence the term 'freeze the balls off a brass monkey'."

"Well I never!" said the other officer.

Beecham caught Hawkins out of the corner of his eye.

"Excuse me."

"Of course, sir."

Beecham walked towards Hawkins. The two officers' faces said *Thank fuck the old sod's found another victim!*

"How's it going Graham?"

"Twenty-eight experienced men, sir."

"Well done."

"Transport is being arranged as I speak."

"Excellent. I've taken the liberty of getting the cooks to knock something up for us." He gave his cup and saucer to a passing orderly.

"Right you are, sir." The kitchen was closed; Hawkins knew that for a fact. Bugger, what now? Beecham gestured towards a table laid for two, it was by a window and to one side was a painted latticework screen which created some privacy.

"Better than a stuffy office, eh?"

"Quite so sir."

Two kitchen orderlies appeared and drew back their chairs.

"Thank you," Hawkins said as he sat down.

"Not the Grosvenor House Hotel is it?" Beecham said tongue in cheek. "Still, I'm sure they'll make the effort." He smiled.

"I'm sure they will, sir." Hawkins picked up his napkin, he was wary of what was coming next.

"Sir?"

Beecham raised his hand politely, Hawkins leant back as they were served bowls of soup.

"Ah, cockaleekee... well done." Beecham gave the slightest nod to the orderly. He leant forward, "Time to bring you up to speed."

Thank Christ for that! Hawkins thought to himself.

"Sorry to keep you in the dark for so long."

"I'm sure you have good reason, sir."

"The thing is..." Beecham was now quite serious, "things in the East, as I'm sure you're aware, haven't been going our way." A resolute look came over Beecham's face. "But that's about to change."

Hawkins made to interrupt, again Beecham's hand was there, he was in full flow.

"We desperately need to get supplies to China. So as they can give the Japs a good kick up the arse from their side. The Chinese need supplies of just about everything." Beecham took a mouthful of soup.

So do we, Hawkins thought, and started spooning his own soup.

"Guns, ammo, materials, men trained in all aspects of modern warfare. We've got hardly any transports for the job and the ones we do have are flying nonstop." A plate of sliced bread appeared.

"Sounds like we're on a bit of a sticky wicket, sir." Hawkins took a slice and dunked it.

"Nothing a good batsman can't sort out. Anyway, as I said, that's about to change." Beecham took a mouthful of bread.

Hawkins wanted to ask a multitude of questions, but decided to stay silent.

"Starting now –" Beecham swallowed "– air transport command is taking up the reins to supply our Chinese allies. More aircraft of all types will be made available over the next few months. Our American cousins are being most helpful in that respect. We will be flying as often as possible to get as much as we can to them. I cannot overemphasise the importance of these supply drops."

"I understand, sir."

"I hope you do!"

Here comes the axe, Hawkins thought.

"Your job is to reinforce our somewhat depleted contingent of trained men."

And my head falls into the basket. Sod it!'

Beecham paused. He held up his spoon. "Don't misunderstand me. The chaps we've got out there are doing exemplary work in deplorable conditions. They work miracles every day and deserve every bit of praise going." He took another mouthful of soup. "But they're almost exhausted." He dunked some bread. "Disease is rife." He put the bread in his mouth and talked over it. "Poor bastards are dropping like flies." He swallowed. "As soon as you and your chaps get there, you are to start training as many available men as you can lay your hands on, got that?"

"Yes sir." Hawkins hesitated for a moment and then asked the one questions he didn't want to hear the answer to. "When do I leave, sir?"

"There's a convoy going out day after tomorrow."

Hawkins was not surprised.

"Your chaps should all be here by then." Another mouthful of soup. "You'll get your written orders tomorrow." Beecham stared at Hawkins's soup. "Eat up, old chap. Roast beef next!"

Hawkins gave a bitter smile.

***

After around six and a half hours' flying, Padshaw got up yet again to stretch his legs. His head had been buzzing with the news of his promotion and what went with it. As expected, Stone was not impressed by the fact he was now an officer. Padshaw had found him in the galley. Stone looked up as Padshaw had entered.

"You haven't got that bastard with you have you, Terry?"

Padshaw glanced behind for effect. "He's reading his orders, I think."

Stone reached for a mug and gestured towards the steaming pot on the stove.

"Not for me, thanks." Padshaw said politely. Stone sipped his tea quietly "He's got a bloody awful job to do, Jacko," Padshaw said in Smith's defence.

Stone nodded with a grunt. "I know. But he gets right up my nose."

There was a short silence. Into the breach once more! Padshaw thought, as he pulled the envelope out of his pocket.

"More bloody orders?" Stone asked.

"For you." Padshaw handed Stone the envelope.

"Great." Stone slit it open with a finger. "More bloody bullshit." He began reading. After a couple of lines his eyes started to widen: *Your professionalism in the air against such daunting…* Stone's eyes darted around the page *the fact that your aircraft had suffered… the losses the enemy sustained… the manner in which you…* His eyes went to the last paragraph. *You are hereby promoted to the rank of Pilot Officer with immediate…*

"Am I fuck! Te—" Stone looked up. Padshaw had gone. He stood and shouted, "Bastards! I don't want to be a bloody officer! Are you listening?" He stormed towards the rear bunk area shouting obscenities.

"Told him then," Smith grinned.

"I'm not joking Terry," Stone said as he entered the bunk area. He saw Padshaw putting on his new tunic. Padshaw turned to face him. For a moment Stone was silent.

"And you think you've got problems," Smith said laughing.

"Bugger me!" Stone replied. "Does that mean I have to salute you now?" he asked with a tight smile.

"If you do, Jacko, I'll promote you to flying officer!"

Stone knew that he was beaten. "Sod it all... the boys are gonna make my life hell! Congratulations, Terry," he added.

"Thanks, you too."

"Yeah right." Stone turned towards the cockpit. "Lucky fucking me! One of the chaps now, don't you know," he added, with a bloody awful clipped accent.

Padshaw was dozing when Chris James appeared. "Congratulations on your promotion, wing commander." There was just enough satire in James' voice to come through.

"Thank you," Padshaw replied in the same tone.

"Pilot Officer Stone –" Padshaw could see James was enjoying himself "– as skipper of this boat, orders the wing commander to come and fly it for the last couple of hours to Qatar." James wore a huge grin.

"He's forgiven you then?" Smith said.

Padshaw smiled and went forward, apart from anything else, he was glad of something to do.

Just over two hours later, they were floating on the water. Illman and Pither were taking turns retracting the nose turret. (The Sunderland flying boat's nose turret could be retracted into the fuselage by manual operation of a chain drive. Once inside, a folding mooring bollard was locked into position and an anchor could be lowered.)

Stone scanned the immediate shore. "No sign of Mr Smith's imaginary re-fuelling arrangements!" he said curtly.

"Oh come on, Skipper," Pelt said in Smith's defence, "he's got everything else right."

"Nevertheless," Stone replied with satisfaction in his voice, "I will take great pleasure of informing him of his failure." Stone had a satisfied smirk on his face as he got up. "I shall enjoy this!" As he started his way back, Padshaw too, got up.

"I'm beginning to feel like a tennis net between those two," he said lightly, as he passed by Pelt. Pelt smiled.

"Give us a hand with the anchor Josh!" Illman called.

"Coming."

Smith was looking out of one of the portholes at the shore as Stone walked in.

"Doesn't seem to be anybody here to help, old boy." Stone was relishing every word. Smith's face was one of mild annoyance. He gently bit his lower lip. "Are you sure we're in the right place?" Stone cocked his head in anticipation. Smith remained silent.

"Oh well." Satisfaction and sarcasm flowed copiously. "Best laid plans of mice and men, eh?" Stone turned to go and found himself facing Padshaw.

"Not so bloody clever this time, was he?" Stone made his way forward and started whistling a very cheerful rendition of *Waltzing Matilda*. Padshaw, now in the doorway, looked at Smith.

"What do you think happened?" Padshaw asked, mildly concerned.

"To what?"

"The re-fuel–" Padshaw stopped in his tracks. Smith was desperately trying not to laugh.

"You knew...?" Padshaw ran out of words.

"Well, Jacko wasn't going to happily fly all the way here knowing he had to re-fuel this beast himself was he?" Smith was just about containing his laughter.

Padshaw stared for a moment and then turned his head and laughed. "We'll say no more about it, eh, Terry?" Padshaw waved his agreement as he stifled his laughter with the other hand.

It took two hours to manhandle the cans of petrol up through the engineer's hatch, and top up the tanks. On this occasion Stone had Smith mucking in as well. All things considered, it was the least he could do. Though Smith was constantly grinning to himself, which caused even more annoyance to Stone. It was bloody hot work, everybody was stripped down to the waist and working their bollocks

315

off. Padshaw, however, had been given the task of fishing from the nose of the Sunderland, whether this was because Stone felt uncomfortable with having a wing commander muck in with the others, Padshaw wasn't sure. What he was sure of was the fact that he couldn't fish!

With re-fuelling complete, Stone made sure everyone took turns to eat, but more importantly drink. He then checked with Pelt.

"What d'ya reckon, Josh?"

Pelt was writing down figures while munching a biscuit. "Ask me later, Skip." Pelt was concentrating very hard. Stone gave him a gentle pat on his shoulder and left him alone.

Illman and Pither had raised the anchor and just finished winching the turret back out. "Turret locked and secured, Skipper!" Illman shouted.

"OK."

Padshaw was in the co-pilot's seat.

"I forgot to ask: any luck, Terry?" Stone asked, strapping himself in.

"Nothing biting I'm afraid," Padshaw replied.

"You were using the wrong rod, Terry."

"Wrong rod?" There was only one, he thought to himself.

"When we fish," Stone said knowingly, "we use a hand grenade!" Stone gave a broad smile.

"I'll know next time," Padshaw replied understandingly. They began checking off instruments.

As Lenny was making his way back to his turret, he noticed what looked like more cans of fuel under some hessian sacks. He lifted one of the sacks out of the way. They'd missed eight cans.

"Bugger... the Skipper will have a fit!" he said out loud.

"Not if you don't tell him," Smith said quietly. He was sitting in the corner of a bunk. Lenny hadn't noticed him. He turned to face Smith.

"Don't be daft," Lenny said smiling, "we need every can we can get."

"Not those you don't!" Smith's voice had turned as cold as ice. Lenny held Smith's stare for a moment and then briefly glanced at the remaining cans. He faced Smith again, and then with a sigh said, "Skullduggery?" It wasn't really a question, more a knowing statement of fact.

"How pleasant it is to have another Englishman on board," Smith replied very courteously.

Lenny gently shrugged his shoulders. He gave Smith a sharp wink and then turned for his turret.

"Christ almighty," he said as he strapped himself in, "am I glad all I have to do is shoot people." He stared out at the sea as dusk began to fall.

The Sunderland droned on throughout the day. It was easy for boredom to set in, so Stone had his crew regularly rotate positions. Some caught a little shut-eye when possible. Stone, Pither and Padshaw took turns at the wheel. Lenny was back in the tail again, having had a spell in the nose and then half an hour's restless sleep. He looked around to his right, which was now greenery and hills, to his left, the sea. We're over halfway, he thought.

Josh Pelt was keeping an eye on his engines and the fuel consumption. He was continually scribbling down figures and then, forty minutes later, drawing lines through them.

"How are we doing?" Padshaw asked.

Pelt was leaning over the seats looking at dials. "All right so far… we've used less fuel than I thought. Tail wind helps." Josh turned, Stone was holding two mugs. "Pilot Officer Stone, sir. Excuse me sir… very sorry sir." He bowed very graciously.

"Fuck off!"

"Yes, sir." Pelt left, sniggering to himself.

"Bastards!" Stone exclaimed, handing Padshaw a mug. "You've ruined my life, chum," he stated accusingly.

"Don't blame me." Padshaw took the mug. "I didn't promote you."

"Oh, sure, you had nothing to do with it." Sarcasm flowed like the Niagara Falls.

"Your professionalism in the air..." Padshaw said airily.

"Don't you fucking start. Drink your bloody tea."

Padshaw grinned into his mug.

Chris James came forward. He was holding a map. Stone turned slightly in his seat as James leant forwards.

"By my reckoning we're here, Skipper, give or take a few miles." James used the point of a pencil to indicate their position. "Chahbahar is on our left, I reckon... so we've got another 450 miles to go... ish."

"How's our fuel?" Stone asked.

"Josh says it'll be tight but we'll be OK so long as the winds don't change too much."

"OK."

James turned to leave.

"... Chris?"

"Skipper?"

"I want a position and fuel report every hour till we get to Karachi."

"Will do Skip."

James left.

***

Blackman and Naylor were making good time. The terrain was pretty bone-jarring and they'd had to change a flat tyre, but apart from that the going was as good as it could get.

"I reckon we're almost on them."

"Right sir."

318

"Mind you, we could easily drive straight past with all this." Blackman gestured at the thick wall of greenery on all sides. The day was coming to an end and the light was beginning to fade.

"Bastard!" Naylor shouted as he slapped his left arm. "Some bugger just bit me!"

"They're not fussy then."

Naylor stared at Blackman who was smiling to himself. Just then Blackman slapped the back of his neck.

"You're right sir... they're not are they?"

"That's insubordination Corporal."

"Yes sir."

"You can be court–" Blackman raised his hand "–pull up... cut the engine."

Naylor stopped abruptly. They were both listening.

"Get your rifle."

Naylor's faith in Blackman's judgment was total. He grabbed his rifle and stood by the jeep, searching the trees.

"Smell it?" Blackman asked.

Naylor sniffed, at the same time, giving Blackman a puzzled look.

"No sir..." he moved a couple of yards forward of the jeep. "Cigarette smoke!" he said quickly. "To the left." Naylor pointed his rifle.

"Let's go... Slowly, Corporal."

"Sir."

Side by side they moved forward. After a few yards Blackman gently put his hand on Naylor's left shoulder.

"Don't move..." he whispered, drawing his revolver. "Quietly now."

A few more yards and they broke cover, the cigarette smoke was coming from behind a framework of bamboo.

"Christ almighty," came the somewhat high pitched, unseen voice. "I'd give my left bollock for a solid turd!"

"I think we're in the right place, sir," Naylor said quietly, and grinned. "So to speak, that is."

"Who goes there?" came a curt voice behind them. Blackman and Naylor turned slowly to be confronted with a Lee Enfield rifle pointed at them. "Captain Blackman and Corporal Naylor," Blackman replied, in an authoritative tone. "Advance party for the supply train for this squadron." The sentry lowered his rifle. Blackman holstered his revolver. In a more relaxed voice he added, "Looking for the front door. Perhaps you'd be kind enough to show us?"

Marsland was standing outside his office with Hollingsworth and Jennings.

"Turns out the engine's shot as well, sir. So I'll get the lads to use Vine's Kitty for spares."

"Righto, Punchy. Let me know how many aircraft are available for the morning, soon as you can."

"Will do."

"We have guests." Hollingsworth announced, pointing at the jeep coming towards them. As it drew up the sentry was the first out.

"Found these gentleman by the latrines, sir."

"Well done, Carver. That'll be all."

"Sir."

As they both got out of the jeep, Jennings' face lit up. "Blackie… you old bastard!"

"Hello Punchy! Nearly drove straight past you."

They shook hands vigorously. The others looked on with amused interest.

"Glad you didn't… did you manage to? Ahem?"

"The supplies you requested are on route."

"Excellent. Captain Blackman, this is Squadron Leader Marsland." Jennings introduced them. "Captain Blackman is my cousin," he added.

"Aha," the adjutant murmured quietly.

"Squadron Leader."

"Captain."

They shook hands. Both had a good firm grip and looked at each other in a confident and relaxed manner.

"This is my adjutant–"

"Hollingsworth," Hollingsworth interrupted. "Pleasure to meet you."

"Likewise old chap."

As they shook hands Blackman half turned. "This is my corporal, Naylor."

Naylor saluted very smartly. "Sir."

Marsland noted a look of respect in Blackman's eyes as he introduced Naylor. He returned the salute and then looked at Jennings.

"Punchy?"

"Sir?"

"Find a spot for the captain and his corporal to bunk down later and tell the cooks we have guests."

"Will do, sir." Jennings smiled at Naylor.

"This way Corporal."

"Naylor!" Blackman called.

"Sir."

"Be kind enough to give Mr Jennings the box in the back of the jeep."

"Will do sir."

"Captain?" Marsland politely gestured Blackman into his office.

"Thank you."

Connors was looking up at what he could see of the night sky, smoking, as Lieutenant Portman came alongside him. There was a light drizzle, but everyone was so wet with sweat anyway, it made no difference.

"I've posted the sentries and put them on three-hour spells sir."

"Jolly good… have you eaten?"

"Just about to, sir. Mr Mercer would like to see you if you could spare a moment, sir."

Connors sighed. "Will do." He found Mercer and Lance Corporal Fenn sitting on boxes, comparing notes on paper that was so sodden it was almost tearing.

"More bad news Doc?" Connors asked.

"Not yet. A couple of these chaps really need to get to base hospital for treatment, ASAP. Otherwise..."

"Mmmm," Connors was thoughtful. "Well, let's hope we can get them flown out tomorrow, eh?"

There wasn't much more Connors could say. In the past, he had had to make some soul-destroying decisions which on more than one occasion had ended in him leaving wounded men to die.

He'd had a pretty shitty war so far. A lot of his friends were dead. Most of them killed by disease rather than enemy action. Some had gone mad, some had got lost, which was pretty common. Others had been posted to other theatres and he'd lost touch for one reason or another. He didn't feel bitter or in any way sorry for himself. He just sometimes wondered where the bloody hell it was all going. In fact, the more he thought about it, the more he understood that his main battle was with the surroundings he was in, rather than the enemy. His thoughts were broken by Sergeant Bell handing him a mess tin.

"Cook says you haven't eaten, sir."

"Bugger... thought he hadn't noticed." Connors grudgingly accepted the mess tin.

Mercer and Fenn smiled at each other. Connors forked out a lump of bully beef. He stared at it for a moment.

"I want to be on the move by 0630 hours, George."

"Right you are sir."

He put the fork in his mouth and winced.

Blackman pulled back the flap on 'Punchy' Jennings' tent. "Permission to come aboard?"

Jennings gave a broad smile. "Granted."

Blackman sat on a small, tired cane chair. He had just come from the mess hut. He'd eaten pretty well and had been given a warm welcome by everyone he'd spoken to. For some time, he found he was the center of attention. After all, he was a different face, who offered a change of conversation.

"I hear you're 'Punchy's cousin," Harris proffered.

"Well, you can't choose your family can you?" Blackman replied haughtily.

Harris smiled and then saw Valentine walk in.

"I say, 'Snobby'?"

Valentine walked over.

"Captain Blackman, 'Punchy's cousin. This is 'Snobby'."

"Good evening old chap."

"How do you do?"

They shook hands.

"If you find these chaps are boring you, I can easily have them shot –" Blackman's eyebrows went up "– no trouble, really."

"That's very kind of you... I'll let you know."

"Anytime old chap." Valentine turned politely away, he then glanced back over his shoulder. "And don't lend them any money either... they'll buy sweets. Very bad for their teeth."

Blackman nodded reassuringly. "I won't."

Valentine wandered off.

"Is he always like that?" he asked Harris.

"Like what?"

Blackman grinned. He liked Valentine.

As the evening had gone on through, he had learnt of the day's losses, which put something of a damper on things. Now in Jennings' tent, he brought the subject up.

"Not a good day, then?" he said gently.

"No... poor buggers only just got here, too."

"I didn't want to ask any pertinent questions in the mess, but what happened?"

Jennings recited the day's events.

323

"Christ..." Blackman said. "And I thought we had a bad time of it."

"We lose more aircraft to the weather than we do to the Japs... still, it's the same for them I suppose."

"Yeah, but they deserve it!"

Jennings reached under his camp bed.

"Thanks for these." He was holding up two bottles of Bells whisky. "You're a gent, 'Blackie'."

Blackman smiled.

"The rest will be arriving tomorrow."

"Just in time –" Blackman looked at him quizzically "– CO's birthday," Jennings informed him.

"Ah... I did wonder."

"He works bloody miracles, he does. Never stops."

"Holly and I..."

"Holly?"

"The adjutant."

"Got it."

"We thought we'd surprise the bugger. Besides, the chaps haven't had a blowout for months."

"All in a good cause, then?"

"We like to think so. They could bloody well do with one after a day like today." He put one bottle down and pulled the cork of the other. "After you."

"Thanks."

Marsland was in his hut on his own. The adjutant had popped his head in fleetingly but had seen that the CO was writing and the only time the CO didn't get Hollingsworth to do the bumf was when those letters had to be written. He could see that the CO was struggling a bit and decided to leave him to it. He'd written quite a few of these now, Marsland was thinking to himself. Why was he having such trouble this time?

He sat back... he'd only known them a few days... hadn't really even had a proper chat with any of them. Maybe he should make more of an effort? On the other hand, if the silly buggers are going to get themselves killed, maybe they should write their own letters in advance. Help the CO out, for God's sake. His thoughts came back to the Squadron. Five aircraft and two pilots gone in one day. Not forgetting another pilot crocked... and no doubt the brown jobs will be screaming out for air support in the morning. On the upside, what with more supplies arriving tomorrow, he had never been so well equipped. "No excuses," he said to himself aloud and felt better for it. "In fact... I think I'll fly tomorrow. After all, it's my birthday!"

He looked at the blank piece of paper. A few seconds passed and then he picked up his pen.

***

It was now less than half an hour to Karachi. They'd been flying in semi-darkness almost from the off and Chris James had got his work cut out. If nothing else, he did enjoy a challenge. The tail wind they'd encountered earlier had been kind enough to still be following them. Stone was at the wheel when Pelt came forward, reading his notes with a small torch.

"Fuel's looking OK, Skipper. Even got a little to spare."

"Thanks Josh."

As Pelt moved away, Chris James came forward.

"Just received word from Karachi, Skipper. There's a good moon but they're laying on fire pots to help us in."

"I'm glad of that. Let's hope the sea's not too choppy."

"And we're to approach from east to west, keeping the flare path on our starboard side."

"Roger that. Tell Simon to come up, he needs the practice."

"Will do."

Half an hour later they were on the water being towed by a small launch towards a mooring buoy. As soon as the

Sunderland had settled on the water, Smith and Padshaw made their way forward.

"You made good time Jacko," Smith commented politely.

"Yeah well, if you wanna get a job done right, get an Aussie to do it."

Padshaw gave the slightest of grins. Pelt and Illman were again retracting the turret prior to dropping anchor. A few minutes later, having completed their task, they climbed the staircase up to the cockpit.

"Where do we eat and bunk down?" Pelt asked, as he got to the top.

"Arrangements have been made," Smith replied.

As if on cue, Mike Illman called out:

"There's a launch laying up alongside, Skipper!"

"Shall we?" Smith added. One by one they climbed down into the launch, Stone last. The man at the helm looked like a local vagrant. He wore a very old, white captain's cap, yellowed by the sun. A shirt with only one sleeve, khaki shorts and odd sandals. He didn't seem to speak any English.

"Good evening," Lenny had said as he climbed in.

"Yeh, yeh," the man replied with a huge smile, revealing only five, bright, shiny teeth. Lenny gave up.

The crew were sitting on benches fixed to the hull. The gentle *phut*, *phut*, *phut* from the engine was almost relaxing. As they pulled up alongside a rather rickety-looking pontoon, they were met by a mass of a man smoking a large pipe. His deep matted beard hid a well-lined seafarer's face.

As they climbed out of the launch he welcomed them with a rather gruff manner.

"Good evening... or is it morning?" He had a hard Hampshire accent and didn't look happy to be kept from his bed.

"They all roll into one, really," Smith said politely.

"You must be Smith," the man said just as gruffly.

Stone smirked. Before Smith could reply the man turned and started to walk off. "This way..."

Padshaw glanced at Smith and raised his eyebrows. They followed him down the short walk to the concrete slipway. There were various buildings and huts constructed out of just about everything, lining the waterfront.

"I've laid on some hot food and some bunks."

"We're most grat–" Padshaw tried to reply.

"Over there's a washroom and latrines," he pointed vaguely in the direction of two smaller huts. He reached a corrugated iron fronted building and turned to face them. "Eat here. Bunk rooms round the back." He took a long draw on his pipe and exhaled. "You'll be refueled by 0600. Goodnight." He methodically placed his pipe between his teeth and shoved his hands in his pockets. With that, he walked off into the night.

They walked into a large, dingy, badly lit room. There was one large table and six chairs plus a couple of wooden benches, one with a broken leg. On the table was a stack of odd-sized plates and some mugs, together with a huge pot of something hot, which didn't smell too bad. There were two jugs of water, and, apart from a wooden box with spoons in it, that was it.

"Christ, what a shit hole," Stone said with feeling. Even Smith was silent. Stone was thinking. It was around two a.m. local time. They'd had a bloody long flight and everyone was dog tired, him included. He looked at his surroundings. Bugger this!

"Take-off at 0630," he added with some authority. Nobody wanted to argue with that. They were looking at the pot of food.

"Any volunteers?" Lenny asked.

At 0630 the Sunderland's hull left the water.

327

The day after his meeting with Beecham, Hawkins had taken his wife out for the day. They'd had a light lunch and then he'd taken her to a matinee. He followed this with a restaurant meal in the evening. The conversation was very matter of fact. Chit-chat about the neighbours, the tight rationing, one of the locals had been arrested for black marketeering, and so on. He let her do most of the talking. His imminent departure was avoided.

The following afternoon Hawkins found himself on a train heading for Plymouth.

"I'm relying on you," Beecham said as Hawkins got out of his car.

"Yes sir."

"You'll like the hotel. By the way, have a good trip. Driver?" Beecham tapped the driver's shoulder.

Hawkins watched Beecham's car pull away. He continued to watch it until it turned off, though he didn't know why. He then picked up his bags and walked towards the station waiting room. Standing in the doorway, he glanced about the room. Various uniforms were milling about, a couple actually saluted him but most didn't. Why would they? he thought. He was just another uniform, too. Hawkins bought a newspaper and found himself a seat. After staring at the front page for a while, he realised he wasn't even reading it as he put it down.

"May I see your pass please, sir?"

Hawkins looked up at an MP.

"Yes, of course." Hawkins smiled as he gave him his pass. The smile wasn't returned. The MP glanced at it.

"Thank you sir," the MP said as he gave it back. Still no smile. He walked off.

Fifteen minutes later the train pulled into the station, people stood up and joined the crowded platform. It took Hawkins a minute or so to find a seat. Placing his luggage in the rack above him, Hawkins sat down. Sitting opposite was a woman in her fifties, knitting furiously. After a few minutes of listening to the click-clack of knitting needles, he thought of his wife.

He'd risen early that morning to finish packing. To his surprise his wife was already up. He'd had a quick wash, dressed and then methodically placed everything into his bags. Carrying them downstairs, his wife called:

"Breakfast!"

She laid out the table for the two of them. Not much was said. Forty difficult minutes later there was a knock on the door. Hawkins looked out the window.

"My car," he said quietly.

Her eyes began to well up. Hawkins found himself re-assuring her and making light of everything. He gave up and instead gave her a firm hug and a long, passionate kiss. Walking out to the car, the tears began to roll. As the car pulled away, she forced a huge smile and waved. Hawkins waved back, blowing a kiss. Hawkins was brought to the present:

"Tickets please."

He showed his ticket.

"Thank you sir."

He looked out the window. The English countryside raced past. After an hour or so he tried to sleep, but that eluded him. He read the paper for a while. Only then did he inadvertently doze off. As the train slowed he awoke. Walking away from the platform, an RAF corporal approached him.

"Squadron Leader Hawkins, sir."

"That's me," he replied quietly.

"This way sir." At the same time, he took Hawkins' luggage. He drove Hawkins to the Royal Hotel, it took but a few minutes. Hawkins felt a little outside himself.

"Here we are sir."

The corporal got out and opened Hawkins' door. He then retrieved Hawkins' bags from the boot and put them down as a hotel doorman approached.

"Will that be all, sir?" the corporal asked.

"Yes. Thank you, Corporal."

"Right you are, sir."

"Welcome to the Royal Hotel, sir," said the doorman as he picked up Hawkins' luggage. "The grill room is open all day if you wish to eat sir, and the restaurant is available from seven."

In silence, Hawkins followed the doorman up the steps, at which point a bellboy took the bags from him and they both escorted him to the reception desk.

"Will there be anything else, sir?" the doorman asked.

"No, thank you."

"Sir." He nodded and walked away.

"You're in room twelve, sir," the receptionist said politely and nodded at the bellboy who then disappeared.

"Thank you." Hawkins took the key.

"Can I help you with anything else, sir?"

"No. Thank you." Hawkins looked at the key. "Yes, where's the bar?"

Marsland had had a good night's sleep which was unusual. He was also in good humour, which he couldn't explain. Then again, it was late morning and they'd not yet received any orders to fly. Maybe the chaps at Chittagong are having all the fun, he thought.

'Punchy' Jennings popped his head round the door. "Morning, sir."

"Top of the morning to you too, 'Punchy'."

Jennings' eyebrows went up in pleasant surprise at the CO's jaunty reply.

"To what do I owe the pleasure?"

"You asked me for aircraft availability." Jennings reminded him.

"I did, quite right. Read on."

"Well..." Jennings was curious. "I can give you five Kittyhawks."

"Five?"

"One's got a cracked fuel line. They're cannibalising Vine's Kitty now."

"Ah."

"And we've got six Hurricanes –" Marsland opened his mouth but Jennings got in quick "– oil pressure, the lads are stripping it down now."

"Excellent."

"Happy Birthday, sir," the adjutant said cheerfully as he walked in.

"I completely forgot," Jennings said convincingly.

"Just another day in paradise," Marsland replied flippantly.

"Neane's just received this, sir." The adjutant passed Marsland a piece of paper. He read it quickly.

"'Punchy'...?"

"Yes Sir."

"One flight of eight aircraft... four Hurris, four Kitties. Bloody quick if you please."

"Sir." Jennings hurried out to ready the aircraft.

"Pilots?" Hollingsworth asked.

"Hacker with Banner, Chalmers and Miller. They'll make up Blue section. Cavendish, Spencer, Cracken and myself will make up Red section."

"Right sir."

"Where are we going?"

"Cox's Bazaar again. It would appear the Japs are moving up from Akyab in some force. Getting a bit sticky, by all accounts."

"Briefing outside the mess hut. Ten minutes."

"Good as done sir." Hollingsworth left. Outside ground crews were readying the aircraft. Thirty minutes later, Marsland was coming to the end of his briefing. "To sum up, same routine as yesterday, red smoke call for help, .yellow smoke is there to indicate the target. Hopefully

331

we'll be in radio contact with our chaps as we were yesterday. Keith?" Hacker raised his head from his notes. "Your section's got the Hurricanes."

"Right sir."

"'Snobby'." Valentine pretended to pick his nose. "You're in charge."

"Oh goody," he replied childishly.

"Any questions?" There were none. "Good. Empty your bladders. Take off in twenty minutes."

Some pilots went for a pee, the others stood together and had a smoke or indulged in idle chit-chat. Decker was standing by the MO's hut. He looked bloody awful. Banner saw him and walked over.

"Y'all right, cobber?"

"Yeah, not bad... what's on?"

"Same as yesterday I reckon."

"Smoke?" Banner pulled out a packet.

"Thanks."

"I hear you've not been making yourself too popular chum," Banner said politely. Decker took a cigarette and pulled out his lighter. He looked a bit sheepish. "They're a good bunch of chaps here," Banner added and puffed as Decker lit his cigarette and then his own.

"I reckon," Decker replied quietly. Engines coughed into life.

"Gotta go... see you later."

"Good luck."

Banner was already running.

Blackman and Naylor were standing by their jeep. The bonnet was up and Naylor was wiping oil off his hands as they both watched the last two aircraft leave the ground.

"All fixed sir."

"Well done. Fuel line again?"

"It's got a new one now, sir. Courtesy of your cousin."

Blackman was about to comment when the adjutant walked over smiling. "Captain Blackman."

"Just 'Blackie' is fine."

"Right you are. The chaps call me 'Holly'." Hollingsworth was holding his clipboard. "Just wondered if we could go through today's delivery of supplies?"

"Of course."

"Just a general run-down will do. Only I'm trying to get my chaps organised, before your chaps arrive."

"No problem."

Hollingsworth led him towards his hut.

Massey, Jones and Clarke were working on the faulty Hurricane. The day was getting hot again and the Hurricane wasn't playing ball. Tempers were getting a little frayed around the edges.

"Pass me a shorter one," Massey said, sweating like a pig, "this one's too long. I can't get any purch– fuck it!" with a loud *clong* the spanner bounced off at the side of the engine onto the ground. Massey had also nicked his hand. "Bollocks and bugger, he sucked it."

As he looked down from his ladder for the traitorous spanner, he found himself looking at Decker who then leant under the starboard wheel and retrieved the spanner. He passed it up to Massey. Massey wore a stony face and said nothing as he took it off him.

"I haven't thanked you all for–" Decker began.

"All part of the service," Massey interrupted bluntly and resumed his battle. Decker looked at his back for a short moment and then glanced at Jones. Jones gave the beginnings of a smile and then nodded politely. Decker returned the nod and walked off.

"What's with you?" Jones asked. "You wanted an apology, and that was as near as you were going to get!"

Massey mumbled something incoherent and toiled on.

Valentine had been chatting to 'Jiff' Verster and Midgeham. Both were laying next to each other on stretchers.

"Well our chaps are still trying to advance south, obviously," he answered Verster, "but it looks like the Japs are moving north in large numbers, so they've got their work cut out."

"That Captain Blackman says his chaps bumped into a bunch of Japs on the way here. Nearly got wiped out!"

"Bloody Nips are everywhere," Verster stated.

Midgeham's eye was caught by Neane waving.

"'Snobby'." He gestured towards Neane.

"Be right back," Valentine replied casually. He wandered off towards Neane. "Morning old boy, what's up?"

"That Lysander should be with us midafternoon," Neane replied cheerfully.

"Good egg."

"We're to have the wounded ready for it."

"Jolly good. I'll let the Doc know."

"I should tell you that we inadvertently received some supplies this week," the adjutant informed Blackman. Blackman's eyebrows went up in surprise. Hollingsworth first explained about the unexpected arrival of the Hurricanes and that they were, at that time, not equipped for them. Blackman then explained about the confusion they'd had due to bad communications, and at one point didn't know where they were supposed to be and that they'd made the decision to press on here. Hollingsworth then gave Blackman a run-down on the unexpected supplies.

"Thing is, they were meant for Chittagong airstrip but they ended up here. Got lost, apparently."

"I suggest we don't tell my major that. At least not straight away. We've had a bit of a battle getting here and he'll be none too pleased to find out. Got lost? How can you miss Chittagong?"

"No idea. But they did, and we're grateful. Nevertheless, we've got next to nothing in the way of medical supplies and we're short of just about everything else. We're not too bad for grub but whatever your chaps can help us with will be a godsend."

"Adj?" Neane interrupted, holding some paperwork. "This just came in."

"Thank you." He unfolded it as Neane turned back towards his tent. "One moment we have no communications at all and the next..." he began reading. Valentine walked up.

"The Lysander will be here this afternoon Adj. What's that? Love letter?"

"Hrrmph." Hollingsworth looked up. "This'll please the CO. It would appear that this officer who's supposed to be joining us, isn't. How odd."

"Nothing odd about it, old boy," Valentine said casually... it's just another balls up."

Hollingsworth looked sharply at Valentine and gruffly asked: "...Have you told the MO about the Lysander?"

"He's getting Jiff and Midgeham ready as we speak."

"...Good," the Adjutant said firmly, ending all conversation.

'Punchy' Jennings joined them. "Blackie..." he pointed to the other side of the strip. Connors' trucks were approaching. Blackman grinned. By the time they'd walked over to meet them the newcomers were being cheerfully welcomed by half the Squadron.

Blackman made what introduction he could.

"Major Connors –" Blackman started.

"Hollingsworth," the adjutant interrupted warmly. "'Holly' to the chaps."

"Don". They shook hands.

"And this is 'Punchy' Jennings, my cousin." Blackman introduced Jennings with a sweep of his hand as if royalty had arrived.

Connors smiled. "'Punchy'." He shook Jennings' hand and glanced at Blackman. "I didn't realise you had any relations Blackie –" Blackman's eyebrows went up "– thought you were hatched from an egg."

Blackman gave a sour face.

"It had two yolks, Major," Jennings enlightened him, smiling back.

"Shall we get out of this sun, Major?" The adjutant gestured towards his hut. Connors removed his hat and wiped his brow.

"How's your war going?" Connors asked genially as they walked away.

"Still working on it, old chap. Nearly got it right."

'Punchy' Jennings and Sergeant Bell also hit it off on being introduced. Within ten minutes they'd got every available man shifting the supplies. Mercer had sought out Holden and, between the two of them, started checking over the medical supplies and discussing their various casualties.

On completion of unloading the trucks, Bell had the vehicles dispersed so that they were in some cover. At that moment Lieutenant Portman, who'd been lagging behind with a lame mule, broke cover.

"I take it he's with you?" Hollingsworth said politely, gesturing through the open door.

Connors turned in his chair and smiled.

"That he is," Connors replied observing the approaching mules. "Would you excuse me a moment?"

"Of course old boy."

Connors got up and made his way towards Portman.

"Well done, Portman."

"Thank you, sir!"

"Any problems?"

"None, sir."

"Excellent. Get yourself and the chaps a brew and something to eat."

"Yes sir."

An hour or so later, all the supplies for the Squadron had been unloaded and stashed away, apart from several boxes that Blackman had helped with. They were now in the mess hut. Thirty minutes later, Red and Blue flights had returned. No losses.

As Marsland walked away from his aircraft, Hollingsworth met him with Connors and did the introductions. At the same time Mercer and Holden were tending to the various casualties inside and outside Holden's medical hut. A large tent had been erected to make more room for them to cope.

"You've had your hands pretty full," Holden commented, while carefully removing a bloodied bandage off one of the wounded men outside.

"We've certainly had a rough few days... take this." Mercer raised another wounded man's head and popped a couple of pills in his mouth. Fenn passed him a canteen.

"Thanks."

"Two more have come down with dysentery, sir," Fenn informed him.

"This is going to be a very busy day," Holden stated resignedly.

"No peace for the wicked. Next!"

***

As Hacker climbed down from his Hurricane, Jennings sauntered over to him. "Any luck?" he asked.

"Bloody well hope so, 'Punchy'! We clobbered the area they gave us."

"Any problems with the bus?" Jennings nodded towards his Hurricane.

"The mice have been at the tailplane I'm afraid." Hacker gestured. The elevators and rudder had picked up several rounds of ground fire. They went for a closer look. Jennings stuck his right index finger into one of the holes.

"Bloody sharp teeth they've got. I'll get the chaps on it straight away. Shouldn't take long."

"Thanks 'Punchy'."

"By the way." Hacker looked attentive. "CO's birthday party tonight. Mess hut, around sixish."

"Good show. Any booze?"

"All arranged." Jennings smiled knowingly.

"Pass it on to the other chaps, won't you?"

"Absolutely."

"Right then." Jennings examined some of the other holes. "I'd better go and find some sticking plaster, hadn't I!" He wandered off.

Making his way to the mess hut, Hacker glanced over at Holden and Mercer. Holden gestured with his head at the medical hut. Hacker looked on curiously and walked over. Mercer looked up.

"How do you do," Mercer said, trimming off some fresh stitches.

"This is Hacker," Holden informed him.

"I'd shake hands," Hacker said, "but I can see you're busy."

Mercer smiled.

"Someone to see you inside," Holden told him. Raising his eyebrows, Hacker entered the MO's hut. A very battered and bruised 'Bobby' Graham looked up from his bunk at him. Hacker stopped in his tracks.

"I'll be damned! We all thought... How on earth did you ..."

Graham raised his hand. "Pull up a chair."

By three o'clock the Squadron had been called on again. But before they'd even got airborne the mission was scrubbed. As the pilots walked away from their aircraft, the drone of a radial engine could be heard. They all stopped, people started looking up.

At either end of the airstrip were two gunpits surrounded by sandbags. Each pit had a pair of Vickers K machine guns. The covers were being pulled off and men were manning various Bren guns attached to five-foot poles which were scattered around the strip.

"What d'you think, Hack?" Vine asked, searching the empty sky.

Hacker was about to reply when a Westland Lysander appeared over the trees flying very slowly.

"Good show," the adjutant said, as the Lysander came into view from his hut. The gun covers quickly went back on. Marsland walked up to Hollingsworth who was now watching the Lysander's approach.

"Better late than never sir, eh?"

The Lysander deftly came in over the trees, skillfully rounded out and landed without a bounce.

"You're right there. Best you have a word with the MO, Adj. Find out how many ..."

"On my way." Hollingsworth interrupted him and trotted off with some haste. Unbeknown to the CO, he still had a few things to sort out in the mess.

"And I'll talk to the pilot," Marsland said indignantly to thin air.

Between them, the adjutant, Holden and Mercer had decided to fly Verster and Graham out first. Marsland had briefed the pilot on the casualty situation and then had a word with Valentine.

"He says he can do one trip today, but he's at our disposal for all of tomorrow."

"Jolly decent of him. Perhaps you could ask him to bring me a new manicure set, only the last one..."

Connors had sidled up to them. "I believe we're somewhat indebted to you and your chaps," he said sincerely.

"How so?" Marsland replied.

Connors explained their earlier altercation with the Japanese patrol they'd encountered and that several of his men had been chatting to the pilots.

"On the contrary," Marsland said, pointing at a medical orderly making a list of the much needed medical supplies.

"Nevertheless," Connors offered his hand.

"Our pleasure old boy."

Two hours later, Verster and Graham were placed on stretchers to carry them out to the waiting Lysander.

"What about me?" Midgeham said childishly.

"You're going out tomorrow," Holden informed him.

"Fine by me," Midgeham replied very jovially. "Didn't want to miss the party anyway." He giggled a little. Holden glanced at Mercer.

"Had to give him a shot of morphine. His ankles are killing him."

"Ah. Having his own party, then." Holden smiled.

Hacker walked alongside Graham as he was carried out to the Lysander.

"All the best chum," Hacker said encouragingly.

"And to you. Keep your head down."

"Will do." Hacker then made his way to the mess. Ten minutes later Verster was about to be put on the Lysander as Marsland came up to see him off. He put on a smile.

"Good luck Jiff."

"Don't you worry about me Skipper. I hear they've got nurses back at that hospital. I'll be just fine!"

Marsland gave him a broad grin. They shook hands.

A few minutes later, the Lysander was clearing the trees. Marsland watched it fly away. Valentine came up beside him.

"That South African bastard'll be back in no time!"

Marsland turned his head to face Valentine.

"No doubt about that. Any problems?"

Valentine put on a concerned frown.

"Just a small flap on. You're wanted in the mess."

"Oh bloody hell," Marsland replied irritably, "what now?" He started off for the mess hut. "Are you coming or not?"

Valentine grinned. "Right behind you old chap."

The hustle and bustle of Calcutta was almost overwhelming after so many hours flying in the confines of the Sunderland. The streets were milling with sailors, Army types, RAF and civilians. For a majority of the military personnel, there was a waiting game for postings, or a ship to serve on. It was an organised confusion.

Stone and his crew were in the Grand Hotel on Calcutta's Red Road, chatting with other aircrew and each other. The heat was stifling. The smallest movement seemed to require so much effort.

"Christ it's hot," Pelt stated needlessly.

"I'd never thought I'd say this," Hardcastle had his eyes shut and was sweating buckets, "but I'd kill for a rainy day in Ireland and a Guinness." Groans came from various quarters at the thought. A rolled-up piece of sodden paper flew through the air and bounced off Hardcastle's forehead. He didn't flinch.

"If you're trying to make friends Vinny, it's not working," Illman said, as he threw again, missing.

"How long do we have to hang around here Skip?" Lenny asked languidly.

"Buggered if I know. We've been told to wait for orders."

"So we wait for orders. Hours, days, weeks?"

Beer mats and bits of paper flew Stone's way.

They'd touched down just after 1500 hours. No sooner had they finished walking up the slipway than Padshaw and Smith were met by a couple of officers and a civilian wearing a very soiled linen suit. Smith and the civilian shook hands warmly and had a bit of a joke about something, it was obvious they'd met before.

"Christ, don't tell me there's more than one of 'em," Stone said quite loudly. He and his crew were a few yards behind them.

Padshaw, talking to the two officers, turned and gestured in their direction. The officers smiled and nodded at Padshaw. As they walked away, Padshaw approached Stone. "Well, Jacko," he said casually, "I guess this is where we part company."

Stone stretched out his hand. "Gonna miss ya Terry." They shook hands slowly but firmly. "Where for you now?"

"That's something I can't tell you."

"No doubt he's involved." Stone glanced at Smith who was wandering towards them. Padshaw thought for a moment and then said, "Actually, it's his job to look after me., point me in the right direction so to speak, make sure I don't walk down the wrong alleyway." Padshaw was smiling.

Stone's face had taken on a look of understanding. "I see... at least I think I do."

"Good luck, sir," Lenny said, shaking Padshaw's hand. One by one the crew bade their farewells. Smith was standing in front of Stone.

"Thanks for getting us here, Jacko," Smith smiled warmly and offered his hand. Stone took it.

"You've been a right pain in the arse, chum! But you seem to know what you're doing." Stone broke into a smile. "Don't lose him, will you."

"No, I won't."

"There's transport laid on to take you into town, Jacko," Padshaw said. "Food and a billet have all been taken care of. All you have to do is wait for your orders."

Stone looked at Padshaw for a brief moment and then stood to attention and saluted. "Thank you, sir."

The rest of the crew did the same. Padshaw returned the salute smartly and gave a gentle nod. He and Smith then turned and walked away.

Three days later, Stone and his crew were still waiting for orders. The insufferable heat continued to bear down on everything and everyone. In the short time they'd been in Calcutta, they'd realised what a difficult environment this could be. Not just the intense heat, as if that were not enough, but also the diseases that were going around, claiming one victim after another. If it wasn't jaundice it was dysentery, if it wasn't dysentery it was malaria and so on. And the flies were everywhere. "I resign," Pelt said flatly. They ignored him. Stone had been talking to a couple of sergeant pilots. He went back over and sat with Chris James.

"I've had about all I can take of this," James said.

"Think yourself lucky." James raised his eyebrows. "Those poor bastards over there have been here over a year."

"You're kidding!"

"Pilot Officer Stone!"

Illman's ears pricked up.

"Is there a Pilot Officer Stone here?"

"Skipper?" Illman nudged him.

"What?"

Illman pointed at the corporal who then walked over to them. "Pilot Officer Stone, sir."

"Yes, that's me."

"Your orders, sir."

"Thank you." Stone began reading. His crew gathered round. "Back to Blighty for us, boys," he announced.

There were satisfied nods and smiles.

"Make sure you get a good night's kip. We're taking off at 0700."

For the rest of the day they were in good humour and enthusiastic for morning to come. As it turned out, nobody slept that well, it was a challenge just to doze off for a few minutes, not that any of them cared. They were going back to Blighty.

The following morning they were all waiting for the launch to arrive to take them out to their Sunderland, when a car pulled up and a squadron leader got out. He walked up to Stone.

"Morning, sir," Stone said and gave a casual salute.

"Morning." The officer was a little put out by Stone's lax effort. "There's been a slight change of plan."

"Sir?"

"This gentleman will be flying with you back to England."

Stone stared at the officer's car. Taking his bags out of it was the civilian he'd seen talking to Smith.

"We need him there as quickly as possible, understood?"

Stone's jaw dropped, before he could stop himself.

"I don't bloody believe it!"

The squadron leader was wide-eyed, but before he could comment, the civilian had his hand out, offering it to Stone. "My name's Harper."

Stone dumbly shook his hand.

"According to old 'Smithy' you're the best man for the job, so let's get off then, eh?" he walked past Stone who then stared at the back of Harper's head. "Oh, and I need to speak to your navigator. Got a few things to do on the way back."

Stone's face turned to thunder. "God hates me," he said loudly.

Harper was grinning. The squadron leader looked completely lost.

"Here we fucking go again," Lenny said under his breath.

***

The party had gone down very well. Everybody had been invited and had a bottled beer each. The ground crew

344

rotated with those on duty so as everyone got involved at some point.

As Marsland had got within twenty feet of the mess, the adjutant gave Carver a perceptive nod. Carver gently pulled on some twine and a small tarpaulin unravelled itself down the mess hut wall. In whitewash was written 'Happy Birthday Skipper!'

"Bugger me!" Marsland blurted putting his hands on his waist. 'Punchy' Jennings walked up to him with a bottle of beer on a small wooden panel, fashioned to the shape of a round tray.

"Good afternoon sir." Marsland nodded, smiling, and took the beer. "Your table is waiting for you, sir. This way." Jennings turned and walked back into the mess hut, still holding the tray up like a waiter.

The cooks had cobbled together a rich stew with various tinned meats and vegetables plus, for pudding, there was tinned fruit and slightly watered-down condensed milk. To add to the merriment, Valentine had managed to concoct a punch made up of the juices from the tinned fruit, a few bottles of beer and a lot of gin.

Everybody talked to everybody. An hour in, and Hacker was doing what he did best: pastimes detrimental to keeping ones rank.

"'Stubby!'" Hacker called.

Hillman was chatting to Massey. "Yes old chap? Excuse me," he said to Massey and wandered over.

"Do you know how to play 'Bomber'?" Hacker asked.

"Of course! Who is the victim?"

"I thought Vine would make a good engine."

'Stubby' glanced over to Vine who was chatting to Valentine. "Excellent choice, you get it organised and I'll set him up. Tally ho, I say! Vine!"

Hacker went recruiting.

Ten minutes later, word had got round and space was made in the centre of the hut floor. Connors was standing next to Marsland.

"Dare I ask?" said Connors grinning.

"Just don't volunteer," Marsland replied.

Connors looked on, intrigued.

"OK chaps," Hacker announced with his hands up. Silence fell. "This is the story of a bomber coming back after a night raid. I shall need some volunteers."

Cavendish enthusiastically thrust up his hand. "I'm in!" and he walked forward.

"You're the pilot. You sit here," Hacker said. Cavendish sat.

"And me!" shouted 'Spence'.

"Me too!" This from Miller.

"You're the rear gunner," Hacker instructed Miller. "You sit here facing the other way." He indicated a spot six feet behind Cavendish. "You're the port inner engine, 'Spence'."

"Er... right," 'Spence' replied, feigning ignorance.

"All you do," Hacker pretended to inform him, "is lie face down with your arms folded under your chin and make a noise like an engine."

"Oh, right... of course." 'Spence' got down, lying a couple of feet from Cavendish.

"Come on, I need three more engines!" Hacker called.

Cracken and Parish were now standing either side of Vine.

"Shall we, chaps?" Cracken asked, moving forward. As Parish followed, Vine was one step ahead. "Which engine am I?" he asked cheerfully.

"You're the starboard outer. Paul? You're starboard inner." Parish took up the final position of port outer as the other two lay down.

"It's nighttime." Hacker began, "having completed a successful raid." Hacker sounded like he was narrating a play, "Come on, I can't hear the engines!" The pilots started imitating engine noises as the onlookers started chuckling.

"The bomber is returning home... suddenly, the rear gunner spots Jerry!"

"Bandit coming in Skipper!" Miller shouted.

"The pilot opens the throttles," Hacker informed the audience. At once the pilots made louder engine noises, Vine following suit. Walking to the left of Miller, Valentine loudly came out with, "Tackatackatackatack!"

"The port engine gets hit," Hacker continued, "but the pilot feathers it and there's no fire." Parish fell silent.

"The enemy fighter attacks again, but the rear gunner has a bead on him." Both Valentine and Miller competed with their *tackatackatacks*. "The fighter pulls away to the right and gives the starboard outer a peppering." Valentine continued with his limited lines.

"The engine immediately catches fire," Hacker's voice was semi-serious, "but the pilot quickly hits the extinguisher!" At that point 'Punchy' Jennings threw a bucket of water over the prostrate Vine. The hut erupted in laughter as Vine leaped up in shock, arms raised.

Hacker casually added, "And the bomber made it safely home on two engines." He could hardly get the words out. Vine didn't know who to have a go at first, before he could even find the words, Jennings thrust a beer into his hand. Vine was surrounded by laughter. He gave a wry grin, held up his beer and shouted, "Bastards!" Everyone cheered.

During the evening, Marsland learnt from the adjutant that the officer due to join the Squadron, wasn't. His evening went from good, to excellent!

What had been a boisterous and jovial evening the night before was quickly becoming a distant memory. As early as 0600 Neane had been receiving desperate requests for air support. Jennings had got everyone he could muster working on the aircraft. Armourers were checking belts of ammunition, others were topping up the tanks. Massey and Jones were now working feverishly on the Hurricane with the oil leak.

'Punchy' Jennings walked over to them. "How's it going, chaps?"

"Nearly there, 'Punchy'," Jones replied.

Massey was covered in grease and oil, his hands were cut in various places and he was getting pissed off.

"Another pair of hands would help," he stated.

Jennings sympathised. "Well, just do your best."

"Anything I can do?" Decker asked as he came round the port wing. He still had impaired vision in one eye, so the MO had grounded him. Jones gave Massey a nudge. Massey sighed. He stared at Decker for a moment. Jennings was about to speak, but Massey got in first:

"Well you can get your fat Australian arse up here and help with this, if you want?" Massey continued with his fight with the oil pump. Decker grinned. Massey gave Decker a genial stare and then said dryly, "Well don't just stand there, get up here!"

"I'm coming you pommie bastard... I'm coming!"

Jennings nodded courteously at Decker, winked and then walked on.

Just under an hour later, 'Punchy' was walking briskly towards the CO's hut. He looked over at Massey Jones and Decker expectantly, who were sweating over the unserviceable Hurricane. Massey raised his hands and shook his head. Jennings nodded. "I can give you twelve aircraft, sir," Jennings said as he walked in.

"Excellent! Well done 'Punchy'." Marsland, Valentine, Hacker and Harris were studying a map. Jennings joined them. Pointing with a pencil, Marsland continued. "That puts the main contingent of Japs about here... Now, accurate bombing is paramount," he emphasised. "If you are in any doubt at all, don't bomb. They're on top of each other in some places and we don't want any stupid mistakes. Got that?"

"Got it, Skipper," Harris replied seriously.

"Right. Two flights, six aircraft each," Marsland gave Jennings a courteous nod. "'A' flight with me and Keith. Three Hurris, three Kittyhawks. 'Snobby', you and 'Chancer' take the rest." Valentine and Harris nodded. "Squadron call sign remains 'Guillotine'. Theirs is 'Teapot'. Any questions?"

"What happened to 'Fighting Cocks'?" Harris asked.

"God knows," Marsland replied flatly, "let's hope they've linked up with 'Teapot'."

"Any chance of having the day off?" Valentine asked politely. Jennings glanced at the ceiling.

"All right then. 'A' flight up first. 'B' flight an hour later. 'Punchy'?"

"Sir?"

"Looks like we're going to have a busy day of it, so you chaps may have to break a few records refueling and re-arming us."

"We'll cope sir," Jennings replied confidently.

"Jolly good." Marsland gave him a knowing smile. "Anything else? Good. I'll talk to the chaps."

The pilots were gathered outside the mess hut, Vine looked a little jaded.

"I see the starboard outer's not firing on all twelve cylinders," 'Stubby' commented.

"Anybody got a fire extinguisher?" Cracken said loudly.

"Sod off!" Vine said. Some of the pilots laughed.

"Here comes the skipper!" Spence observed. Those pilots sitting on the ground stood up.

"Right chaps." Marsland looked them over. "'A' flight: Miller, 'Spence', Cracken and Cavendish. 'B' flight: Banner, 'Stubby', Chalmers and Parish. 'A' flight to take off in thirty minutes, 'B' flight one hour later. That's all." Marsland went back to his hut.

Looking on from outside the MO's tent, Connors and Blackman were talking with Mercer and Holden.

"According to our radio OP, Neane, the Lysander's due back in an hour," Holden informed them. "By all accounts, it's allocated to us until all the hospital cases have been flown out."

"Excellent," Connors replied. "We're most grateful."

"Our pleasure," Holden replied. "And talk of the Devil."

Neane was approaching them with a piece of paper.

"This just came in for you Major." Neane passed Connors the message.

Connors read it. "This could be worse," he said, in a relaxed voice.

"Keep us in suspense, why don't you?" Blackman commented sarcastically.

"We're to make our way north to Chittagong," Connors informed him, "and await further orders."

"That's it?" Blackman asked, a little surprised.

"Apparently, yes."

"Does it say when?"

"No." Connors was a little puzzled, normally he was being harassed from all directions. The adjutant joined them. Connors turned to him.

"Would it be all right if my chaps stayed another night?"

"Absolutely old boy. No problems there."

The pop and crackle of aero engines coughing into life took their attention.

"By the way," said the adjutant, "the CO said he'd catch up with you as soon as he gets back. Apologies and all that, but we've got something of a flap on."

"Yes of course," Connors replied raising his voice.

"I take it our chaps are still advancing then?" Blackman said over the thunder of engines.

"They're trying, but the Japs aren't making it easy for them," Hollingsworth answered. "Latest reports say they're moving north in large numbers."

They stood and watched 'A' flight take off.

Fifty minutes later, at around two thousand feet, 'A' flight were approaching Cox's Bazaar. Marsland's headphones crackled once, the voice sounded distant but audible:

"Guillotine, this is Teapot, over."

"Receiving you Teapot."

"Guillotine, can you see the smoke rising ahead of you and to your left? Over."

Marsland looked down to his left.

"Anybody see it?" There was a short silence, then...

"This is Green leader, I see it."

"Teapot, this is Guillotine, we see it, over."

"Guillotine. Your target is 200 yards directly south of the smoke. Over."

"Roger that, Teapot."

"Green section, you lead. Red section to follow. Bomb and strafe first, then come back round and strafe again."

"Wilco, leader. Green section... turning port. GO!"

Green section turned as one and dived towards the smoke.

"Green section... line abreast and keep it tight! Miller at Green two and 'Spence' at Green three: spread out, flanking Hacker's Kittyhawk. Drop your eggs when I do."

As they flew down through the dissipating smoke, Hacker focused on his invisible target.

"Open fire."

The three Kittyhawks shook as round after round saturated the target, tracer lanced its glittering way into the undergrowth.

"Bomb... now!"

Almost simultaneously, the three Kittyhawks dropped their load.

"Green section. Break left and climb, go!"

As Green section climbed away, the ground below them erupted in flashes of flame, men not cut down in the initial strafe were torn to pieces by the bomb blasts or

351

pieces of flying shrapnel. Through the smoke came Red section. The next moment, small trees seemed to explode as cannon shells punched through them, and anything else that got in their way. Again the whistle of bombs.

"Bombs gone!"

The whop of cannon ceased.

"Red section, break left and climb."

Wheeling around in a sweeping curve, Hacker brought Green section in for its second strafe.

"Keep it tight."

Again the sparkle of tracer tore its way into the trees. Red section was climbing around for another go when Cracken's voice came over the RT. "Bandits above! Bandits above! Coming down now!"

"I see them," Marsland replied calmly. "Guillotine aircraft, make angels."

Red section corrected their turn and opened their throttles wide, desperately clawing for height. But it was Green section who were in real trouble. Height was everything and Hacker had none of it.

"Green section, full throttle and spread out. Don't bunch up!"

"Roger leader."

"Wilco."

"This isn't fucking funny," Hacker said to himself seriously. "Rats in a barrel. Shit!"

The flight of four Japanese Nakajima Ki43s or Oscars' hadn't actually spotted 'A' flight until the bomb bursts got their attention. It was only then that they spotted the three Hurricanes. At just under five thousand feet, all four 'Oscars' dropped a wing and made a beeline for the Hurricanes.

Hacker saw this and realised they hadn't been spotted yet. We may still get away with this, he thought. The gap between the falling Oscars and climbing Hurricanes disappeared in seconds. Red section was still in a relatively loose line abreast formation.

Cracken, at Red two, opened fire first, then Marsland and Cavendish opened up. At that moment, the Oscars split into pairs. The two on the right headed straight for the hapless Kittyhawks. Hacker saw what was coming.

Bugger and fuck!

"Tallyho Green section. We'll take them on the climb."

Spence glanced at his leader. Confident bugger isn't he, he thought.

The two Oscars on the left were suicidally close when they both opened fire on Red section. Marsland and Cracken took various hits as the Oscars knifed through them. Once through, they too turned on the climbing Kittyhawks. Cracken found his forward vision reduced by the starring of his cockpit canopy. As he looked at his starboard wing, he could see various holes and his wingtip was missing. As he looked to his left he was horrified to see two more 'OSCARS' coming in.

"Bandits! Nine o'clock!"

"Red section, break, break, break." Marsland calmly ordered.

Cracken pulled back on the stick with all his strength, sending his Hurricane into a loop. Marsland and Cavendish broke left towards the oncoming Oscars. At this moment they were at the same height heading straight at each other. Both the Oscars saw Cracken's Hurricane coming out at the bottom of its loop. Neither were tempted by the manoeuvre. Cracken looked up. Worth a try, he thought, and then broke hard right.

It was Marsland's cannon that opened up just before Cavendish thumbed the button. Of Marsland's opening rounds, three cannon shells hit the port wing of the Oscar on the left. It buckled immediately. At the same time, two consecutive rounds took out the prop, the top of the engine cowling and the pilot's head. The momentum left in them carried them through the fuselage and into the tail. Bursting into flames it fell from the sky shedding its other wing. Cavendish's opening rounds missed by a whisker. He corrected slightly and was rewarded by his target exploding with such ferocity that all he saw was bits of wing fluttering down.

Both the Kittyhawks and the first pair of Oscars opened fire at the same time. All the rounds from the Oscars were wildly off the mark. Miller's tracer fell just short of his target. Spence's washed over one of them while Hacker saw smoke start to billow from the exhaust stubs of the other. Both Jap fighters broke to their left.

"Leave them!" Hacker shouted. He'd seen the other two breaking away from Red section and coming down on them. "Keep climbing!"

As Green section continued their climb, they were caught in a hail of fire from the descending fighters. The back of Miller's cockpit, fuselage and tail plane were peppered by 7.7mm rounds. To Miller, the thuds and bangs of rounds hitting his aircraft momentarily terrified him. He was still pulling up to meet them when several rounds hit his engine. Part of his engine cowling bounced off the cockpit hood, flames began to leak out of his exhaust stubs.

Hacker to his right took various hits but suffered only superficial damage. Spence took a dozen rounds in his tail and immediately felt the lack of response from his rudder. A few more rounds randomly hit his engine, there was a muffled bang and his Kittyhawk lost speed.

'Bloody hell!' Spence searched his instruments to locate the problem. 'Keep going for Christ's sake!'

Then the Oscars were through them. Opening their throttles, the Ki43s started to pull around to the right. The maneuverability of the Oscar was unmatched but the Kittyhawk was faster.

Hacker looked over at Miller's labouring Kittyhawk. Flames were licking over the top of the engine. He glanced at his altimeter. About 1800 feet. He was just about to call Miller up when Miller's cockpit hood slid back. Smoke billowed out. He saw Miller pulling at his leads and harness release and then partially stand, he was steadying himself with his hands on the sides of the cockpit rim, then he was gone.

Both still climbing, Hacker looked round at Spence, his rudder was barely intact.

"Green three. Head for home. I'll cover you."

"Roger Green leader." Hacker dropped back a couple of lengths.

Spence kept his throttle wide open, but the engine was missing on at least one cylinder, it sounded like it was beating itself to death. Intermittent streams of black smoke began spluttering from the exhaust. Hacker's ASI was reading a paltry 250: they'd be on them again at this rate, and he knew it.

Sure enough, the two Oscars had completed their turn and were now in a shallow climb in pursuit of the crippled P40. Cracken, flying at Red two, glimpsed one of the first pairs of Oscars to attack Green section fly straight into the ground. The other was some distance away, heading south, wobbling and coughing smoke.

Then he saw the second pair of fighters complete their turn and start to climb.

"Green section. Bandits gaining on you, behind and to your left." Cracken gave the Merlin full throttle.

"Roger that. Keep going Spence."

Hacker dropped his port wing and opened her up. Seeing this, the two Oscars spread out.

Marsland, having seen both his Oscars disappear in flames, went to throttle back; only then did he realise his arm ached and was streaked with blood. He looked down, his left leg was bleeding as well. Buggeration!

"This is Red leader. I've been hit... am heading back. Continue without me." Marsland could feel his left leg begin to throb.

Cavendish looked over at Marsland's Hurricane. He could clearly see bullet holes and streaks around Marsland's cockpit.

"Oh sure," he said to himself. He came up alongside Marsland's Hurricane.

"Didn't get that Red leader. I think my RT's on the blink."

Marsland smiled bitterly, he wasn't going to argue. Cracken was now flat out and coming up on Hacker's starboard side. Hacker's headphones crackled.

"Green leader. I'll take the bastard on the right!"

"Roger that Red two!"

Hacker deftly jinked a little to the left as the Oscar filled his gunsight. He pulled the trigger. His tracer seemed to follow an erratic path and then suddenly converge all at once into the Jap fighter. It literally fell to pieces. At the same moment Cracken's cannons pumped round after round into the path of the other oncoming Oscar. Before the pilot could avoid them he was suddenly caught in a merciless onslaught. He didn't know what hit him. Cracken watched his radial engine fly on its own for a split second and then start to fall below.

Hacker called out, "Red two, break left and climb, time to go. Bloody well done!"

"Right behind you, Green leader."

With 'B' flight gone, the LGI now looked more like a private flying club on a quiet day. Apart from the now repaired Hurricane and the Lysander, the strip was void of aircraft.

Both Jennings and the Lysander pilot, Sergeant Pilot Sullivan, were in conversation with Holden and Mercer, discussing in which order to fly out the casualties. Hollingsworth was taking notes.

Lieutenant Portman and three other men were feeding the mules. At the same time, Sergeant Bell and Corporal Naylor were overseeing the servicing of the vehicles. And for once, there was no sign of rain.

Connors and Blackman, meanwhile, were discussing their choice of routes to Chittagong.

"I'll go along with that, Don," Blackman agreed. "Apart from this section here –" Blackman indicated on the map spread over the jeep's bonnet with his unlit cigarette, "– we should make reasonable progress. What time do you want to leave tomorrow?"

"If the weather stays like this," Connors looked up at the sky, "the lieutenant and his mules at 1000 hours and the vehicles at midday."

Connors pulled out a lighter, Blackman put on a wide-eyed look of surprise.

"Wonders will never cease!"

They both turned their heads to the radio tent as they heard Neane's raised voice.

"Adj!"

Hollingsworth looked up from his notes, Neane ran up to him.

"The CO's been hit. Terry says to have the MO ready!"

Jennings ran like a sprinter off the blocks for the fire bell, at the same time shouting orders. Mercer grabbed a stretcher. As Holden went into his hut for his medical kit, the adjutant called over to Connors.

"Don! We need you."

Connors had already started the engine.

Marsland was beginning to feel light-headed. Now his chest hurt as well, it was an effort to breathe. He struggled to focus on his instruments, he could hear Cavendish talking to him but nothing seemed to make sense. He knew that he should be doing something, but he couldn't quite put his finger on what. His eyes were getting heavier, he was opening and closing them.

Cavendish, flying alongside, could see Marsland's head lolling. Cavendish put on his best authoritative voice:

"Squadron Leader Marsland! You are to land immediately!"

Marsland's head jerked up. He looked about the cockpit, everything seemed a little clearer. Check

357

airspeed... undercarriage down... Marsland struggled with this, but it felt like someone else was doing it and he was just watching... and locked. Check landing area's clear... he looked down, but couldn't focus properly... flaps... a little more throttle... down... down.... He cleared the tree line by bugger all. Jennings and the other onlookers winced. More by luck than judgement, Marsland drifted down on a perfect attitude... Down... down... flare now! The Hurricane's main wheels touched the ground, at the same time Marsland had just enough left in him to cut the engine. As the tail wheel touched the ground, the propeller came to a halt. A few more yards and so did the Hurricane.

Marsland didn't move, his head was slumped and his hands hung lifelessly. The jeep raced forward with men running behind it towards the stationary Hurricane. It ticked gently and patiently waited for them.

As soon as he had said goodbye to Stone, Padshaw had been whisked off by Smith for a private briefing. They were sitting at a table on a covered veranda. The clammy heat seemed to drain the very life out of Padshaw. To add to the heat was the almost constant aroma of bad sewage, intermixed with the occasional waft of vehicle fumes, topped by that of ripe body odour. Probably his, he thought. But to look at Smith, you would think he revelled in it. Padshaw was quietly impressed. Smith, as wily as ever, had managed to scrounge some tea and some biscuits.

"Before you ask, Harper put me onto a few people before he left."

Padshaw sipped his tea.

"The doubt didn't enter my head."

Smith grinned. At his feet was a leather satchel. He picked it up and placed it on the table. Padshaw simply glanced at it.

"Everything you need is in here, Terry. Questions to ask, requirements, options, what we can offer – and what we can't."

"Aren't you coming with me?" Padshaw asked quietly.

"Oh yes. Be assured of that, but a civilian in such meetings would be frowned upon, even raise suspicion, and we don't want that, do we?"

"Good point."

There was a short silence. Smith saw the patient look on Padshaw's face.

"You see, the thing is, when all this is over, there are a lot of political and business issues to be discussed. We – that's the British government – firmly believe that we can all benefit each other. Not just then, but now."

Padshaw was about to speak, but Smith continued.

"The point is, that the Americans feel the same way and–"

"Hang on. Aren't we all in this together?" Padshaw interrupted a little puzzled.

"Of course we are." Smith was very re-assuring. "But we'd just like to get a foothold first."

Padshaw's eyebrows went up, he looked slightly amused.

"Besides, what they don't know won't hurt them." Smith sipped some tea.

"What happens next?"

"Firstly, we have a meeting with various intelligence types and then we have to get you to Dinjan."

"Dinjan?"

"It's in Assam. It's one of the airstrips used to get supplies to China. From there we fly straight to Kunming, where, I've been led to believe, various ranking Chinese types will be there to meet us. That's it really, in a nutshell."

"You certainly make it sound straightforward. Let's hope it is."

Smith dunked a biscuit.

"Well, as it stands at the moment, I don't foresee any major problems."

Half his biscuit fell into his tea.

Two days later, Padshaw found himself staring out of an open-fronted tent. As he looked about him, there was a constant movement of men, boxes, pallets, sacks and God knew what else. He was mildly amused at the efforts of six men trying to get a less than helpful mule into the DC3.

"Put up a fight," he said lightly. "I would!"

Smith, who was standing a few feet from the mule pointed at what looked to be stacked fuel tins, and then gestured towards the Dakota. Of the three men he was talking with, two of them nodded. Smith and the third man then made their way towards Padshaw. Padshaw got up. The third man was a pilot, as he approached he saluted.

"Sir."

Padshaw returned the man's salute.

"At ease. It's too hot."

"Pilot Officer Marham, sir." He stood relaxed.

"He's known as 'Chunky' apparently," Smith advised Padshaw.

Marham was slightly built. Standard RAF humour, Padshaw thought. "We'll have finished loading in about half an hour, sir. As soon as we're completed, we'll get you both on board."

Padshaw nodded. Marham did look awfully young.

"I take it you know the way?" he said in a relaxed manner.

"Yes, sir." Marham had an engaging smile. "This will be my twenty-fifth trip over the 'Hump', sir."

"Well, 'Chunky', as soon as you're ready, so are we."

"Sir." He left.

"According to his CO," Smith said, "he's an exceptional pilot. Pulled off some pretty hairy trips, by all accounts."

Padshaw walked back into the tent and as he sat down, said, "Join me, why don't you?"

Padshaw had a mischievous look on his face. As Smith sat down, Padshaw produced one of the bottles of gin supposedly meant for Marsland.

"I say, topping suggestion."

"I gave the rest to Lenny, to share with 'Jacko' and the others."

He passed Smith a tin mug and poured. They toasted each other.

"Here's mud in your eye."

"Cheers."

Once the Japanese had cut the final road with which to send supplies to China, the only option available to the Allies was to supply the Chinese from the air. Separating the area of Assam and Kunming were the great Himalayan Mountains. At over 500 miles across and over 16, 000 feet high, they were a formidable challenge to cross. To make things worse for the aircrews of these mainly unarmed transports, to avoid Japanese fighters they were required to fly around and through the most horrendous weather conditions. The nimbocumulus clouds were far higher than the operational ceiling of a Dakota. Flying through one could easily rip an aircraft to pieces. Flying as best to avoid them required exceptional navigation.

Flying the 'Hump' was not for the faint-hearted.

One hour into what had been a relatively smooth flight was beginning to become anything but. The Dakota was starting to buck and shake quite violently. Padshaw unstrapped himself and went forward. As he reached the cockpit a huge downdraft sent him colliding into the side of the fuselage. Nursing a badly bruised shoulder he grasped the back of the co-pilot's seat. Dark brown cloud was everywhere. It was almost impossible to see anything else.

"I must ask you to get yourself strapped back in sir!" Marham shouted.

Before Padshaw could reply the co-pilot shouted back:

"Starboard engine loosing revs, Skipper!"

"I see it!" The co-pilot looked out at the engine.

"It's cut out, dammit!"

The Dakota immediately started losing height. Marham repeatedly tried to re-start the engine.

"Come on! Come on for Christ's sakes!"

"It's not having it Skipper!"

Smith came up alongside Padshaw, clinging on to restraining straps as the Dakota was thrown about. The altimeter was winding down their loss of height rapidly. The co-pilot again and again tried to restart the engine as Marham fought with the controls. The moment they dropped out of the thick cloud base, the starboard engine began to cough into life.

"She's trying, Skipper!"

The canopy of trees was getting closer. Marham had the port engine at full throttle, but was still losing height.

"I can't keep her up!" Marham shouted despairingly.

Padshaw glanced at Smith, all the lines of stress seemed to have left his face. He looked younger, and relaxed.

"Do look where you're going, 'Chunky'," Smith said casually.

Padshaw looked forward. At just a few hundred feet and rapidly coming up to meet them, was their own personal mountain.

"Oh Christ," Padshaw said emptily.

***

After being at sea for three days, Hawkins had bugger all left to bring up. He'd tried various remedies suggested to him by various people who had sod all knowledge of what they were talking about. He had now simply resigned himself to the fact he would never keep anything down until he was on dry land again. Not for the first time since he came aboard, he cursed the fact he'd ever met Beecham.

During his first day at sea, he'd assembled all the men he'd recruited, and given them a general briefing as to what would be required of them. When he'd finished, half of them had already been sick. Outside, the swell of the sea was getting worse and it was blowing a gale. The bad weather continued into the next day.

By the third day it had calmed down. Nevertheless, Hawkins found himself clutching the guard rail on the port side, trying to bring up something from his already empty stomach. An Army captain came up alongside him.

"Try this old chap." He offered Hawkins a hip flask.

"Thanks, but I don't think –"

"You'd be surprised," the captain interrupted and stuck the flask under Hawkins' nose. Hawkins forced a grin and took it.

"Take a big swig old boy."

It was rum, and it coursed through Hawkins' body like wildfire. Hawkins' chin was on his chest.

"Christ almighty!"

"Better?"

Hawkins breathed out slowly.

"Yes... actually." He was a little surprised.

"Have another."

Hawkins dutifully had another mouthful and passed the flask back.

"You've saved my life old chap," Hawkins said, choking slightly.

"Pleasure." The captain took a large gulp and put the cap back on.

For a few moments, they both stared out across at one of the other merchant ships. The captain turned to Hawkins. "Harry Gresham."

"Graham Hawkins." They shook hands.

They both continued their stare. Thirty seconds passed.

"I bloody hate these things," the captain said, matter of factly. "That's why I joined the Army."

"I can't stand ships either." Hawkins took a deep breath, thinking he was going to vomit again. "Hence..." he gestured at his own uniform. Another few seconds passed, again the captain glanced at Hawkins.

"Fancy a game of poker?"

Hawkins didn't really like gambling of any sort. Then again, there was bugger all else to do.

"Why not?"

An hour later, sitting in a store room and Hawkins was half a crown down. He hadn't had one decent hand. Of the five of them who started playing they were now down to three. Gresham wasn't faring well either. A Sub Lieutenant Russell, who had joined them earlier, couldn't seem to do a thing wrong.

"Where are you headed?" he asked Hawkins as he dealt.

"India," Hawkins replied and looked at his cards. Total rubbish. Gresham frowned as he looked at his hand.

"How many?" Russell asked Hawkins.

"Two... and you?"

"No idea," he looked at Gresham.

"One."

Hawkins looked at Gresham.

"I fold," Hawkins said dejectedly.

"Here," Gresham filled Hawkins' glass with rum. "Your luck can only improve."

"Don't you believe–"

The crash was deafening, all three of them were flung violently to the floor as the entire ship seemed to jump a hundred feet to one side. Boxes and containers of all descriptions rained down from the shelves above. One of them hit Gresham as he struggled on to all fours, knocking him out. Hawkins struggled to get up, he was clutching at a metal shelf support. The ship began to list.

"Give me a hand with him!" Hawkins shouted.

With difficulty, Russell clambered over the debris on the floor. Between them they heaved the unconscious

364

Gresham up. They staggered for what seemed an eternity to the open door to the passageway. Again the ship was hit.

"Come on!" Hawkins shouted.

They fought against the listing ship, foot by foot, to the stairwell. It seemed to get further away the nearer they got to it.

"You first!" Hawkins ordered.

Russell had Gresham's right arm around his neck and held on to it with his left hand like a grim death, his right hand grasped the stairwell support. Hawkins had most of Gresham's weight on his right shoulder, one hand clasping at a leg and the other jumping from step to step. With only five feet to go, the water came in with a rush.

'B' flight had returned without loss. 'Punchy' had all his ground crew working flat out to re-fuel and re-arm all the serviceable aircraft. Banner's Hurricane had been hit by ground fire and had been leaking glycol all the way back. Parish had also taken a few hits and his starboard elevator looked like a sieve.

On hearing the CO had been badly hit, all of the pilots were milling about around the mess, continually glancing over to where they could see Holden and Mercer working on him.

Valentine was in Marsland's hut, staring at his empty cane chair. He poured himself another gin and necked it. Hacker came in, Valentine was still staring. Hacker looked at Valentine and then to the empty chair.

"You all right 'Snobby'?" he asked softly.

Valentine poured another. "Oh I'm fine," he replied gruffly, taking a mouthful.

"Anything I can do?"

Valentine didn't move for a moment. He then poured gin into the willowware cup and passed it to Hacker.

"Here... you can drink this."

Hacker took the cup.

"Cheers." Valentine's voice was empty.

"Cheers," Hacker replied gently and drank. There was a short silence.

"Any news on 'Spence'?" Valentine asked curtly.

"I'm afraid not..."

"Excellent. What a spiffing day!

Hollingsworth came in. Hacker turned and gave him a frown at the same time gesturing his head towards Valentine. The adjutant nodded.

"Can I have a word?" Hollingsworth looked straight at Valentine.

Hacker knew to leave. "I'll go and organise the flights." He put down his tea cup and hastily left.

"What is it, Adj?" Valentine asked without interest.

The adjutant was silent for a moment.

"I've just received this." He was holding a piece of paper.

"What is it?"

"I think you should read it."

"Have you?"

"Yes, of course."

"Then you read it."

He looked at the piece of paper and then back at Valentine. Valentine's face turned to one of impatience.

"You're the new CO," the adjutant said bluntly.

Valentine was silent for a moment.

"No I'm fucking not!" Valentine exploded. "Not a fucking hope. You can shove that right up your arse. I've been down that street before, and I'm not going down it again! Got that?" Valentine swallowed the remains of the glass. He stood silently fuming. The adjutant gave it a few moments and then said:

"These are orders from above. You're the best man for the job and you know it. You don't have a choice, 'Snobby'."

Valentine glared at him, but Hollingsworth had been around a long time and wasn't to be intimidated. He stepped forward and placed some paperwork next to the

366

bottle of gin. He then turned and walked to the door. As he reached it, Valentine stared down at the desk.

"What's this?" he asked curtly.

In the same manner, Hollingsworth replied:

"As CO, you have some letters to write." He left.

As Hollingsworth walked around the hut, Massey was walking towards him.

Valentine could be heard shouting: "Fuck! Fuck! Fuck! Fuck! Fuck! With a side order of Fuck! And lashings of fuck on top!"

Massey stopped walking and stared at the hut.

"Massey?"

"Yes, Adj?"

"Bugger off."

"Sir." He trotted away

***

Pullman knocked gently on Beecham's door.

"Come."

"Morning, sir," Pullman said quite quietly, making him sound a little timid.

Beecham stared at him expectantly. Pullman was hesitant.

"Oh, what is it man? You look like you just lost fifty quid. Get it off your chest!"

"It's Squadron Leader Hawkins, sir."

"What about him?" Beecham dropped his pen on his desk and leant back, he looked impatient.

"Reports are vague –" Beecham's eyes were now wide and piercing "–.but we believe his transport has been sunk, sir."

Beecham lent forward and carefully placed his pen next to a writing pad.

"Go on."

"Apparently the escort lost three of four merchantmen in fog sir, during that time there were several explosions

367

and only one merchantman emerged. Damaged, but not the on Squadron Leader Hawkins was on, sir."

Beecham's head dropped a little, he had a sad smile on his face. Pullman had never seen that before.

"Thank you Pullman... that'll be all."

"Yes, sir." Pullman turned for the door and then stopped. "Sir?" Beecham raised his eyebrows. "There's a Squadron Leader Baxter to see you."

"Ah," Beecham's smile was back. "Send him in would you?"

"Yes sir." Pullman politely gestured to the squadron leader to enter.

Baxter walked in and gave a very smart salute. "Morning sir."

"Please... have a seat." Beecham had his left arm extended, his hand open in invitation.

"Thank you, sir." Baxter sat opposite Beecham. Beecham gave his best smile. "I've been led to believe you have a grasp of Chinese languages..."